THE RAZOR AND THE GUN

A. TRAURING

This edition published in 2022 by AT Press, Atlanta, Georgia

ISBN 978-1-7338339-0-5

© 2022 AT Press, Atlanta, Georgia
v 6.16

If you believe this is a documentary, seek professional help. THIS IS A WORK OF FICTION! People don't just turn up in someone else's head, right? Names, characters, and incidents are products of the author's dubious imagination; all persons and events depicted are fictional. Any resemblance to actual persons living or dead is an unintended coincidence.

While some places depicted may exist in what some refer to as the real world, they are used fictitiously.

Other books by A Trauring in the *Amy & Paul Saga*:

A Different Kind of Twin

The Beaded Necklace

The Wedding Fatality

The Rothschild Jewels

The Strawberry Birthmark

Available at Amazon.com at
https://www.amazon.com/A-
Trauring/e/B00JCC9RCO?ref=sr_ntt_srch_lnk_2&qid=1650070963
&sr=1-2

Dedicated to the quill pens of Jane Austen and the Brönte sisters, and the Remington typewriter of William Faulkner. Thanks, y'all.

Thanks to Barbara Greenstein for editorial support. She has made this a better book.

Thanks to the EPC Book Club for fellowship, good reading, and wonderful support.

Amy and Paul live at
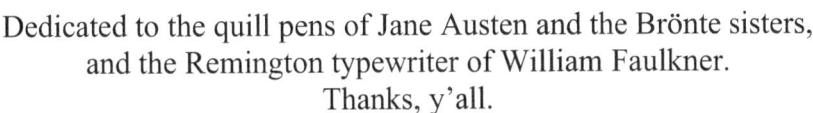
http://atrauring.weebly.com

WEDNESDAY, DECEMBER 10, 2036

"I've got another job for you."

I was thrilled to hear these words come out of my phone. The woman speaking was Melanie Goode, owner and head of the legal firm Goode at Law. She was my most reliable client. I'm Amy Clear of Clear, Hodges & Owens. I'm a private investigator. Some people call it a private eye, but I call it a living.

"Tell me, tell me, tell me," I answered. *God knows I need the work*, I thought silently to my dyad Paul. I patted down my cluttered desk until I found a legal pad, and dragged it to me.

"Paralax Insurance wants an evaluation of a claim for fire damages," Melanie said. "I need someone to do the legwork." As always, Melanie explained things succinctly. "Come in to the office this afternoon, I'll have details for you."

Paul Owens thought to me, *Insurance? At least it's not a divorce.* This dyad and me, we can think to each other. In fact, we do it all the time. He lives inside my head. While I may be crazy, this is not the proof. Paul showed up in my head when I was eleven years old, and everything he told me and my parents about himself turned out to be fact. He's real. You may not believe it, but I know it's true.

Hush, I thought back. *I need the work. Melanie pays well.* To the lawyer I said, "Give me an hour, I'll be there. And thanks."

When I hung up Paul spoke out loud, using my mouth and my voice. "Insurance investigation. That's so boring!" Yes, he can talk out loud, too. After all these years I trust him, and sometimes I let him control things like my voice. Even my private investigator gun. Although I'm a better shot than he is.

"Yes, it is." I walked to the bedroom and my closet to change clothes. "But we need to eat. I haven't had a paying job in three weeks." Clear, Hodges & Owens LLC was not the financial success Paul and I had counted on when I left the New Orleans Police Department to start my own private investigating company. I pulled a yellow blouse off a hanger, and then a blue maxi-skirt.

"We're supposed to be bringing down drug smugglers," Paul said, our voice muffled as I pulled my sweatshirt off over my head. "Mother-rapers. Father-rapers." I dropped my jeans. "Not boring insurance investigations. Do you really want to spend your time verifying addresses and claim numbers?"

"Fine," I said, "you stay home." That was a joke.

I looked down to watch my fingers while I buttoned my blouse. "Me, I'm willing to dig up someone's old medical records to see if they're lying about when they got hurt. I'll even talk to their neighbors if the price is right." I stepped into the skirt and pulled it up. "Belt. Where's my belt?" I sang, "Oh, be-elt, oh be-elt–" Ah, there it was, under a chair. "Besides, I don't know what kind of investigation Melanie wants."

"How about if it's a legitimate claim but the insurance company doesn't want to pay?"

I blew air out, making a dismissive sound I found very satisfying. "I'm an equal opportunity shamus. Pay my fee and I'm your girl."

I sat on the edge of my typically unmade bed. First, I pulled up the hem of my skirt; then I took an elastic holster from the drawer in the end-table and fastened it around my left thigh. When I was on the NOLA police force a woman detective showed me how to hide all the police hardware under a skirt. She also demonstrated that she didn't wear underwear, which pleased Paul entirely too much.

It's so petty, he thought to me. *It's demeaning to them. And to us.*

I took my Ruger 9mm from the night stand and inserted it into the thigh holster. "Maybe to them," I said as I stood up and shook my skirt until it fell over the butt of the gun. "But I don't have a problem doing the work." I checked myself in the closet door mirror to make sure I looked properly outfitted for a business call. "Or do you want to plant a vegetable garden in the courtyard for food?"

I was locking the front door to head for the car when Paul thought to me, *Shit. Okay, let's snoop.*

Think to me. It's not like he and I can read each other's minds. We have to purposely direct a thought to each other. We can even do it to other, normal people near us. If he doesn't think something to me, I have no idea what's going on in his part of what I still think of as my own head.

I laughed, but cautioned him, "Trash mouth." Paul has a foul mouth—well, no, his mouth is my mouth and there's nothing wrong with my mouth that a crown on a back tooth wouldn't cure. And it's not like I can't do a fair impersonation of a sailor when I'm surprised or really, really angry. But mostly I don't like to use those words. I'm a lady. No, really.

I was smiling as I opened the door to my wonderful old yellow Benz. I like my Benz. Bought it used when a killer set fire to my previous chariot. Great thing about a diesel, it doesn't care how cold or how hot it is, you mash the glow plugs, count to ten, and it cranks.

When Paul woke up in my head, I was eleven. Among the things he complained about missing while I was growing up was driving. Beer, too, but mostly driving. He had to wait six years until I was old enough to get my own Louisiana Cheaters' Permit before he could try to convince me–or my parents–to let him roll down the left window and ignore speed limits the way he had when he lived in his own body. Even now, in 2036, Paul acted like a teenager with a brand-new drivers' license; if the engine was cranked, he wanted to be the one turning the wheel and mashing the pedals. And usually, I let him. Fortunately, he's a good driver.

Goode at Law was in the CBD, New Orleans' Central Business District.[1] Even with mid-afternoon traffic it was no more than a twenty-minute drive from my house in the Carrollton section. Paul parked us in an outdoor lot two blocks south of the law firm, an automated concern considerably cheaper than the ritzy parking deck across Girod Street from Goode at Law's front door. Melanie had been emphatic about refusing to validate my parking.

Don't know why I didn't button up my sweater when I got out of the car. I just pulled it close while I walked up Carondelet, fighting the December chill. *I hope I can get a week's work out of this,* I thought to Paul. *How much will that get me?*

Two-fifty a day, five days, he thought back. We shared the same head, but he could do complicated math in it and I couldn't. *That's one thousand, two hundred and fifty bucks.*

I turned the corner onto Girod. *That'll cover the mortgage and some red beans and rice.*

At the entrance to the two-story office building that housed the law firm, Paul led long enough to open the door. What a gentleman. "Why, thank you, kind sir," I said softly. True, it was my left arm that had reached out, and my left hand that had pulled the door, but Paul was the one applying the effort. *Anytime, young lady. Will there be anything else?*

Down a hallway to the glass and chrome door etched with the name 'Goode at Law.' The same anorexic receptionist was behind the desk, clacking away at a computer keyboard. "How are you,

---

[1] 'CBD,' the Central Business District, is upriver from the French Quarter, sandwiched between *Vieux Carré*, the Garden District, Central City, and Tulane/Gravier. If you've got a map, look for the Superdome—that's right smack in the middle of CBD.

Harper?" I called out. Aside from being infuriatingly skinny, she was a reliable ally.

The woman looked up and smiled. She had straight blonde hair that came to her jawline, and a row of braces gleaming on her upper teeth. Paul thought she was cute. "Hey, Amy," she replied. "Mel is backed up. I'll let you know when she's ready for you."

I want to throw her on the ground and cram a cheeseburger down her throat. Among other things. I told you he was a trash mouth.

So, I smiled blankly at the two men and one woman who were seated in the waiting room. They all were in business attire, one reading the *Wall Street Journal* and the other two looking at their iPads. *Seeing Harper,* I thought, *maybe I'll skip dinner.* It's not like I'm overweight; I'm five-six and I weighed one hundred and nine the last time I got on a scale. But Paul and I do like our Dixie Beer. If I'm not careful I'll blimp out by the time I'm forty. Four years to go.

I sat two chairs away from the woman whose eyes kept darting between iPad and wrist watch. The floor vibrated from the way she tapped her foot.

Mineral, Paul thought. *Bigger than a breadbox.* Paul and I played 20 Questions to kill time if people could see us. By ourselves we preferred Rock Paper Scissors, but I learned the hard way that people get nervous watching me go 'paper' with my right hand and 'scissor' with my left. Paul is left-handed.

I was so wrapped up in our game that I didn't see the client leaving Melanie's office until Harper called me. I picked up my portfolio and ignored the frowns of the others who had been waiting longer.

"You're late, damn it!"

I closed the office door behind her. "Good to see you, Melanie. How's business?"

"I said you're late."

Paul barged in front—mentally, it's something we can do—to say, "We've been here twenty minutes, but you were busy with Mister Client. How can we help you?"

Melanie Goode was in her mid-40s. Stocky, with a stunning head of black Medusa curls, she was used to Paul's unfortunate attachment to the first-person plural. She waved a hand and sat down. "Paralax got a claim for a fire loss on the West Bank," the lawyer said. "They want to know if they can subrogate the claim. And they want to know the cause of the fire." She held out a manila file.

I took the folder and sat back to leaf through it. "How long ago was the loss?"

"Nine or ten days ago. The insured is a client of mine, but I still want it checked out."

I turned a couple of pages to a color photo of smoldering ruins: cement footprint, parts of two walls, and a foundation full of unidentifiable charred things. "Looks total."

"That's what the claim says. Check it out, talk to the Parish fire department. See if my client is broke and torched it himself."

Paul thought, *BOR-RING! I want a beer.*

"Is that likely?" I countered to Melanie; to Paul I thought, *Behave now and I'll get us a Dixie.*

"Not really. George runs a real estate agency." Melanie opened a desk drawer and patted a hand inside until she came out with a bag of hard candy. As she put one in her mouth she added, "But anything can happen."

Usually does, Paul thought.

Looking at the pictures in the file, I asked, "Residence? Office? Where?"

"A warehouse in Waggaman, on the west bank. The claim is for the building, not contents."

"What was he using it for?"

Melanie Goode stood up. "You'll tell me when you find out. Go. Report back."

I said, "Uh, my usual rates?" This began the traditional Arab street bazaar charade we always went through. I stayed in the chair.

"You charge too damn much!" Melanie folded her arms in front of her chest. "What do you say to $125 a day?"

Paul laughed out loud. I said, "You did say $250 a day, right? Plus expenses."

Melanie sat on the edge of her desk, one leg crossed above a pudgy knee. "One fifty. You're driving me to the poorhouse."

I shook my head and said, "Every time you hire me for an investigation we go through this routine. Why?"

"Because you charge too much. Be reasonable, do—"

Paul interrupted her. "Two fifty a day," he said, sounding just like me, "or three camels, your eldest son, and a goat."

"Tempting," Melanie smiled. "Do you have any idea what it's like to have a fourteen-year-old boy?"

"I'd sell him to Tulane for medical research. Come on, Melanie! We always go through this rigmarole and you always finally agree to my price because it's the going rate, and you know it. Two-fifty a day, plus expenses. And you can keep the goat."

The woman stood up again and pointed at the door. "Alright, damn it. Now, go!" Paul thought, *She's trying to hide a smirk. We got her.*

Why did you think about a goat? I thought to him. *What would I do with a goat?* I walked through the waiting room, nodding at the impatient clients waiting for their turn in Melanie's office.

We could sacrifice it in the courtyard, then eat it. Hey, didn't you say something about a beer?

"Ah. First, I want to look at the smoking ruins of the warehouse." I walked around the corner to the parking lot on Caroldalet where my beloved ancient yellow Benz was waiting. "You want to drive to Waggaman?"

Stop twisting my arm, Paul thought. He would drive anywhere, anytime, for any reason or, just as well, for no reason. *I love to feel the wind in your hair,* he thought.

"You get to brush it afterwards," I said.

Carondalet being one-way the wrong way, Paul drove up to Poydras, made a bunch of New Orleans left turns to get to Loyola Avenue, and finally made it to the Pontchartrain Expressway, heading across the Mississippi river. Once over the Crescent City Connection bridge we were in what everyone referred to as the west bank, despite it being east at this point. To compound the confusion, the name of Business Interstate 90 changed after passing the Oakwood Center to the Westbank Expressway. It would be another twelve miles before we would truly be west of New Orleans. And you thought your town was weird.

Waggaman is a small community of ten thousand souls in thirty-five hundred homes between railroad tracks and the river levee, where they bravely make a stand against an encroaching swamp.

While we were stopped at a red light, I took out my phone and opened the GPS application. It hadn't fully loaded by the time the light turned green, so Paul drove across the intersection and pulled to the side of the road. "2...9...1...6...Live...Oak...Boulevard," I said as I keyed in the address. A moment later a piece of map appeared on the screen. "There! Keep going."

"What are we going to learn from looking at a burned-out foundation?" Paul asked. When we were in the privacy of my car or my living room, we both liked to speak out loud. Keep the throat muscles exercised, I guess. Actually, even now it was a reaction against how we used to try to keep Paul hidden from the rest of the world so we didn't end up in a padded cell in Mandeville[2].

I shrugged. "Maybe nothing. But maybe seeing it will make it more real to me. I've never seen what's left after a serious fire."

---

[2] An anachronism. Through the last half of the 20th century the town of Mandeville hosted the Louisiana State hospital for the insane. Even though the facility was moved to an already-existing asylum in Jackson in 2012, people still used 'Mandeville' as a code for the loony bin.

The rural roadway was surrounded by spindly trees and wild bushes, barely obscuring the swamp beyond. No sidewalks; no mailboxes; no nothing.

"A movie theatre in Falling Spring burned when I was seven or eight," Paul said. He grew up in a town in West Virginia. I checked; census records say a Paul Owens really did come from there. "Me and my parents and my sister and all our neighbors stood around to watch. It was nothing like a tame fireplace, I tell you what. I remember being scared and fascinated." He snorted. "And then there were no more movies in town."

"You won't have any flashbacks, will you? You're not going to see blackened ruins and start crying, are you?"

Paul answered, "I don't think this made it to my anxiety closet. But I did miss the movies."

When the GPS prompted, Paul turned us onto Live Oak Boulevard. We passed an Entergy sub-station, a concrete island with an outsized tinker-toy display of insulators, wires, and transformers. There was another eight miles of scrub and swamp before we crossed the CSX tracks and Siri told us we had arrived at our destination. Paul turned into a driveway and stopped at one edge. Nearby were ruins, scattered debris, and fire department do-not-cross tape.

The remains were a blackened exoskeleton of brick with burned out openings that once had been windows, and jagged, broken walls. Charred timbers were strewn about the parking area, and more were visible through the former windows, hanging inside from what little remained of the roof. In the cool December air there were competing odors: marine, from the swamp and nearby river; burned wood from the warehouse ruins; and a small, noxious smell that prompted me to remark, "Something here is rank." I stepped out of the car to explore.

What is that smell? Paul thought. I guessed we were talking about the same scent.

"I know it," I replied, "but I can't put the name on it." I ducked under the yellow warning tape and approached what had been the front door, stepping over rafters and debris. "It's like someone says, 'taste this,' and you know what the taste is, but the name of the taste isn't there. And then they say 'Coconut,' and you slap your head and go, 'Oh, of course!'"

Paul tried to sniff, working around my dominant breathing pattern. Trouble was, it was distracting me. "He-hey, what are you doing?" I asked.

Paul said, "Let me sniff, okay?" Thus prepared, I nodded and let Paul take in a few deep breaths through our nose.

Whoa! I'm getting dizzy! I thought. I shook my head and stumbled in place.

"I think I got it," he said. He walked us to the back of the large fire footprint. "We were at a pajama party when you were a senior at St. Giles Academy—"

I remember, I interrupted. *You were perving over all my classmates.*

Paul laughed. "Damn right, I was. Half a dozen seventeen-year-old girls in nightgowns. But, remember, you leaned over one of the candles and—"

I singed my hair! You're right! That's the smell here.

"Was the warehouse full of natural hair wigs?"

Melanie didn't say. This may mean there were people inside during the fire. Come on, and I took back the lead to step around the detritus of the fire. The lead, that's what Paul and I call it. Whichever one of us is leading mostly controls my body. I guess it's weird, but I just think of it as my life.

When we had finished our circuit and were back at the remains of the front of the warehouse I leaned back against the side of my car and took in the scene. "There's scorch everywhere," I observed. "What gets a building this large totally involved?"

"Lightning?" Paul said. "Arson? Nuclear detonation?"

I rubbed my arms against the chill. "I'm not dressed to wade into what's left. You think there might be a piece of kryptonite in the middle?"

Can't rule it out. But—no, not really.

"It would be fun, though. Next time I'll wear old jeans." I opened the door to my car and slid behind the wheel. "But first, I'd better visit the Parish Fire Department. Maybe they found the reactor cooling rods."

More like graphite dowels, Paul corrected.

"And there's a difference?" I lit the glow plugs and started counting.

"Ah, yup. Cooling rods when they're in the atomic reactor so it doesn't go all Chernobyl, boom, boom," Paul said. "When they're graphite dowels you can sharpen one end and write a book."

"Are you making that up?" I let the clutch out and found a big enough piece of parking lot to turn around. "Or are you teasing me for sleeping through my science classes."

"Guilty as charged. Sometimes reality is too—too—too real."

I made a left out of the warehouse driveway. The trees, scrub, and swamp all looked the same in this direction, as they had when I came out to Waggaman. When your only landmarks might be a gnarled tree, it's too easy to get lost—thank God for my GPS. I figured I'd drive back over the river to the fire station in Harahan, where I expected the Jefferson Parish headquarters to be. "I should get a straight answer if I show up in person with my P.I. ID," I told Paul. But when I turned left onto US 90 he shouted, "Fire house on the left!" Do you have any idea how disorienting it is when, out of the blue, your dyad uses your own mouth to shout something? I swerved, but I managed not to sideswipe the semitrailer in the next lane.

After I was sure we weren't about to die on the roadway I said, "Well, that's convenient." I took advantage of a break in the neutral zone[3] to turn up a side street, past the exit-only driveway the fire

---

[3] In the New Orleans area we call it the neutral zone. In your town it may

trucks used, and turned into the employee parking area. *Glad you saw that,* I thought as I undid my seat belt. *I'd have zipped right by.* Our usual pattern was whichever one of us was leading looked straight ahead, and the other paid attention to our peripheral vision. You'd be surprised how well that worked.

A firehouse is not like any office or business. There is no lobby, no tidy chairs next to small tables with three-month old general interest magazines, no receptionist. No, the purpose of a firehouse is preparedness to save lives and property. Anything else is a bonus.

I pushed the glass door to go in the entry foyer. It was a moderately sized area; the floor was made of those twelve-inch linoleum squares with a mottled dark and light gray pattern. Posters with fire safety slogans lined a wall on the left, and a small decorated Christmas tree was in a corner. *So, where is everyone?* Paul thought.

Right on cue I heard a man's voice from around a corner. "It's about damn time, Larry! You get enough burgers for lunch this time?" There was the sound of a chair scraping against linoleum, and then footsteps getting louder. "I'll get the guys and–Whoa, you're not Larry." The man, who also was not Larry, wore a short-sleeved light blue workshirt with official insignia on the shoulders; his dark blue Red Kap pants were held up by a gold set of suspenders.

"Call me whatever you like," Paul said, "but don't call me late for lunch. Me for ketchup and pickles."

The tall, middle-aged man wore a look of embarrassment on his pudgy face. "I'm sorry. Uh, I'm Captain Broussard. Wasn't expecting visitors. Uh, Larry, uh, he went to pick up lunch and..." His voice trailed off in cadence and volume.

"Nice to meet you, Captain Broussard," I said brightly, holding out my right hand. "I'm Private Investigator Amy Clear. I think you

---

be a median or central reservation. It's the physical division between oncoming lanes of a road, usually but not always covered in vegetation.

are exactly the person I need to talk to. And lunch besides, I can't believe how lucky I am." I heard Paul think, *Ask if we get fries with that.*

The captain shook my hand. His lost look slowly turned into a professional smile. "Talk away. Would you like to step into my office?" With his other arm he motioned to a large open area around the corner from the foyer, where a desk held an inbox overflowing with sheets of goldenrod paper. It looked like my cubicle when I was with New Orleans PD.

He put his hands on the back of a simple wooden chair across from the desk, holding it out for me. I am a sucker for the traditional vestiges of chivalry. I said, "Thank you, Captain," and took the seat he offered. He went to the same type of chair on the working side of the desk. "So, what brings you to Station number 76?"

"I'm working for Paralax Insurance," I started. "There was a fire a week-and-a-half ago at a warehouse up Live Oak Boulevard? My employer needs some information to process the owner's claim." I held my clipboard on my lap, and put my pen in Paul's hand, my left hand. Did I say he's left-handed?

"Oh, Jeez, that was awful." Broussard sat with arms extended, hands on desk top, as he looked down. "Looks like a fatality or two." Still looking down he shook his head. "You hate that."

Fatalities? Paul thought; before I had a chance to respond he went on aloud, "We were just out there. We thought we smelled burn, uh, burn damage."

"Burned flesh is unmistakable. I don't think the parish sheriff's office has identified what was left yet." He shook his head again and repeated, "You hate that."

"That's awful," I commiserated. "What were the circumstances?" I thought to Paul, *You've got the pen. Take notes, you.*

Just then there was noise from the lobby, and a man shouted, "Little help with lunch, please!"

It was Paul who said, "Ah. The real Larry."

Captain Broussard stood up and went to his crewman, who was struggling under a big cardboard box and a gallon jug of iced tea. "I've got it!" the captain called, taking the box of burgers, fries, shakes, and pies. When he hefted it, Broussard said, "This feels like it'll be enough." As the two men began walking into the interior of the building, the captain turned his head and called, "Come along, Detective. I believe we'll have that lunch for you."

Oh boy, free food! Paul shouted silently. I thought back, *Only one. I'm watching my weight.* If I ate as much as he wanted, I'd look like Jabba the Hutt. And no slave girls, neither. I trotted to catch up with the men. "Can I help?" she asked.

"If you can make the kitchen come closer," Broussard muttered under the awkward box.

I like him, Paul thought.

We went down the central hallway and turned right into the firehouse kitchen. It was brightly lit with overhead fluorescents, showing sparkling clean countertops and a gleaming range. The white double-door refrigerator glowed. I thought, *My house hasn't been this clean since the day I moved in.*

The captain dropped the big cardboard box onto the table, while Larry placed the tea containers beside it. "Lunch!" the captain called.

Sounds of movement outside the room began; within a minute eight firemen and one fire lady were in the kitchen, all talking at once. "Did you get my root beer?" "No mustard!" "Are there enough fries to go around?" "I get the fish sandwich." Larry didn't try to respond individually; he kept saying, "Yeah, yeah. Sure. Uh-huh. Plenty. Yup."

Like the captain, all were dressed in their working uniform— blue pants and light blue shirts with badges and JPFD patches, although the fire lady also sported red suspenders. Seated noisily at the large round table, they divided up the contents of the box.

"Here," the captain said, sliding something edible wrapped in yellow wax paper to me. "There's enough to go around."

"Hey! Is that my fish sandwich?"

I unwrapped it and peeled the top piece of bun off. "Burger with ketchup, mustard, and pickle," I said, and looked around. Hungry Paul added, "Going once, going twice, GONE to the ravenous private detective." *Thanks for introducing me,* I thought.

The man two seats away said, "Detective? Well, welcome to Station 76. Why are you here?" He was talking around his hamburger; it sounded like 'wy ar uhr?'

"Branson, you were on duty with me for the warehouse fire up Live Oak," Broussard called. "She's got questions."

I finished chewing my oh-so-petite bite of burger. Then I wiped my dainty lips with one of the paper towels that had been brainwashed into thinking it was a napkin. "I'm investigating the fire for Paralax Insurance. Captain Broussard says there were fatalities?"

Branson nodded vigorously. "Yeah, looked like it. And it may have been set on purpose."

I put the burger down on its yellow wrapper. "On purpose? You mean, murder?"

"I mean arson," Broussard broke in. "We found evidence of accelerants. When we found the remains, I turned it over to the parish sheriff's office."

"Yeah," Branson went on. "It's unusual for such a big building to be fully involved so quickly. A typical fire might start in the kitchen, or the fuse box, but then it takes a while for flame to work its way out." He bit off part of a French fry. "Sixteen percent of fires are arson, and this looks like one of 'em."

The captain said, "I was the incident commander. Branson here was a big help."

Branson nodded and answered while still chewing, "The captain handed it off to the sheriff's office, but I saw him doing most of the evaluation and isolation."

"Yeah," one of the other firemen offered. "What do the cops know about fires?"

And I thought to Paul, *And what do firemen know about preserving evidence?*

I asked Branson, "What about the victims?"

He answered, "Don't know. Burned up. Not even sure they were human, but what else would they be? We haven't heard IDs yet."

I nodded, and held my right arm out toward Broussard. "What did it look like?"

"They were in a long hallway, and someone had poured accelerant around." A shake of the head, "You hate that. Whoever they were, they didn't have a chance."

"Cause of death?"

There were harrumphs around the table. "Might be smoke inhalation," the captain said, "or it might be 14th degree burns. I tell you they didn't have a chance."

Suddenly I wasn't hungry anymore. I put the remains of my burger down. Immediately I heard Paul think, *Are you done with that? Can I finish it?* I pushed it a little further away with my right hand, but then Paul used my left arm to reach across me and pull it back. I rolled my eyes and let Paul take another bite.

Between Paul's huge and rude chews, I managed to ask, "Can I get your report for Paralax? And who at the Jefferson Parish Sheriff's Office should I talk to?"

"Mmmmph," came out of Broussard's mouth, along with little pieces of his sandwich. He mopped up with a paper towel while saying, "It's only preliminary, but it's sitting on my desk." He went back to chewing, then swallowed. "And the sheriff's office is up highway 90 in Harvey."

While I started to plan my next stop, Paul said, "Thanks for lunch. Who are all—"

The alarm was very, very loud. I swear, firemen should have to wear earplugs because of the alarm, like I did when I was on the police pistol range. Instantly each of the firefighters was up from the table, running for the vehicle bays that contained their uniform lockers. "Grab that report off my desk. We can talk later," Captain Broussard called as he sprinted away.

In less than a minute me and Paul were alone at the lunch table. *You want what's left of that fish sandwich?* he thought.

I wouldn't say no to a leftover beer if there was one, I thought back. Then, aloud, "I wonder if I should lock the door on my way out." When I stood up Paul bent over and grabbed someone's half-eaten sandwich, and took a bite out of the un-used part. *No cheese,* he thought. *Ours was better.*

I hope the Board of Health agrees with you. I can't believe you just bit part of a stranger's meal. Even though I was surprised by Paul's omnivorous action, it didn't gross me out. After all, he did go after the pristine half of the sandwich.

So, I went down the long hallway, and I recognized the entryway. The preliminary report was indeed sitting on Captain Broussard's desk, under a coffee mug. When I picked it up, I saw the round, brown stain on the cover.

"Okay, let us see what the parish sheriff has to say."

"Can I drive?" Paul asked.

I placed my keys in my left hand, Paul's hand. "Be my guest. But let me do the talking when we get to the station house."

Paul made a left turn onto US90 East, and later stayed to the right for the Westbank Expressway frontage road. Suddenly the luxuriant but creepy swamp on both sides of the road blossomed into bustling urban activity, from gas stations to fast food joints, from factories to industrial sized employee parking lots. All that remained of the rural Louisiana we had seen in Waggaman were the wide neutral zone of the highway and the occasional empty lot that had not yet recovered from Hurricane Olaf or Rodrigo. A few more miles down the road we crossed over the Destrehan Canal and entered the town of Harvey, population 25,000, give or take. We passed a TraveLodge, then the seven-story red brick block of the parish motor vehicle bureau and probation office that looked out of place, deserted, surrounded by a nearly empty parking lot. A funeral home. A string of car dealerships–Kia, Mazda, Chevrolet, Mitsubishi, Suzuki, and Jeep; Paul thought, *We're up to 93,000 miles and the left turn blinker is wonky. Should we check out our next ride while we're here?*

"Not hardly. My old Blue Beast had twice that when Skyler Blunt[4] torched it."

We passed the cracked slab of a fast-food restaurant that was rumored to have been hit by a meteorite in 1996, a place so cursed by local legend that not even Richelieu and RE/Max had been able to sell it in almost forty years.

On my left was the glorified neutral zone beneath the elevated lanes of the Westbank Expressway. Although Paul concentrated on the roadway, I used my peripheral vision to look at the more entertaining commercial scenery on the right.

Between the gas stations and car rentals and nameless factories and strip malls, we crossed several small canals, really open drains, as in Verret Canal and Drainage Ditch Number 7.

"Where, exactly, is the sheriff's office?" Paul asked. "We're getting close to your Aunt Peggy's in Gretna." He came to a stop at a traffic light.

The big green road sign at the intersection had a big white arrow pointing to the right, along with the words 'Belle Chasse.' "Aw, crap and a half," I muttered, my standard oath. "It must be on the north side of the expressway." Paul nodded and flicked the wonky turn signal; when the light changed someone—possibly afraid the erratic blinker might mutate into a James Bond weapon—let him merge left, and then he took the turnaround that snaked through the neutral zone, between the elevated road's pylons, on the way to the westbound frontage road. When he honked at an oblivious cyclist on the bike path that wound under the Westbank Expressway proper, I shouted, "Hey!" *It's okay*, he thought back; *If*

---

[4] In *The Rothschild Jewels* by A. Trauring, 2016. Oh, you read that already? Good!

I hit him and it damages the car, we can go back to one of those dealerships.

"If we have a wreck—" I began, thought, and started again, "If you have a wreck, I'm going home and I'll let you deal with the police all by your lonesome." I was trying not to smile as I spun a variation on our favorite kind of threat, "And I'll visit you in their dungeon the day before your execution. But I'll smuggle in a file and a hacksaw blade and a bottle of Dixie."

Yes! I'll slash a dozen guards with the saw, and you and I can split the Dixie as we watch them all die. I like it!

"I thought you would," I snickered. "I think the sheriff's in that big ugly thing up ahead."

Paul saw the five-story block of white concrete and black glass, set far back from the frontage road. "It looks like your dad's hospital," he offered, turning into the campus. My father, Doctor James Clear, had been an emergency room surgeon at the Jefferson Parish Medical Center in Metairie back when Paul turned up in my head; he was semi-retired now, running a private medical practice in the same complex. Dad had stitched me up countless times from the mistakes I've made as a detective. He was one of the handful of people who knew about Paul. Actually, they had become friends. Go figure.

Halfway down the drive we came to the small guardhouse, its plywood pike blocking the pavement. *You lead!* Paul thought.

"Can I help you, Miss?" the guard called when I powered down the driver's window. He was some flavor of officer, in a light blue shirt with metal badge and fabric insignia.

I unfurled my Private Investigator's ID. "Captain Broussard at fire station 76 sent me. I'm working for Paralax Insurance and I need information on a warehouse fire."

The officer's brow wrinkled. "You couldn't get that from the fire captain?"

"I wouldn't be bothering you if I had." I smiled the smile that always made my dad give in. "Who do I need to see?"

"Ah. You park in the front of the building—" he pointed toward the tall structure at the end of the driveway "—and you go in that main door. The guard'll ask for ID. Tell him you need the Public Information Office. He'll set you right."

So, I waved and let the clutch out in first gear. I heard Paul think, *Can we get lunch after this? And a beer?*

"Maybe," I said, but I was already thinking about a frosty bottle of Dixie. "We'll see."

I parked my yellow chariot at the far left side of the front of the Harry Lee Law Enforcement Complex. It was named in honor of a beloved sheriff who died during a re-election campaign in the early 21st century. I was undoing the safety belt when Paul said, "Why do you keep dragging me to police stations? You know John Law makes me break out in hives."

Because it's how I make my living, I thought back as I opened the driver's side door. *At least I'm not on the force anymore. That should make you happy.*

Yeah. It's not a daily thing now. As I walked toward the building entryway he went on, *Sometimes we go a week without hanging around cops. And because of you they never yell and tell me to put our hands on our head.*

You've never told me what it is you did before you came to me that has you so spooked by law enforcement.

Paul laughed out loud, then thought, *Nothing felonious. Uh, not in 2036, anyway. Could have gotten in a lot of trouble in the 1980s, though.* Silently he sang, *'It increases my paranoia Like looking in my rear-view mirror and seeing a police car.'*[5]

"And you wonder why I have a taste for bad boys?" I smirked. Actually, my taste in men was fairly omnivorous, but the complications from the bad boys tended to linger. I took the steps

---

[5] Crosby Stills & Nash: "Almost Cut My Hair" (David Crosby) Stay Straight Music BMI. Paul was only 16 when he bought the *Deja Vu* album that contains the song, but it made a BIG impression on his youthful outlaw attitude.

two at a time and nearly fell forward when the door I was about to push opened all by its lonesome.

The wide and deep lobby was dimly lit by small hanging fixtures suspended from the fifteen-foot ceiling. A Christmas tree was visible on the other side of the security kiosk, with blinking lights and a sign informing the world that the gift-wrapped packages underneath were destined for the parish *Toys for Tots* program. Meanwhile the marble walls displayed crime prevention posters. In the front, velvet ropes formed a weir that forced anyone entering the building into the line for the security desk, where an older sergeant with his cast-enclosed left leg propped on a chair sat reading the *Times-Picayune* next to the officer-and-employee gate.

"I.D. please," the sergeant said from behind the desk. Two other officers were behind him, intent on some hidden work.

"I need the Public Information Office," I said as I retrieved my wallet and opened my PI license. I tried on my dad smile while the sergeant examined the credentials.

"Investigator, huh? Are you armed?"

"Sure," I said. "Aren't you?"

He snickered, "Yeah, but I work here. You can check your gear with me."

Even though there were two people on line behind me, and those other officers behind the man I was talking to, I reached up under my skirt and undid the thigh holster, then handed it to the sergeant. While I smoothed down my skirt I said, "It pulls a little to the left, in case you need to use it."

"Get on with you," he grinned. "I'll have it for you when you leave. He snapped my ID case shut and returned it. "Take the elevator to the fifth floor, then make a left," he said. "There are signs all over the hall."

I nodded, but before I could say 'thank you' the sergeant was challenging the next person in line, an older black man in a sport jacket. She heard Paul think, *That was fairly painless. I hope they have a fast elevator; those are the fun kind.*

It was not to be. The elevator was painfully slow. *Come on, come on!* Paul thought as we watched the door consider closing, ever so sloowwwllllyyyyy. *This elevator is made by Zeno, not Otis!*

I glanced up at the information plaque over the floor buttons. *It's an Otis,* I thought. *Somebody named Zeno makes elevators?*

Paul's silent snicker made me realize I had misunderstood something. As the door finally closed, I said, "Okay, I'm an uneducated brat. What's a Zeno?"

"Dead Greek guy," he answered. "He's the reason we're growing old in this elevator." The car inched upwards; it was fifteen seconds before a computerized 'ding!' indicated we had passed the second floor. "He said if you go half the distance to something, and then half again, and then half of that, that you'd never get to where you were going."

I dropped my jaw. "I never heard of Zeno," I said, "but even I know that's a load of crap. A double load."

'Ding!' Third floor.

"Yeah, well." He snorted. "And I thought I was being so erudite and intellectual."

"Oh, you were!" I assured him, "You are. Just wrong, is all."

'Ding!' Fourth floor.

"I want a beer with lunch."

I said, "And maybe Santa will hear your prayers." After a pause I added, "Mine, too."

A double 'Ding!' and the door began its agonizingly slow movement. Concerned about being overheard, Paul thought, *You tell Santa I've been a good boy. I deserve a beer. You, too.*

Oh, sure. I've got that hot-line to the North Pole. Which is why I'm still waiting for a pony.

Finally, finally! the door opened. I stepped into the hallway and looked for signs. "Let's see, he said turn left, right?"

Left. I set off down the narrow hallway, toward the patch of light coming through glass doors to some office.

The lettering on the glass indicated it was the entrance to the Accounts Receivable department. *This ain't it*, Paul thought, helpfully. I turned to look at the opposite wall, where a sign at face height said, "Public Information Office, room 522," with an arrow pointing farther down the hall.

So, I followed the sign's instructions. I pushed open the door to room 522 and found a well-lighted anteroom with two desks, one on each side of the pathway in. One was completely bare, but the other sported a phone, in— and out—baskets, and a young civilian woman frowning at the computer monitor. As I entered, she looked up and said, "Can I help you?" She was dark-haired, with fair skin and a mouth that showed several of her upper teeth. For years Paul had gone on about how he craved women with a short upper lip, so I figured he was mentally combing his hair and checking his breath.

I said "Hi," and stuck out my hand. "I'm a P-I working for Paralax Insurance. Captain Broussard of the Parish Fire Department suggested I talk to someone here about a recent fire with fatalities." I kept smiling at the woman.

"Uh, okay," the receptionist said, "just a sec." She picked up her phone and punched three numbers for an extension. "Lieutenant? A woman is here, she wants to talk to someone about a fire with deaths." She looked up at Amy while she heard the response. "Uh-huh. Uh-Huh. O-o-okay, okay, I'll tell her. Okay."

She put the handset back in the phone receiver and said, "Lieutenant Lucky will be out for you in a minute." Pointing to some chairs on the far side of the other desk, she said, "You can wait over there."

I said, "Thank you," but then good old Paul added, "Lucky? That's a nickname, right?"

"No, ma'am. Lieutenant Richard Lucky. He's our Public Information officer."

Paul raised my eyebrows—trust me, if feels weird when someone else raises your eyebrows. I sat us in one of the available chairs. *Lieutenant Lucky*, I thought. *I hope he can tell us if Paralax is off the hook for this loss.*

We were in our silent second round of 20 Questions when a tall man in dark gray military uniform stood before them. "Miss? You're waiting on me?"

It took me a moment to switch mental gears from a mineral, bigger than a breadbox, to Paralax Insurance and official business. "Yes, Lucky. Uh—Lieutenant. Lieutenant Lucky." I stood up, clipboard under my arm, and held out my right hand. "I'm Amy Clear. I've been hired by—"

"Come in my office and tell me about it," he interrupted. *The man must have fifty teeth*, I heard Paul think with a tone of awe. Indeed, the officer had a mouth full of perfect, shiny, white enamel that sparkled through his broad smile. *At least*, I thought back. *Maybe sixty.*

The office was lit by bright overhead fluorescents, which made the white walls and white furniture—desk, chairs, credenza, filing cabinets—gleam unnaturally. You'd have to wear sunglasses to work here. As in the other parts of the building, crime-fighting posters were prominent decor; behind the lieutenant's chair was a picture of Crimedog McGruff in a trench coat, with the legend "Take a bite out of crime."

"So, what's this about a fire with fatalities?" the officer asked. He motioned for me to use a white chair in front of his desk, and then he sat himself. He made unwavering eye contact, with a look of concern across his face. I heard Paul think, *Uh-oh. Hang on to your wallet.*

So, I started in. "Captain Broussard—uh, fire Captain Broussard—said his people worked a warehouse fire a week or so ago. They turned it over to the Parish Sheriff because they found bodies."

"And why does this concern you?"

Not cool, Paul thought.

I said, "The building is insured by Paralax, and they've asked Goode At Law to do a subrogation investigation, and Goode At Law hired me. I want to know what fire and police think before I approach the property owner."

"Well, let me look," as he turned his attention to his computer screen. "When was this fire?"

Paul spoke up. "December second or third, I think."

"Ah!" The lieutenant peered at the screen for a few moments, until the smile slipped off his face.

Turning back to me, he said, "I will not discuss an ongoing investigation with an outsider." His unnerving eye contact resumed.

Somebody got up on the wrong side of the bed, Paul thought.

"Uh—outsider? Do you consider the company being dinged for insurance payments an outsider?"

The lieutenant nodded. "We think there was a fatality. This may be a criminal matter. Who the insurer is doesn't matter."

So, I reached for my wallet and started to fish out my New Orleans Police ID—since I sometimes consult for Commander Ramirez, he's kept me on the PD roster, although he didn't agree to the retainer I wanted; I only get paid when I consult. What kind of world is this?

About the time I held the ID out Paul said, "So, how long before you will talk to us about it?"

"Don't know," the officer shrugged. "Could be two days, could be two months. Jefferson Parish has to finish its own investigation first." His eyes dropped to the document in my hand. "So, what's this?"

"I'm no outsider," I said, and I dropped my ID on the desk in front of him. "Three years New Orleans Police detective, and I still consult for Commander Ramirez." I unloaded the daddy smile again. "You can tell me what's going on."

True, the officer seemed amused at my attempt to flirt past his refusal to talk about the fire. "You're a clever woman," he offered, and leaned back in his chair, touching the fingers of his hands together. "I can tell you that we're not sure about the remains we found. Not really enough to be anything but a small child, but that doesn't make any sense. The Parish medical examiner has the remains and we're waiting on a report."

I started to say, "Thank you, Lieu—" but he cut me off. "And that's all I'm going to say. Is there anything else I can help you with today?" Lucky stood up behind his desk to show the interview was over.

So, I shook my head and stood up. Paul thought, *What a maroon.*[6] *Let's go back to the firehouse.* I said to the lieutenant, "Apparently not. I guess I'll go talk to the property owner. Or is he an outsider, too?"

He held up his right hand, palm out. "I'd rather you didn't do that just yet."

Duly noted, I thought. And Paul said, "Is that an order, Lieutenant?

"Just some friendly advice."

I don't like this guy, Paul thought. Aloud, he added, "Am I free to go?"

"Just trying to help," the officer said, and he shrugged. I got us out of the jerk's office without offering to shake hands, or even noticing if the lieutenant had extended his.

Let's ask Melanie for the owner's contact information, Paul thought. I stamped my feet in the hallway as I walked toward the elevator lobby. He went on, *NOPD wasn't that stingy with information, was it?*

I wasn't, I thought back. *Crap. Crap. Crap and a half.* When I pushed the call button, Paul muttered, "We're waiting for Zeno again."

Who? Oh, him. Well, never mind. I headed to the stairwell exit instead.

---

[6] It was Bugs Bunny who first used 'maroon' as an insulting pun on the word 'moron.' (He also popularized 'nimrod' as an insult instead of a Biblical reference.)

As I bounced down the stairs I thought, *I may go back to the firehouse after I read the report. Captain Broussard'll tell me everything he knows, I bet.*

Can we get lunch first?

No! I shouted silently. *Melanie gives me such a hard time about taking too long to come up with answers. I need something to bring back to her first.*

Fuel cells getting low, Paul thought to me, using a funny mechanical voice, *must recharge with food. And alcohol.*

I ignored his whining about lunch and beer. "Why would Lucky be such a jerk?" I asked. "NOPD talks to insurance reps. I don't believe Jefferson Parish Sheriff's Office has a rule against it."

Do we know who owned the warehouse?

"Melanie said it's a client. Wait 'til I tell her the Sheriff's office asked me not to interview them."

First things first, Paul thought. *Beer. Lunch. Beer.*

"The owner can tell us what he kept in the warehouse," I said. Paul was going to go on and on about food and beer until we finally got some of each, so I kept ignoring his pleas. "Who were his employees that may be the fatalities?"

I'm thinking a Dixie—no, we can be fancy and have an Abita. You like the sweet ones.

"And maybe he has some enemy who was ready to burn the place down. Somebody he crossed? Someone he owes money to?"

When I got down to the ground floor, I saw a long line waiting for the elevator. Shame on me, I had mashed the button up on the fifth floor, and now all those people and sheriffs were probably wondering if that old Greek guy Paul talked about wasn't on to something.

I stopped at the secure area and waited until the sergeant with the broken leg turned to me.

"You done?" He reached under the counter and then handed my holstered pistol to me. I stood close to the counter so he couldn't see what I was doing, and lifted my skirt to replace my thigh holster. It was an unwieldy position; there was a metallic clatter as my Ruger fell to the marble floor. Although that made it easier to fasten the holster. Paul said, "Whoopsy, heavy gravity out here." I crouched to retrieve the pistol, and holstered it while I was hunkered down.

"Careful, lady," the sergeant said. "That's no toy."

"Oh, that little thing?" I said as I straightened up. "Do you know how hard it was to find pink bullets for it?" We grinned at each other, and I headed out to the December afternoon.

Lunch! Paul shouted silently. *I know you want a beer, and a shrimp po-boy would do me good.*

As I opened the door to my car I thought, *I've got to talk to Melanie first. I'll talk to the owner, maybe find out why Lucky was so close-lipped about things.*

Makes sense, Paul responded. *But can't it wait until after lunch? Don't you feel that hole in our stomach?*

"Melanie first. Then lunch. Then the owner. You can drive." That last one always shut him up.

He mashed the glow plug button, counted to ten, and released the clutch. We headed for highway 90 and Goode At Law beyond.

"You call yourself a detective, but you can't get the sheriff's office to tell you what's going on? What do I pay you for? And your rates are extortionate!"

It was Paul who said to the lawyer, "We've got the preliminary report from the team that handled the fire. That might be enough for Paralax to know if it's on the hook for the loss."

"What do you mean, 'we'? I hate the way you use the royal we. Who do you think you are, Queen Kate?" Standing behind her desk, Melanie Goode was drumming the fingers of her right hand against her left upper arm. I thought she was having a good time giving me grief.

I said, "Some of the beat officers at NOPD called me Queen Bitch. I—uh, WE rather like that."

Melanie ducked her head, trying to hide her smile. I (and the Paul Owens she did not know existed) was the only colleague who gave back as good as she gave. Despite our running disagreements, particularly the daily fee, we both enjoyed our dueling.

"Anyway," I went on, "I'll go over Captain Broussard's report later today. And since Lucky won't tell me what the sheriff's of—"

"Lucky?" Melanie interrupted. "Dick Lucky? A million teeth?"

"That's him. Lieutenant Richard Lucky. He's the—"

"I know that sonofabitch. His father was a client."

"Does that mean he'll talk to you? That's embarrassing." It's hard to justify $250 a day plus expenses when your client can do the job easier than you can.

Melanie shook her head, but didn't attempt to hide her smile. As she sat behind her desk she said, "No. I had an okay relationship with his father for years, doing family estate planning. Little Lucky would come along. But as little Lucky turned into bigger Lucky he'd come with dad and be a prick. Always asking the wrong questions. He seemed to assume I was trying to cheat his father. When the old man died, Dick transferred execution of the will to Bludgeon and Maim, and I've never seen him since."

"I don't remember if I mentioned Goode At Law to him," I admitted. "I see that might have made a difference."

Melanie opened a desk drawer and took out a container of hard candy. She offered one to me—I shook my head even while I heard Paul go, *Ooh! Ooh! Yeah!*—then she popped something red and sticky in her mouth. "The property owner is George Locaviche. He lives uptown, and his office is probably near mine, somewhere in the CBD. His file's been sitting on my desk since Paralax called me—" she waved a manila folder "—so here. Leave it with Harper after you get what you need. Meanwhile, I've got some clients waiting on me. Go away."

I can tell when I'm being dismissed. I stood up and said, "I'll check in in a day or two. Thanks, Melanie."

Squinting, but with a smile, the lawyer said, "Didn't I tell you to go away? Go on, get lost."

I sat in the office waiting room and copied George Locaviche's contact information onto my clipboard pad. Real estate office on Poydras, near the Superdome. Home in an especially ritzy part of uptown, way more upscale than my place in the Carrollton section. Leafing through the file, I saw there was a wife, Eustacia Donna, and an adult son, Cody. Professionally, George Locaviche had begun Hometown Realty in 2019, then sold it to RE/Max in 2027. After a few years of retirement, George started his current business, GL Estates.

You promised lunch.

Wait—didn't I have a burger at the firehouse? I thought back. "Harper?"

The receptionist looked up from her crossword puzzle.

"Melanie asked me to give this back to you." I handed over the file.

"Oh. Uh, thanks."

"Casa," I said. She looked up at me. I pointed at 12 across on her puzzle. "Four letter word in Spanish for house. C-A-S-A."

It took her a few moments to find 12 across. "How about that!" She looked up at me with a real smile. "Thanks."

Beer? I said, "See you," and I left the office.

Beer. Lunch is over, but beer.

I led to drive a few blocks to a restaurant and bar with a World War II theme. Not even Paul had firsthand knowledge of that confrontation, born as he was in 1955; now, eighty years later there were precious few real veterans left. The food, which I was going to avoid, was good but expensive; but the beer was cold and reasonably priced. Besides, some of the old-timers in there would flirt with me. Harmless, but enough to make a girl feel good about herself. So, I parked at a meter displaying 'Expired' and put my outdated New Orleans Police Department ID on the dashboard.

Let's see if they have some high gravity brew, Paul thought as I walked up Poeyfarre Street to the 55th Fighter Group restaurant. *Something with a little more oomph than Dixie.*

The vestibule walls and ceiling were made to look like sandbags. Just inside the doorway, barely out of the way for a customer, was a vintage jeep; complete with jerry cans and bullet holes, the hood featured a big five-pointed star in a circle. A manikin in green fatigues was behind the wheel, an unlit cigarette glued to its lower lip. *That guy makes me laugh,* Paul thought of the faux soldier, *I expect him to jump up and say 'smoke 'em if you got 'em.'*

The place was sparsely populated, it being only 3:30 on a winter weekday. I dropped my clipboard on the bar and sat in one of the high stools. The bartender came over before I'd finished reading the first page of the fire report. "What can I get you, miss?"

I smiled. "Something a little heavier than the usual, I think."

He was tall, he was burly, he was older than me. I saw pieces of tattoos peeking out of the neck of his uniform polo shirt. "Give me a hint. What's the usual?"

"Dixie."

The man let out a guffaw. It was a mixture of surprise, a sudden exhale, and perhaps shock. "Your usual is...Dixie beer?"

"Hey!" Paul exclaimed, taking the lead. "We won't make fun of your tattoos if you don't make fun of our drinks." Thank God it's my voice that comes out of my mouth, even when Paul is doing the talking. If a guy had said that to the barkeep, they'd be sweeping blood and teeth off the floor.

Instead, the bartender exerted the considerable effort to drop the smile from his face. "Fair enough."

"We'd like something with gravitas," Paul went on.

"We've got Guinness on draft, and Parish—"

I shook my head. "Bottle," I interrupted. "I can only handle so much change at a time."

"I've got Founders Imperial Stout. Thicker and darker than Dixie, but smooth."

Paul asked, "Sweet or bitter? ABV?"

"Not as sweet. And ten percent, I think."

"What else you got?"

In classic bartender style, he began polishing a clean beer glass with a bar rag. "Green Flash, it's sweeter but not as, uh, potent."

I raised my eyebrows to encourage him to continue.

"Squatters Outer Darkness. A little sweet, very thick, and more of a bang than the Founders."

Sounds like what we need, Paul thought.

"Indeed," I said. "Bring it on. I love the name."

He stepped away to the cooler, then brought out a huge brown bottle. He took the top off on the bar opener, then placed the brew on a cocktail napkin in front of me. Then the polished glass. He reached for the bottle as if to decant it, but I waved him away. "Okay. Well, let me know what you think," he said.

Paul leaned forward to inhale over the open bottle. *Sweet. Tart. Is that some licorice?*

No! I thought back, *I hate absinthe.* Still, why take his word for it? I took my own sniff. *Oh. That's good. It smells so, so solid. You ready?*

I felt Paul nod inside. Yes, that's something we can do. So, I held the brown bottle to my lips and took a moderate sip.

A rich and complex flavor flooded my mouth. The beer was thick, and rich, with bits of chocolate and hops and yes, even licorice. The sweetness was balanced by the sharpness of the alcohol. My mouth watered from the combinations. I took another swallow, slow, so I could enjoy the smooth refrigerated warmth as it slid down my throat.

"Oh! That's good! That is a big girl beer."

The bartender, dealing with a customer several stools away, turned to me and said, "Told you."

You're going to love this, I thought to Paul. I held the bottle out, and let him take it into my left hand, 'his' hand.

As little as I could taste it, he thought, *it was, uh, intriguing. Really good, huh?* Whichever one of us is leading gets the full taste, while the other gets only a washed-out shadow. That's true for food, alcohol, and sex. I have no idea how it works, but that's my life with dyad Paul. I nodded, and he went ahead with the ritual. Bottle neck to lips; lift the container, lean our head back a bit; and the full flavor of all those tastes, of sweet and tart, of softness on our tongue, and a bit of warmth on the way down to a happy, happy stomach.

Paul held the bottle out with our eyes closed. He was savoring the aftertaste, the hint of bitterness behind the chocolate. I wanted to know what he thought. *So?*

I am in love, he thought back. *This is great. Fantastic. Tremendous. Faboo.*

Faboo? I snickered.

"Barkeep!" he called. "Can we get a twelve pack of this to go?"

Can we never drink Dixie again? I thought. *Can we stick to oodles and oodles of whatever this is?* I took a close look at the dark label; the only color was the yellow border and what seemed to be red ghoulish eyes. "Squatters Outer Darkness," I said to the bottle. "It's a pleasure to make your acquaintance."

Paul did something funny with his voice when he thought to me, *Just call me Squat. I'll be taking care of your beer needs from now on. Shall I send a 'Dear John' message to Dixie?*

"Oh, Squat," I smiled, "we're going to get along fine." And I took another sip.

I started reading the rest of Captain Broussard's report on the warehouse fire. He was sure it was arson; not just the rapid full involvement, but the use of accelerants—that's tech talk for stuff that burns, like kerosene or even gasoline. Paul pointed out that Broussard said accelerant was used in many places, not just at the hallway where they found remains. *I don't think the firebug was trying to kill anyone,* he thought. *He may not have known that anyone was there.*

"He could have been a she," I said. It was a lesson I learned early in my career, that the natural assumption that a perp was a man can be very wrong.

"That sort of thing confuses me," a voice said. I turned my head and found one of those older darlings standing by my barstool, holding a highball glass. "I'm used to the men staying men and the women, well, you know."

He was cute. I mean, in a seventy-year-old way, like how I remember my PePaw. He had some wispy grey hair that had retreated from an otherwise gleaming head. Blue eyes. Lots of lines on his face. And brave enough to walk up to a woman half his age. I was impressed.

Paul, who lived and breathed for Bugs Bunny and some old rock band called the Beatles, sang, "I am he and you are she and we are all together."[7] I smiled at the man and patted the chair next to me.

I liked how he kept his eyes on mine as he sat down. "Really. There was a time when long hair and a skirt meant a woman. And short hair and pants meant a man. It really was easier then to know which end was up." He smiled, then juggled his drink to hold out his right hand. "I'm Edgar, by the way. And you are…?"

Before I could respond Paul said, "I'm Paulette. You're a man, right?"

"Indeed. And you're a woman."

"I was this morning," Paul said. "But things could change." I thought to my dyad, *Have a little fun, but I really have to finish this fire report.*

Silently he blew a raspberry at me. Years ago, when I was depressed about my then-recent flame turning out to be a murder

---

[7] That's not what John Lennon sang, but it's what Paul thought he heard on "I Am The Walrus." He and his sister wore out a copy of *Magical Mystery Tour* when he was 13.

suspect, Paul dragged us out to a bar and he led, claiming to be Paulette. Some little cutie lesbian hit on him—uh, on us, I guess— and since Paul had spent the first 55 years of his life in a man's body, he still thinks of himself that way. Long story short, Christine has been Paul's—Paulette's—girlfriend for something like five years. I put up with their romance, but the woman has turned into my very best friend. Uh, next to Paul, that is.

"I don't want to consider it," Edgar said. He pointed at our beer and asked, "Can I get you another one?"

"Sure, daddy."

He's being nice, I thought. *Don't make fun of him.*

Edgar flagged down the bartender and signaled for another Squatters.

"So, what do you do, Ed? Uh, can I call you Ed? Is that okay?"

"You can call me anything you like, Paulette." He tugged at his open shirt collar. "Actually, I'm retired. Just hanging out uptown all day, cutting coupons."

"Sweet!" Paul nodded at the bartender and took the full bottle of Squat in our left hand. "I think I'd get bored if I ever retired."

The man harrumphed, he really did. "Bored? After I retired, I wondered how I ever had time to do everything I do while I was working. What do you do, Paulette? May I ask?"

I was curious what he'd say. When he still had his own body, before he turned up in my head, Paul had done market research. In fact, he helped me earn my Masters in statistics, and for a few years that's what I did for a living. But now that he lives in my head, it's not like he can go to his job while I go to mine. It always makes me anxious when someone talks to Paulette—he once told a car mechanic that he was a professional sky diver. Just what is he going to say now?

"Private detective," he said. He pulled one of my business cards out, for Clear, Owens and Hodges LLC. "Huh, I got my partner's cards," he said, handing over one for Amy Clear. "I'm the Owens."

Edgar leaned back, sitting very erect. "A private detective! How exciting! Do you find murderers and dangerous criminals?" I must say, Edgar seemed quite impressed.

"Sometimes," Paul said, and took a very long pull on our Squat. *Hey!* I thought, *Save some for me.* When he was done, he slid the bottle into my right hand. "But mostly it's lost dogs, and pinning the goods on a straying husband, and insurance investigations." He held up the fire report, then dropped it on the bar. I felt him put a smile on our face. "It's not like on TV. It's a living, you know?"

"That's fascinating," the man said. "How did you ever get to be a private eye?" Like I say, he seemed to be most impressed with us.

Paul said, "I was a police detective for three years. Would you like me to pat you down and read you your rights? I've got my handcuffs."

I couldn't help it, I burst out laughing. I could tell Edgar's feelings were hurt because there was no doubt Paulette was goofing on him. He didn't deserve it. I led to say, "I'm sorry, Edgar. Sometimes I just crack me up." I lifted the report in my left hand and held the Squat in my right; I took a nice, long, not-so-dainty glug. "I'm doing an insurance investigation now, and I have to wade through this report this afternoon."

I feel bad to see how disappointed Edgar is, I thought to Paul. *Really, he's just being nice. Maybe he's a little lonely, but he isn't being ugly or creepy. And he made me feel good by striking up a conversation with me.*

Suddenly Paul leaned me toward Edgar. I was amazed when he kissed the man on the cheek. He smelled like bourbon. "Thanks for the beer," Paul said. "I really liked talking to you, but I have to get to work."

Edgar had been so pert and sparkly when he first sat down. Now he seemed slumped and tired as he shuffled toward a dimly lit part of the bar, away from me.

What was that all about? I thought to Paul. *You actually kissed a man?*

I used to kiss my father, he thought back. *He smelled like Scotch. No, I thought if I had been in his place, a kiss from the girl would make me feel better.*

"Huh!" I said out loud. Then, *Well, that was nice of you. Considerate. Good.*

Why did you laugh at him? Paul thought.

I wasn't laughing at him, I thought back. *Your line about patting him down was so off the wall funny. I couldn't help it.*

Drink? It was Paul's way of asking to lead so he could get all the taste and wallop of a drink.

"Sure," I said out loud. *There's a circle in hell for women like me,* I thought to him while he sucked down half the Squatters.

"I can't get too smashed," I whispered. "I really have to go through this report for Melanie." *You can have the rest of the beer.*

I guess Edgar told his friends about me, because no one else tried to talk to me while I went over the dossier. Even the bartender seemed to stand farther away when he asked if I wanted another Squat, although that may have been my guilty conscience.

Overall, I had maybe three sips from three beers. Paul was loopy, a funny drunk. I wasn't going to let him drive us home. The report was straightforward, laying out a damning case of arson, but not of murder. If the property owner set the blaze, Paralax Insurance was off the hook.

I thought it was strange that the report gave no hint of contents. It's like the warehouse was vacant except for whoever had been in the crematory hallway. I had questions for owner George Loco-something.

It was after six when I finished writing up my notes. Too late to call Melanie; that would have to wait until tomorrow. I threw a twenty down on the bar and collected my gear. *Let's go home, Paul. I'll drive.*

Nooo! Let me drive! I'm fine. I retreated inside to let him lead, and he promptly walked us into the side of the jeep. If that cigarette hadn't been glued to the manikin GI it would have gone flying.

That's okay, I thought to him as I straightened my skirt. *You enjoy the ride.*

Back at the house Paul insisted on phoning his girlfriend. He turns cranky if he doesn't get his minimum daily allowance of Christine. Fortunately, I love the woman; she and I have turned into best buddies over the last five years. You're probably wondering, so let me get this out of the way right now: Paul has to borrow my body when the two of them have, uh, intimate relations. I've learned to deal with it. Don't get me wrong—I like men. But the only way I get to be with men is if I let Paul be with Christine. It's a deal we made when I was in college. He used to be a basket case when I had a date (with a man, of course), but he's calmed down with time. With Christine, so have I.

"Paulette!" she cried. "How was your day? How is Amy?" What a sweetheart, she remembers me.

"I'm doing great, now that I'm talking to you. Amy got a gig today, so we were doing some research."

"Nothing dangerous, I hope. I worry when you have to deal with bad people with guns."

I chimed in, "I do, too, Christine. How are—"

"Amy! Good for you," she interrupted. Somehow, even on the phone, she always knew which one of us was leading. Nobody else can do it. I swear, Paul and I aren't all that sure sometimes. "Is it exciting stuff? Will I see you and Paulette on the TV news?"

We coughed; that's the sound that comes out when we both try to talk at once. Since we were talking to Paul's sweetie, I let him speak. "Not hardly. It's an insurance investigation. Not very exciting, not dangerous, and it pays okay." I nodded, but not even Christine could see that through the phone.

They talked about Paul—and me, of course—coming over to her double in West End on Saturday. Maybe a movie, maybe cook up a storm, maybe a walk over the canal lock to my *alma mater*, the University of New Orleans Lakewood. It rarely mattered what we did, because the point was how comfortable and close we were. All three of us in these two bodies. Christine has introduced us to some of her friends, although she calls us Paulette and he does most of the leading. I brought her to dinner at mom and dad's a few times, which was almost as awkward as you imagine. I remember the day Paul told my dad he had a girlfriend, everyone in a two-mile radius was embarrassed, including me. Have you ever found yourself saying, "Daddy, I swear I'm not a lesbian"? I didn't think so.

"I kissed a guy today," Paul told his honey.

"You what? Amy, what is Paulette talking about?" said the lesbian girlfriend.

He explained about the 55th Fighter Group and Edgar the sweet old man, and how I broke the fellow's heart by laughing inappropriately.

I had to defend myself. "What do you mean, 'inappropriately'? Paul told Edgar that he used to be a cop, and would the man like to get patted down and have his rights read. And 'I've got my handcuffs.' I laughed because it was funny."

I could hear Christine laughing on her end of the phone. She saw my point; she thought it was funny, too. After a moment she calmed down and asked, "So, Paulette, why did you kiss him?"

"I felt bad for the guy. I thought about if I had been trying to make some time with a woman—you know, back in the old days, when I had my old body—and the woman laughed at me, I'd feel crushed. Mortified. Filled with shame and—"

"I get the point," his girlfriend interrupted. "And so, you kissed him?"

"Well, yeah. I knew he thought I was a woman. And if I'd been in his shoes, the woman kissing me on the cheek would have, uh, lightened the blow. You know. So, yeah, I kissed him."

"Why any woman likes boys is beyond me," Christine said, "but I think it's sweet that the man came over to talk to you. I'm sure he thought you were pretty. And Paulette, that was so, so kind of you to do that. Just to make him feel better."

I started to giggle. "If Paul hadn't made me laugh, it would have been a pleasant fifteen minutes. Instead, I felt like some kind of evil monster."

Paul thought, *I have yet to find an evil bone in our body.* In my ear I heard Christine say, "You weren't trying to be mean. It's unfortunate, but you're not a bad person." There was a pause. "I couldn't be friends with a bad person, and you're the sister I never had."

"Christine Hodges," I said, "You make my day. You always know what to say to make me feel good. Plus, I hear Paul likes you a lot."

She played along. "Oooh, I like her too. But don't tell her I said so. I don't want Paulette to think I'm easy."

☿ THURSDAY, DECEMBER 11, 2016 ☿

I waited until ten AM to dial George Locaviche's office number. An automated attendant welcomed me to GL Estates. It rattled off several options; when I heard "For George, press 14," I did so. When did those phone machines learn to take two-digit numbers? I heard it ring one and a half times, and then a man's voice said, "Good morning. Welcome to GL Estates. Are you buying or selling?"

"I'm looking for George Locaviche," I said.

"Loca-veech," he corrected. "That's me. Who are you?" Paul thought, *The man is all business.*

So, I introduced myself. "I'm acting as a representative for Paralax Insurance," I went on. "It's a routine check on your property loss in Waggaman." If you tell them it's routine, maybe they won't get all hysterical. Maybe.

"I've been in touch with my agent," the man said. "He's taking care of everything."

"I don't know about that," I said, "but Paralax hired a lawyer who hired me. I want to discuss the fire with you."

"But my agent told me—"

Paul interrupted the man. "And I'm telling you I'm the one doing the research. Why don't you take me to lunch today?" That Paul, always thinking about food.

"But my agent said—"

"Tell you what," my aggressive dyad said, "I'll be at your office at noon and we can go someplace decent to talk." I heard Locaviche start to say something, but Paul drowned him out with, "See you at noon, George," and he ended the call.

"Did you used to sell encyclopedias or something?" I asked him. "Talk about a foot in the door!"

You hold your elbow out, lean forward, and keep moving. It's a little harder on the phone, but it's really the same thing.

I opted for slacks. That means I carry some hardware on my belt—cuffs, phone, ID, that sort of thing. I don't bother with a baton when I'm not working for NOPD, although there's one in the trunk of the Benz. My other concession to polite society is a concealed hip holster for my lovely Ruger 9mm. It's easier to access than the thigh holster, and it doesn't make my leg turn colors. Also, I can wear underwear. It makes a girl feel more secure, you know? Well, the gun, obviously. But I mean the underwear. Really.

I needed to go over the fire report again. To keep Paul from thinking rude noises to me, I got him involved; we alternated reading paragraphs aloud. When only your eyeballs are at work you miss things that your brain catches when your ears are in play.

He read, "Evidence of accelerants was found at each of the three outside entrances to the building, as well as at two internal doors that only could have been accessed by someone inside. Jefferson Parish Fire Department was unable to determine if the outside doors were or were not locked before the fire began."

"How did I miss that before?" I asked. I re-read the paragraph. *Was the building locked?* I thought to Paul. *If that was the case, only someone with a key could have poured gasoline under the inside doors. That would limit suspects to the owner and any tenants.*

"Was there a burglar alarm?" Paul asked. "Don't all business have them? Was it turned on?" Paul said he hated police, apparently because he was some low-level bad boy when he had his own body. But he liked detective work; he said it was like solving a puzzle. Sometimes he was a huge help.

I let the fire report drop to the floor and started making notes on my clipboard pad. Questions to ask George Loca-veech at noon. A, did he have a tenant? B, if so, who were they? C, if so, what was their business? D, if not, was the building locked up? and E, did it have the kind of burglar alarm that notified police, or just annoyed all the neighbors?

Paul saw my notes—after all, we both use the same eyes. He said, "Are you going to start easy? You know, 'When did you buy the property?' 'How long have you used Paralax Insurance?' 'What's your shoe size?' Or will you start with the sixty-four-thousand-dollar questions?"

"Sixty-four thousand—Oh, is that like—" right pinky at the side of my mouth— "'One meelyon dollars'?"[8]

I heard him laugh inside. *Yup. You got me. Cracko-jacko, another teenage hoodlum bites the dust.*[9]

---

[8] *The $64,000 Question* was a TV program in the golden age of TV quiz shows. Paul was too young to remember it, but the show title remained a common euphemism for any vital question as he got older, and he continued to use the expression even though Amy knew nothing about the TV program. Likewise, Paul's use of the Austin Powers movie's "one meelyon dollars," complete with pinkie move, had entered Amy's vocabulary despite her ignorance of the real source.

[9] Paul was in a college production of *West Side Story*. It was a long time ago, and this is how he mis-remembered a line of dialogue.

I had no idea what he was talking about. Sometimes when he does things like this I wonder if he's having a stroke. And then I wonder if I could stay healthy and sane if that happened. I mean, we share the same brain. Not that I'm in a hurry to find out, mind you, but it's an exchange like this that gets me considering the possibility.

Paul drove to the lunch date he'd crammed down George Locaviche's throat. His office was in the ritzy 650 Poydras Center in the Central Business District, almost within spitting distance of Melanie Goode's place on Carondalet—up Carrollton and a right on Earhart; but by the time Paul turned left on Loyola the streets were narrow and the CBD traffic was worse. I didn't want to walk from the parking lot I used for Melanie, so I told Paul to try the building's deck. It was four dollars an hour, remarkably cheap for NOLA. Besides, Melanie was paying my expenses.

I'd never seen a building whose lobby was on the ninth floor. This being New Orleans, anything described as below-ground parking would really be underwater parking; the first eight floors of this huge building were dedicated to cars. The elevator up to GL Estates on the twelfth floor was not made by Zeno. *Is our stomach in your feet?* Paul thought, *That's where it is for me.* There were other people in the elevator so I couldn't just slap the side of my head like I sometimes did when Paul was being silly. *Right behind my belly button*, I silently hissed back at him.

There was a simple building-provided sign next to the wooden double-doors, black plastic with etched numbers and letters in white that said "1215 GL Estates." Gentleman that he is, Paul led to open the door for me.

What a letdown. The place was tiny. There was an empty desk with a multi-line phone blinking like a lying thug in a police interrogation. I could see three doorways that led to who knows where. "Hello!" I called. "Anyone home?"

There were noises. A thin, tall woman wearing pearls and a print dress came out of one of the doorways and said, "Can I help you?" She was attractive, about my parents' age, with short blonde hair and a winning smile.

"Good morning," I said, trying to sound as chipper as she looked. "I'm the investigator for Paralax Insurance. Amy Clear. Is George Loca-veech here?" I heard Paul think, *She must have been stunning when she was young because she still looks great.*

As the woman said, "He's expecting you," I heard a deep voice from beyond one of the doorways, "I'm here! Give me a minute." The woman shook her head and said, "I'm Donna. George's wife. He told me we're going to lunch?"

"That's what I understand," I replied. No use explaining that I was as surprised by my dyad's instructions for luncheon as she was. I followed Donna into an adjoining room where George Locaviche was working on a calculator and writing figures on a columnar pad. She stood by me while her husband repeated, "Give me a minute." He seemed to be finishing up some project.

From above and behind, George appeared robust. Broad shoulders in a dark suit jacket, neatly trimmed grey hair combed left to right, and huge but nimble fingers on his ten-key calculator.

Amy heard Paul think, *Where do you think he's taking us for lunch? You said Melanie's paying expenses, we can go someplace nice.*

I guess we're going wherever George takes us, I thought back. *I'm not pushy.*

He wrote some numbers; he keyed in some more and mashed the equal sign on his calculator; he added those figures to his columnar pad; he sat back, saying, "Done!" He stood up and turned to me with his right hand extended. "George Locaviche," he said. A double-take: "You're the agent from Paralax?"

Like his wife, the man was in his early sixties. He was eight inches taller than me, with an attractive and easy smile. Paul thought, *What is it about him? He looks so comfortable in his own skin—uh, suit.*

I took his hand to shake. "Amy Clear," I said, "glad to meet you." Paul barged to the lead to add, "Something about lunch?" He must have weighed four hundred pounds when he had his own body.

George smiled and nodded. "Have you met my wife—"

"I introduced myself," Donna interrupted. The woman stood beside her husband and put a hand on his shoulder. Paul's not all that sentimental, but he thought *Don't they look like they're still in love. L'amour. Le sigh.* I learned French from Sister Agnetha and some Cajuns, but Paul learned it from watching Pepe Le Pew cartoons.

"The building cafeteria is convenient and quick," George said.

I should have known what was going to happen when I heard Paul silently swear. He got the first two syllables of the word 'cafeteria' out of my mouth before I realized what he was doing. I tried to say something, which made us cough; then I took the lead and said, "Cafeteria. That would be great." *You were going to complain, weren't you?*

Well, yeah! he thought back. *I remember the lunchroom at St. Giles Academy. Mystery meat, English peas, and those tiny red milk containers. Feh!*

George called to agents hidden in the other rooms, "Vanessa! Pete! I'm going to lunch. Don't give away the home planet."[10] He put an arm around his wife, and looked back at me. "Come on," he prompted.

Cafeteria. Fucking cafeteria food, Paul thought. *I'll bet the only beer they have is Olde English 800.*

Too bad, trashmouth, I answered in kind. *I can't drink on a business lunch anyway.* He continued to think uncomplimentary things about cafeterias, steam tables, and heat lamps keeping food warm.

---

[10] Originally instructions from Londo Mollari, the Centauri Ambassador on the TV series *Babylon 5,* to his assistant, Vir.

As it turned out, the building lunch place wasn't bad. I got a garden salad and a tuna melt. Paul wanted a hamburger and chess pie, but I told him no. *We can go back to 55th Fighter Group tonight for some more Squat*, I thought. Suddenly he was silently claiming to be my newest BFF.

George and Donna chatted about some home things, but eventually he turned to me and said, "What does Paralax need to know? I thought you knew everything about me. I've been using Paralax for seven or eight years."

Remembering Paul's biting question from the morning, I started with, "What all does Paralax insure for you?" I had pen in hand, over my clipboard pad.

"Home. Office contents and liability. Three cars. And our cabin in Pass Christian. I'm sure I've helped Paralax's bottom line for years." He was working on a bowl of gumbo. Donna, befitting her trim figure, had her own salad.

"Have you ever filed a claim before?" I heard Paul think, *If you really worked for Paralax you'd know.*

"Our son was in a bad wreck in Kenner three years ago. Cody spent some time in a hospital and in rehab. The woman who ran into him died, but she was at fault."

I started aiming at my money questions. "You've filed a claim for—" I had to look at some printout under my pad—"for, let's see, $385,000. Is that just the structure, or does it include contents?"

He pushed his spoon through his soup a few times before he said, "Just the building. It was empty."

"My God," Paul blurted, "Why did you own it?" *Shush*, I thought to him. *Don't make the man defensive.*

"I was between tenants." A shrug.

"What kind of alarm system did you have?" On my legal pad I wrote 'Alarm—?'.

"I don't remember the brand name. It was for fire and intrusion. It was wired into the Parish Sheriff's office."

Are you going to ask him?

Now's the time, I thought back to Paul. "The night of the fire—was the system armed?"

"I guess. Why wouldn't it be?"

"The Fire Department report says the fire was arson," I went on. "They found accelerant had been used inside the building. Either you're the only person who had a key, or you didn't set the alarm." My heart was racing; I always get this rush of excitement and anxiety when I confront someone.

George turned to his wife and said, "Honey? Would you get me another cup of water? And get yourself that piece of pie you wanted."

Smiling, Donna Locaviche stood up. "Can I get you anything?" she asked me. What a gracious woman! I thanked her but said no.

When it was just George and me at the table he hissed, "Why did you accuse me of arson in front of my wife?" I heard Paul, ever the pedant, think, *You didn't say his wife watched him set the fire.*

I tried to look offended and hurt. "My only concern is Paralax Insurance's liability," I said. "The fire report—" I pulled it off my clipboard and tossed it to him, splashing butternut squash soup onto the front page—"makes no accusation, but it does say their evidence shows the fire was set." I paused, but George was silent; I went on, "Logic says if you forgot to set the alarm, anyone might have come in and done the deed. That would mean you were negligent, but probably not enough to get Paralax off the hook. But if the alarm was primed, and you had no tenant, you are the only person who would have had access. In which case, Paralax not only wouldn't accept liability, but might sue for insurance fraud."

As Donna came back to the table, I saw George deliberately drop his spoon on the floor. "Oh, I am such a doofus!" He took the water and pie from his wife, while she smiled and went back to the cafeteria line to fetch another soup spoon.

He hissed, "I don't appreciate your implication, young lady." There were furrows between his eyebrows, quite a stern expression.

"Does Paralax cover your loss, or does it deny it?" I answered;
I don't know why I whispered it. "I'm not acting as a law
enforcement officer. Just an agent for Paralax." That mixture of
excitement and anxiety had me feeling like I was vibrating.

George glanced over his shoulder and saw his wife returning
with two spoons. "I want you to go."

Paul said, "We didn't know your wife was going to be here. We
didn't mean to embarrass you."

"Embarrass George?" Donna said as she sat down. "I don't
think that's possible." She smiled at her husband, and rested a hand
on his suit-jacketed arm. The man leaned toward her and kissed her
on the cheek. I heard Paul think, *Does this mean we're supposed to
go home? Did I miss something?*

No, I replied silently, *you got it.* Aloud I said, "This has been
productive, but I have to go back to the office to check in."

"Oh, please stay!" Donna said. "I want to know what you think
could embarrass my husband." I didn't hear any snark or sarcasm;
she really seemed curious.

"Thank you, no," and I stood up. I fished my Clear, Hodges &
Owens business cards out of a little pouch on my belt and gave one
to George and another to Donna. "If you think of anything Paralax
needs to know, please contact me." When I picked up my clipboard
and pad Paul said, "Thank you for lunch. Do you think they'll start
selling beer here?"

I would have slapped my head but I was in public. *Sure, ruin
my reputation. Let's see how much beer you can have when I can't
earn a living because everyone thinks I'm an alkie.* I rolled my eyes;
I waved; I escaped.

I was angry at my dyad, so I did not think anything to him
while I retrieved my Benz. I ignored him when he thought, *Can I
drive?* I went down Carondelet to Tchoupitoulas, then followed the
river to Rouses, my favorite grocery market.

It's always exciting when you start hearing Christmas songs the
day after Thanksgiving. Christmas is on the way, with pretty lights,

presents, time with friends, and, even for this non-believing alumna of a Catholic school, the advent of the baby Jesus. But now it's three weeks later and I am so sick of hearing all the Santa songs and snowman songs and tree songs and presents songs that are blaring from the speakers in Rouses. If I hear "Little Drummer Boy" one more time I will scream, and Paul keeps silently singing about his poor grandmother getting slammed by a reindeer. I started humming some nonsense to block out the seasonal Muzak and to keep Paul from speaking out loud, and I kept ignoring him when he thought things to me, like *What did I do?* And *Are you there?* And *Am I here all alone?* I put two green cabbages in my cart, and a pound of carrots, a head of iceberg lettuce, and a case of sparkling water. When I started looking at tofu, I heard Paul scream silently, *WHAT IS GOING ON?*

Did you say something? I have only the vaguest idea of what to do with tofu, but I guessed it was a victual that would get Paul's attention. Eight ounces has ten grams of protein and only 94 calories. Who knew? Maybe it was something I should be eating.

Somehow Paul managed to take the lead. He let go of the cart and sat on the floor in the middle of the dairy section. *Amy*, he thought. *May I ask you a question?* Meanwhile people were nearly running over me with their carts.

Oh, Paul. What would you like to know?

Why are you ignoring me? He sounded hurt. *Did I do something wrong?* Ignoring him was the most potent weapon I had for disciplining him. Every now and then I have to remind him that this body and brain are mine, and he's just a guest—generally a welcome one, but still, a guest.

Now that you mention it, I thought back, *we need to have a conversation about alcohol.*

Not again!

"Yes, again!" I said out loud. An older woman with a four-pronged cane in her cart and maybe her daughter beside her stopped a few inches from me and swerved down the frozen food aisle. I could imagine her telling her child, "Don't look at the crazy lady." It's what I would have said.

I heard Paul's dramatic but silent sigh. *Okay. What?*

I seem to have a problem with beer, I thought to him, *and so do you. As long as it's just the two of us, we'll muddle through. Gatorade and aspirin are a wonderful combination. But Paul Dominic Owens, you can't be telling strangers about our problem!*

Oh.

That's all you have to say? We're sitting on the floor in Rouses causing a scene and all you can say is 'oh'?

I'm sorry, Amy. I thought I was being funny. I didn't know I was divulging state secrets.

I laughed. *You think everyone knows you and I have a beer problem?*

There was a pause, as if he was thinking of the best way of phrasing an apology. Instead, he thought, *Well, yeah. I mean, isn't it obvious? We like beer and wine, and we like to get buzzed. Yeah, everybody knows.*

That knocked me back. "Really?" I whispered. "Everybody knows?" And I thought I'd done a great job of hiding it. I wrapped my arms around me as I sat and began to rock slowly.

Well, not anyone at the police station, Paul thought to me. *But Christine does. And even though we don't see Florence often, she does. Your sister and Eddie know. I'm pretty sure—*

Don't tell me mom and dad know! I moaned silently.

Okay, I won't tell you that. His voice in my head wasn't nasty or judgmental, just honest. I heard what he wasn't saying.

"Miss? Do you need any help?" A store manager was crouching beside me.

I probably looked like I didn't know who or where I was. "Uh...I—I guess I'm blocking traffic." I started to hoist myself up, and the man was nice enough to take my right arm and help me stand.

"No, I'm fine. Thank you."

"You're sure, Miss?" Would you like to rest in the employee lounge?"

I shook my head. "I'm sorry," I said. I looked up at him—he was taller than me—and added, "Did you ever realize that the whole world knows your deepest secret?"

"Really," he said, "you can sit or lie down on our couch. Is there anyone I can call?"

Paul, bless his brutally honest heart, led and said, "No, I'm good." He peered at the manager's name tag. "Bert? I appreciate your concern, and I'm sorry if I bothered anyone. Really, I'm okay." He stood up straight, which was when I realized I had been standing hunched over. *Let's pay up and go home,* I heard him think. I nodded, which probably added to Bert's evaluation that there was a crazy lady cleanup on aisle seven.

Paul put our hands on the cart and started pushing it toward the front of the store and the sixteen cashier lines. Last I saw Bert he was standing with hands on hips, peering after me. Possibly worried that I'd burst into flames and incinerate their entire stock of rotisserie chicken.

We don't need any of this, I thought, meaning the items in my cart. *I only picked them because I was mad at you.* I heard Paul laugh, *It was the tofu. That's when I knew you were serious.*

I saw a young lady stocking cans of soup. "Excuse me, Miss," I called to her as I pushed the cart towards her. "I forgot my wallet. Can you put these things back before they spoil?" Before she had a chance to protest, I added, "Thank you," and turned toward the front of the store and escape.

That was bad of me, I thought as I walked through the parking lot. *The lady is busy and I threw more work at her. I'm really a bad person.*

You're not a bad person, Paul thought back, *you're a customer. It's not your job to stock the shelves. Besides, the customer is always right.*

Even when she's wrong?

Yeah, he thought as I opened the driver's side door to my Benz, *even when she's wrong.*

Inside my car we were comfortable talking. "I'm so doomed," I moaned. "Do you want to drive?"

"That depends. Are you still pissed off at me?"

"Am I—?" His words caught up to my brain and stopped my mouth. I had to laugh. "Yes, but not like before. Give me twenty minutes and you'll be off the hook." I leaned back in the seat and let Paul wrap our arms around us. In a perfect world he'd still have a man's body and we'd be able to hold hands, or kiss, or, or, you know. But this is the best we can do. When I was eleven years old and Paul was a new and exciting part of my life, we learned to hug each other like this. Sometimes it was for support, like when my life or his seemed to be falling apart. Like when he discovered his wife had had him declared legally dead. Like the various times some man did me wrong. But sometimes it was just for affection, like now.

"Okay, you silver-tongued devil. You can drive." Paul made a left on Tchoupitoulas and headed for the Carrollton neighborhood and my humble abode.

As soon as I was home, I telephoned Goode At Law and asked Harper to relay a message to Melanie, that I'd bring a report to her the next day. "If it's not complicated," the skinny receptionist said, "why don't you tell me what you found?"

"If I do that," I answered with an anxiety-free burst of honesty, "Mel will take ninety days to pay my invoice. If I come in tomorrow, I'll harass her into writing me a check right away."

It sounded as if the woman was trying to stifle a snicker. "I see your point," she said.

Paul started laughing when I hung up. "You've got a future doing collections," he said. What a terrible thought! Although I guess it's good to have a future doing anything. I don't know about collections, though. Edgar had the right idea—clipping coupons. That's the future I want to get used to.

Paul and I are a good team in the kitchen. Between us we boiled up some rice, chopped onions and red bell peppers, and stir-fried them with sliced chicken strips. I call it my 'Not Fajitas.' Uh, don't hold your breath waiting for "Cooking With Amy and Paul" to show up at your neighborhood book store. While the chicken was cooking, Paul got a wine glass out of a cabinet and took a bottle of Landry Merlot Blackberry from my little countertop wine rack. It was a collapsible wooden contraption that could sit landscape if I had as many as ten bottles; since I never have more than three it usually takes up less counter space standing portrait. Not the sturdiest thing, but I trust it with my extensive and expensive wine collection of vintage October reds.

I let Paul open the bottle and pour our glass. I took a sip—not too terribly sweet for blackberry wine from West Monroe, Louisiana—and then Paul led to take a huge swig. Sometimes I wonder why he bothers with a glass. I let him pour a refill.

I took the glass to a table by the stove and went back to poking the stir-fry with a wooden spoon. "What are we going to do about our problem?" I asked. I think he was as surprised as I was to hear the words.

"First, do we have a problem? Lots of people drink but it's not a problem."

I shook my head while I stirred the wok. "I don't drink before work," I said. "I don't drink at lunch when I'm on a job. And I haven't had a drink for breakfast since I was in college."

"Okay. So?"

"I'm afraid I'm going to do all those things. I want to do them." I stood still, wooden spoon in hand over the softly bubbling wok. "I work so hard not to do them."

"I didn't know," he said.

"And then there's my health. I mean, my skin is getting slack and I've gained a few pounds."

"Yeah. You've mentioned that bef—"

"And I can see myself sleeping on my parents' couch and sneaking drinks from dad's liquor cabinet. And I wake up some mornings and I just want to keep hitting the snooze alarm until the clock mysteriously breaks into a zillion pieces against the far wall."

The chicken is going to burn, Paul thought. I stirred. I turned the gas off. I stirred some more. "And I know it's not your fault," I babbled on, still stirring, "but you like to drink as much as I do. Paul, we're going to be the dipsomaniac duo!" I felt my nose drip. "The tipsy twins. The drunken dyad. The pixilated pair." I'm not going to cry, I said to myself, I will not cry. I wiped my cheek with my sleeve. No, I will not cry.

No. We're always going to be Amy and Paul.

"I've got to stop," I said. I sat at one of the ladderback chairs in the kitchen. No sooner had I settled down, Paul stood us up and finished making dinner. A nice thing about the way we live: since he was leading, he was the one who felt the effort. Of course, if he overdoes things—say, cleaning the rain gutters—it's my one and only body that's sore the next day.

I'm discouraged, I thought to him. *I like to drink. I like the way it makes me feel while I'm drinking. But I hate being all dragged out the next morning. And losing my looks, I hate that even more.*

"Okay," he said. "I understand that. When I was in my twenties and thirties, I smoked cigarettes. Quitting was like you describe: I wanted to quit, but I also wanted a smoke. It was a bitch; I tell you what." He had dumped the Basmati into a bowl, and then threw the stir-fry on top. I thought to myself that I'd done a great job making dinner but I wasn't hungry. I wanted a Dixie. No—I wanted a Squat.

"I want a Squat!" I shouted.

Paul sat us back down. "Yeah," he said. "Me, too. They were great." He picked up a fork in my left hand and said, "You want to start?" I shook my head and mumbled, "Not hungry anymore."

"Well, I am," he said. "You're a good cook, you know that?" He was leading, so I barely got the taste of the chicken or the texture of the rice—thank God. I might have spewed otherwise. "Umm—this is really good. Thanks for making dinner," and he took another forkful.

I understand from seeing my parents, and watching my sister Kaylee and her Eddie, that people have different ways of saying 'I love you.' Kaylee and Eddie are always nagging, calling each other what I think of as bad names that must be part of their personal script. Sometimes I get uncomfortable around them because they act so negative, but they've got three kids and they still hold hands.

Paul and I have a different pattern. He stopped calling me names by the time I was thirteen or fourteen, once he came to grips with his new reality of living inside my head and body. I pointed out to him that he could have still been inside his old body when it died in my father's hospital ICU.[11]

Paul is good to me. He loves me, but even more, he's nice to me. When I mess up, he never ever says 'I warned you,' even if he had counselled against whatever it was that I messed up. He pays attention to the things I do, and he says things like, 'You're a good cook.' Ask yourself—when is the last time someone in your life said something like that? 'You're a good cook.' 'That was really smart.' 'I'm glad I know you.' And so, on those very rare occasions when I melt down like I'm doing now, he's a help. He doesn't tell me what I should do, or how I should feel. He just acknowledges whatever I tell him I'm feeling, and lets me be me.

Of course I love Paul.

I'm not nearly that good to him. True, the only names I call him are 'trashmouth' and 'garbagemouth,' because he could teach a pirate captain new and different ways to curse. And sometimes I call him 'geezer,' which is left over from when I was eleven and he would call me 'kid.'

The place where I fall down and treat Paul badly is over boundaries. Can you imagine what it's like to have someone else move your hands, and speak out of your mouth? I'd say ninety-five

---

[11] In *A Different Kind of Twin* by A. Trauring, 2014.

percent of the time it's fine, because we're used to each other. But that other five percent! I have to remind him that this is MY body, and no, he can't go on a zip-line expedition. And it's MY life, which he might ruin if he makes all my clients think I'm an inebriate. And the argument we recycle the most, NO I won't let him marry Christine because that would kill my pathetic little chances to find me a flesh-and-blood man. I'm thirty-seven and Christine is a year older, so we're both afraid she might give up on Paulette and find herself someone else, but please, can't I find a man for myself? Please?

I'm not as good to him as he is to me. But he loves me anyway, and he knows I love him.

Paul was chewing my Not Fajitas, so he thought, *What do you want to do?*

I want to stop drinking. I want a drink while I stop drinking.

I drink because I like the taste of beer, he thought, and I like the tingle of getting a buzz. Why do you do it?

Uh—I guess—I mean—uh— I had never considered it. How do we miss the basic questions? When he had swallowed I said, "I don't know. I think—I think maybe, maybe I'm bored." I felt sudden waves of heat come off my face. It was embarrassing to admit it. Crap. That's the sort of response that means it's probably true.

Okay, Paul thought. *Is there something you wish we were doing instead?* He was back at my Not Fajitas. He must really like them.

Well, what do I do now? We see Christine every two or three days. I see Florence once in a blue moon, when she's here from Los Angeles. And...and...

Hmmm?

He sipped some wine. Then I said, "When I'm working, my days and sometimes my nights can be intense. I want to come home and put my feet up."

And have a drink?

"Yes, Paul. And have a drink."

He stood up to put the bowl in the sink. "I've heard that the easiest way to get rid of a habit you don't like is to replace it with a different one. I used to collect coins. I had a friend who made stained glass. Nice stuff, too."

"PePaw had a huge model railroad layout in the basement," I recalled. "Sometimes he'd let me and Kaylee run the throttle. You could even make smoke come out of the engine chimney."

As he washed the bowl and flatware he said, "We don't use the spare bedroom for much. We can set up a Lionel system. Or H-O trains." Paul wasn't telling me to do this; he was offering possibilities in answer to my dilemma.

I shook my head. "With PePaw gone, there's not much point," I said. "You know—I'm not looking for you to sympathize with poor, poor pitiful me. But I don't know that you can solve this for me, either."

"Nope. Sure can't." He dried our hands on the dishtowel and sat back down at the kitchen table. "You want some coffee?" he asked.

"Maybe…maybe you and I and Christine can go somewhere some weekend. Camp out on the north shore. Take that shrimp boat trip in Biloxi. Or, we can go see a play—ah, crap, everyone's doing *A Christmas Carol*. There's no theatre worth seeing in December." I drummed my fingertips on the table. Crap. I really want a beer.

"What?" Paul asked. Like I've said, he doesn't know what I'm thinking unless I think it to him. No, I have no idea how we do it; it's just something we can do.

"I want a beer," I said out loud.

"Me, too."

I thought about going to the refrigerator for a Dixie, but something occurred to me. "How come you aren't upset about drinking?" I don't know how I'm going to quit if he isn't on my side. The temperance two, that's what I need us to be.

I felt him shrug. "I don't feel bad about drinking. I drank when I had my own body. Yeah, I was bald and overweight, but Mary

Pat—" she was Paul's wife "—drank with me. We had a good time. We didn't fight, we just enjoyed it." He paused a moment. "She may have gained some weight, too, but I didn't notice because I didn't care. I loved her." A longer pause. "Damn, I wish we'd had kids."

We sat there for a minute or three. Then I had a revelation. "So, drinking has never interfered with your life. Or with your self-image?"

Huh. I guess not.

"So why does my drinking bother me so much?"

Because you're not me?

I laughed. I love how Paul can be dead serious and make me laugh. "Hey, not me," I called, "Let me have some of that wine."

You sure?

"I think so. My strategy is to figure out how to be okay about drinking." I lifted the glass in my right hand and took what for me was a big gulp. It was sweet and a little biting, and, frankly, not the best red I've ever had. I made a show of wiping my mouth on my right arm. "It's got to be easier than quitting."

Later in the evening, when my dyad and I were comfortable with an alcohol cushion, I said, "I need your help at the computer. I've got to give Melanie a final report on the fire business."

"And an invoice," Paul helpfully added.

"And an invoice."

My relationship with a keyboard is strained at best. I'm your basic two-finger typist. Florence said I'm a Christopher Columbus typist: "First you find it, then you land on it." Meanwhile, Paul sometimes sprouts an eleventh finger on my left hand when he sets to work. I have no idea why a male in a backwater like West Virginia in the '60s and '70s was taught how to type, but I'm grateful. When I had to take an office skills test for my first market research job, I let Paul do the typing. Can you believe the man got sixty-two words a minute? I get more mistakes than that.

So, Paul was nice enough to prepare an invoice for three days' work, at $250 a day for a subtotal of $750, and then $23.41 for parking lot receipts and a fast half-muffuletta from Rouses' steam table. $773.41, not bad for a week's work. If only I worked more than one week a month.

And the final report. Fire department says arson. Sheriff's office investigating a possible fatality. And the property owner declined to answer questions about the state of the building alarm or door locks. I didn't think Paralax would be paying anything on this claim.

✄ FRIDAY, DECEMBER 12, 2036 ℧

The next morning, I was at Goode at Law bright and early for me, around 10:30. It was chilly, even by New Orleans standards, with low overcast. People think of New Orleans as non-stop Mardi Gras, but winter is not an attractive season here. It's not like you need a snow shovel, so we should be grateful, I know; but there's something about 45 degrees at 90 percent humidity that is just unpleasant. And after you survive a New Orleans summer, 45 degrees feels like a dry ice compress all over your body. The Chamber of Commerce is not asking me for an endorsement.

"Melanie's in a terrible mood," the receptionist, Harper, whispered to me. "She called me 'fatso' when she came in." A reminder: Harper is the ninety-pound anorexic that Paul wants to force-feed a cheeseburger. A Melanie in a bad mood was going to argue over my invoice.

Maybe I should take off the expenses, I thought to Paul.

Nah. But you can offer to as a compromise.

I sat in the lobby, playing twenty questions with Paul to pass the time. After he beat me three times, Harper told me it was my turn. I walked in with a small portfolio holding the papers I had for my boss.

"Ah, my least favorite person," Melanie declared as I entered. She was sitting at her desk; the bag of hard candy was on its side, its contents spilled across her calendar.

Paul responded out loud, "And you're looking like a ten-car pileup on the Pontchartrain Causeway this morning." It wasn't true, of course. Melanie was as pretty as ever, with that Irish complexion and amazing Medusa curls. But then, I doubt I'm her least favorite person.

Melanie broke into a grin and motion for me to sit. "Actually, that last client is my least favorite person. He thinks all the stuff I do for him should be pro bono. I'm this close to sending him to Bludgeon & Maim. What do you have for me?"

I handed her the single sheet Paul had typed up for me. "Paralax is off the hook," I said. "Jefferson Parish Fire says it was arson, and the parish Sheriff is investigating a possible fatality. And your client, Loca-veech, is an oily weasel who sent me home when I began asking the money questions."

She scanned my report, which basically said the same thing.

"Damn," she said. "George has been a client for forever." She shook her head. "It'll be a shame to have to visit him in Angola."

"And here's my bill," I said. I held my breath while Melanie looked at it. I swear, her eyeballs bulged so much they knocked pieces of candy off the desk.

"$773.41?" she bellowed, then dropped the page and looked up at me. "$773.41? Are you serious?"

"How much is Paralax paying you for this?" I asked, feeling that mixture of adrenalin and anxiety. I heard Paul think, *Good question.*

"Uh, twenty-two hun—wait, that's irrelevant!"

The anxiety evaporated. "Bingo," I said. "Tens and twenties would be nice, but I'll settle for a check."

It was funny, the way Melanie's face collapsed into a frown. Squinting at me, she said, "I don't know why I put up with you."

"Oh, Mel. It's because we have such a good time together. And I got you your answers in three days instead of a whole week." I was pretty sure that last part spoke to the woman's stingy heart. It's an open secret that private investigators routinely charge by the week, even when they find what they're looking for in the first fifteen minutes.

"You are so exasperating!" she shouted; I was sure heads turned in the waiting room, beyond her closed office door. "I want you to go away. And never come back unless I call you!" She was staring at me while her right hand was feeling around the desk for one of those sticky red candies.

It was Paul who said, "Then write me a check so I don't have to come back." He was almost as good as me at wearing that sweet smile that always worked on my dad.

"You are such a piece of work," the lawyer muttered as she stood up. "C'mon," she said when she opened her door, and she walked me to her bookkeeper's office. "Pay the wench and get her out of here," Melanie ordered.

"Hey, Mel?" I called. "Since I probably won't see you, Merry Christmas."

Eyes flashing, she aimed an index finger at me. "You! You get a lump of coal." Then she walked to Harper's reception desk and asked who was next.

Check in hand, I walked up Carondalet toward the parking lot where my yellow Benz awaited. Paul was whistling; I asked him how he did that. "You can feel where I'm putting your lips and your tongue, right?" he asked. "Do that and blow. Here," and he retreated. *Go ahead*, he prompted me, *you can do it*.

For the umpteenth time I tried. Some odd sounds came out of my mouth, but nothing I'd call whistling. *You almost got it*, he thought to me. I tried some more. What I was imagining to be a careless tune sounded like 'wheeze, wheeze, chirp, wheeze, wheeze.' *There, you got one.* I love how supportive Paul is, even when I'm an abject failure.

"I don't get it," I said. "Same mouth. Same tongue. Same lungs. Same bent front tooth. You make it sound like a symphony and for me it's a tuba with indigestion."

More like a jew's harp, my helpful dyad thought to me. *With indigestion.* Hah! When we got to the car, I turned on the radio. It was Paul's favorite Sirius/XM station, the 60s oldies channel. I forgot about whistling and let Paul sing along with a bunch of songs from before I was born.

I was dreading the 'discussion' we were bound to have at home. It wasn't even one o'clock. Paul was going to want a 2,000-calorie lunch, and I was going to want a couple of beers. But after we talked last night, something he coaxed out of me was still bouncing around my half of my head. "I think maybe I'm bored," I had said. Just thinking it now made me feel bad, like a worthless wino with no will power. Hey! I come from a good home! I've got a Masters in statistics! I'm no dum-dum!

But maybe I'm a bored not-dum-dum. Before Paul began his plea for food, I went in to the bedroom and started changing clothes. A sports bra. A green tank-top for the Zephyrs baseball team, with mascot Boudreaux D Nutria playing a bright red saxophone. Running shorts I realized I had not worn since the day in August that the thermometer hit 104°. A black fanny pack for my phone, my wallet, and my backup snub-nosed revolver. And my hot pink running shoes—I swear, there were cobwebs in them. *Uh-oh,* I heard Paul think. *What are we going to do?*

"Last night you made me think I'm bored. So, I'm going to run around the block to get un-bored. If that doesn't work, I'll run a second lap." Holding on to the chifferobe, I started stretching out my hamstrings.

"Are we bringing water?" he asked between my grunts. "Oxygen? Insurance card?"

We used to run a lot, I thought to him. *You liked it when I was a kid.*

"You're the one doing the work. I'm just along for the ride."

I snickered. *I may run until I collapse. Then you'll have to get us home.*

My house is in a safe part of Carrollton, maybe three blocks from the river. When I was still just a consultant for Commander Ramirez—well, he was only a captain then—Paul and I brought down a drug kingpin in Bywater. I found his inventory, it was huge. Turned out I got a joint task force reward. Had to pay taxes on it, but still. My father's advice was to buy a nice house in a good neighborhood, and let his tax consultant set up an investment plan. I think I was twenty-six when that happened. It's not normal to be that young and realize you'll never have to work for a living. Dad told me I needed to stay employed for my own sanity, and Paul said pretty much the same thing. So, I actually joined New Orleans Police as a detective. It's ten or eleven years later and I'm used to working for a living, even though I paid cash for the house. I complain about my mortgage just like everyone else, except I don't have a mortgage; but I don't want to turn into a lazy slug. Well, except for the part of me that agrees with sweet old thing Edgar, about clipping coupons.

They're doing repair work on my street, so there's no sidewalk in front of my place. I started jogging in the gravel outside my fence, heading up toward Dominican Street. It was a chilly December day, but I figured the exercise would keep me warm. By the time I turned the corner I was warmed up and shifted gears. Paul was making silent sounds of joy as I ran under trees, in front of houses traditional and modern, and past the occasional repairman working on roofs or plumbing. I was breathing heavy, but feeling good about doing something—something that didn't involve food or alcohol.

It's great to accomplish something, I thought to Paul. *Healthy. Good for me. Not bored.*

I waved at an older woman standing by her mailbox as I raced past her.

This still amazes me, Paul thought. *Like when you and your friend Josie used to run when you were a kid. If I were in my old body, I'd be lying on the side of the street with Xs instead of eyeballs.*

You said you were fat and bald before you came to me, I thought back.

I rounded the next corner and headed toward the river down Millaudon. Some of the houses on this street were grand affairs. Needless to say, after ten years I still haven't met most of my neighbors.

Halfway down the block a stitch started in my side. I tried to downshift back to jogging, but even that hurt. *Whoa! What's going on?* Paul thought when I stopped and bent over, hands just above my knees, panting.

Hit a wall, I thought to him. I was looking at my pink running shoes. Not so much looking at them as that's where my eyes were aimed. My main concern was oxygen.

Hit a--? Oh, Paul finally figured out what I meant. I was leading, so I guess he didn't feel that painful knot in my side. *Can I do anything?*

The muscle cramp was unstitching, so I stood up. *Sing me a song,* I thought. He was a fount of ancient melodies and lyrics from artists with strange names like Animals, Zombies, Kinks, and Exclamation Mark and the Somethings. Generally good for a laugh. I started walking the rest of the way to Benjamin Street.

"You always make fun of me when I sing," Paul said.

I smiled. "So be grateful I'm asking you to." I happen to have a good singing voice, and when Paul uses it, so does he.

"Oh, baby this town rips the bones from your back," he started. "It's a death trap, it's a suicide rap, We gotta get out while we're young, 'Cause tramps like us, baby we were born to run!"[12]

I'd never heard the song before, so the way Paul was emphasizing some syllables and holding some notes was funny.

---

[12] Bruce Springsteen, "Born To Run," 1975, Sony/ATV, Universal, Downtown Music. It was the first song Paul thought of that had anything to do with running. Yeah, it was a stretch.

Still, I sort of promised I wouldn't laugh at him. And besides, he was singing, so I couldn't say anything out loud.

What a treat, I thought, honestly. *I'm walking down the street with my very own soundtrack. Where's the camera?*

My side didn't hurt anymore and I was starting to feel the chill, so I resumed jogging. I had passed my house and started on the second lap when my cellphone rang. *If that's Christine,* Paul thought, *I want to talk to her.*

I stopped in the gravel sward between pavement and front yards to answer the phone. I didn't recognize the incoming number, so I sounded official and said, "Clear, Owens and Hodges. How can I—"

"You're the detective lady, right?" a woman's voice leapt from my phone.

"Yes, ma'am. This is Detective Clear. How can I—"

"I'm Donna Locaviche. Somebody beat up George and just threw him out of a car in the driveway." The longer she spoke, the faster the words came out and the higher her voice went. "Please help us!"

"Be right there," I said. "Where are you?"

She barked, "25 Richmond Place. Hurry, please!"

Are you getting a new job? Paul thought.

"Hmm. Maybe," I said. I turned and went back to my car. "Right now, though, she sounds like she needs help."

I programmed my GPS while I sat for a red light at St. Charles. When the map came up, I said, "You want to drive?"

Please fasten your seatbelt and return your seat tray to the upright and locked position. The light turned and Paul sped off to the Uptown neighborhood and the Locaviche homestead.

There are many enclaves of wealth and style in New Orleans, places where millionaires live, aided of necessity by butlers, gardeners, chauffeurs, chambermaids, and tax advisors. As neighborhoods go, the area referred to as Uptown[13] houses much prosperity and surprisingly little ostentation. When the little Garmin told me we had arrived at our destination, I was looking at a two-story beige stucco structure with lots and lots of windows. There was a peculiar dormer sticking out above the red tile roof. Most striking was the wide semi-circular driveway of textured concrete. Meanwhile, Paul parked across the street from the bulky block of an abode.

There's no fence, Paul thought. *Even we have a fence. Where is George's fence?*

I was standing outside the car, buckling my fanny pack. It gave me a moment to look down the one-way street. *Huh. Nobody has a fence.*

"Zoning?" he hypothesized.

"Maybe some people are so rich they don't need fences?" Even as the words came out of my mouth, I realized that couldn't be right. "No," I added, "must be zoning."

I headed for the seven marble steps—marble! The steps were marble! The wrought iron outer doors were open, and so was one of the two practical wood doors. "Hello! Hello!" I shouted as I walked in. Immediately I heard a woman's voice call, "Coming!" and the sound of footsteps on the hardwood floors.

Donna Locaviche looked frazzled; her hair was ignoring gravity, and there appeared to be blood on the left sleeve of her blouse. "Thank heavens you're here!" she shouted. "Please, come with me." I followed as she retreated to an inner room.

I guess it was the living room. It was the size of a hotel ballroom, with two chandeliers ablaze. Two walls seemed made out of windows, and the others were mirrored to make the room seem even larger. A huge artificial Christmas tree was in a corner, sparkling with blinking white lights. Sprawled on a brown leather sofa, clothes torn and with a steak over what I guessed to be a blackening eye, was George Locaviche.

---

[13] "Uptown" in New Orleans means upriver from the French Quarter.

Donna was crouched next to him, whispering something, trying to comfort him. I could see his uncovered eye blink and move, so I gathered he was conscious. Maybe even alert. I stood behind his wife and said, "Hey, George. What's the other guy look like?" Detective humor.

His voice was barely a whisper. "I thought I told you to go away."

"I did," I assured him. "I finished my job with Paralax, and then Donna called me. I'm available."

He groaned, while his wife cooed and patted him. He managed to say, "Available for what?"

"To protect you from whoever beat the holy living crap out of you," I said. "By the way, I told Paralax they shouldn't pay your claim." I heard Paul think, *Yep, that ought to convince him to hire you.*

"I don't need—Ouch! Oh, oh, oh," down to a wimper. "George, please let me call the doctor," Donna pleaded. "I'm afraid you may be hurt worse than you think."

"No!" and then his voice fell to a murmur, "I don't need a doctor."

"I'm thinking you need to call the police," I offered. "I know a lot of those people. Let m—"

"No!" louder this time. "No, no police." He winced as Donna adjusted the slab of beef over his eye. "Honey," he whispered, but with unmistakable annoyance, "it's okay. Let me be, okay?" Donna leaned back, her hands still on the couch cushion. "I—I just need to rest. Please."

His wife stood up, looking confused and embarrassed. "I don't know what to do," she said. "What should we do?" She looked up at me, expectantly.

I whispered, "Can we talk somewhere else?" I wanted to find out just what happened, and it was obvious George wasn't about to be helpful.

"The kitchen," she whispered back, and led me down a hall and into what must have been the grand prize winner of the *Better Homes and Gardens* kitchen competition for 2036. It wasn't as big as the living room, true; but I could have fit three of my kitchens in there and there'd have been room for a chest freezer and a Jacuzzi. Paul, who is a better cook than I am, said, "This room is magnificent. I'd kill for an island sink like that."

Donna ignored him and sank into one of the elaborate soda fountain chairs. I took the one next to her. Before I could say anything, Paul said, "Okay, what the hell happened?"

She took a tissue from the box on the table and daubed at her eyes. "About five minutes before I called you," she began. "I was working on dinner, when I heard car tires screech, and a car horn. We don't hear things like that on this street." She was nodding. Paul thought, *She agrees with herself, that's a good sign.* "I went into the hall and opened the door, and there was George in the driveway, on his hands and knees. An SUV was pulling out of our driveway, but I ran to George." The nod turned into a slow head shake. "His shirt was bloody and torn. His slacks were torn. His nose was bleeding, and—" She turned her head and tried to collect herself. I could tell the Locaviches' world did not usually include much in the way of physical violence.

She applied the tissue more forcefully for a moment. "I—I helped him into the house. I got him to the sofa. I kept saying, "What happened? What happened?" All he said was, 'I don't know.'" She hiccupped a few times—I've seen lots of people do that when they've been crying—and then finished, "That's when I called you. I didn't know what else to do."

"That's good," I said; I thought she needed some support and validation. "I'd call the police, but your husband said no. And I'd call a doctor, but he said no. Donna, I don't know what else to tell you. Does this sort of thing happen often?"

"No!" she said, horrified. "Nothing like this, never."

"Phone calls in the middle of the night?" A head shake. "Door bell ring and you find a flaming bag of dog crap on the porch?" Another head shake, and not even the hint of a smile.

Paul thought, *Does he have enemies? I don't think muggers administering random beatings take you home afterwards.*

I nodded, and began, "Does George—"

"I'm so sorry," the woman interrupted, "I feel so rude. Would you like some coffee? Water? Anything?" By the end her voice was barely audible.

"Coffee would be great," I said. It occurred to me that Donna might hold her crap together better if she had a task to accomplish.

It also occurred to me that she must be feeling overwhelmed to overlook my running attire—green Zephyr's tank-top, running shorts, and hot pink running shoes. I probably didn't look like the most reliable fount of advice or protection, but Donna was too upset to notice.

"Thank you. Look, does George have any enemies that you know of?"

"George? You have got to be kidding." She was spooning beans into an electric grinder. Paul thought, *I don't see chicory in our future.*

I fell back on the line of questions I learned when I was on the police force. "Does he owe anyone a lot of money? Does he do drugs—No, Donna, I'm not accusing him of anything. I'm trying to figure out why someone dropped an anvil on him. No judgement. Please, just tell me truthfully. Does George gamble?" Another shake. "Does he drink a lot? Is someone blackmailing him?" Donna poured three cups of water into her Cuisinart, then placed a filter for the fresh grind she'd made. I had stopped asking questions, but she continued shaking her head. She pushed some buttons on the coffee maker display, then came back to the chair next to me.

"Why would anyone want to hurt George?" she asked. "He doesn't do any of those—those things you were asking about. Maybe a client misunderstood what they were buying from him?"

Poor woman, Paul thought. *I'm betting she really has no idea why anyone would mess him up.*

"I don't know the answer, Donna," I told her. "But I can give you and him some advice on how to protect yourselves."

"I don't want a gun!"

For a fleeting moment I wanted to slap her. Paul thought, *I don't want to need a gun either, but meanwhile I live in the real world.* I managed to keep my voice level as I said, "Target hardening. There are some things you can do to make trouble less likely to fall on you."

"You sound like you think this will happen again." The coffee maker went 'beep beep beep beep beep." Donna went back to the counter and poured two cups. "I forgot to ask—do you take sugar? Cream?" Holding each by its saucer, she brought the liquid caffeine to the table we were sharing. I heard Paul quote a terrible movie he once made me watch, *I like my coffee the way I like my men—strong and black.*[14]

Tell me you didn't say that out loud!

I don't think I did, he replied silently. *Nah. Donna's head hasn't exploded. We're good.*

"Walk me through your house. I'll show you things you can do to make everyone safer."

The poor lady nodded, and sipped at her coffee. When she put it down, a pint or so spilled into the saucer. She didn't seem to notice. "Let me check on George first," she said, and she stood up.

"I'll wait here," I said, and took advantage of the coffee she had poured. It didn't have the kick-you-in-the-teeth punch of chicory, but it made up for it in a smooth, sweet taste. I told Paul, "I'm drinking liquid gold."

Donna was back quickly. "He's sleeping," she informed me. "I put a throw over him. Oh, his face is going to look like a painter's palette tomorrow."

---

[14] More or less from the movie *Airplane* (1980). Paul likes puns and verbal slapstick. He is a big fan of Leslie Nielsen. And don't call him Shirley.

"Yes, I think it will." Since she didn't let me answer earlier, I returned to a comment she had made before the coffee maker derailed us. As I stood up to follow her around the house I said, "Look. We know George wasn't robbed. The fact that he doesn't want to call a doctor or the police tells me he knows who beat him up. And yes, I expect it to happen again. And if I'm right, each episode will be nastier and nastier."

We had gotten as far as a wide, modern wooden staircase. She stopped abruptly; I nearly walked into her. "How can you think that?" she asked, looking at me as if she'd just noticed my fabulous neon green and hot pink couture. "Do you have such a low opinion of your fellow man?"

Uh, that seems to be a serious question, from Paul. *You want to answer? Or shall I?*

All yours, I thought back.

Paul said, "Occupational hazard. Three years on the New Orleans Police Department. It does tend to dim one's view of humanity."

"But—" suddenly Donna was standing with her hands on her hips "—my husband said he doesn't know who beat him or why. He's an honest man, I assure you, after thirty-one years of marriage."

Paul shook our head, genuinely sadly. "I can't tell you how many times we've heard that from battered wives, extortion victims, and petty drug dealers. Uh, no offense! I don't mean your husband is doing anything wrong. Just..."

Thanks, Paul. I'll take it from here. "...Just that I wouldn't believe Mother Teresa if she said she didn't know who spit in the holy water."

There was a long silence while Donna stood looking at me, her mouth open. Finally, she said, "I'm sure you are not lying to me, detective. Let me say I am grateful that my life has been different from yours."

I nodded. I heard Paul think, *Hey! Our life is fine, thank you very much, you prissy little tight-ass.* Although I agreed with my trashmouth dyad, I said, "That's fair. Show me your house so I can help you protect yourself."

The wide stairs took us to a long hallway with a light blue carpet. There were portrait paintings along the walls, and at intervals there were antique tables with fancy old chairs. It made me think of my visits to Oak Alley Plantation up river: that super-tasteful and classic old-fashioned taste. If the people in this family ran for exercise, they would not mix and match neon green and hot pink.

"This is my son's room," Donna said as she took us into a super-sized bedroom. It had a twin bed, neatly made, with an ornate dark wood headboard. There was a sofa at one end, a desk with one book on it, a few chairs, and a built-in bookcase chock full of, well, books.

New Orleans, right smack in the middle of the central time zone, is pitch-black by 6:15 PM this close to the Winter solstice. The two wide windows overlooked the front of the house, but the nearest lights I saw were from a Richmond Place street-light and the houses across the street. "Jack the Ripper could walk right up to your front door and no one would notice," I said; I took Donna by the shoulders and positioned her to look outside. I watched her blink a few times. Finally, she said, "We usually have the front porch light on by now."

"And you turn it off when everyone goes to bed, right?"

Donna turned to look at me. "Of course. Doesn't everybody?"

It was Paul who replied, "And everybody knows bad guys don't do anything after you go to sleep." I tacked on, "You need floodlights on the outside of the house. If you don't want to burn up electrons all day and all night, put motion detectors on them. Lumens are your friend."

"I—I didn't know," the woman said softly, looking at her shoes.

"Nobody does until it's explained to them. Don't feel bad; just fix it." Then I stepped back and looked at the windows. Both sets of openings were made of three conventional double-hung sash units, topped by a transom window that I've seen over old inside doors, but never before on an outside wall. Not that I'm an architect or anything. The most obvious thing to me was the cheap locks on the window units. Flimsy as they were, all but one were in the unlocked position. You might as well hang a neon sign flashing the word 'open.' I tapped the frame of one window to see what it was made of; the solid thunk said it was wood.

"These windows. If a sentient and awake human is not in the room, they should be locked. And when I say locked, I don't mean these bargain-basement window sash latches. Have George drill a hole through the top of the lower window unit," I was pointing, "and into but not through the bottom of the upper unit. Then put a bolt eye in the hole. No one will be able to force them open, but in case of fire you can pull the bolts out easily."

Paul thought, *Take it easy. I think she's about to cry.* I looked, and saw what he meant. "Look, Donna," I said, softly, "I'm sorry if I'm barking at you or making you feel bad. Ninety-nine out of a hundred people are oblivious to this kind of personal security, and most of them will never suffer for it. It's not your fault that you didn't know."

She looked up and gave a faint smile. "Thank you," she said.

Thanks for telling me, I thought. *I'm so wrapped up in what she needs to do that I wasn't paying any attention to her.*

Yeah. There was a time I didn't know any of this shit that you learned in the police force. I feel for her. Even if she is a prissy tight-ass.

I snickered. *Prissy tight-asses need to know home security too.*

The other rooms upstairs had similar windows and deficiencies; and as it got later and darker outside, the lack of outdoor security lighting became more obvious.

"This is the master bedroom," Donna said as she ushered me into it. The same double-hung sash window arrangement greeted us, although the view was of the tiny backyard and Nashville Avenue behind it.

"Your garage," I pointed. "I saw your driveway off Richmond goes by the side of your house. Is that the only way into your garage?"

The answer I dreaded was what I got. "We can go in and out onto Nashville." She sounded as if she was proud of the convenience.

I slapped the side of my head, and this time it wasn't because of Paul. "That's a nightmare!" I exclaimed. "Until whatever is going on with your husband is resolved, you've got to barricade that entrance. I recommend a fence to keep uninvited guests from coming in that way. Think barbed wire. Broken glass. A trip shotgun. That really—"

Look.

So I looked. Donna was wearing a brave face, but tears were streaking her makeup. *Oh, crap. Crap and a half.*

"I'm sorry, Donna. Really, there is no reason why you should have known any of this. Don't beat yourself up." I put a hand on her shoulder.

"You are making me see that George is in serious trouble. Well-not trouble trouble, it's not like he's done anything wrong. But that this situation is serious." She met my eyes to add, "And he's in danger."

I nodded. "I'm afraid so."

The silence got awkward for me, so I tried a different tack. "I think this will make a great safe room."

"I thought I knew what those words mean," the woman said, "but I expect you will teach me new definitions."

Paul laughed. Out loud. "I like word play," he said, "and that was clever." I rolled my eyes, which, come to think of it, probably did not reassure Donna Locaviche of my maturity, if not sanity. Oh well, it was crazy lady Amy week.

I explained that a safe room was a room somewhat fortified and with necessary supplies, like the attached bathroom, flashlights, weapons if you have them, and a reliable phone. "If a burglar or worse is in the house, you retreat to the safe room for protection until you notify the police and they arrive. I recommend a metal door with a long dead bolt. That way a bad guy can't kick the door down or shoot through it."

"When I was a child," she mused, "my grandfather built a bomb shelter. He was worried the Russians or the Cubans were going to start World War Three."

I heard Paul think, *My father did that! I used to take girls down there to make out. Tried to, anyway.*

"Let's look downstairs." Donna seemed still to be thinking of her pepaw. "Is that all right? Can we—"

"Oh, of course. I can look in on George first." I followed her down the wide wooden stairs.

I stood in the hallway, watching Donna tend her husband. He was awake, and the icepack steak was lying in a pink puddle on the floor by the couch. *Is that his blood or the cow's blood?* Paul asked. God help me, but I laughed. Paul has permanently warped my sense of humor. Black, the way I like my coffee.

I could see they were talking, but I couldn't hear what they said. After a few more moments Donna stood up and came back to me. "How is he doing?" I asked.

"He said he's hungry," the woman replied. "That has to mean he's doing better." Paul thought, *If I spent an hour smelling a raw steak, I'd be hungry, too. Hush,* I told him, *You're always hungry.*

Her next words surprised me. "You may as well stay for dinner. I was working on a casserole when all this started. I'll heat it up when you're done telling me everything we've done wrong with our house."

Paul lept to say, "That's so nice! Thank you, Donna. We're glad to stay." Then I said, "But I'm a bit underdressed for dinner."

The woman smiled. "Coat and tie not required," she parried, "but we'll find something for you." She extended an arm and said, "Now, this is our breakfast nook."

Not as big as the living room, or even the kitchen, but an inviting area. There were windows on three sides; I was imagining the room flooded by morning sunlight. There was a large, rustic table surrounded by glorified picnic benches. 'Nook' was a good word to describe it.

I examined the structure. "These are casement windows," I said. "They're harder for a perpetrator to open from the outside than the ones upstairs." The locks were the effective standard for the units that swung out: levers with a sturdy hook that securely held the window tight against the frame. "Good locks, too," I said. I hoped the woman was feeling less beat up by my inventory. "The bushes, on the other hand…"

"Bushes? We want some privacy. A few years ago, we were eating breakfast on a Saturday and the Corals—" she pointed at the sumptuous house next door "—waved at us."

"I understand," I told her, "but what you think of as your privacy is also privacy for a perp trying to open a window from the outside."

Donna's expression made it clear she had never considered that unintended consequence. "Really. You've got to have your man cut the bushes back. Way back." I heard Paul laugh and think, *Good call. I'm sure they have a Mexican gardener to do just that.*

"Miss Clear, we have an alarm system. Isn't that enough?"

Paul answered, "Probably not." I felt him retreat (it's something we can do, and I don't know how) so I expanded. "Do you use somebody local?"

"ADT. I don't know, are they in New Orleans?"

"I'm sure the sales staff is. I mean the response team. The closer the monitoring, the faster police will be able to respond. But don't forget: when seconds count, the police are minutes away. And I say that as a consultant for the parish force."

Donna asked, "Anything else?"

"Where's your back door?" I said.

So we returned to the kitchen, and then went to the adjoining laundry room. That's where the alternate access was. "Please excuse the mess," she said. "I don't do laundry until Friday." Paul thought, *Our laundry room look like a tornado touched down even after we've done the clothes. This place is spotless.*

The door was white, with nine window panes set from waist to head. "This piece of glass—" I pointed to the one nearest the doorknob "—A burglar smashes it and he can reach inside to unlock the door. I know people who would be holding you hostage in five seconds."

Donna winced.

"And these wood panels underneath the windows. If I were wearing high heels I'd still be able to kick my way in."

She winced again.

"And this lock!" I turned to face her. "You have to get deadbolts. Really long deadbolts. Fasten the lock and the door strike with long screws. Really long screws. And get a solid door." Paul made a noise by blowing air out of my mouth. He said, "It's a wonder you haven't been burgled already."

When I met her yesterday, Donna had a ready smile and seemed totally poised. Today, not so much. Granted, her husband was resting up after the worst beating he'd probably gotten since he was ten years old. My guess? The battle between hearing how much needed to be done to protect her family and having to hear it from a virtual stranger in tanktop and pink running shoes was killing her self-confidence. I felt bad for the woman, I really did; but if she and her husband didn't upgrade their security, George would be getting a worse beat-down.

She looked so discouraged. I couldn't blame her. I said, "You may need to upgrade your front door and locks, too."

"Probably so." She let out a sigh that made my heart go out to her.

"I think you've heard enough bad news for one session," and I saw her smile. "Is there anything else you want me to evaluate before we call it a day?"

"My son's studio," she said, and she began walking back through the kitchen and the hallway. I followed her into a large, brightly lit room where I heard a man saying, "That's it—yes, that's it—good one, yes, yes." I could see a young Japanese woman in a cultural school uniform, striking poses as she sat in a wicker chair. Why do those anime wannabes always flash peace signs and play with their hair? Maybe to make people like my dyad think, *Oh, what a cutie! She's adorable! Cute, cute, cute!* If so, she was a stunning success.

I turned toward the voice, and the clicks and whirrs of a single lens reflex digital camera. His face was obscured by the device, but I saw a man, skinny as a pencil and wearing a gray tunic over blue jeans. He was glued to the back of his camera. As he moved sideways for a fresh point of view on his model, it seemed he had a limp. Donna and I waited off to one side as the two of them continued and finished their session. "Cody is so creative," she whispered to me. "He has a, uh, a disability, but he figured out how to earn a living and enjoy life." She turned her head to look right at me. "I'm so proud of him."

It was Paul who replied, "And well you should be." What else can you say to a proud mother? 'No?' Get real.

When the son placed his camera on a table, I took a few steps toward him. Donna grabbed my arm and whispered, "Let him finish with his client. It'll only be another minute."

So, I watched him exchange small talk with the woman, and get her to sign a waiting invoice; he took her credit card, and run it through his computer Square dongle. "I'll have the files for you on Monday, and we can go over what prints you want then." His voice was baritone, with a typical New Orleans 'Yat' accent.

The customer waved at me and Donna as the photographer, indeed limping, walked her out of the room and, I assumed, to the front door of the house.

"The limp?" I know it was rude to mention it, but his mother did mention a disability. And it's not like I expected I would ever see her or George again. Well, maybe if I got a part-time job spraying unsuspecting shoppers with unwanted perfume at Neiman-Marcus.

"He was in an auto accident three years ago," Donna explained in a low tone, as if she were afraid her son might hear her. "He's coped well with that damage. There were some other things that are more of a problem. But—"

"Mother, who is your friend?" Sonny boy was hobbling back to his studio. I turned to take a look at him and I was stunned. Cody Locaviche missed his calling behind a camera; he ought to be in front of the lens. *Oh. My. God.* I thought to Paul. The man's face was all angles, with a narrow jaw that went up and out to cheekbones that were at least two inches beyond the outside of his head. He could cut a steak with those cheekbones. And the hair! Not a mullet; that's so before-I-was-born. It was a dark sandy brown that seemed to fall from a natural part in the center of his scalp. It dropped in an unruly but attractive curl to just above his shoulders. He could have disciplined it into what Paul has taught me is called a Prince Valiant, whoever he was. I liked it the way it was, untamed. It was so, so, so magnetic. It invited a woman to be the one to tame it.

As Donna cooed, "Cody, let me look at you," he clenched his eyes closed for a moment. "The headache?" She played with his hair, trying to train it, and then she kissed him on the cheek. Careful, woman—you could cut yourself doing that! "I love watching you do your photography," she enthused. "Your clients love your work."

He nodded, his face back to planes and angles. "They seem to be happy with the pictures. I am grateful." He turned his head, and with a more forceful tone of voice he said, "Hi, I'm Cody Locaviche. I'd love to take pictures of you. What's your name?"

Later Paul told me I stood there with what felt to him like a goofy look on my face for so long that he took the lead to say, "Amy Clear. Nice to meet you, Cody. I'm a private investigator."

"Uh-oh." He looked at his mother. "What's dad done now?"

I was still looking at the man through bokeh eyes, vaseline on the lens. Paul went on, "He's gone and had the stuffing beat out of him. We're trying to make sure that doesn't happen again."

"You're joking, right?" Sadly, Donna shook her head. "Dad got in a fight? Someone beat him up?"

I had recovered enough to butt in and say, "Yes, indeedy."

"Miss Clear is doing a, what do you call it? A safety inspection? She's going to make sure this can't happen again."

"Security inventory," I corrected her. "Your mom asked me to include your studio."

He stepped back and shrugged, although I quite liked the way I thought he was looking at me. "I have liability insurance in case a client slips and falls, if that's what you mean."

"Not quite. Target hardening. I want to make it more difficult for an intruder to, to, well, to intrude." I looked around the room and finally noticed there were white, green, and blue screens on three walls. "What kind of windows do you have?"

The man laughed. I like the way it rumbled out of his chest. "I put the scrims up so long ago, I don't remember what's behind them. Mom?"

Donna shook her head, but I noticed she was smiling. This was a woman who loved her son dearly.

"Can I get behind the screens to look?" I asked. Paul thought, *I'm betting on casement windows. That should be the back yard that way,* and he pointed.

Cody and Donna both turned their heads in the direction Paul was pointing. "What?" Donna said.

"Back yard?" Still pointing.

She thought a moment; then, "Yes. Nashville Avenue is that way."

I went to the green scrim, where the anime wannabe had been posing, and pulled one end away from the wall. Paul fished in my fanny pack for his little LED flashlight and pointed it at the hidden windows. "Casement," he said. They had soap or paper on the glass, making them opaque.

"That one," I said, aiming the light at one of the windows. The lever that kept them fastened was lifted up. "That one is unlocked." I looked back; all I could see was the back of Donna hand as she hid her face.

So, I squeezed behind the green screen and pulled the lever down into the closed position. *We're in here, so let's look at the rest,* I thought to Paul. For some reason I thought it was a good idea to tap at the photography screens with my left hand as I sidled toward the next group of windows; I thought it would be funny if Donna and Cody could trace my progress. Until I heard something object to my tapping and fall over, and confused words from the two of them. *What did we just break?* I thought to Paul.

It's not our fault, he thought back. *It's not like anyone saw us. There's another unlocked window.*

It took some effort to pull the lever down. Was it rusted? It had been in the open position for how many years since Cody had created his studio?

Turning the corner was tricky. Maybe your back can fold ninety degrees in a narrow passage, but mine didn't want to. A rare bad word came out of my mouth, and I heard Paul think, *Trash mouth!* And I heard something else fall over on the other side of the scrim.

"Stop!" Cody barked. I heard movement from the room. Surely, he was moving anything else in harm's way to safety! After all, it's not like I could see what was on his side of the photo backdrops.

Everything was locked on that wall. I moved sideways, back to the screen and face just an inch or two from the windows. Then there was the final left turn. This time I refrained from un-ladylike language, although my thoughts would have led Sister Caligula from my tenure at St. Giles Academy in eighth grade to make me recite a dozen Hail Marys at the least.

That final hidden wall of windows seemed secure.

I emerged from behind the blue scrim. *Uh-oh*, Paul thought. The remains of a Tiffany lamp knockoff were laying on its side. Cody was crouched over the corpse, picking up large pieces of broken shade. Donna had gotten a broom and dustpan from somewhere and was headed toward him.

"Crap!" I shouted. "I'm sorry, I'm sorry!" *I barely know these people and already they hate me*, I thought. "What can I do?"

"Stand there," Cody said. "Just—just stand there." He held the dustpan while his mother swept the smaller shards of colored glass into it.

"Now, Cody, you know she didn't do it on purpose. Bless her heart."

No! Paul bellowed silently. *'Bless your heart,' that's the southern insult. It means 'he's a loser, but he can't help it.'*

"Wait, mom," Cody said in a choked voice. With his free hand he was rubbing his left temple, and muttering to himself, "Quiet. Please, quiet."

"Oh, Cody, dear. Is the headache bad?"

"Just for a minute," he said. A moment later he looked up at her and smiled. "Gone."

"Donna. Cody. I'm so sorry I broke the lamp. Let me get a replacement for you. It may have to be a reproduction—"

They both interrupted. Donna was saying, "Don't be silly!" while Cody said, "That's fair. I'll take you to Shades of Light or First Light, they're bound to have something that'll work." He was still crouched over the dustpan and the earthly remains of that lamp, but he was looking up at me. And he was smiling. I swear, it made my little heart go pitty-pat. Nothing like the attention of a good-looking man to make a woman feel good, you know?

Paul took it upon himself to announce, "A couple of the windows behind your screens were unlocked. You've been lucky so far. Anyway, they're fastened now."

We heard something from outside the door and across the hall. It was George, but I couldn't make out what he was saying. Donna handed the broom to Cody and left to tend her husband.

So, it was me and Cody and a big, brightly lit room. Trying to be the cool police veteran that I am, I asked, "So, is Sunday good for running down a new lamp?"

I got the feeling a smile was not Cody's at-rest expression. But all those angles of jaw and cheekbones, when they were bisected by the charming arc of a smile—well, I'm intrigued. Besides, he said he wants to take pictures of me.

Before he could respond, Donna was back to say, "Your father is ready for dinner now, so we'll eat that casserole I made." She started to turn back to the kitchen but stopped to tell Cody, "I've invited Amy to stay."

"But I'm not dressed for dinner," I whined, thinking the tank top, running shorts, and hot pink sneakers made that obvious.

Cody said, "I'll get a shirt for you. It'll be too big, but it's what I've got." He didn't wait for an answer; he headed for the stairs, and I'm guessing, his bedroom on the second floor.

"Thank you," I said again. "I feel bad for breaking the lamp, and for being, uh, brusque about the inventory. It's really sweet of you to have me stay."

"Nonsense," she said, for just a moment reminding me of my own mother's typical response. "You're being a great help to my family, and I appreciate that."

I bent down to take the dust pan and broom. "Where's a trash can?" I asked.

"You don't have to do that," Donna said, but she led me to the kitchen to dispose of the debris, and to return the tools to their closet.

"There you are," Cody said as he limped into the kitchen. He was holding a blue oxford cloth dress shirt. "Here, you can wear this."

I stuck my arms into the sleeves and realized how much bigger than me Cody was. I'm only five-six, and he must be a little more than six feet tall. My hands were invisible inside the cuffs, and when I buttoned the shirt, it looked as if I was not wearing running shorts, or anything, on my bottom half. For a second I remembered college, staying over with an old boyfriend, getting up in the middle of the night to use the bathroom and slipping on his shirt over my birthday suit. Good times, good times. He became the main suspect in a murder investigation, although he turned out to be innocent. Of murder, anyway.[15] Creep.

"Good fit," I said as I rolled up the sleeves so I'd be able to wield a fork. "Thank you, Cody. I'll wash it before I give it back."

"You don't need to do that."

Paul jumped to lead and said, "Yes I do. I'm a sloppy eater." I love how his half of my brain looks out for me, even when I'm not thinking about things. *If I wash the shirt,* I thought to Paul, *I have to see Cody again to return it.* Pretty sly, actually.

Donna shooed us into the breakfast nook, where she'd already set up plates and flatware. When she left us to help George, I sat next to Cody and asked, "What's with the headaches?"

"Very well, thank you," he said. "And you? Where will you vacation next year? My, isn't it chilly for this time of year." The combination of the vocal sarcasm and the smiling face made me laugh. "I'm a detective," I replied. "I'm used to asking blunt questions about essentials." I beamed at him smiling at me. "So? Headaches?"

This is going great, Paul thought. *He likes you as much as you like him.*

---

[15] You remember this—you read *The Beaded Necklace* by A Trauring (2014), right? No? What are you waiting for? These books won't read themselves!

Cody closed his eyes tightly for a moment. "They come out of nowhere. At least they don't last long." I felt relief when his face relaxed into those angles, like facets of a gemstone. "They started after I was in that car wreck."

"And the doctors say…?"

A shrug. "They say nothing's wrong. Sometimes I go for a week without any. Tonight was rough. Don't know why."

Donna entered, half lifting and half pushing her husband. George had washed the blood off his face, but the purple creeping around his eye wouldn't be so easy to remove. "You sit with me, dear," his wife said. I realized she was still wearing the blouse with George's blood on the sleeve. The man was moving like he needed WD-40 in his back and legs.

"Dad, what happened? I was working in my studio and I missed it all."

"Just as well, Cody." He was moving side to side on the bench, as if he was looking for the one spot that didn't hurt. "I wish I missed it, too." He looked up and said, "I remember you. Didn't I tell you to go away?"

Bad sign, Paul thought. *He doesn't remember we had this conversation already.* "Donna called me. I've been working with her about home security. How are you feeling?"

Cody half-rose from the bench. He took a potholder and picked up the CorningWare with the casserole. What a gentleman! He dished out some for his mother, and then for George. He turned to me and apologized, "Moselle was off tonight, but mother knows her way around a kitchen. This is going to be good." I lifted my plate and smiled. "Please."

"Like a beer truck fell on me," George answered. I watched him dig into the tuna casserole with enthusiasm. *Good sign,* I thought. *Appetite intact, he can't be too messed up.*

As we sat eating Cody talked about his client, and Donna clucked over the price of shallots at Rouses. Then Cody dropped his fork and started a breathing exercise. Paul thought, *What is wrong with the man?*

"It's been a bad evening, Cody, I'm so sorry. Did you take the pills the doctor gave you?"

"Yes, mom, I did. And I'm doing better now. I—I'm sorry if I alarmed you. I'm okay."

So, this was the disability Donna hinted at, the thing worse or different from the limp. Headaches. *At least they don't last long,* Paul observed.

I need to know more about what's going on, I thought back. *Doctor's daughter.*

Not to mention detective, he snickered silently.

In contrast to Donna's concern, George barely noticed his son's difficulties. I guess he was used to it after, what, three years since the accident? Besides, George had his own pain to deal with tonight, literally if not figuratively.

The tuna casserole was extremely good—lots of tuna, and whatever the cheese was, it was a whole lot better than Velveeta. "Donna, this is excellent," I said between my mouthfuls and Paul's. "I could learn a lot from you."

"Thank you, dear," she said. "I learned a lot from you today."

"Mmm?" came from George, and the inflection indicated it was a question.

Adrenalin and anxiety. I jumped in to start a sales pitch. "You had a problem today. I think I can protect you from an instant replay. And I'd like to see the sons of bitches who did this to you pay for it in court." See? I can talk, uh, vulgar when it's called for.

"Why do you think I need protecting?" he asked. "You sound like you expect this to happen again."

"I do." Adrenalin and anxiety up another twenty percent.

His face folded, an expression I took to mean utter disregard. Or maybe a pang from his eye, which was swollen just about shut. "I don't."

"And why is that? Did you give whoever they were what they wanted?" I noticed Cody was looking at me with a mixture of surprise and disbelief.

"I don't know what they wanted."

"So how could you give it to them?"

He put his fork down and squinted his open eye. "Why do you think they wanted anything?"

I couldn't help it, I laughed. "It's a lot of work to beat up someone. Only psychopaths in the movies do it for no reason. At NOPD I saw it's usually for robbery, for some twisted idea of honor, or for intimidation. So, which was it with you?"

Donna put her hand on her husband's arm. I hoped she didn't think she needed to keep him from leaping across the table and throttling me. Even so, I unzipped part of my fanny pack, just in case I needed Roskette Junior in there.

"Can this wait until after dinner?" he asked.

"Of course," I said. I could feel my face turning red. I'm a thirty-seven-year-old ex-cop, and I still get embarrassed when I feel like a 'grown up' puts me in my place. *Uh-oh,* I thought to Paul, *Daddy's going to spank me later.*

What? I don't remember James ever taking a hand to you! James is my dad, Doctor Clear.

You didn't come to me until I was eleven. He had stopped by then.

Oh.

Donna and Cody exchanged some domestic comments. At a pause I said, "I forgot to wash my hands. Where is your, umm, your rest room?"

Even though he had a good mouthful of mama's tuna casserole Cody said, "Back through the kitchen, into the hall, and second door on the left."

"Thanks," Paul replied. "I'll let you know if I find Nemo." I blotted my lips, then retreated to some privacy so Paul and I could converse.

As it turned out, the second door on the left was the linen closet, where I nearly caused an avalanche of fitted sheets and bath towels. The necessary was the first door on that side of the hall.

"Let's whisper," I whispered from the safety of the largest bathroom I've seen this side of my old college dorm. A third world country could camp out comfortably in here. "I wonder if us thinking to each other is causing these headaches."

I was looking in the vanity mirror, noticing my unibrow needed a little work. It's strange to see your lips move when you are not the one moving them: Paul said, "He's had them for three years and we just met him."

"So—You mean—Uh—" It dawned on me that I was hoping Cody had a dyad, too. "So, he's not like us?"

It's something we've talked about. Back when I still did market research, we did encounter a man with someone living inside his head. Granted, I found him in a lunatic bin, but I gave him to my parents and they reported there was nothing wrong with the man, and his female dyad was a sweet young woman. I would love to find more people like him. Like me. Like me and Paul.

"Maybe, but I don't think so."

I nodded. "Well, thank you very much, Mister Bringdown."

"Am I really a wet blanket?" he whispered.

I thought to myself. No, not really. So, I said, "Sure, sometimes." See what I mean about Paul being nicer to me than I am to him?

He ignored my sass, which I expected. He changed the subject: "When did you decide to make a pitch to be George's bodyguard?"

"Halfway through Donna's home security tour," I answered. "But I was as surprised as you when I said it at dinner. What do you think he's going to say later?"

Paul laughed. "That's easy. He's going to say he doesn't need no steenkin' bodyguard, and you're going to explain to him why he does. Are you going for the usual $250 a day?"

"Think I should?"

"Shit, yeah!"

"Shhh," I whispered. "They think I'm just washing my hands, not gabbing on a phone."

"Or talking to your dyad," he whispered, dramatically.

I flushed the toilet so the family would think I had a legitimate reason to absent myself from dinner. I half expected the bowl to fill with liquid gold, but no. Just New Orleans' weird water.

The dinner nook was silent when I returned. "What did I miss?" I asked Cody. He shook his head and pushed the casserole around on his plate. George looked like his head hurt, which I'm sure it did. And Donna looked as if she was thinking about crying. Oh, boy. What <u>did</u> I miss?

"This casserole is excellent," Paul said. No one seemed to notice our pattern of moving the fork from left hand for him and right hand for me, so each of us could taste and enjoy this flavorsome dinner. "Thank you for inviting me to share it."

"Coffee, anyone?" Donna asked. Her perky tone didn't sound enthusiastic. "I'm afraid I didn't get around to making dessert."

George nearly tilted the table over as he put both palms on it by his plate and used his arms and shoulders to do the job his legs didn't want to. "I'm going in to the study. Miss Clear, would you join me?"

Pep talk! I called to Paul *I need a pep talk!* as the adrenaline and anxiety burst over me. George shuffled down the hall, and I followed behind. I felt like I was back at St. Giles Academy, off to the Mother Superior's office to be caned.

The study was larger than the laundry room and the breakfast nook, but smaller than any of the other rooms I'd visited that day. Blonde wood paneling; a bookcase, a desk, two wing chairs, a low table between them, and several framed lithographs of old buildings on the walls. George dropped himself into one of the upholstered chairs with a groan.

I sat on the front edge of the other wing chair, watching him. "How bad is it?" I asked, concerned. He looked like two-day-old crap.

"Nothing compared to what it will feel like tomorrow," he answered. "They worked me over pretty good."

"Why?" I asked. "Why did they beat you up?"

He shook his head. "I have to tell you, Miss Clear, you are a very difficult person."

I heard Paul think, *Bullshit!*

"Difficult?" Anxiety was leading adrenalin, but it was still a close race.

The man let out a big sigh. "You ask impertinent questions. You embarrass me in front of my family. And even though I tell you to go away, you're still here. Yes, difficult."

"I used to be a police detective for Orleans Parish," I said, adrenalin catching up. "I ask direct questions about relevant things. I don't sugarcoat, and I don't lie." It was my turn for a deep breath. "It is not my intention to embarrass you. If I said things in front of Donna or Cody that you'd rather had been private, I do apologize. All I'm trying to do is figure out what happened to you so I can protect you."

He frowned. Maybe he didn't like what I said; maybe his body hurt. "I don't understand why you think I'm in danger," he finally said. "And why do you want to protect me?"

I wished I had time to talk to Paul about it! "Police training tells me you continue to be a target," I offered. "And even though I think you and Donna and Cody are all peachy people, I charge for being a bodyguard. I can use the work. Trouble is, you need a bodyguard." The anxiety peaked and dissolved; I'd told him I want a job. Now it was all adrenalin.

The door creaked open. I couldn't see who was behind it, but I heard Donna's voice say, "Honey, would you like a drink? You've earned it."

"That. Would. Be. GREAT!" He held out his hand, and I finally could see Donna. She handed a highball glass to her husband, then withdrew without acknowledging me. He took a sip, then closed his eyes as he swirled the liquid around in his mouth. He held the glass against his forehead, rolling it left and right. When he finally swallowed, he said, "Oh, that's good." He held the glass out and stared at it for a moment before putting it on the low table between us. I noticed he didn't bother with a pretty glass coaster only a few inches from his drink.

"Better?" I ventured.

"Better."

"George, who beat you up?"

"I don't know."

"BAAAAAH![16] Amyfacts says that's a big Pinocchio. Let's try again: who beat you up?"

"What's wrong with you!" He leaned forward, but the pain of his thrashing pushed him back into the wing chair. "You're treating me like a criminal. Stop that!"

"Correction," I said, "I'm treating you like someone who is hiding important information. Who are you protecting, and why?"

"I told you. I don't know who did this."

"Were you robbed?" I asked. He shook his head. "Still have your wallet? Your watch? Your cellphone?" The way he hung his head told me he indeed was still in possession of those things. "Where's your car?"

"Still in the lot where I parked, I hope," he answered.

"So, you maintain that person or persons, unknown to you, who were not interested in depriving you of money or other valuables, beat you to a pulp and then dropped you off at your home? Am— am I understanding this right?"

His head was still hanging.

---

[16] Amy has never heard of the '50s and '60s TV show *Truth or Consequences*, but she has heard Paul cite Beulah the Buzzer when accusing her, or someone else, of lying. This is her innocent 2036 take on it.

I lowered my voice, prepared to speak a little slower, and tried to put honest concern into my words. "I can't protect you if I don't know who I'm protecting you from. Please, George. Tell me. You can trust me. I've got references if you want them."

He picked up his glass and took several quick sips. This time he did not pause to savor the flavor.

"How can I trust you?" he exploded, turning in my direction and holding his empty highball glass out at me as if it were an index finger. "You told the insurance company not to pay me."

"Well, yes," I said. "But that was when I was working for Paralax. If you hire me, my first advice to you is to withdraw your claim. I'm pretty sure it's legal in Louisiana to burn down your own property, but insurance fraud is not."

"Oh, sure. You're my new best friend and you think I torched my warehouse?"

"Uh, yes. Yes, I do. Until I see proof that someone else had a reason to do it, yes."

He started to shake his head but stopped short, probably when one of the big purple splotches on his jaw complained. "Great, you're my new best friend and you think I had reason to burn my building down?"

"Well, yes. I might change my opinion when you stop lying to me and start telling me what really happened today."

George swirled the ice cubes around in his glass.

I went on. "At least call your lawyer. You need help staying out of jail, and you need help staying out of the Ochner Hospital system. Staying out of the morgue, if I'm not mistaken. Who did you piss off this badly?"

I waited for a response. I heard Paul think, *You got him. Wait to see what he says.*

So, I kept my mouth shut. It seemed like forever before George said, "I'm too tired to make a decision tonight. Can you come back tomorrow? I—I really need to talk to you."

Paul jumped to the lead. "Tomorrow's Saturday, I've got plans," meaning his non-negotiable Christine time. "How about Sunday?"

"Sure," George Locaviche said. "Assuming I'm still alive."

"Yes," I said, "let us assume that. I'll be here early in the afternoon—I broke a lamp while I was taking the security inventory, so Cody is taking me to some fancy store so I can pay for a replacement. We can talk afterwards. Okay?"

George Locaviche nodded. He even smiled. And then his eyelids and his chin lowered, and he began to snore.

If there had been a throw or blanket around, I'd have spread it out over the man. I mean, isn't that what everyone does in the movies when someone falls asleep? Paul, ever the literate one, came forward to say, "Good night, sweet prince, and flights of angels sing thee to thy rest."[17] I don't know where he gets these things, but he is endlessly entertaining. If I hadn't been concerned about waking George I'd have let loose with a guffaw; instead, I just snickered. I picked myself up and left the study, trying to find my way back to everyone else.

Donna was in the living room, some domestic sewing gear in her lap and on the sofa cushion next to her. "Your husband nodded out," I said softly. "He looks like he can use the rest. Look—"

"Does he need anything?" she interrupted, her big needles suddenly silent and still in her hands.

"Maybe a blanket. Whatever was in that highball glass seems to have done him a world of good."

"He does like his Haig & Haig." The woman went back to her needlework.

"So, uh, I, uh, I want to thank you for dinner. The tuna was excellent. I wouldn't have had room for dessert, so as far as I'm concerned, it's just as well you didn't get that far."

She nodded. When I was little, my mother taught me to hem clothes and even make skirts and things from those tracing-paper

---

[17] He gets them from William Shakespeare, Amy. *Hamlet*, to be precise.

patterns. But crocheting? Knitting? Tatting lace? They all are the same to me. Donna probably was doing one of those.

"I made a job proposal to George about being the family bodyguard," I went on. "He asked me to come back out on Sunday to discuss it. And Cody and I made a sort-of plan for Sunday for me to buy a lamp to replace the one I broke. Can I talk to him to set a time?"

"I believe he's transferring the pictures we watched him take. He'll be in his studio. Do you remember how to get there?" She paused, and I guess she noticed my out-to-lunch eyes. She dropped her sewing and stood up. "I'll show you."

It was just down the hall, a big room on the right that faced the back of the house. Donna left me on my own when I knocked on the open door frame. Cody looked up from the computer, and, ohmygod, he smiled. I'm telling you, the curves his lips made when he smiled in the middle of that face of geometric angles was a treat. Down girl, down.

I walked in and sat in a chair facing the back of his computer monitor and the front of his head. He had doused the klieg lights, so the room once blindingly bright now was lit normally.

"Was Dad rough on you?" he asked.

"He tried to be," I admitted. "He said I was a difficult person. But he invited me to talk business Sunday afternoon." I nodded, in full agreement with myself. "When should I come over so I can replace that lamp?"

A little laugh came out of his mouth. "You don't have to do that. It was just a cheap reproduction."

"Detective's honor," I protested, shaking my head. "I broke it, I replace it. What time?"

"Saturday would be better for me, now that I think about it."

Paul, ever protective of his Christine time, said, "Too bad, I'm not available Saturday."

"Oh," Cody teased, "busy with your boyfriend?"

I could feel Paul keep the lead, but he didn't speak. The look on Cody's face explained everything: he heard Paul's masculine voice think something directly to him. One of the changes I'd like to see in the Amy&Paul upgrade (are you reading this, A. Trauring?) is that I'd hear what Paul thought to someone else. But I can't, so I did what I always do when this deficiency is apparent. I said, "What?"

"I could have sworn I heard a man say that—that he would be spending the day with—with his girlfriend?"

I tried to hide my face because I was smiling; he described such a perfect Paul thing. I said, "I can't hear him when he does that. And I don't usually talk about the weirdness until I know someone better." Actually, I've only ever talked about Paul and me to a handful of people outside of my family. I have to know someone really well before I take that risk.

The room was silent for what seemed like an hour. Maybe it was time to say good night and run away. I shrugged and stood up. Crap. Crap and a half. Double crap.

"I don't have headaches," Cody said abruptly. "It's just easier to explain it to my parents that way."

I sat back down. "Something is going on. What?"

"I hear a woman's voice."

Oh. "What does she say?"

There was a furlong of silence. "Sometimes the voice yells. Sometimes it calls my name. Sometimes it sounds like crying."

"Have you tried talking to her?"

"Actually, yeah. This started when I was hospitalized after the wreck. I was groggy and they were giving me drugs, and I thought at first a woman was talking to me. But no answer. After I was off the pain pills, I decided that was a good thing. You may be a little crazy to hear voices, but I decided I'd have been very crazy if I thought the voice was answering me."

Well, crap! I thought to Paul. What a disappointment. I was just now becoming aware of how much I had been hoping Cody was like me and Paul

He thought back, *I'll poke around in there anyway.*

"That was pretty brave," I said. "OxyContin or not, I'm impressed that you considered the possibility."

Cody seemed to be examining his shoes. Finally, he looked up at me and said, "You—you're okay with this?" Was that in his voice—surprise? Disbelief? Relief?

I nodded. And I smiled. *He's worried what I think. He doesn't have a problem with us.*

Cody sat back in his chair and took a deep breath. Well, actually three or four; I lost count. "For the last three years I've been told I'm crazy or a psychosomatic basket case. I lost my fiancé, I lost my job, I lost my friends. My parents, when they look at me there's such sadness in their faces." Just the tiniest piece of a smile crept into his face. "You are the first person who believes me but doesn't hold it against me."

I couldn't help it. I reached out and put my hand on the back of his closer hand, his right. Immediately he put his other hand on top of mine. He whispered, "Thank you."

Wow. I'm not exactly a ball of emotion, but what Cody said, and the way he said it, moved me. Before I could think of something to say, Paul said, "We need to get home. How about noon on Sunday? Can you deal with us then?"

He didn't exactly implode like Edgar did at the 55th Fighter Group, but Paul's words did put a damper on Cody. Wordlessly, he nodded. I took over. "I'll tell you my story. And you can tell me more about yours. Okay?"

"Let me walk you out," he said listlessly, but he stood up. I grabbed his hand, and we walked to the front door. I couldn't believe it was open. Here I am, trying to save George's life, and his front door has been standing open for hours? And...

I was surprised, but I liked it when Cody suddenly held me. His head was towering over me, while my face was buried in the front of his shirt. "Thank you," he whispered, and he clutched me tighter. I put my arms around him as far as they'd go—did I say how much bigger than me Cody is?—and tried to return the strength in his grasp. "It's okay, Cody," I told his clavicle. "I'll see you Sunday. We'll talk more."

He loosened his grip and leaned back, as if to take me in. There were two parts of that that I liked. First, it struck me that we had sidestepped a lot of the usual social walls people have; I'm a people and I have walls and I was grateful to have this personal intimacy break them down. And second, even though I wasn't feeling particularly romantic, a woman always appreciates it when a good man, a man who isn't being creepy or mookish, takes a good look at her. For my part, Cody was an eyeful, too.

"Is there anything I can bring over on Sunday?" I asked. I wasn't in a hurry to break this physical connection.

"Just you and your brain. And money, if you're really going to buy a lamp."

I laughed. "Oh, sure. No, I meant…ice cream? Bottle of wine? The head of Alfredo Garcia?"[18]

"Surprise me," he said. He gave me a quick squeeze, then let me go.

Cody watched me as I unlocked the Benzmobile. He was still watching when Paul mashed the glow plugs, and when I let out the clutch. And I know he was still watching as I drove up Richmond Place because I was still watching him.

"I don't know," Paul said, "but maybe he's got a dyad." He was leading, driving us up St. Charles toward home.

"Maybe," I answered, trying to balance hope with practical reality. "I'm looking forward to hearing his story."

"But you will introduce us. Right?"

I – I don't know. When I was twelve, I told my best friend Josie Binkowski about Paul. Alas, Josie's mother had certifiable mental problems. Josie thought I was making fun of her mom. Let us just

---

[18] *Bring Me the Head of Alfredo Garcia,* a 1974 movie by Sam Peckinpah with Warren Oates, Gig Young, and Kris Kristofferson. I need to ask Amy how she knows the film.

say by the time I was thirteen Jamie no longer was my best friend. You see why I'm cautious about introducing Paul to the world.

On the other hand, Paul's girlfriend is perfectly cool with us as a dyad. And when I was in college, I told my best friend Florence about Paul. She didn't believe me for the longest time, but it didn't interfere with our friendship.

"RIGHT?"

"Yes," I finally said. Cody had confided in me about the woman's voice in his head. I owed it to him to be honest about Paul. "Yes. I'll make a formal introduction on Sunday." I had done this mental score card, should I or shouldn't I tell Cody about Paul. The balance sheet said yes. So why did anxiety flood over me when I told Paul I'd do it? As it was, Cody acted as if there was nothing strange about hearing Paul's male voice in his head.

It must have been nine o'clock by the time Paul parked in the gravel strip in front of my house. Cody's oversized shirt was a help, but a December night in New Orleans is a tad chilly for running shorts. I was looking forward to pants at the least; a blanket at best. As he locked the car Paul declared, "I have to call Christine. Make a plan for tomorrow." Silently he continued, *Tell her about Cody?*

"Are you kidding? She's my best friend. Even though she doesn't like men, I absolutely must tell her all about him."

I led to unlock my front door. The living room was warm, thank God. "You want some wine?" I asked as I headed for the kitchen and my countertop wine cellar.

"You're feeling better about booze? Good. I'll help demolish a bottle of something red."

Anxious or not, I was feeling hyper-alive. I was pleased about my left-over police chops with the security inventory at the Locaviches' house; I was excited to encounter another human being who might have a dyad inside them; and I couldn't help but hope that maybe, just maybe, I was at the start of something worthwhile with Cody. I took an empty peanut butter jar out of the cabinet and plopped it on the kitchen table. "Fill 'er up, barkeep!"

I took a sip, something called Chateau Voodoo, some blend that I paid no attention to after I saw it was red. Paul poured most but not all of half the glass into my mouth—crap, I really was going to have to wash Cody's shirt. Even though I was dripping—literally— I took another sip for luck and pulled my phone out of my fanny pack.

Paul speed dialed Christine's number. It rang twice, and then we heard her adorable outgoing message: "You've reached Christine's phone. And if this is Paulette, I love you!"

"Sweetie!" Paul said. "We need a plan! When do you want me and Amy to come over? Oh, I am soooo looking forward to being with you tomorrow. And Amy's got some news—I hope she leaves any time for you and me to talk. Call if you can, or I'll call in the morning. I love you, Christine. 'Night!"

"Crap," I said after he ended the call. "I want to talk to her about Cody."

"She's always been so cool about you and me being a dyad," he mused. "We have to introduce her to Cody." He reached for peanut butter glass that now only had an inch of wine; a moment later it was empty. He could teach Penn & Teller a thing or two about making stuff disappear.

"It's Friday night," I said. "Why isn't she home? I really want to talk to her."

I could feel Paul laughing inside, although he let a snicker or two escape out of my mouth. "She's probably up at Sappho Rising," he said, "hanging out with Gina and Shawna." I admire Paul for being devoid of jealousy. Gina was Christine's girlfriend before Paul—uh, Paulette—came along. Gina moved on to Shawna; they even got married after the law changed.[19] If she's had enough to drink, Shawna apologizes for having stolen Gina. But they all are friends. Paul and I sometimes hang out with them at the club, too,

---

[19] Yes! You read *The Wedding Fatality* by A. Trauring (2016). And you know what? Amy and Paul and Christine lived it. What, you think they cease to exist when you close the cover of the book? Get real!

but they don't know I exist. That's why I can empathize with Paul now, when he complains about being hidden and wanting to play with more people than just me and Christine.

In the laundry room, I put a stopper in the sink drain and poured in some soap powder. While I let three or four inches of hot water build up, I undid the many buttons on Cody's shirt, slipped it off, and took a look. Yup, red wine from the pocket down to the hem. That probably meant a stain on my leg, too. I wadded up the shirt and dropped it into the sink. I used the empty broomstick I keep back there to slosh the garment around. Good. In the morning I'd do a load of clothes, so the shirt would be clean and dry for my return to Chez Locaviche on Sunday. It's bad enough I have to spend money on the lamp I broke; I don't want to have to replace a ruined shirt.

ॐ SATURDAY, DECEMBER 13, 2036 ॐ

In the morning I managed to girl up against the temptation of Dixie Beer for breakfast and settled for Cheerios with vanilla yogurt. A look out the window showed low, gray clouds and intermittent rain. Great. Then Paul and I watched my clothes and Cody's shirt go around and around and around and around in the dryer. He was waiting for the stroke of ten-oh-five to telephone Christine. "Come on," I said, "it would be fun to wake her up and razz her for being a sleepyhead."

"Yeah, I'm sure you're right," he answered, "but 'no.' Maybe you haven't noticed after all these years, but I like Christine. I want to make her life happier. She's a big girl, she's allowed to sleep in."

I lay down on the cement slab in the laundry room. "It's such a dreary day," I complained. "What are we going to do with your lady love?"

"How about a romantic walk in the rain?"

"Forty five degrees. That's not romantic."

"If it was Tuesday, we could go to the Crescent City Farmers' Market."

"Yes. Yes, I suppose we could. If it were Tuesday. Where is their Saturday location?"

"I think they moved it near Lafayette Square. Shit, who wants to go downtown on a Saturday?"

For some reason, Paul started tickling me. He was jiggling the fingers on my left hand, 'his' hand, along my side. Think about this: It's a known scientific fact that you cannot tickle yourself. Go ahead, try; I'll wait. There. See? So, the absolute proof that Paul is his own distinct personality living inside my head is that he can tickle me. I suppose I could tickle him, but I'm not that mean. Besides, I got that out of my system when my kid sister was eight or nine. So, I was trying not to laugh, and I was sliding and wriggling to get away from him, but how do you get away from your own left hand? Inside of two minutes I was screaming with laughter, pounding my free hand on the concrete floor.

Feeling less grumpy now? he thought to me.

"You mean this was therapy?" I pretended to be insulted.

"Nah!" He teased one last finger across my ribs, setting my hysterics off again. "This was because I'm just a mean bastard who gets off on making your life hell."

I used my right hand to grab my left arm to keep him from any more hellraising. A moment later we were hugging each other, the way we sometimes do. I try not to admit this to him very often, but I am a happy woman that he lives inside me. And considering the alternative for him was still being inside his body when it died, I'd say he's one lucky man.

I had barely noticed my phone ringing when Paul jumped up and grabbed it off the laundry sorting table. It must have been ten-oh-six.

"Hey, ma belle," he said; he cracks me up when he tries to talk Cajun. "How are you doing?"

"Paulette!" she cried, "I miss you!"

"We can do something about that, as soon as we're done with this load of laundry. When will you be ready for Amy and me?"

"It's a little after ten," she said, mostly to herself. "Shower, sweep the kitchen, change the sheets;" then her voice changed and she was telling Paul—uh, Paulette— "why don't you come over around noon? We can have lunch at that place I've been telling you about, JuJu Bag. They have a fried catfish sandwich that is yummy."

"Sounds gr—"

"And you can get a haircut."

"Say what?"

"That's their gimmick. A restaurant and salon, all in one. Uh, you don't have to get a haircut. But you can."

I piped up, "I don't think I need a trim, but the catfish sounds good. I've got—"

"Amy!" she squealed. "What's the news Paulette mentioned in the voice mail? Oh, wait, don't tell me now. But I want to hear all about it at lunch."

"I hope I don't gross you out," I warned, "part of it's about a guy I met."

"As long as I'm holding Paulette's hand, you can talk about boys. I'm a big girl, I can take it." Bless her heart, but Christine is one of that minority of lesbians who actually dislikes men in all ways, not just in the bedroom. She told Paul the reason about five minutes into our knowing each other, and, alas, it is a good one. It's a mark of our friendship that she listens to me talk about men at all.

She went on, "And I can use your help on a project. I sold a house in the good part of Terrytown last week and I've taken on another one. I want to put flyers on people's front doors to advertise it."

Paul said, "There's a good part of Terrytown?" It's a suburb on the west bank, next to where my Aunt Peggy lives in Gretna. No two ways around it, it's a down-scale area. Considering New Orleans proper remains a cesspool of crime rates, Terrytown is not bad by comparison. Just...just poor. Except for this newly discovered 'good part' I'd never heard about before.

"Silly," she laughed. "I got $289,000 for it. And six percent of that is what keeps me in kibble and wine. That's why I can treat my Paulette well."

Paul sat us on the concrete, our back against the toasty dryer. "You've helped Amy with some of her investigations," he told her. "It'll be nice to be able to pay you back. As long as it doesn't involve moving a piano."

"If I had to move a piano," she said, "I'd raise my commission rate. You're safe. I love you, Paulette! See you at noontime. Amy. Bye."

Paul ended the call, and leaned back. There was a big smile on our face. *Hey, hellraiser. Are you happy?*

He pointed at our face. "There's a picture of this in the dictionary. I love her, love her, LOVE HER!"

Good. You deserve it. Plus, the woman had turned into my best buddy. Win, win, win.

"I told you their catfish was great!" Christine bragged. Paul and I were changing the fork from hand to hand, and alternating bites of a superb open sandwich of fried catfish. Lightly battered, crunchy crust and moist inside, with no trace of an oil slick on the plate. And the sweet potato fries were good, too.

"You're right," I agreed, between bites and swallows.

Paul said, "If only they had Squat."

Christine smiled and said, "What are you talking about, Paulette?"

"Squatters Outer Darkness," he clarified. "It's a beer Amy and I got introduced to—it was the day I kissed that geezer at the World War II Bar and Grill."

Still smiling, she mused, "World War II Bar—"

"55th Fighter Group," I interrupted. "It's got a war theme. And great beer. And old gentlemen who know how to boost a woman's ego."

She nodded, and perused the menu. "They have seven, eight, nine different Abitas. Huh. Not even the Dixie that you and Paulette like." She looked up. "Sorry." Her smile showed off the way her top front tooth was twisted just a little, just like mine.

"We're trying to cut back on the alcohol," Paul offered. "Although my college English teacher made a big impression on me. He was an Irishman, a tax dodger from at least three countries. He said if you only have enough money for a sandwich or a Guinness, go with the Guinness. Plenty of protein there."[20]

"This week, I can afford both," Christine said. "Do you know, I sold eleven houses this year."

We left bills on the table to cover the check. As we walked to Christine's old Smart Car, Paul said, "I'm so proud of you. When I met you, you were answering phones for that real estate agency."

"I was thrilled to have the job, too." She unlocked the doors, and we all got in. If I were any taller, I would not have fit in that tiny toy car. "That was just before I met you. I wasn't careful about my medication, so I'd spend days where I was sure the King of Nutopia wanted to kill me." She shuddered. "I didn't deserve that job. I didn't deserve you when I met you."

I jumped in. "But it was because you were ill and hearing voices that it didn't bother you that Paul and I share my body."

"That's for sure." She was driving us back to her double in Fillmore so we could work on the arts-and-crafts project she needed. "Besides, you and Paulette both are nice. My other voices weren't."

"Yesterday I met a man who, I think, may be like me and Paul. I hope. Only he doesn't know it yet."

She looked at me sideways and said, "What is Amy talking about?" Then it was eyes back on the road.

---

[20] This one is based on the author's writer-in-residence instructor. Benedict Kiely had a wonderful accent, I'd have listened to him recite the phone book. He had just gotten a story in *The New Yorker*, *A Great God's Angel Standing*. Amongst us wannabe authors, *The New Yorker* was the holy grail, paying more than $3,000 for a short story in those days. He offered the Guinness advice while drinking with students at a college watering hole. Kiely said he had left Ireland to teach in Canada because of a problem with the Office of the Revenue Commissioners, then came south to the US to avoid a tax bill with the Canada Revenue Agency. God knows if the IRS ever saw a penny from the man.

Paul explained everything to her: the insurance investigation, the unpleasant interview with George (he dwelled on the cafeteria experience), the report to Melanie Goode, and the frantic phone call from Donna Locaviche. Sometimes you see things differently when another witness tells the story, but that didn't happen this time.

Paul had gotten to the security inventory when Christine reached her double. "I don't mean to interrupt, Honey," she told my dyad, "but you can finish the story while we make these publicity packages." We all climbed out of the dog-cage of a car and went in the door to Christine's living room. As it had been since the day we met, the walls were mostly bare, and the furniture tops unblemished by anything except a lamp. Her idea of Christmas cheer was a six-inch pine bough sitting on the back of the sofa.

In the kitchen, Christine pulled the table away from the wall. "Paulette, you sit here and I'll sit over there. We can work off the same stacks."

Stacks? There was half a ream of color printout of the house she was trying to sell, a long box of her business cards, and a pile of clear colorless plastic sleeves with a doorknob hole at the open end.

"This is pretty slick," I offered. I lifted one of the publicity sheets. Nice color picture that probably made the house look better than it was in real life, and smaller pictures showing the interior of three different rooms. You can't be sure what the purpose is of a room is when it's empty of furniture, but the honking big refrigerator was a giveaway for the kitchen.

At the bottom of the page was a picture of Christine, looking serious; the lighting obscured the multitude of colors in her hair. And without a smile on her face, you couldn't see her turned front tooth that Paul loved. "I sold a home at 2130 Carol Sue Avenue for $289,000, and I can sell yours next!" Her contact information at Lincoln Properties almost finished the page—at the very bottom was some disclaimer in three-point type that I didn't even try to read.

When I turned it over the real estate photos were replaced by a large blue box with big white letters: OPEN HOUSE. It had the address and hours for Sunday week, and invited the recipient to "bring any friends and family you believe may be interested in a home in your neighborhood. I look forward to meeting you!"

"Do these things work?" I asked. I slipped the sheet and a business card into a plastic sleeve and dropped it into a wicker bowl.

Christine smiled, giving me and Paul a delightful glimpse of that tooth. "I've never done it before. One of the top sellers in the office showed all of us how he does this." A shrug. "What do I have to lose? A ream of paper and business cards I give out by the boxcar load." She began assembling another package.

"What a clever idea," Paul offered. "After we put all these together, then what?"

"We go around that neighborhood and put 'em on people's doors." She was concentrating on the project, with the tip of her tongue sticking out at the side of her mouth. I heard Paul think, *Isn't she adorable?* True, Christine didn't turn me on the way she does Paul, but I had to agree. Her straight hair, once just blonde, now had streaks of pink and green and blue; it still fell in various lengths between her jaw and her shoulders. Me, I was grateful there were no tattoos or body piercings to go with it. Paul may have had a different opinion, but I have never thought to ask him about it.

So, with Christine on one side of the table and me (and Paul) on the other, we set to putting together these packages for the people of Terrytown, bragging about the previous sale in the previously unknown nice part of town, and inviting them to the upcoming open house.

"Paulette, you were telling me about your exciting day yesterday with Amy," she prompted.

"Ah. Where was I? Umm—Amy led the wife around the house and kept pointing out problems that a bad guy could take advantage of to get in their house. She was—"

"Is that really likely?" she interrupted. "Amy, do you think someone wants to hurt that man?"

"In this case, yes. The man is in danger. His wife understands it, but George is being some tough macho idiot who kept saying no."

"Boys do that, don't they?" she said. "But not my Paulette." Long ago I gave up on trying to understand how other people think. Christine knows Paul is a man—she has called him the only boy who will ever touch her; when he thinks directly to her, she must hear his unmistakably masculine voice. But she insists on calling him Paulette, and referring to him as 'she.' Well, it works for her. Me, I'm just used to it. She went on, "What makes you sure it wasn't some kind of, you know, random thing?"

"Oh, he was targeted," I explained. "They didn't rob him. And they dropped him off at his home. Well, pushed him out of their car onto his driveway."

"So, it couldn't be random?"

"There's something about the ride home that says 'we know who you are.'"

Paul said, "I was there when Amy was learning this stuff on the police force. I'm amazed she remembers it, because I sure didn't."

Christine smiled and dropped her business card to put her hand on Paul's—uh, Paulette's—actually, mine. "She's so smart," the woman said to my dyad. It was as if I weren't there, hearing her though the same ears Paul was using, and seeing her through the same eyeballs. As if she heard me—which she didn't, because I didn't think anything to her—she added, "You're so smart, Amy."

That caught me by surprise. "Uh, thank you," I managed to say. Then I heard Paul laugh, "We're cute when we blush, aren't we?"

We worked in silence for a few moments, and then I went back to my story. "Whoever hurt George, they're trying to intimidate him for some reason. He needs security. I made a pitch to be his bodyguard, and he told me to come back tomorrow to discuss it."

Christine sat back. "You think this George person is in danger, and you want the job of standing between him and the bad guys?" Her eyes were open wide, like cartoon ping-pong balls someone had drawn pupils on with a Sharpie.

"Well, yes. He needs someone to—"

"Amy, I worry about Paulette and you. I mean, you're so brave, but it's dangerous and, and, and I worry." Those ping-pong eyeballs were aimed down. She worried about her Paulette. She has always worried about her Paulette. She will always have worried about him.[21] He's a lucky man. Lucky dyad, at least.

"Tomorrow I'll talk to George," I said, trying to console her and calm her down. "I'll make him tell me who beat him up. Then I can go after the bad guy instead of waiting for him to surprise us."

"Go after the bad guy?" she echoed. "You're going to find trouble?" You know, when someone has her heart set on worrying, there is nothing you can say to dissuade her. Still, I tried. "It's safer to be in control of the moment of contact than to be surprised. Really."

Paul spoke up, "Once Amy knows who the villain is, she might can get her police buddies to do anything that might be, you know, dangerous." He's right, but I don't think that's how things play out most of the time.

Christine sat upright with a flounce and announced, "I am not going to worry. You and Amy are professionals and I trust that you will be safe." She picked up a flyer, and a business card, and shoved them in a plastic sleeve. The assembly line was up again.

"The amazing thing about all this," Paul began, "is that Amy thinks the would-be client's son may be like her and me."

"How do you figure?"

I took over. "He was complaining about momentary headaches that seemed severe, but passed quickly. His parents were used to it."

---

[21] A reader sent a letter to a hippie erotic comic book, *Cherry Poptart*, later shortened to *Cherry* when Kellogg's complained. "How old is Cherry?" the reader asked. Artist Larry Welz replied, "She has just turned 18. She has always just turned 18. She will always have just turned 18."

Flyer, business card, plastic sleeve, into the basket. "When we were alone, he admitted it's not headaches. Instead, he hears a woman's voice. And it isn't mine."

Paul let out a laugh and barged in. "When Amy declined his invitation to spend today shopping for a lamp we broke, he said something like, 'Oh, you're going to spend Saturday with your boyfriend.' I startled him, I'm sure, but he didn't freak out when I thought to him, 'No, I'm spending the day with my girlfriend.' He even commented that he heard a man's voice saying it."

Christine was getting three packages finished for every one Paul and I were able to toss into the wicker basket. "Maybe he can tell which one of you is leading, like I can."

"Well—well, maybe. Tomorrow he's taking Amy and me to some upscale lighting store so we can get a replacement for something we broke."

"I'm excited about this," I added. "Six or seven years ago, when I was still doing market research, I met a study subject from a local loony bin who had a dyad. Paul and I got to teach him and his dyad—Paul, what was her name? —anyway, we rescued them from an institution. Best gift I ever gave my parents."

"I don't understand that," Christine said, narrowing her eyes. "What did you give your parents?"

Paul rescued me. "Amy brought the man to James and Tracey and asked them to take care of him while he learned to deal with his dyad. I think her name was Vicky? Tracey said it was almost like having Amy and me back at home."

"So, there are other people like you? A lot?"

I said, "Let's see. We've met one person like me in the, uh, the twenty-six years I've been a person like me. So, not a lot. But at least one, and now maybe two."

"Is this going to interfere with us?"

It felt like the temperature in Christine's apartment dropped in half.

"I won't let it," Paul finally said. "Like when Amy's had boyfriends before, alternate days are ours. It wouldn't be fair for us to keep her from being happy with a boyfriend, just like it wouldn't be fair for her to keep you and me apart."

"Boyfriend?" Christine stopped, flyer and business card in one hand and plastic sleeve in the other. "Did you say 'boyfriend'?"

What is it about Christine that I am able to blush in front of her?

"No!" I shouted. "No, no, no." I folded my arms in front of my chest, dropping one of her business cards to the floor. "Not yet, anyway."

Christine broke into a smile and pointed at me, going, "Ahhhh! Amy's got a boyfriend! Amy's got a boyfriend!" in schoolyard sing-song.

It was embarrassing. I don't know why; maybe because Cody is gorgeous and he's been open with me and I like him. I felt defensive. "From the woman who once told me she waits until the first date before she plans the wedding?"

Her laughter stopped. "I'm sorry, Amy," she said. "I didn't realize I was hitting a sore spot." Oh, Jesus, when her lower lip trembles like that I want to throw my checkbook at her, change my will, anything to make that chin quit quivering. I heard Paul think, *She's serious. She's really apologizing.*

So, I took a deep breath. I leaned forward, over the table, and I said, "The man should be a model. He's got a face like a geometry textbook, it's all angles. And I get the feeling I'm the first person he's ever told that what upsets him is hearing a woman's voice in his head."

I sat back and resumed the real estate package assembly line work. "You know how you have a conversation with someone, and out of nowhere there's a comment, an admission, a piece of honesty that blows away all the crap? Some intimacy? It's rare, and it has the potential to, to, to change your world." Into the plastic sleeve, over to the wicker basket. "Or you misread something and you're about to make a first-class fool of yourself." I shrugged. "Either way, I want to pursue this."

Out of the blue Paul sang, "I don't care what consequence it brings, I have been a fool for lesser things.'"[22]

Christine squinted at us, and finally said, "I love your voice, Paulette, Amy. What's that song?"

I felt him roll our eyes and shrug. "Just something from one of those old dead rockers I used to like," he mumbled. "Don't mind me."

"So, it's important to you," Christine said, rewinding past Paul's interruption. "You have to go for it. You deserve to be happy. Amy, I don't understand boys, but you do, so, good. And Paul and I will still be here if things—nah, we'll still be here, but things will be great."

Do you see why Christine is my best friend?

And then she said, "MORE PACKAGES! My God, it's already after three, I want to finish this while it's still daylight. Get to work, you slacker!" But she was smiling.

"Would you do something for me, honey?" Christine whined to her Paulette. We were leaning back on her futon sofa, wiped out from delivering all those real estate promotional door hangers, and making a serious dent in a big bottle of Fairbanks' sherry.

"Sure thing," he said.

"Rub my feet? My feet are killing me."

I felt his smile across my face. "Sure thing," he repeated. Christine gave us a peck on the cheek, then lay down with her head on a pillow and her feet in our lap. We had discarded our tennis shoes the instant we got to her house—actually, I got a head start so mine were sitting in the Benz. Paul peeled the powder blue anklets

---

[22] Billy Joel "The Longest Time," ©1984 Universal Music. This is the last doo-wop song to be a pop hit in the US. Paul really liked it, but it's no wonder that neither Christine nor Amy (born in 1998 and 1999) never heard of Billy Joel or any of his songs.

off, and gave each foot a vigorous starting rub. I thought, *I'm glad her feet aren't foul.*

Doesn't matter if they were, he thought back. *Old friend taught me the best complement you can give a person is to tell them their feet smell like roses.*

I almost laughed, but Paul spoke. "Your feet are burning up! Damn, we must have walked ten miles to hang all those packages."

"You were so smart," she said. The look on her face was of delight as Paul worked our thumbs in the sole of one foot, then the other. "Taking both cars. We drove together to the south end of Terrytown, parked my car, and then you drove us to the north end. That way we didn't have to walk back anywhere." Paul was twisting one foot to the side, and if a voyeur were looking in the window and saw Christine's face they might think it wasn't her feet that were being massaged. "If we hadn't done that, I think I'd be dead on the side of Terry Parkway. Oooh, that feels good!"

"Why Terrytown?" I asked. "Home prices have to be higher on this side of the river."

"Competition is higher, too," she explained. "If thirty agents claim to represent this area—" Fillmore and St Anthony, the neighborhood where Christine lived "—maybe only ten handle the West Bank." Paul was silently rubbing and pushing and caressing her feet while his lover and I talked economics. "Home prices are lower in places like Terrytown, and Marrero, and Westwego, but I sell more of them. Eleven houses this year."

We sat quietly for awhile, Christine giggling and moaning and sighing as Paul used those magic hands to restore her feet. Then she said, "That's much better," and she sat up, leaning against us. Paul led to hug her. I couldn't hear what he thought to her, but I figured it out when Christine said, "Let's have dinner first." My kind of woman, she knows the stomach is the prime erogenous organ.

Paul was still leading, even though he didn't say anything, so I thought to both of them, *I'm too wiped to cook or to go out. Can we order in a pizza? Chinese?*

Christine said, "What a great idea." But then she just sat there.

Somebody's got to make a phone call, I thought to them both.

All three of us in these two bodies just sat there.

Finally, I rocked my body until I unglued myself from the back of the futon, and I grabbed the bottle of sherry. "I'm thinking a nap may be in order." I pulled a Paul, guzzling right out of the bottle. Most of it went in my mouth.

Good idea, Paul thought. Things were quiet, and I heard Christine snoring. *I'm next*, I thought.

☙ SUNDAY, DECEMBER 14, 2036 ☙

When I woke up, I was on my side in Christine's bed. My left arm—Paul's arm—was over her bare waist. I needed to pee, and I needed to cough.

It sometimes happened that Paul or I fell asleep before the other did, or woke up before the other. He must have stayed coherent after I passed out, and there we were, naked in his lover's bed. Carefully, to not wake her, I moved my arm and rubbed my face. Wait—that smell. Hah! I know where those fingers have been. Somehow, I missed out on the erotic dream that tells me what Paul and my body were up to overnight. I pulled myself up from Christine's floor bed and shuffled off to her spacious bathroom to relieve myself. Paul and I might divide our drinking, but it all ends up in my one and only bladder. And in a moment, it'll be out of there.

As soon as I closed the door from the bedroom I leaned over the sink and coughed, and coughed, and coughed. It took a couple handfuls of water from that same sink before my throat began to calm down. Christine has an evening ritual that includes a bowl or three of marijuana. I always decline—I was a cop, for crying out loud, and my dad the doctor warned me about the evils of non-Rx drugs—but if I'm asleep, bad boy Paul makes up for lost time. I'm sure he has a good time, but I hate the feeling of hawking up half a lung the next morning. Still, what can I do? I've told him again and again not to smoke Christine's locoweed, but when I'm asleep and away, the dyad will play.

The clock radio said it was 7:19 in the morning. So I took a shower, which miraculously did not revive a sputtering and cursing Paul. Back in the bedroom, I took clean clothes out of Paulette's stash. Considering I was to spend part of the day with Cody Locaviche, the Daisy Dukes were tempting. Nah. Overruled by December temperatures. So: underpants; a green bra mottled from a bleach accident; a pair of jeans; and an ancient, faded long-sleeve T-shirt for Rodeo New Orleans. That was the rodeo where my then-boyfriend Timmy lasted about two-tenths of a second on a bull and ended up at Touro Infirmary with a broken leg. Auspicious for a first planned meeting with Cody, no? Yes, that would do.

I was ready to go home, but I thought it would be mean to deprive Paul of the chance to say goodbye to his sweetie, or at least leave her a note in his barely legible left-handed scrawl. Really, it was unusual for him still to be asleep after I'd be up and at 'em for so long. So, I poked at him internally (my dad said it's our equivalent of computer pinging) a few times until I finally got a response. As I expected, it was hostile and filled with obscenities. *Yo, trashmouth,* I thought to him. *Do you want to wake Christine or leave her a note before we go home?*

Why are you awake? he thought back. *Isn't it still night?*

Just how late did you and Christine stay up canoodling?

Canoodling? What century are you in? We swived, we podgered, we charvered. I felt him shake our head, then snicker. *Yeah, we had a good time. Didn't you have a hot dream or anything?*

No. I slept the dreamless sleep of the just and the tipsy. How late did you stay up?

I dunno. He yawned, which to all the world looked as if I yawned. *Five? Six?*

I was sitting at Christine's kitchen table, bereft of real estate promotional items and restored to its rightful position against the wall. I had one foot up on the chair she would have been in if she weren't unconscious in her bedroom. *It's about eight now. Do you want to leave a note for Christine?*

Good idea, he thought. *Can I use your lipstick?*

Uh—I've got a pen. Just a second.

He yawned again. *Nope, it's got to be lipstick. I'm going to write 'I love you' on her bathroom mirror.*

I laughed and whispered, "Why not use spray paint and put it on her living room wall?" It still bothered me that Christine had no pictures or posters hanging in that room. There was a lot of wall that could be turned into a canvas by a child with crayons or Paul with a can of Krylon.

Too much work. I'd have to move the sofa.

I fished a pen out of my purse, and tore a sheet of paper towel off the roll on the table. "Here," I whispered. "Get poetic."

Goddam. I ask for a fucking lipstick and all you've got is a pen? A fucking Bic pen?

"Yes, my dear demonic dyad. All I've got is a pen. I like men, but I'm not a lipstick kind of gal. I thought you knew that by now. Now, write your note so you can go back to sleep and I can go home."

Paper towel is not the most cooperative medium, particularly when a cranky lefty who's not entirely awake tries to work it. After poking a couple of holes in the towel he grabbed the pen in our left fist and managed to write, in uneven but large block letters, 'ME LUV YU.'

He let go of the pen. "Where are you going to put it?" I asked. No luck—he was back asleep. So, I added a tidy PS in my frilly, girly handwriting, 'Me too. Wish me luck with Cody. Talk to you soon.' I snuck back into the bedroom, and left the love note on the empty pillow beside the sleeping Christine. "Thanks for a fun day,"

I whispered, even though I knew she couldn't hear me; I had to say it though, because it was true and I was grateful.

Good or bad, you get used to things. If you live near the airport, after a while you don't hear the planes. If you wear pearls every day, eventually you forget to take them off when you go swimming. After 26 years I am used to Paul being a part of me. So, I'm sitting in the Benz, parked on Richmond Place across from the Locaviche homestead, feeling weirdly naked that Paul is asleep. I'm waiting for the magic hour of twelve noon to strike before I walk up their semi-circular driveway and knock at their double doors. I'm auditioning with George for the job of bodyguard. I'm auditioning with Cody for the job of girlfriend, if not dyad guide. I want to win both contracts, but I'm not sure which one is making me more anxious.

I took another look at my watch. It was time. Just as I had been visualizing, I got out of my car, hefted my bag of surprises, locked the door behind me, and headed up the semi-circular driveway. I walked up those seven marble stairs. I rang the bell next to the double doors. And I wished fervently that Paul would awake, rested and optimistic, to lend his support.

Donna opened the door. "You're right on time," she smiled, then stepped back to let me in. "George is doing much better today, but you can tell to look at him that he was in a fight."

"And how are you doing?" I asked. I realized that I liked the woman a lot. Irrational, I suppose. I hope when I am her age I look half as good as she does; she seems to have a positive attitude; she clearly loves her husband; and she is the mother to that beautiful adult child Cody.

"I've been in touch with our contractor," she replied. "He's going to implement that security inventory. I may need a reminder on some of the details."

I was impressed, and said so. "I threw a lot at you, and you weren't even taking notes. You are one sharp woman."

"Thank you, detective Amy," she laughed, and held out one arm to usher me into the great room. "George is expecting you in his office."

She walked me back to that room where I'd finished talking with him on Friday: small, for this house, with light paneling, a desk, and two wing chairs. Today George was behind his desk, writing notes on a yellow legal pad. "Good morning, George," I volunteered as Donna closed the door behind me. "Your wife tells me you're feeling some improvement."

He was startled at the interruption to his concentration, but he quickly pulled himself together. "Good morning, Miss Clear," he said, and, half-standing, motioned me to take one of the wing chairs. Although he was wearing a smile, his face was also wearing the yellow and purple hues of his recent beating. If it were me, I'd hide for a week until the colors subsided before I allowed anyone to see me.

"Yes. Well. Amy—Miss Clear? We need to talk."

Indeed, we did. "You go first," I said. "And 'Amy' is fine."

He was sitting in some modern caster chair that twirled and bobbed in every direction. He seemed to be rocking up and down, which was disconcerting to watch. Still, he said, "I've given a lot of thought to what you said the other day. I still think you are a difficult person, but I realize your time on the Parish police may have taught you some things I need to learn." Suddenly he and his chair came to a halt. "What do you propose?"

"You admit you know who hurt you?"

"Maybe. Why?"

I was tempted to go ballistic on the stubborn man, but my greedy desire for the job of being his bodyguard helped me keep my voice calm. "If you know who beat you," I offered, "then you know why they beat you. And that's the clue to what has to happen so they don't beat you again."

"You really think they'll interfere with me again?" He was tapping a pencil on his desk top.

"Did you give them what they wanted after they beat you up? If you didn't, yes, they will come back at you."

There was a long pause. Paul had taught me the importance of being silent when a suspect or a client was having trouble with a question or statement. Used to be, the gap would make me nervous and I'd babble. Even though Paul was asleep now, I remembered the lesson and I know better now. Although it still makes me nervous.

Finally, he lowered his head into his hands, both elbows planted on his desk top. "I'm in trouble."

At that moment Donna knocked and opened the door. She had a tray with a teapot and glasses. I stood up and took the tray. "Thank you," I said, "now, leave. We're talking private in here."

Poor woman! There was a mixture of offense and outrage in her face. If I hadn't already developed a good opinion of her, I'd have expected her to say, 'Well, I never!' Instead, she said, "George and I have no secrets."

"Ah. But you and I do. Leave."

She looked toward her husband, but all she saw was the top of his head, held between his hands. "Uh, well—"

"Thank you, Donna," I smiled. I somehow was holding the tray with my left hand while I was shoving her back toward the door with my right. "We won't be long."

As soon as she was gone, I placed the tray on the floor away from me, then turned the bolt on the door.

"George!" I said. "What trouble are you in?"

"A cup of tea would be nice." He was still hiding his face.

"Tea later, George." I felt like I was trying to control one of my sister's kids when they were trying to dance around their Aunt Amy's edicts. "Now tell me, what trouble are you in?"

"It started three years ago," he said to the top of his desk. "I was—"

"Look at me!" I barked.

He did so, with knotted eyebrows. "Wh-what?"

I was standing on the other side of his desk, my fists on my hips. "I'm not a priest," I said sternly, "I'm not going to grant absolution. I'm a woman with a P-I license and a gun who's trying to save your damn life."

He stared up at me, mouth open, head tilted slightly. I'm sure he was not used to people talking to him like this, but I needed his complete attention. I can't save someone if they don't want to be saved. So, I'm trying to make sure he wants it.

It wasn't becoming to see this handsome, self-assured man catching flies with his gaping maw. I sat back down, and in what I hoped was a more soothing voice, I said, "Okay. Tell me the story."

He closed his slack jaw. He nodded. And he began, "Three years ago I was approached by two men to rent a warehouse. I'd recently bought the property in Waggaman but it was vacant. And they offered me $3,000 a month. If they had asked me, I'd have quoted them $2,500, but the customer is always right, right?"

"Go on."

"Three months ago, they informed me they would only be paying me $1,500 a month. I thought they were kidding, but after I left and I counted what was in the envelope, it was only $1,500."

"Wait a minute. Envelope? They were paying your rent in cash?"

Sheepishly, he nodded.

"That one time? Or all along?"

"Yeah, well…" he turned his head and scratched behind his ears.

If what George was finally telling me was true—and that remained to be seen—it was obvious from day one that he was dealing with people who were trying to hide something, and had an extra three grand a month with which to do so. I asked an honest question: "Why on earth did you do this?"

"Free money," he answered just as sincerely. "It was off the books—wouldn't you like an extra $36,000 a year that no one knew about?"

"Oh, sure. I mean, aside from the tax evasion, and the likelihood that there was some kind of excrement all over the money."

"You don't approve."

Of course I didn't approve. But his comment made me realize I was being inappropriately judgmental when what I had claimed to be doing was trying to protect him.

"You're right," I said, "but that's beside the point. Any idea what these people were doing at your property?"

He shook his head. "I'd go out there on the first of the month to pick up the envelope, that's all."

I considered that. "Was the parking lot crowded, like there were customers or a lot of employees"

"I…uh, I never noticed. I don't think so."

Why would he notice? To be honest, if I'd been in his shoes, I probably wouldn't have noticed, either. "Any clues from the utility bills? Were you paying for a lot of natural gas or water or electricity?"

"The warehouse was 40,000 square feet. None of the utility bills seemed out of line."

Okay, they weren't cooking meth or growing marijuana or brewing hooch. What other sort of criminal activity leaves $36,000 a year available for volunteered rent? I didn't like where this was going.

I stood up and walked around the study, rubbing my chin, thinking. Out loud. "No drugs. No liquor. Maybe knock-off designer goods. No; the likely option is prostitution."

George looked genuinely surprised. "My warehouse was a whorehouse?"

"Possibly," I laughed at the idea, "but probably not. I think it must have been a holding pen for prostitutes. White slavery, which Jefferson Parish Fire and Rescue seems to think may have included a dead body. Sexual trafficking." I stopped in front of his desk, and leaned over it, both palms on the desk top. Our faces weren't twelve inches apart. "Very profitable. Very illegal."

We stared at each other for a very long time before he finally said, "Can you blame me for not wanting to know?"

And we stared for another long time before I answered, "No. On a human level, of course not." I pushed myself upright. "The law might think different. So, you need protection from the people who maybe you know. I can do that. And you might need protection from the Parish sheriff. I'll do what I can, but I hope you trust your lawyer."

He was rubbing a particularly purple patch alongside his left eye. "I'm in real estate; of course I have a lawyer," he said along with the movement. "And I have a friend in the Jefferson Parish Sheriff's office."

It took me a few seconds to process what I thought George meant. "Do you think your friend can make things go away?"

He smiled wistfully. "One can hope," he said. "I sold a house to Dick, and he and his wife found a cache of silver bullion hidden in a wall when they did a renovation. He thinks I'm great."

"Can't hurt," I said, "as long as it's not a jury you have to win over."

"What? I haven't done anything wrong!"

I smiled and got up again, pacing the small studio office. "Why did these people you still haven't identified burn your warehouse?"

There was so much silence I turned toward the desk, afraid I'd find George laying on the floor with his legs in the air. Once again, he was holding his face in his hands, elbows set on the desk. Was that a tear? It startled me so bad, I said softly, "George? You okay?"

The way he looked at me! It was like my sister's youngest, Little Charlie, when he was insisting he hadn't eaten the cookie whose crumbs were all over his shirt.

I sighed. I dragged a wing chair so I was alongside the desk instead of opposite George, and I read him Amy's Rules of Life: "George. Do not lie to your doctor. Do not lie to your lawyer. If you have any religion, do not lie to your priest. And do not lie to the person who is trying to save your life. You got that?"

There was the merest hint of a smile on his mouth, distorted by the way his hands were supporting his cheeks. He whispered something.

"Say what? I'm sorry, George, I didn't get that."

The whisper was a little louder, but still incomprehensible.

Eloquently I said, "Huh?"

I finally heard him say, "I set the fire."

What? George torched his warehouse? Despite all appearances, it seemed the man is unmoored from reality. Do I really want the job of saving him? Well, he sure needed protection, but perhaps as much from himself as from the shadowy people who beat him up.

I noticed he was waiting for me to say something.

"When I wrote up my report for Paralax, I said it looked like you did. But the more you told me about your, uh, your tenants, you had convinced me they must have done it. This is a shock."

"When they cut their rent in half, it dawned on me the next step was they would stop paying any rent. Because it all was off the books, I couldn't get the sheriff to evict them. I evicted them the only way I could."

There was a certain logic to his reasoning. Twisted, but logic. Many times in my police days Paul had quoted some poet from his childhood, 'To live outside the law you must be honest.'[23] When he accepted the deal for an off-the-books tenant, George put that part of his life 'outside the law.'

"Okay, then," I said, struggling to order my thoughts. "First thing, withdraw your insurance claim. If Paralax takes you to court,

---

[23] Paul was eleven when Bob Dylan sang those words in "Absolutely Sweet Marie" on *Blonde On Blonde*. When he saw the movie *Day of the Jackal*, the scene of the document forger trying to blackmail the Jackal brought home to him what Dylan's words meant: If you live a life where you cannot count on the courts to enforce contracts, you'd better be honest or face severe consequences. The movie's illicit armorer was honest and lived, but the forger was not—and paid the price.

all this will come out, and we don't want that. I don't think it's against the law to burn your own building. At the worst, Jefferson Parish will want you to reimburse them for the cost of putting out the fire. That's bad, but it beats going to jail."

And my half of my brain continued to churn. "So that's why they beat you up. You took away their headquarters. And you burned some of their inventory."

George countered, "They don't know I was the one who burned the warehouse."

It made me laugh. "They darn well know they didn't do it."

"My friend the Lieutenant says the police don't know who set the fire."

"You think the people you've been dealing with need proof? I'm sure they think you torched the building. And even if some vagrant did it by accident, you are no longer their soft touch and I'll bet they're angry about it."

George hung his head. I leaned back in the wing chair. I was hungry. I wanted to go lamp shopping with Cody. I wanted a beer. I really wanted to talk to Paul.

Finally, I said, "Who are they? Your, uh, your ex-tenants."

He shook his head.

"Don't tell me you don't know their names!"

He shook his head again. This time he said, "I just don't believe I'm in danger."

I was ready to slap the man. "This beating—" I pointed at his multi-hued face "—was a warning. There's more where it came from. And it's heading your way." In my head I was screaming, but I managed to behave civilly. I really wanted the job.

He must have heard some urgency in my tone. "I mean, you've been a big help. Donna thinks you're the best thing that could happen to this family. Do you know she's already hired our contractor?"

Nice to know the missus understands danger and preparation. I wish Paul were awake, he might know an approach that would work on this stubborn fool. "She said something about that," I offered, trying to be gracious.

"But I just don't feel like I'm in danger."

"I wish you were using your thinking instead of your feeling, George. I'll be mad if the next time I see you, you're the guest of honor at your funeral."

"Look, you've been a big help already." He was opening a drawer in his desk; it made me nervous, and I put my right hand on the butt of my Ruger in my hip pack. But it was a checkbook that he pulled out and dropped on the desk top. "You gave a lot of good advice to Donna. And I think I'll listen to you and withdraw the insurance claim. Let me pay you."

"First rule of private detecting," I said, relieved, "never say no to money."

"How's $400?"

"My usual rate is $250 a day plus expenses," I laughed. "Four hundred sounds right." I fished my business card out of a pouch on my belt and gave it to him. "Make it out to Clear, Owens, and Hodges LLC."

"Do I get to meet them?" He was really writing me a check!

"I've discussed this with Owens and Hodges. He's asleep and she's working another job. But anything could happen."

I love the sound that comes with tearing a check out of a checkbook. And I love the feel of a check as I fold it and put it in my pocket. "If anything else happens, George, you've got my phone number. Remember what I said, though; I can't protect you if I don't know who I'm protecting you from."

He nodded and stood up. Two steps later he kicked the teapot against the far wall. "Shit!" he cried, "I forgot about that!" He bent over to clean up his mess.

"I'm done here," I said. "Now to spend some of the money you just gave me. I broke one of Cody's lamps and he's taking me to find a replacement. Do you know where the nearest Goodwill is?"

"Be nice to Cody," he said over his shoulder from the puddle of tea on the floor. "The boy is a little, uh, delicate."

We had gone from business to family. I felt like a high school boy picking up his date for the prom. I'm sure Paul would have thought of something clever to say, but all I could do was mumble, "Yes, sir." I'll have him home before ten o'clock. And I won't feed him liquor.

When I opened the office door, Donna Locaviche practically fell into the room. I expected to see her holding a water glass that she had been pressing against the door to try to listen to our conversation. Embarrassed, she picked herself up, saying, "I was coming for the tea things."

"It's okay," I told her. "I'm sure George will tell you all about our discussion. Uh—where's Cody?"

"George!" she shouted. "Leave that, I'll get it." She scurried to where her husband was trying to mop up the tea spill with the cocktail napkins that had been on the tray.

I'm easily amused, I know. For some reason I was tickled to see George and Donna on their hands and knees, working together to solve that little wet crisis. They were a good-looking couple, and they really behaved like they cared about each other. Sweet.

But the day was marching on. I went into the living room and found Cody sitting on the huge couch that had served as George's litter when I responded to Donna's call on Friday. He was wearing chinos and what looked like a ruffled shirt with a peculiar stain across the chest. He was swiping his way through an iPad.

"Good morning, Cody," I called as I approached him.

"Good afternoon, you mean." He had looked up and was smiling at me, the curve of lips and expression surrounded by the sharp lines of his face. He stood up with some difficulty. "How did it go with my father?"

"It was peachy. He's got his blind spots, but I suppose we all do."

"That he does," the man chuckled. He dropped his iPad on the couch behind him and said, "Well. Are you ready to go shopping?"

I nodded. "Look, since this is all necessary because I broke the lamp, I volunteer to drive. You have to navigate, though."

"I was going to ask you," he said, and now he seemed to be examining the tops of his old black-and-white Converses. "My license is suspended."

"Oh," I blurted out, "that accident?"

He was still meditating on his shoes. "No, that was three years ago. Louisiana thinks I have seizures. They won't let me drive."

"I'm double-glad I volunteered, then. Let's head out."

Cody smiled, maybe relieved that I made no indication of thinking less of him. Some people have psoriasis, some people have epilepsy. It's not them, it's just a condition that they have. It's not their fault.

In the car, Cody saw my GPS. "We don't need that," he said. "I'll get you there." I wondered about the advisability of letting a non-driver give road directions, but I didn't want to start my social time with Cody by challenging him over a relatively minor thing. Besides, if we get lost, that's more time I get to learn if he really has a dyad, and how that came to be.

"Sure thing, boss," I replied. Glow plugs, starter, clutch. "Where are we going?"

"Harahan. Hunter-Kray is the only good lighting store that's open on a Sunday." Oh, is that why he would have preferred Saturday?

We were on our way up Richmond Place. I took St. Charles to the river, then snaked north on Leake Avenue, which paralleled the levee. What started as a pretty residential street gradually became a not-so-pretty residential area, When I made a left onto Oak and then River Road the scenery morphed into industrial and maritime. We were on our way to Harahan.

"Something that happened Friday," Cody said, somewhere around Freret or Maple. "I told you I sometimes hear a woman's voice that's not there. But we were talking, and suddenly I heard a man say something."

I nodded. The incident was etched in my emotional memory.

"And what the voice said was an answer to a question I'd asked."

Anxiety, fear, excitement all flooded me. If I somehow cut my finger, all that emotion would spurt out of me like blood from a severed artery. I nodded again, and said, "I remember."

There was a long silence. I was already on River Road when Cody said, "What was that?"

I glanced in his direction. His arms were folded in front of his chest. Whatever the stain was on his shirt, it looked like a parody of an Izod alligator.

"I don't want to explain while I'm driving," I said. "We can stop somewhere for coffee and we can talk. It's every bit as, uh, as unusual as the voices you sometimes hear."

"Voice. There's only one."

"Yes. Me, too. Only one." I was bursting with apprehension, and we hadn't gotten to the lamp place yet. And I needed sleepyhead Paul to be awake before I'd be able to show Cody that I was like him—if, indeed, he had a woman living in his head and wasn't garden variety stark raving blathering crazy.

"But you'll tell me, right?" Another glance, I could see him chewing on the side of his thumb. "Three years, I've been afraid I've gone crazy. But I don't feel crazy—I figured out how to make a living, I'm usually a happy man." There was silence, but I was watching the road to make sure I didn't get creamed by some joyrider taking advantage of the absence of traffic lights on River Road. "And then I hear her voice…" and his trailed off.

"Where do I turn to get to this place?" I asked. It was a relief to change the subject, because I didn't want to talk about Paul and dyads until we were sitting down alone somewhere. We were passing simple residences and the occasional empty lot on the landward side; to the left was the grassy slope of the levee, with the tops of leafless trees visible from the batture beyond. "What is it? Hunter Gatherer?"

"Hunter Kray," he corrected. "Go under the bridge road, then take the second right. It's not far now."

The Huey P. Long Bridge was hard to miss. It's a massive cantilever erector set, with three truss sections. Traffic is horrible at all hours because, believe it or not, my Texian[24] friends, it is one of only three—count them, one, two, three—bridges across the river in metro New Orleans, and the I-310 bridge doesn't really count because it's way west, past the airport. When I have the time to kill, I like using one of the ferries. After all, if you're stuck behind someone else's back bumper, you may as well be able to get out of your car and enjoy the view of the water.

We don't have a lot of tunnels in Louisiana—you have to go to Mobile for one of them. But, leftover from childhood games, I still hold my breath when I go under any overpass. The bridge ramp from Clearview Parkway cast strong shadows across the road and across the windshield; I could hear the thunk-a-thunk-a-thunk of overhead traffic. "Are you all right?" Cody asked.

I nodded. A moment later, when we were back in the December sun, I explained. It was sweet to see Cody's reaction, a smile and a nod.

We passed parking lots and warehouses.

"Look," he said, "A PJ's is near here. Can we get some coffee first and talk? Hunter-Kray is open until five." I glanced and saw begging in his half-smile, half-squint, half-frown.

"Sure." The stupid lamp was just a convenient excuse; what I wanted to know about was Cody and his dyad. Or his not dyad. "Where is it?"

"It's behind Elmwood Shopping Center. Turn right." I am good, I obey. Without Cody's directions, I'd have been lost. I was surrounded by warehouses. He gave more directions, and I drove us

---

[24] When a Cajun uses the word 'Texian' it means one who doesn't speak Cajun French. More loosely, it means outsider, foreigner, or even ignoramus.

down an alleyway alongside a self-storage place, into a sorry shopping center with acres of empty parking places. Well, it was a Sunday.

"Over there," Cody pointed.

The man who doesn't drive knows his way around. I'd never have found the place, even though it had a sign over the door and window. In my own defense, PJ's signage was dwarfed by the red and blue neon SELF STORAGE sign on the tower above it. And to think, I grew up in Jefferson Parish.

Cody had a little difficulty getting out of the Benz, and then he limped along with me to the PJ's entrance. He didn't look to be in pain; it was more a matter of his right leg no longer having the full range of motion. Remind me never to be in a car wreck. Even so, he opened the front door for me. What a gentleman!

We stood at the counter to order our coffees. They had lots of fancy French-roast-fair-trade-grind-'em-in-front-of-you brews. The whole place smelled like candy. So much for my preference for that bitter wake-the-hell-up taste of chicory. Why is there a coffee shop in New Orleans that does not sell the single most popular blend—with chicory—that no one else in America likes? I'll bet they'd be helpless if Boudreaux and Thibodeaux[25] came in here and placed an order in their Cajun French. Still, the coffee was as much an excuse as the lamp. It was just a necessary step on the way to The Conversation.

In an ill-thought-out plan, I ordered a double espresso; maybe it would wake Paul up for the conversation. When the young barista brought it and Cody's Vienna double crème, I brought out my wallet. "This whole trip is because I broke the lamp," I insisted, "I'll pay." Holy crap, nine dollars for two glorified coffees! I hope George hires me for ongoing work so I can continue to live this fast-paced high-life.

---

[25] Cajuns can tell Boudreaux and Thibodeaux jokes. You Texicans maybe shouldn't. I'm just saying.

Cody picked up both drinks, gentleman that he was, and limped to a tiny table in a far corner of the shop. We fussed about napkins, then sat and looked at each other. Finally, he asked, "How did you do that?" I knew what he was talking about.

"I was eleven years old when something impossible happened to me," I began. "It was a little scary and a little annoying and very, very exciting." I stirred my espresso. The smell was the coffee equivalent of three-day-old raw fish, overpowering and unpleasant. "So, all these million years later, I still have a man who lives in my head. He can think directly to people. That's what happened."

Cody was staring at me, mouth open. He was ignoring his candy coffee drink. A couple of moments after I finished, he snorted. "Right. You expect me to believe there's a man who lives inside you who silently said that he was going to spend Saturday with his girlfriend?"

I forced myself to shrug, despite the anxiety racing through me. "Okay. What's your explanation?" His mouth closed, then opened again, and finally closed into a thoughtful purse, accompanied by frown lines around his eyes. There was no answer.

"This is why I don't tell many people about him," I said. "Just like you don't tell many people about the woman's voice you hear."

"But, but, but—" I got the feeling his mouth was waiting for his brain to catch up "—but that's not possible. You can't just think into another person's head."

I smiled. And with my mouth clamped shut I thought to him, *Yes I can.* This was the rubber-meets-the-road moment. Either Cody had his own dyad and we were going to be best of friends, or he was going to freak out, tell me to forget the lamp, and call a taxi to get him home.

The poor man. First, his jaw bounced off the table top, which made his spoon bounce, which knocked a cute little ceramic contraption full of yellow and pink sugar substitutes onto the floor, with the unfortunate sound of breaking crockery. Then, after a few seconds of seeming recovery, he tilted his head and said, "That's scary. That's not possible."

"Absolutely," I nodded. "Not possible. But there it is."

"So, why did it sound like a man's voice last time?" He was blinking rapidly but his eyes were aimed at mine.

"Because Paul was a man. Is. Is a man."

"Make him talk to me again."

"He's asleep," I said, shaking my head. "He and his girlfriend stayed up way after I conked out last night."

Cody managed a smile. "That's convenient."

So much for my fantasy of love and romance. I took a deep breath. "Look, I told you what's going on with me. You don't have to believe it. But our coffee is getting cold and we have a lamp to buy, right?" We both looked at our elaborate cardboard cups. "Besides, he'll wake up eventually."

He sipped his coffee slowly and silently. Oh, I wished Paul were awake! He wouldn't like being asked to bark on command like a circus seal, but at least I'd be able to compare notes with him. That would make this ominous silence a little easier to endure.

Finally, Cody offered, "You don't have to do this. Replace the lamp, I mean. It's okay, really."

"Are you kidding?" I replied. "You said you want to take my picture, and I want that lamp in it." It looked as if he was done with his coffee, and I was more than tired of mine, so I stood up, gathering our debris for the trash can. "How close are we to that place?" I asked. "Hunter Safety Orange?" That was something Paul had talked about from his days in the woods in West Virginia.

"Hunter Kray," he corrected me. "Yeah, we're about two minutes away."

Back in the car, Cody's silence was oppressive. "I don't know what I did wrong, but I didn't mean to do it." I started driving, making a right out of the shopping center.

"I felt like you were making fun of me." His arms were folded in front of his chest, and he was looking at my car's dirty floorboard.

I pulled over, right wheels on the sidewalk, and turned off the engine. "No," I said. "I'm not making fun. Everything I told you about me and Paul is true. If you've got a voice inside you, maybe you're not alone."

"I guess." He was looking out the passenger window, at a TJ Maxx and a laser tag place.

"Cody. Please. Look at me."

He turned his head, but his eyes were aimed in the direction of my seatbelt. I put my hand under his chin and lifted his head until he finally met my gaze. "I've had Paul inside me since I was eleven years old. I told my best friend after it happened and she freaked out. Christine is the last person I've told about him, and that was years ago. I understand being afraid to tell anyone." I let my palm go up to the side of his face. "You are a brave man for admitting this to me, and I admire you for it. I'm grateful. I'm—" And I leaned forward and kissed him on the mouth.

"I'm glad you trusted me," I said when we were hugging. "I won't let you down." Cody was silent, but he was moving his hands on my back, petting and rubbing. It made me feel like I hadn't utterly ruined the intimacy between us.

Hunter-Kray was two streets over, on Distributor's Row. It was at the end of a long row of faceless warehouses, punctuated by a cellphone tower.

The showroom was huge. I think the Superdome could have fit inside with room left over for City Park and maybe a Delta hangar from Armstrong International Airport. Cody introduced me to Karl, who had been handling his lighting account ever since he started his photography studio.

While Cody was asking Karl about reproduction Tiffany lamps, Paul awoke with an unfortunate slinging of my arms and an awfully loud, "Who? What the fuck? Where are we?"

Cody got whacked across the back by Paul's profligate awakening; he fell forward but managed to keep his unsteady feet. Silently I hissed, *Be quiet. We're in public.* Aloud, I apologized to Cody and Karl, "Tourette's. I am so sorry. Is there a restroom I can use?"

Karl took a few steps back, away from me, but pointed to the far corner of the warehouse, "Past the ugly floor lamps."

"Please forgive me," I said to Cody, and set out for the ladies' restroom in the south forty.

Since only those poor unfortunates who actually suffer from Tourette's know what that disease actually involves, my shamefaced apology and quick run to the powder room usually fool people into believing I must have the condition. Actually, the embarrassment is quite real. It takes a private lecture to Paul, with his own promises of contrition, before I calm down enough to be willing to show my face in public again.

From years of experience, Paul led with his regrets as I legged it to the sanctuary of the ladies' room. *I didn't know!* he thought. *I was sound asleep, with a wonderful nasty dream about Christine, and all of a sudden, I heard some guy saying something.*

Well, my garbage-mouth dyad, you may have loused up my getting a job as George's bodyguard, you may have ruined any chance I had of getting to know Cody, and you probably terrified his dyad, if he has one.

Terrified his—You mean—You really think he has one? That would be great. There was a pause. *We could double date.*

First, I need to make sure that woman's voice he hears is connected to someone living in his head. But I'm sure Christine would love to know your dating plans, I thought.

The ladies' room was small and underwhelming, with three stalls and a tiny sink; Hunter-Kray must sell more twenty dollar reproductions than thousand dollar originals. Still, it served the purpose of privacy. Out loud I said, very loud, "Do you always swear first thing when you wake up?"

Before Paul could reply, a woman's voice came from one of the stalls: "Most days, yeah. I hate alarm clocks."

Nothing like laughter to blunt your anger. And I had been so looking forward to giving Paul a what-for. Silently I told him, *I won't skin you alive while we have an audience. But really, do you always wake up with the word 'fuck' on our lips?*

Not really, he replied silently. *There are mornings when I wake up first and get out of bed. When you wake up, you just ease into the day. You're a cheerful morning person. I wish I were.* It's like I said earlier, Paul is nicer to me than I am to him. On the other hand, he doesn't have to pretend to have some exotic neurological condition because of me.

I heard a toilet flush, and a heavy-set young woman let herself out of the far stall. She saw me staring at myself in the mirror— really me staring at the Paul Owens I know is on the other side of my eyeballs—and stood next to me to use the sink. "Oh, I'm sorry," I said, and moved to the side.

"Did your husband embarrass you by swearing this morning?" she asked.

"Kind of," I answered. How could I explain what really happened?

She was drying her hands on an ancient endless towel gizmo on the wall. "My husband says I'm an embarrassment for the first hour I'm awake. I don't tell him he's always an embarrassment."

I laughed politely, which seemed to be what the light social situation required. Paul thought, *Why are so many married people unhappy? Mary Pat*—Paul's wife when he had his own body—*and I liked each other.*

Just another example of the different ways people have of saying 'I love you.'

Paul snorted silently as the woman left the rest room. *Lady Nancy Astor told Winston Churchill that, if she were his wife, she'd give him poison. He said that if she were his wife, he'd take it.*

"I've heard of Winston Churchill," I said softly, even though I knew Paul would laugh at me for not knowing the prehistoric figures he grew up with. "Who is Lady Astor?"

"She used to be famous," he said with a sigh. "*Tempus fugit.*"

"Gesundheit," I said. I thought it was appropriate after I didn't understand the last thing he said and decided it was some kind of sneeze. I'm not stupid; I have a Masters in statistics. But I was born in 1999, and Sister Caligula at St. Giles was not the most, uh, engaging history teacher in school. Meanwhile, Paul was born in 1955, so a lot of what would be history to me is what he lived through. No wonder he knows who Lady What's-her-name is. He keeps mentioning singers I've never heard of who he tells me were hot stuff back in the day. We all are prisoners of when we were born.

Paul thought, *Tell me, what did I miss? You really think Cody may have a dyad?*

"Yes," I said. "Uh—maybe. I need you to make contact with her. If she's there."

If there's a she there.

"Well, I guess. Cody seems happy to hear me say he's not crazy, that's nice. Oh, and I auditioned to be daddy's bodyguard. He put me off again, but he's beginning to understand he's in danger. He wrote me a check."

"I'm sorry I missed all this," he said, "but Christine and me had a good time after you conked out."

"In English?"

"What?" I think he reviewed what he'd said, because he went on, "Oh. Conked out. Passed out, fell asleep, slipped the surly bonds of consciousness. When did I turn into a Thesaurus?"

"You're so entertaining," I said. "I think I'll keep you."

"That means I don't have to update my resumé. Hallelujah."

This kind of repartee is our idea of fun. I guess that's our strange way of saying 'I love you.' I hope we don't make you uncomfortable.

I leaned against the wall alongside the sink, arms crossed. "We used to worry that people would find out about you and we'd end up in a strait jacket at Mandeville," I mused. "Then I went to college and I discovered a lot of the people there were screaming bonkers, but no one minded. So, I stopped worrying about you and me."

I paused, and Paul said, "Yeah? So?"

"And then, in the midst of Cody's polite introduction to a salesman, you suddenly whack the man almost to the ground and scream, 'What the fuck?' I'm not so much worried about Mandeville as I am of never being able to earn my own living again."

"Yeah," he said, dejected. "I don't know how I can behave better when I get woken up out of the blue in some strange place. But Amy Clear, with God as my witness, I swear I will try to do better."

If I hadn't been trying to scold him, I'd have been rolling on the bathroom floor, laughing. I love Paul. It's not that he can do no wrong, but he always has a plausible excuse and a believable promise for the future. And always entertaining.

"See that you do," I said, sternly, trying not to crack up.

After a minute I said, "I have to pay for whatever lamp Cody picked out. Then I have to convince his father to hire me to guard his body."

"Plus, we haven't had lunch. Breakfast, even."

I shook my head and opened the bathroom door. *Do you know the meaning of the word 'incorrigible'?*

I fear you think it's spelled P-a-u-l. Yeah.

I started the long hike back to where I had left Cody and salesman Karl. *That's about right,* I thought.

When he saw me getting close, Cody turned away from the sales rep and said, "Are you feeling better, Amy?" What I felt was a jolt from hearing him use my name. "Uh, yes. Yes, thank you." I smiled at him, then looked at Karl. "Sorry," I said. "I'm okay now."

Cody resumed his talk with the salesman. Karl was holding a pretty Tiffany styled lamp. The stained-glass shade was a four-sided pyramid. I was a little nervous at how much it was going to cost me to salve my conscience and replace what I had broken. When we first met up with the salesman, Cody had mentioned $400 as the ceiling. I hoped that lamp didn't have a high-priced attic.

"It's a River of Good," Karl was saying, "so you know it's excellent quality for a reproduction. Two seventy-five-watt equivalent bulbs, each with a pull chain." He was holding it by the central pole just above the base, waving it around like it didn't weigh five pounds. "I can let it go for $168."

I had mentally prepared myself to spend $400, so hearing the lamp price made me feel like it was a bargain. "Cody, will this do?"

Nodding, he said, "It's just like the one you—uh, just like the old one."

"Don't wrap it," Paul said to Karl, "I'll eat it here." He held out my Optimo card.

"Thanks again, Amy," Cody said softly. "You really didn't have to do this."

In an unusual burst of courtesy, I heard Paul think to me as well as to Cody, *Amy thinks she has to. It's some kind of personal code of honor.*

Cody stopped in the middle of whatever he was saying to Karl the salesman. He turned his head toward me and squinted. I thought to him, *Paul's awake,* and smiled.

Karl handed me the charge clip on a little clipboard for me to sign. "I broke it, I bought it. Besides, I told you I want this lamp in the picture you said you wanted to take of me." I folded the receipt and slipped it into my right front pocket, alongside some ball-point pens.

"Okay!" he replied. "When we get back to the house, I'll open your account and—"

"Just take my picture," I interrupted. I wanted the connection to be personal, not business.

He was smiling as he limped beside me to the my car. Once we were belted in he said, "I can't wait to plug this in."

We were back on River Road when I thought to Paul, *Did you introduce yourself to Cody?*

Not exactly.

It's time. Let me warn him first. I glanced at the smiling man in the passenger seat, still fondling the new lamp, and said, "You know that voice that just tried to explain why I insisted on paying for the lamp? The one that said he was going to be busy on Saturday?" A vigorous nod. "His name is Paul, and the Tourette's episode was really him waking up. He wants to say hello." Another nod, although not nearly so energetic or enthusiastic. I hope the poor man wasn't ODing on disembodied voices for one day. "Uh, one other thing. When Paul thinks to you, I can't hear what he's saying. I'll be curious, though."

All I got was a confused blink.

Show time, my dyad, I thought.

So, I kept driving us north on River Road, heading for the big bend in the river in the grimy Southport section of the parish, before the street would realign south and hook us back into Leake Avenue. Every now and then I'd glance at Cody, seeing his expression in response to Paul's words that I couldn't hear. But I heard his answers: "You really live inside Amy?" and "Maybe the woman I hear is as real as you?" and "Does everyone who hears voices have someone living in them?" and "But—but—but this is so strange."

Cody asked, "Did you know Amy before this happened?"

"Nope," Paul said aloud. Cody did a double-take, and Paul added, "We only have one set of vocal cords. When I speak out loud, I sound like her. Should I announce myself when I do?"

There was a long pause, but out of the corner of my eye I could see Cody was smiling. "Uh—please?"

"It's Paul. Sure thing, Cody."

"If it's okay with you, Cody, I'd like—" he was squinting and holding his head at an angle. I heard Paul think *You have to announce yourself, too.* "—uh, it's Amy. If you are okay with it, I'd like Paul to try to think to the woman that might be in your head. That way we'll know once and for all."

"I don't know," he said. "This damn voice has ruined my life. It broke my engagement, it lost me my job, and now I'm thirty-eight and I live with my parents. I've spent three years since the accident wishing I could get rid of this voice, and you're saying it might be permanent?" He was glaring at me.

"Oh." I had been so wrapped up in the fantasy of Cody having a dyad and us living happily ever after that I never considered he might have a different definition of happiness. "Look, nothing Paul or I do can turn that voice into a real person. Either she's in you or she's not. Wouldn't you like to know for sure?"

We were going around the big curve where River Road turned into Oak Street and then Leake Avenue. I drove over the railroad grade crossing, and out Cody's window—out of which he was not looking—I saw the big horse stable between the road and the river.

He didn't sound enthusiastic when he said, "I guess." But it was enough for me; I thought to Paul, *See if there's a dyad inside the man.*

"How did this mess up your engagement?" I asked, hoping I didn't sound like the insecure wanna-be-girlfriend that I felt like.

"Rachel," he said. "She was a nursing student at LSUNO, and I was doing freelance photography. Sold a fair number of pictures to the *Times-Picayune*. We were living together for two years when I was in the accident." He wrapped his arms around himself and leaned back against the passenger door.

"After the wreck was when I started hearing that voice. After a while Rachel couldn't deal with it and moved out."

Nothing so far, I heard Paul think.

I put my free hand on his knee. "That must have been awful," I volunteered.

"Mind you, I was a mess. Probably very needy. Not the confident young man she got engaged to."

"Crap and a half. So, what happened?"

He blew out a long breath. "You know, I—I don't want to talk about it right now. It's a pretty day for December, and I'm sitting with a pretty girl. I don't want to think about all that trouble. Some other time I'll tell you the rest of the story."

I drove past the Crossfit NOLA place. Outside my window I saw their logo and street number done to look like graffiti.

"What?" Cody shouted, his face turning into a heated frown. "What did you say?"

Before I could figure out what was going on I heard my own voice say, "It's Paul. Maybe I didn't phrase that well."

"'Your head is empty'? I guess not."

"What I meant was, as best I can tell there is no one in there with you."

Cody was still staring, now open mouthed. "It's Amy," I said. "I think Paul is saying you don't have a dyad."

Yeah. Thanks for translating. Then, "It's Paul. What Amy said. With all my experience living inside another person, I can authoritatively say you do not have such a brain guest."

"Well, that's just dandy, isn't it?" Cody countered. "So, I'm crazy, huh?"

"No crazier than we are," Paul said aloud.

We drove in silence for a minute or two. I could tell Cody was upset, maybe even angry. Hey, I'm just a doctor's daughter, not a medical whiz.

"It's Paul. My girlfriend is schizophrenic. She was a mess when I met her. Now she takes her medication and she's fine. I don't see why you can't be fine."

That encouraged me. I added, "It's Amy. You. Are. Fine."

"I don't know," Cody mused, and he turned to look out the passenger window for the rest of the trip.

Crap-and-a-half. I hope I haven't blown it.

Nah. If he takes the right drugs instead of Ibuprofen, he'll be fine. Too bad the voice isn't real, though. I really was looking forward to a double date.

The monument sign by the credit union was my landmark; I took the next left to get on St. Charles Avenue and head back to the Locaviche estate. "We're almost home," I said to Cody. "Do you want to stop for anything? Ice cream? Bleach? Razor blades? Hemlock?"

At least that got something out of him, somewhere between a guffaw and a chortle. *That's progress*, I thought to Paul.

When I drove into the Locaviche's semi-circular driveway, I nearly ran into the back of a service box truck. "Glass Star" the logo said, the words over a yellow seven-pointed star and what I guessed was supposed to be a cartoon rendering of a pile of broken glass. "Uh-oh," Cody said.

"Uh-oh, indeed," Paul said, sounding like a soap opera announcer.

Oh, crap! I thought to my dyad. *Now what?*

I hadn't turned off the engine when Cody opened his door and, limp be damned, bounded up the seven marble stairs and through the double front doors that were standing open. *These people are not taking security seriously*, I thought to Paul. I turned off the ignition and waited for the afterburning to stop before I got out. You better believe I locked the Benz. And I had my right hand on the butt of my concealed pistol as I tackled the seven marble steps with less speed than Cody.

I heard voices coming through various doors from the rear of the house. I went through the enormous living room, through a hallway, through the kitchen, and looked at the clot of Locaviches crowded into the laundry room. They were watching a young man in white coveralls puttying a piece of metal in the place where a pane of glass had been. When I joined the crowd, I saw it was the very pane I had pointed out to Donna as the one a blind and crippled thief would smash to reach in and turn the door lock.

George was explaining to Cody what had happened in our absence. Around 2:30 he and Donna heard a smash, but it took a while before they located the source. Although the back door was still closed and locked, an empty liquor bottle with a hunk of cotton fabric was resting at an odd angle against the clothes dryer. In fact, the neck of the bottle had broken off and still lay in a sparkly pile of shards. Sort of like the logo on the serviceman's truck outside.

Donna was leaning against the back wall, her head in her hands. After a few moments she saw me and motioned me nearer. I had to squeeze behind the repairman. "Are you alright?" I asked her.

She grabbed me. She threw her arms around me and hugged me like a life raft. She wasn't crying, but her breathing was irregular in my ear. "I wish you'd been here," she finally said. "George told me about your conversation this morning. You're hired."

I wasn't able to escape her grasp, but I leaned my head back to make sure I heard that right. *I'm hired?* I thought to Paul. I did not know he then relayed the message, silently, to Cody.

"I told George my rates—"

"Yes, yes," Donna interrupted. "He may not be ready for you, but I am. I can't—I can't—" and she pulled me close again. I felt like my seven-year-old nephew's Bugs Bunny doll. I imagine I've gained a few pounds from wine and Dixie Beer, but I had no idea I passed the squish test.

"Okay, okay," I said, as I pried myself loose from her understandable quest for comfort and security. "Let me get to work." To Paul I thought, *Show time.*

"Excuse me," I said to the glazier, as I crouched by the clothes dryer to examine the object that had broken the window. *Looks like an unloaded Molotov cocktail,* I heard Paul offer.

I think you're right. That's a warning. The next one will be armed and flaming.

George seemed to be avoiding me, but when he finished explaining things to his son, Cody knelt down beside me. "This is not my idea of fun and excitement," he said softly.

I nodded. "Employment, yes," I told him; "fun, no. Look at this," and I pointed at what was left of the bottle. "This is a warning. Next time it will be full of gasoline and lit." I stood up, accidently bopping the glazier against the back door. I said to anyone who wanted to listen, "We really have to seal off the access from the street back there." Donna said I was hired, so now me and the Locaviches are 'we.'

The repairman was done. George led him off to the office to write him a check. Donna, Cody, and I gathered to look at the metal replacement of the pane of glass in the back door. Donna said, "Why didn't they come in? You said someone could break that window and reach in to unlock the door."

She doesn't believe us? Paul thought, defensive. I replied silently, *No; I think she's curious.* I told Donna, "Yes. They didn't come in because they didn't want to, not because they couldn't. For now, they're not trying to harm George, just terrorize him. And you."

"Well, they've certainly succeeded," she said in clipped words, "and I am angry." She looked up at me and said, "Find out who is doing this—" her blue eyes were blazing "—and make them stop."

"What can I do to help?" I was startled to hear that from Cody; his mother's jaw dropped at the sound of his words.

I looked up at him. "Well, aren't you a sweetheart," I said. "I don't know what yet, but I'll think of something."

I turned to Donna. "Get your contractor out here. Fix those windows I showed you. Replace this door," as I kicked the newly repaired back entrance. "Block off the back of the garage and any access from, what's that street over there?"

"Nashville Avenue," she said, nodding.

"Call your alarm people. Ask them how long before they get someone here if it's 2 AM. If it's more than ten minutes, start looking for somebody local. And cut down those bushes outside your breakfast room."

"All that?" Cody asked, incredulous. Ah, he hadn't heard me on the 2036 Locaviche Home Security Tour, so this was brand new to him.

"This is just for starters. There will be more."

Donna said, "All right," and went into the kitchen and somewhere beyond. Paul thought, *I hope she's making all those phone calls.*

"Why are we doing all this?" Cody asked. It sounded neutral, like he was asking for information.

"Target hardening," I said. "To make it more difficult for the people harassing your dad to throw warnings through your windows. They know where you all live and they are trying to terrorize everyone, not just your dad. I want to stop 'em."

When I left Cody in the laundry room, I was listening for noise or George's voice. I caught up to him in his office, where he was throwing manila file folders onto the Oriental rug. "Are we having a shredding party?" I asked.

He grinned. "Sort of," he said, tossing another file onto the pile. "If those bastards are getting this close, I may as well get rid of anything, uh, dangerous."

"I am not your conscience, and I'm not a cop," I said, meaning I didn't care what sort of incriminating documents he might have. "But Donna says I'm hired, so we have to talk."

He nodded, still paying more attention to the files he was pulling out of a credenza. Paul thought, *He doesn't seem to think a talk is urgent.*

He's wrong about that. I took the three steps toward him and kicked the file drawer closed, nearly catching his fingers. "Sit!" I said, pointing to his chair, which, to be fair, was buried in folders. When he looked at me, stunned at being ordered around, I repeated it: "Sit! Sit down! I work for you now and you need to tell me things."

He backed away from me, toward the chair. I watched him tip it to spill the files off it, and then he sat down carefully. Maybe it was from the exertion of clearing out his office, but it seemed the purple and yellow on his face from his beating were brighter than they'd been this morning.

"Do I have your attention?" I said, standing in front of him with my hands on my hips.

Mouth open a little, eyes glued to mine, he nodded.

"Good. Who beat you up?"

He looked down. I reached over to grab his chin and pull his face up toward me. I leaned in. We couldn't have been six inches apart. "They threw an empty Molotov cocktail into your house. The next one will be full of gasoline and on fire. Donna doesn't deserve to die a painful and crispy death. And neither does Cody."

He leaned back in his desk chair but kept his eyes on mine. Uh, until the chair started to fall over backwards. If you're a normal human being, your first response is concern that a person falling backwards out of a chair might get hurt. Get past that, though, and it's hilarious: flailing arms and facial expressions of surprise and fear. George caught himself, slamming the chair earthward on all five casters. The look of relief on his face was worth the laugh I had surpressed.

"Well, that was embarrassing," he muttered.

"Who beat you up? Tell me, or I'm out of here and you and your family can sink or swim on your own." That was a threat, not a promise. I did not want to walk away from Cody.

"Elwhy," he said. He looked up at me. "I don't know his real name, but everyone calls him Elwhy." Not a name that registered on me, but I'd been gone from NOPD for three years, and besides, this Elwhy may be a Jefferson Parish personality I wouldn't have encountered from my time with the Orleans Parish police.

I pulled a little notebook out of my back pocket, the notebook all police, detectives, and aspiring authors are taught to carry at all times. I wrote 'Elwhy.'

"Anyone else?"

"Ricky something."

I heard Paul think, *Odd surname.*

"His sidekick. Glorified flunky. Yes man. I never saw Elwhy when Ricky wasn't with him."

Into the notebook: 'Ricky something.' "Anyone else?"

"A few times—this last time, yeah. A big baby. He was, what, 25? 30? He must have been six-six and he weighed 300 pounds." George was sitting up, his hands folded but active on the desk. "You know how, sometimes, you can look at a person and you know there's something wrong with them? This guy, I don't know, he was retarded or something. Always had a nice smile on his face, even while he was thrashing me."

Paul jumped to lead to write, in his barely legible, left-handed scrawl, 'Lennie Small.' I thought, *We don't know what his name is.* I started wrestling him to get the pen back into my right hand, which was difficult to do without dropping the notebook. Finally he thought, *Character in a Steinbeck short story. Lennie Small was what George described, but only accidentally violent.*

"Is that all?" I asked, while I was juggling my notebook and pen with Paul. I was watching my fingers, which were not entirely under my control.

There was a moment of silence. I said, "What?" and looked up to see George was nodding in answer to my question. No way to impress a client. Crap.

"Where do they live?" I bit my left index finger and heard Paul think, *Ow!*

A shrug. "Elwhy and Ricky came to my office the first time. After that, I only saw them at the warehouse on rent day."

Paul led to ask, "Did you notice the cars at the warehouse when you met them there? Maybe the same car every time?" Paul told me, many times, that he hates police and was nervous the entire time I was on the force. But he says being a detective is like working a jigsaw puzzle, trying to figure out who the bad guy is. He's got pretty good instincts. He's never told me what he did as a young man on his own to make him so uncomfortable around cops.

"No. Sorry."

"Are you sure?"

"Well—" George held up an index finger "—I think, you know, there was an old pickup truck. The kind with running boards and round fenders." He nodded at his memory. "It wasn't in perfect condition by any means, but it seemed in decent shape. Donna's brother used to have a truck like that."

"Great," Paul prompted. "What color? Louisiana tag?"

The man shook his head.

I picked up the questioning. "Did you always meet them at the same time of day? Was it always the umpteenth of the month, or the first Monday, or what?"

The umpteenth, Paul thought, *my favorite day of the month.*

"Always the first working day of the month. The time had more to do with my schedule than any preference they had."

I scribbled more notes. "Do you have a phone number?"

George looked surprised. "You know, we only talked on the phone once or twice. Elwhy called me out of the blue to make the appointment to come to the office, and once, I think, he was going to be out of town on rent day so we moved it to later in the week."

This was a glimmer, potentially more useful than the old pickup truck of no known color. With help from some of my old colleagues at NOPD, I might—might, I say—pick out the number George's enemy called from—but only if I could pin down a time frame to search for this needle in a haystack. "When did they first contact you?" I shook my notepad to flip to a blank page.

"I don't know, maybe, maybe two o'clock? It was after lunch."

Paul jumped to the front, bristling. "If someone asks you when Christmas is, do you say 'Wednesday'? Or do you say "December 25th?"

"What?" George's head was tilted, looking at me.

I rolled my eyes over Paul's oblique insult, but George probably thought I was aiming them at him. Crap! I want him to hire me! "Time of day may be helpful," I said, conciliatorily, "But only if I have a day. Or a month. And a year. Definitely a year."

"Ohhh," he nodded slowly, finally understanding why I—well, Paul—barked at him. "Yeah. You know, it was a few weeks before Cody's accident. I remember, when we found out how bad he was hurt, that it was good to have that extra rent money coming in for medical expenses." He drummed his fingers on the manila folder that happened to be on his desktop. "So, three years ago. May? April? June? Somewhere in there."

I sat down in the wing chair I'd abandoned earlier. Finally, something to go on. Maybe I was going to earn my way to protect George. I wrote 'April-June 2033. Phone.' "Give me your business card," I said. "I need to know what number they reached you on."

He opened a desk drawer and came up with a card for me. "GL Estates, George Locaviche, Realtor" it said, and several phone numbers. "The main office line," he said. "He didn't call my cell phone."

While I tucked the card into a pocket I offered, "Not much to go on, but it's something. Any guess, maybe do they have friends in the Jefferson Parish sheriff's department? Like you do?"

"But they're criminals," George said, indignant. "They don't know sheriffs—do they?"

"Orleans Parish is not known for being squeaky clean," I answered. "And I say that as a police detective emeritus. I don't know why Jefferson Parish would be any better."

He frowned as he sat, and softly beat his fist on the desk. "What if they know the same guy I know?"

"Who's your guy?"

"Dick Lucky. We went to school together at Centenary. I think he's—"

"We've met," I interrupted. "Now I understand why he stonewalled me. He was protecting you."

George wore a smile so bashful that it was cute, even on a sixty-year-old man. "Like I say, we're friends."

Paul said, "Wait a minute. I don't understand. So, this Lieutenant Lucky, he's a friend of yours, and therefore he wouldn't give Amy the sheriff's office report because why? He was going to lie and say the warehouse wasn't torched?"

George was grinning. "Do you often speak of yourself in the third person?"

"No," I said, "sometimes we talk in first person plural. But is that it? Lucky is going to protect you from charges?"

"I don't know. He told me he'd tie it up long enough that no one would care by the time it was released."

I heard Paul think, *Tell Melanie Goode. She already doesn't like Lucky.*

I rubbed my temples. I was an honest cop when I was a detective, really. I'm willing to slant some things now that I'm in private practice—a client would have to, I don't know, admit killing someone for me to rat them out. But three days ago, I was working for Paralax Insurance, and I still felt some weird loyalty to them. "I'll tell you again, George. Drop your insurance claim for the warehouse fire. Lucky may lie for you, but Paralax will subrogate you into a civil fraud case that'll ruin you."

"Am I interrupting anything?"

Cody had stuck his head in the door. I wonder if he heard me accuse his father of being a cheat.

"Mother wants you for dinner," he went on. "It's past six."

It is? Paul pulled up my left arm to look at my watch. *Holy shit, how did that happen? No wonder I'm hungry.*

You're always hungry, I thought back. Then, out loud, "I guess I'd better skedaddle. George, you call me if anything suspicious is going on around you. And I guess I'll work with Donna about the home security upgrade."

"No skedaddling," Cody said. "Mother insists you stay for dinner. You two come on, now," and he motioned for me and his father to follow.

As we got through the doorway into the hall, George put his arm around my shoulders. "Thank you," he said quietly. "I don't like all the things you say, but I know I need to hear it."

Ding! Ding! Ding! Paul thought to me. *No wonder he's a success in business. He actually listens.* After a moment I heard him think, *I hope Donna is a good cook.*

"You'll call Paralax tomorrow?" I asked the man. He dropped his arm, but nodded, and said, "Do you know the joke about the two gangsters? One says, 'I'm sorry to hear about your warehouse burning.' The other says, 'Shhh! The fire's tonight.'"

I was a bit horrified, but Paul laughed out loud. He likes puns and playing with words and logic. As a former cop I know there are bad people in the world, people who are willing to do bad things. But setting fire to your property to collect the insurance? Huh! And my sister's husband, Eddie, thinks I'm cynical.

Cody led us to the breakfast nook. The various shades of brown from the informal table, the benches beside it, and the paneling gave the room a comfortable, warm glow. Cody took my arm and sat me next to him on one bench. And he patted me on the top of my thigh.

"I hope you like baked chicken," Donna said as I watched George dish out big, golden breasts onto everyone's plates. "I didn't have time to get to Rouses today for steaks." They looked perfect, and smelled even better. As George passed around a tureen with mixed vegetables, I heard Paul think, *Dinner. One of my three favorite meals.* It was a line he used almost daily. Sometimes I imagine his appearance before he came to me as an enormous mouth attached to a 55-gallon drum.

Dinner was excellent, with scalloped potatoes as another side dish, and then blackberry buckle for dessert. Even Paul was stuffed by the time Donna poured coffee for everyone.

"Thank you, Donna," I said, trying to keep Paul from wolfing down the manners' bit of buckle. "It was so nice of you to feed me. And actually, you stuffed me. It's stuffed Amy, and it's time to waddle home."

"I'll need your help tomorrow," the woman said. "My contractor will be here at nine o'clock, and I think it'll go better if you're here to tell him what to do. The window locks, the doors, the grounds, all of that."

I let Paul lead to say, "Yes, ma'am. We'll be here to boss him around." He turned us toward George and said, "We have to figure something out. Do you want me to shadow you? Or is the family house more important?"

"I'm not worried about me," he said, "but I'll call you if anything looks suspicious. Look—" he shifted on the bench; maybe his butt still hurt from Friday's beating "—can't you get Hodges and Owens on this project? Three people, that would be better coverage."

Paul, who, after all, is the Owens on my business cards, said, "Hodges is brilliant with research, but she doesn't do on-site surveillance anymore. And Owens is such a loose cannon—" it was funny to hear him make me sigh "—we really can't count on him anymore. So, it's just Amy."

It's getting late, Paul thought to me. *I want to talk to Christine. Can we visit her tomorrow night?*

When I stood up, Cody stood as well. "I'll walk you out," he said, and took me by the arm. When we were away from the nook and his family, he said, "Why do I believe you more than the doctors? They also say my voice is imaginary."

"Maybe because I've demonstrated that I have experience with a voice that's real. What do your doctors have you taking?"

He shrugged. "I stopped admitting I heard a voice when I came home and saw how upset Mother was. They only prescribe something for the headaches I tell them I have."

"It's funny," I mused, "I'll tell you the same thing I told your dad this morning: Never lie to your lawyer, your doctor, or your priest."

Cody didn't reply, but he stopped us just inside the mercifully closed and locked front door. His arm around me turned into a hug. "They have medicine to deal with voices. Really."

I liked the hug. I said, "It was such a pleasant surprise, your mom inviting me to dinner. You and your parents get along so well."

"I guess we do. Dad can be a bear sometimes, but he knows it and we can laugh about it. Eventually."

I was feeling the excitement of knowing I was about to get kissed, by a man I wanted to have kiss me. I'm thirty-seven years old, but that part of me is still sixteen. "Let's you and me have dinner together. We can—"

"Mother seems to think you're part of the family now," Cody said. "You can count on a meal anytime you're here."

I leaned against him and felt his arms tighten around me. He was warm. He was comfortable. I smiled. "No," I said to some ruffles on the front of his shirt. "I mean you and me. Do you like Chinese food? I know this great place on Broad Street." I wiggled against him because it felt good.

"You don't have to do that."

I pulled my head back, even though the rest of me was still stretched out against him. "You big lug," I said, trying to do Paul's imitation of Humphrey Bogart, "I'm trying to make a pass at you."

He went all stiff for a moment—and no, not in any sort of enjoyable way—and then said, "Ohhh." That's when he bent his head and kissed me on the mouth.

That went on for a long time, although it felt like a split second before we heard Donna calling, "Cody? Come help with these dishes."

The kiss ended, but we both giggled and hugged. "You'll come over tomorrow?" he said to the top of my head.

"Bright and early," I told his collarbone.

"Cody?"

"I have to go," he said, and pulled his arms back. Suddenly I was chilly from the withdrawal of his body heat, but I still felt warm inside.

"Me, too. Good night, Cody."

Once I was ensconced inside the luxury of my old yellow Benz I said to Paul, "That was…you know, that was pretty fantastic."

"I could tell you were having a good time. For a guy, he doesn't smell half bad."

"That's progress," I bantered.

"Can I drive?"

"Be my guest," I assured him, and withdrew to let him mess with the clutch, the gas, and the steering wheel. "You know, I think Cody always knew his voice was a hallucination. I hope I didn't get him too excited about the possibility that it was real. But he's not holding it against me." I thought for a moment as Paul drove up the street. "Plus, Donna and George have hired me. I'd say this was a good day. A great day."

It would be better with that great beer, a Squatter's Outer Darkness.

My place in Carrollton wasn't more than ten minutes away, considering it was eight o'clock on a Sunday night. Paul parked on the gravel swath in front of the house and turned everything off. "When we get inside," he said, "I want to call Christine."

"Good," I said. "I want to tell her about today."

Once I was settled onto my futon sofa, a glass of Chateau Bayou Rouge on the steamer trunk that serves as my coffee table, Paul took my phone and pushed the speed-dial key for Christine. "How's my sweetie?" he began.

"Paulette! Thanks for the excuse to sit down. I've been cleaning house. Hi, Amy!"

"Hey, Christine," I said. "Paul's been hounding me all evening about wanting to call."

I love that Christine always remembers me. She is crazy about Paul—her Paulette—and in person she always limits her lust to when he is leading. But she always asks me how I'm doing. It pleases me that I've become her best friend, because she is mine. Sometimes it feels like we're sisters sharing the same man. Well, almost. After all, Paul always comes home with me.

They chattered on about their boyfriend-girlfriend life. Then Paul offered, "And Amy got kissed by the guy she's interested in. He's the client's son."

"Amy!" Christine squeed. "Good for you! So, he likes you, too."

"I had to tell him I was making a pass at him, but yes, he seems to like me. I think I convinced him to go out to dinner with me."

"You shouldn't need to talk him into these things," she said, like a big sister. "I mean, I don't understand how any girl likes boys, but I know you do. Doesn't he realize how great you are?"

I think I blushed. "Thank you for noticing," I said, trying to make a joke of her unexpected complement. "He'll figure it out. He's kind of a late bloomer."

There was silence, and then I heard Christine say, "Uh-oh. And he lives with his parents, huh?"

"He was in a car wreck three years ago," I explained, defensive. "Everyone thought he was crazy because he started hearing a woman's voice after that. Today Paul explored and—well, you tell her." Paul took the lead and explained, "I spent some time poking around in his head. He doesn't have someone like me in there. That was a disappointment."

"Oh, Paulette. You and Amy were excited that the boy might be like you two. I'm so sorry."

"Yes. But on the front page of the Amy News is I got the job. I am now George Locaviche's official bodyguard. I have to be at the house tomorrow morning to oversee security upgrades."

"You and I both work for ourselves," Christine offered. "I work with Lincoln Properties, sure, but if I don't sell any houses I don't make any money. And if you don't line up work, you go broke."

I waited for more, but she was done. So, I said, "Being a detective for New Orleans Police was a steady paycheck, but I didn't fit over there. I seem to be a little too diverse for most wage-slave jobs. But you were a receptionist at Lincoln for how long?"

"Four and a half years," she answered. "But with Paulette and you in my life, I got stronger and healthier. I decided to take a chance to earn some real money by taking those classes and getting my realtor's license."

It was Paul who said, "I remember telling you, when you were studying for your license, how impressed I was with you. You're still you, I mean, but...I guess you became even more Christine-y. I love it."

"My brother thought I was getting crazier instead of better. I don't think he expected me to be able to take care of myself. But he's still in St Louis, and we only talk every few months. He's family; I guess I forgive him. I've already mailed him a Christmas present."

"You know I never changed my business cards," Amy said. "The client asked if I couldn't put Hodges and Owens on the job for better coverage."

"Oh, Amy," Christine said, with a frown in her voice. "You know that—"

Paul interrupted, "I told the client that you didn't do outside surveillance any more. And that Owens—" that's Paul "—was a loose cannon."

Christine's disapproval turned into a chuckle. When I first started my private detective business, I assumed Christine would rather work for me than answer phones at the real estate agency where she was a receptionist. As it turned out, it was just about the time she began studying to get her realtor's license. We had some fights over it, mostly because I was a bull-headed jerk who hadn't realized I was terrified of going into business by myself. It got pretty surreal; I remember when she wasn't speaking to me and so she'd say things like, "Paulette, you tell Amy that I don't like what she's doing." I guess it's still a sore spot with her. Me, I'm still ashamed of myself.

Paul and Christine planned to have dinner together Tuesday, and I agreed. I hoped Monday–tomorrow—might give me some time with Cody.

MONDAY, DECEMBER 15, 2036

I am not a project leader. The sum total of my event planning was various market research studies when I got out of UNO Lakeside with my masters in statistics. My first grown-up job was crunching numbers, figuring Z-scores and standard deviations, and trying to remember the difference between mean, median, and modal averages. It takes some perseverance to get one hundred people to show up at the same time at some hotel conference room to endure two hours of listening to politicians' recorded statements and twirling joysticks. Of course, the $75 honorarium helped attendance.

So bright and early on Monday I was standing with Donna Locaviche in her living room, telling her contractor, Caleb Jones, what he needed to do. "A-number one," I said, "Is to seal the back entrance to the garage, and to block any access from, what's that street?"

Donna answered, "Nashville Avenue."

"What she said. If you have to put up razor wire or a fence with spikes and broken glass, do it. Anything short of a trip shotgun."

Caleb scribbled notes on the back of an envelope. "I got four guys here," he said. "What else you need doin'?"

"Back door. Replace the frame and install a metal door. No windows, but a peephole would be good. And use a long deadbolt.

A very long one." The man added to his notes. "And a circular key lock. They're a little harder to pick."

"Then, there are some bushes on the left side of the house." I turned to Donna, "You'll show him which ones, so he doesn't cut down what you want to keep?" She nodded. Back to Caleb I said, "Mrs. Locaviche will show you which ones. Chop 'em down. Then salt the ground."

I could see the tip of his tongue peeking out of his mouth as he made more notes on his envelope. "Ma'am, are you serious about the salt?"

I heard Paul think, *Busted!* Then he said, "No, we're not. We were exaggerating for effect. Those bushes must go."

I saw Caleb cross off some words.

He left the house with Donna to learn which bushes to cut, and to corral his employees and set them on their missions. George, of course, was at his office. *I think I'm going to find Cody,* I thought to Paul; *I've got some time to kill.* I went down the hallway and made the right turn to his studio.

The overhead lights were off, but I was blinded by the glare of a klieg aimed at a young woman with her two small children. I heard Cody say, "Hug them tighter, get them in closer. Yes, yes, that's it!" The woman tugged both children in, but the little boy, maybe age three, squalled.

"Wait," Cody said. I saw him come to his photo subjects, and stick a short length of Scotch tape to the boy's right index finger. Immediately the child became silent and concentrated on the tape. He picked at it with his left hand, and then giggled.

Cody retreated out of my view, and said, "That trick always works. Okay, Susan, hug him close. There!" I heard a series of shutter-clicks.

"Do you want to put them in the sailor suits now?" he asked. Susan, the young mother, said yes and stood up, holding her infant girl and tugging at the boy. They went behind a scrim, where I guessed they were changing clothes.

Should I talk to him while his customer is hiding? I thought to Paul

In answer Paul took the lead and entered the studio. Cody was bent over a work table, changing lenses in his digital SLR camera. "Hey, Ansel Adams!" Paul called. "Have you seen Cody anywhere?"

The man looked up; when he saw me, the round circles of a smile broke some of the sharp angles of his jaw and cheeks. It occurred to me that I suddenly was smiling, too.

"Hey, Amy."

I went to Cody and hugged him. "That's a neat trick with the tape," I said. "You're good at this."

"The client wants the lamp in the next set of pictures," he said. We were busy complimenting each other. I think he likes me.

I stepped back to look at him. The smile remained. He was wearing a pale red shirt, open at the collar, over what looked like brand-new blue jeans. And there I was in a faded UNO sweatshirt over khaki shorts.

Susan emerged from behind the screen. *That's like an anime girl,* Paul thought to me. She had on a blue and white sailor dress; her daughter was dressed the same. The little boy's sailor shirt had a huge, red bow tie; his outfit was finished with blue shorts and an odd blue cap with a black ribbon hanging down in back. *And he looks like Donald Duck.*

"Amy, this is my client, Susan Long—" the woman smiled and nodded "—along with little Peter and littler Diane. Susan, meet my colleague, Amy Owens."

I heard Paul laugh silently at the mistake. *I'm Amy Clear!* I thought to Cody, complete with exclamation point. *Paul is the Owens.*

He swung his head to look at me, surprise all over his geometric face. "Colleague?" I smiled, "Thank you. Nice to meet you, Susan, your kids look darling." I actually hate and detest small children, but my sister—who has three of them—has gradually, painfully, taught me the right words to say.

"Yes, don't they? My husband is stationed in Okinawa, so the pictures are his Christmas present." She smiled down at the girl in her arms. Softly she said, "I don't want him to forget us."

"I just wanted to say hello while you had a break," I told Cody. "Donna and I are driving the contractor with a cat of nine tails." I smiled at Susan and added, "It's nice to meet you," and I left them to the photo session.

He got our names mixed up, Paul thought. *That was funny.*

He remembered you, I replied silently. *That's a good sign.*

I found Donna in the breakfast nook, watching Caleb's men tearing into a copse of rhododendron. I plucked some leaves out of her hair and handed them to her. "He's pretty efficient," I offered.

"George found him years ago," she nodded, still looking out the window. "He does all the maintenance on George's holdings. And on our beach place outside of Pass Christian. He and his crew are wonderful."

I looked at my watch; it was a quarter after ten. *Time to find out about Elwhy and Ricky and the big baby,* I thought to Paul. Out loud I said to Donna, "Caleb's going to be busy for a while. You need to call your security company. And I'm going to my old PDHQ to do some digging." I slid a business card out of one of my belt pouches. Before I could hand it over, Paul took my pen to cross out the Owens and Hodges. It probably looked every bit as awkward to her as it felt to me, since I, too, was a bystander: Paul using his, uh, my left hand to find the writing tool in my right front pocket. When he finished his ad hoc editing, I gave the card to Donna. "If anything happens, call me. If you have any questions, call me. If you hear from George, call me. If you need to know who the first baseman for the Zephyrs will be next season, call me. Okay?"

She barely looked at the card, and instead hugged me. "I don't know what we'd do without you, Amy. I finally got a decent night's sleep, knowing you're on the payroll."

Paul, ever the diplomat, said, "We all want the same thing. You and Cody safe, and George out of danger. It's all good."

Personally, I hate the expression 'it's all good.' No, it's not all good. Making a mistake, paying too much for something, getting a speeding ticket, hearing bad news from your doctor…no way is it all good. But Paul never forgets that his body died in 2011 and if it weren't for the impossible miracle that put him in my body and my life, he'd think everything was bad. Assuming there would still be some bit of Paul to think anything at all in 2036. We've argued about it and neither one of us will change. But most people are not the cold-blooded cynic I've become; I've never seen anyone object when Paul has used that phrase. He's a charming devil that way.

On the walk across the street to the my car, Paul asked, *Which one of your old buddies will you ask about this?* He was uncomfortable around anyone in a blue uniform, even the appliance repair guy, although there were a few of my old work partners he liked.

Walter Francks, I thought back. *He won't blab to everyone.*

I like Walter, Paul observed. *He's the only cop who isn't working vice who has a pony-tail. You know, I used to have a—*

"You've told me," I said as I slid behind the steering wheel. "Although it must have been when you were a little kid. I remember that photo your sister showed us. You didn't have any hair at all."

"Wait! That's not true," he protested. "Above the ears, around the back, I had a little. I still had to get haircuts."

"Three times a year, whether you needed it or not. You remember the way to the Rampart Street station?" Offering to let him drive erased any negativity from Paul, something I figured out when I turned seventeen and got my Louisiana Cheaters' Permit. Take my word for it, it's hard to stomach someone in high dudgeon when they live inside your head. It was better for him to drive.

Paul drove north on State Street, past houses that gradually went from grand to disrepair. When we reached the Ursuline Academy's sprawling grounds, he turned right onto South

Claiborne, one of the busiest roads in New Orleans, and the daily site of a dozen auto accidents. When I was on the force, you knew you were being punished when you were assigned to direct traffic on Claiborne, particularly at the intersection with Napoleon Avenue. We went through the concrete spaghetti salad that is the interchange with I-10 and the Pontchartrain Expressway, and made a quick right just past the flying saucer called the Superdome, onto Poydras. Traffic made it take forever to go past Loyola, and then make a left onto Rampart Street. From there it was a straight shot— well, a straight crawl—across Canal and up to the station house that was my professional home for three years.

As he turned into the ramp that led to the underground parking for the police station, Paul said, "That was fun. I love dealing with traffic and crazy drivers."

"Sarcasm?" I asked.

He surprised me by answering, "No. It's a challenge. It's satisfying to get where we're going in one piece." He laughed, then thought, *You know I love to drive.*

If I'm ever desperate for money, I thought, *I'll sign you up for Uber.*

I walked up the creepy cement staircase to the basement of the cop shop. Maybe later I'd visit Doctor Tallant, the parish medical examiner who was always so much fun. Up one more flight to the main floor. I didn't recognize the civilian in the Lucite kiosk that was the reception desk, so I took out my old police credentials and shoved them in the narrow slot. "I'm looking for Sergeant Francks," I told her.

She looked at my ID. She turned it over and looked at the back of my ID. Then she looked at me. "Who are you, exactly?" she asked. Paul thought, *She seems confused.*

Indeed, she did, and I felt like confusing her more. There is no sane way to explain why I'm still on the rolls with New Orleans Police. Indeed, I did consult for Captain, and then Commander, Ramirez. Indeed, he was disappointed when I resigned, but I just didn't fit in with all the rules and procedures, both inside the station house and dealing with perps. So, we made a deal: He'd leave me on the books, although I didn't get paid unless I actually did police work; and I'd be available for those puzzlers where the regulars couldn't get any traction and the Commander thought my off-kilter perspective would work. Once, maybe twice a year he calls me in. In the meantime, I make use of my connections to help my private detective business. That's the truth, but it's not any kind of story this nice lady was prepared to deal with.

"Detective Clear," I said, giving my once and future rank. "I'm Commander Ramirez' consultant. We go 'way back."

"Why haven't I seen you before?" She wasn't in uniform, so I wasn't worried when she put her hands on her hips. Besides, that Lucite cage was for my protection, not hers.

"Usually, I'm wearing a cloak of invisibility," Paul offered. "But it's nice out today, so I decided to travel cognito." He put a decent imitation of the daddy smile on my face.

"I don't know," she said. She was staring at me. Did I have breakfast on my blouse?

"Tell you what," I told her, "you call Sergeant Francks out here. He'll vouch for me."

Without moving her eyes from mine she picked up the phone and punched numbers on the keypad. "Sergeant. Yeah, I know. Desperately. There's a woman out here calls herself Detective Clear. Do you— Oh, sure. Uh-huh. Well, get your sorry butt out here and tell me if I should let her in."

When she was done, she said, "The sergeant will be out after a while. You can lean against that wall." She wasn't kidding; there were no chairs in the waiting area.

"May I have my ID back?" I asked. "I don't want to tie up Walter when he gets here."

Maybe it was using his first name that did it. The reception lady slid my credentials back out the slot. I grabbed them before she changed her mind, and slipped them into my wallet.

It was a mercy that someone else came in and captured her attention. *Do you think Walter will remember me? I haven't seen him in months.* Paul laughed out loud and thought, *It doesn't matter if he doesn't, he always says he remembers every pretty girl he encounters.* That was a fair description of that loveable horn-dog.

"Sugar!" Sergeant Francks bellowed from the security door, even before we could see each other. "I thought you'd forgotten me!" He ran to me and hugged me, lifting me up and turning in a few circles before he let me down. "Damn, Sugar, you get finer and finer every time I see you. Are we eloping today?"

"Maybe, if Cruella here lets me in."

He didn't even look at the receptionist as he waved a hand dismissively. "The less power you have, the more ruthlessly you wield it. C'mon, let's go make out in the evidence locker."

"Walter, you sure know how to push my buttons," I said, laughing. Did the man sound like an old-fashioned sexist pig? Yep. And would he follow through if given half a chance? I have no doubt. But as long as I kept a little distance, Sergeant Walter Francks was a ton of fun. His flirting always made me feel good, and he seemed to own the station house grapevine. He hardly ever bothered with his uniform; he was in jeans and some flannel shirt over a sweatshirt, and, as usual, was sporting his grey hair in a ponytail. He was the precinct weapons specialist, who more than once had counselled me that you can never have too many fingerprints on a firearm. That wasn't true for gathering evidence, but it was probably excellent advice to a civilian.

Walter had an arm around me as he walked me through the reception area and beyond the security gate, into the working area of the precinct. When it was just the two of us, he said, "Is your business going okay, Honey?" I assured him I had just landed a security job, and said, "I need to know about two bad guys who have been bothering my client."

We walked down halls I knew so well, into a work room. There was a huge window onto the hallway, while the other three walls were cinder block, painted a faded and peeling landlady green. "Are they ever going to fix up this room?" I moaned.

"They did," Walter said. "Can't you smell that Terminix was here last week?" I remembered how, on slow days, we detectives and officers would place bets on which palmetto bugs would get to the ceiling first. Trust me, that is no exaggeration.

"Who's the lucky client?" he asked when we sat at a computer cubicle.

"A real estate guy, George Locaviche." Walter shook his head. "He seems to have annoyed a couple of fake friends who are making his life miserable," I went on. "First they beat him up and dropped him off at home—"

"You are shitting me!"

"—And then they threw an unloaded Molotov cocktail through a back window."

"Man, he is dead meat."

"I know! I finally convinced him and his wife that they needed me to watch out for them. Today their contractor is building walls and digging a moat."

Walter laughed, "Well, that is the textbook response to those threats. Who are the bad guys?"

"That's why I need your help," I said. "They may be Jefferson Parish baddies, but I hope you or Kowalski—" my former working partner, now a lieutenant "—recognize the partial names I've got."

"Lay it on me." Bless his heart, when there was trouble, Walter was all business.

"A guy who calls himself Elwhy, and a sidekick name of Ricky."

He rubbed his stubble-encrusted chin. "That Elwhy sounds familiar," he mused. "Let me look—" and he was plinking away at the computer keyboard.

He frowned when the NOPD proprietary software gave him a 'no such entry' answer. He tried Elwhy. He tried LY. Disappointed, I said, "I guess he works out of Jefferson Parish."

"No, no," shaking his head, "I've heard this before." This time he entered L space Y and slammed the enter key.

If it had been one of the slot machines at Harrah's it would have been flashing red and green lights while sounding a claxon. "Yes!" he said, smiling, and he turned the monitor toward me.

The computer showed that L space Y was an alias for Elias Young, age 39, a low-level career criminal. The standard full frontal and profile mug shots were of a thin man in need of a shave, mussed-up curly hair hanging over a large forehead, and a ring in his left ear. The ruler showed he was just five-two. *We can take him,* I heard Paul think.

The comments section included exclamation points and asterisks, and, in all capital letters, the warning that our hoodlum detested his given name and was known to have employed a straight razor on a few people who had mistakenly used it. I heard Paul, *That's not why he's trying to do a number on George. George only knew him as Elwhy.*

L Y, I corrected.

He thought back, *Homonyms are so much fun.*

"Walter, I finally believe that you have magic fingers," I teased the sergeant. I reached out to the keyboard in front of him to scroll the screen down.

"I've been trying to demonstrate that for years," he grinned. His hands were on my back, with his wiggling fingers trying to tickle me.

Ignoring his actions, I saw a home address downriver in Chalmette, across the line in St Bernard Parish. I didn't have my clipboard, so I wrote it on the back of my left hand: 3332 Pakenham. *Hey!* Paul thought, *That's my hand!*

They're both mine, I thought back. *Besides, it'll wash off.* I added the ten digits for the phone number on the screen, but there wasn't a lot of room left on my hand; the last four numbers were on the back of my wrist.

Walter said, "What happens when you run out of room on your hand? Do you write on your legs?"

Smiling, I leaned over to the sergeant, pen at the ready. "No, I write on my friend's shirt." He laughed while I wrote 'Amy was here' on the front of his polo shirt. I heard Paul think, *He'll never wash that shirt again.*

Walter went back to the computer screen. "Been to Angola, two years for extorting the owner of a bar in Central City. Arrested five, six, seven times for petty theft, fencing stolen laptops, identity theft." He scanned ahead. "Only that one conviction, though."

"Associates?"

Walter scrolled down the page in the criminal/suspect/person-of-interest/snitch (CSPS) software devoted to Elias Young. "What's the name? Ricky?" He slowly worked the arrow down key. "I'm not seeing...no 'Ricky'...nah...nah...oh, wait. Here." He clicked to blow up a section of the screen image.

The screen showed Ricky Young, age 33. Cousin of L-Y. No priors. Has a class 2 drivers' license and an ATC Responsible Vendor server card. Address on Poeyfarre Street— "I'll bet that's where the 55th Fighter Group is," I observed. "Do you think he sleeps upstairs?"

"That creature of the night may never sleep," Walter replied. He looked up at me. "This L-Y guy is a piece of work, Sugar. You be careful."

"How about phone numbers?" I asked. "Can you get me a phone log of who called my client?"

"Nah. That's for the phone company. And a warrant."

"Puh-LEASE!" I said, sitting up straight and pressing my right palm against my chest. "We didn't need warrants when I was on the force."

Walter smiled. "Yes, we did. Just sometimes we didn't bother. What time period?"

"2033. April to—"

"They only keep the stuff for two years," Walter interrupted, shaking his head. "If we served a warrant they'd bitch, but they'd send some techs to their Iron Mountain storage and maybe come up with something. But you'd need a warrant for that. You got a warrant, Sugar?"

Paul answered, "I don't even got milk."

"But now I have a name," I said. "That's a big help. Walter, you are a pearl beyond price in this wasteland I call NOPD." I pinched his cheek. "Thanks, buddy."

"Whoa!" he exclaimed. Looking up at the ceiling as if talking to God, Walter said, "She touched me! My life is complete!" Then he looked at me with his usual grin. "My offer for the evidence locker still stands."

I laughed and said, "Maybe next time, Killer. But now I have to go find a guy whose name I must not mention."

Paul moaned, "Oh, great. We're taking on Voldemort?"

The sergeant tilted his head and stared through squinted eyes. "Did you miss your medication this morning?"

Internally I poked Paul, silently laughing at his joke. I said to Walter, "It's gotten so expensive, and business is kind of iffy. Some days I can't afford my Soma." Paul made me read that scary book; I didn't sleep for three days after I finished it, but I remember Bernard Marx. And Soma[26]. Walter's expression did not change, so I smiled. "I'll take it as soon as I get home."

"You do that, Sugar. Sometimes I worry about you, you know."

"Part of why you're so endearing," I replied. I stood up and stretched. "Reserve the evidence locker for next time I'm out here," I teased, "but I've got to get gone right now."

As I walked down the stairs and past Doctor Tallant's cave Paul thought *We've got a name. We've got an address. Do we pay Voldemort a visit?* I felt him pat my pistol holster.

"I think we reconnoiter first. Tomorrow morning, skulk in the bushes in front of his house and see what he drives. Where he goes.

---

[26] Aldous Huxley's *Brave New World*. Amy is right; it is one scary book.

If he's got a gang." I felt Paul nod inside. "Then we visit. But now, it's back to *Casa Locaviche*."

Paul drove back to Richmond Place while we amused each other with fantasies of physically abusing L-Y, possibly to death. In the midst of the black humor, he raised an uncomfortable but accurate point: if, strictly in the world of fantasy, I threw L-Y into a black hole tomorrow, my job would be over. I'd have to refund some money to George, I'd lose my easy access to Cody, and, once again, I'd be between paying jobs. *I understand why some people stretch out a job*, he thought to me as he navigated the endless steel plates up and down St. Charles Avenue, *just so they can make more money for a longer time. But it's still wrong.*

"No argument," I answered; after all, he was absolutely right. "Maybe I can get him and Donna to adopt me instead."

What if he's a bad dad? What if he expects us to be home by ten o'clock? Work for a living?

"There are times I'm convinced the entire universe is a bad dad. I'll survive."

Paul parked the old Benz across the street from the Locaviche's because Caleb and a subcontractor had their trucks in the semi-circular driveway. Four workmen were sitting on one extended lift-gate, joking and eating sandwiches.

"Paul? Are you okay?" I asked.

What? Yeah, I'm fine. You? Uh—why do you ask?

"Because it's lunch time and you haven't moaned for food once." I heard him snicker silently. My life would be a non-stop flagellation if Paul couldn't laugh at himself.

Back inside the house, I followed the voices until I found Donna and Cody in the breakfast nook. They were working on bowls of soup and some kind of sandwich, and will you look at that—there's a plate set for me.

"What did I miss?" I asked as I went to sit on the bench by the window. Before my bottom hit the seat, though, Donna said, "I'm glad you're back. Go wash your hands and you can join us."

You have a new mother, Paul thought to me. The water in the kitchen faucet was hot, the dish soap was slippery, and I could feel my face tinge with red. *Just because she's right*, I thought back, *that makes it worse.* Still, I was grinning. It feels good when people you're starting to care about include you.

I went back to the breakfast nook with my clean hands raised, palms out and fingers spread. Donna smiled and said, "Very good, Amy. I hope you like lentils."

"As a matter of fact," I answered. "And the sandwich?"

Cody swallowed theatrically and said, "Left over roast beef. Mom is a great cook." Before I could respond Paul said, "The carnivore in me says 'thank you'."

I asked Cody about the photo session I had interrupted. "The lady looked sad. I guess looking after two kids on you own can be wearing."

"I'm not supposed to talk about my clients," he began (I heard Paul think, *As he talks about his clients*). "Susan's husband has been stationed overseas since before Diane was born. She's worried he's forgetting her." He took a spoonful of soup, then added, "Oh! Can you help me? Susan wants some, uh, *boudoir* pictures for the husband. Can you sit in when I take them?"

That startled me. "You want me to be part of the erotic photos for the man she's afraid is leaving her?" I'm sure I sounded confused, because I was confused. So was Paul, or so I interpreted his silence.

Donna laughed, then put her napkin to her lips. "No, dear. When a photographer takes nude pictures, there has to be an appropriate observer to make sure the client doesn't claim something improper happened." She was grinning as she told me this. "Usually I do that, but the client might be more comfortable with a witness closer to her own age."

"Not to mention the photographer," Cody added. "It's weird to look at a naked woman while your mother is standing with you."

Paul dropped the spoon he was holding and raised my left hand. "I volunteer." If we weren't sitting with Cody, if we weren't sitting with Cody's mom, Paul might have gone on about having a lesbian girlfriend. I'm barely ready to have that conversation with Cody; it might be a while before I broach the subject to Donna.

Two bites into the sandwich I said, "Donna! You are a good cook." I was talking around a bolus of rare and well-seasoned cow, trying not to spray bread crumbs across the table. "This sandwich is great. You'll put Rouses out of business."

"Told you!" Cody grinned, while his mother graciously said, "Thank you, dear. It would be a shame to ruin such a good piece of meat. George does like his steak and potatoes."

It's not obvious that Paul and I exchange leads for each bite of a sandwich, but a soup spoon is a big clue. The lentil soup was quite good; both of us slurped it with relish. And then Donna said, "May I ask, Amy? Why are you doing that—that—that thing with your spoon?"

I thought to Cody, *Busted!* But Paul, fast thinking devil that he is, said, "It's important to use your body evenly when you eat. If you only use one hand—" he waved the spoon in my right hand "—you get all lopsided. You only use that half of your stomach. Your teeth on the other side will grow too big. One kidney gets overworked and the other one atrophies. You see older people who never changed hands, they lean way to the right when they walk. It's sad. Really, there are studies about it." He grinned and moved the spoon to my left hand for the next swallow.

Everyone laughed. I'll have to check with Donna later to make sure she knows Paul—uh, make sure she knows **I** was joking.

"My trip to my old police department was productive," I said. "I found out the names of the people who beat George. Tomorrow I'll do some detective tricks, see if I can't learn enough to confront him later."

"Have I told you I'm glad you're here?" Donna asked.

"I can't hear it enough," I replied. "I'm greedy that way. I saw Caleb's crew taking lunch," I went on. "How far have they gotten?"

"They've closed the back entrance to the garage," the woman answered. "The fence will take a few weeks, and—"

"Few weeks?" I echoed. "We don't have a few weeks!" I stared at Donna, open mouthed. I heard Paul think, *That's a trusting soul.* I didn't realize the "Hush!" I meant for him came out of my mouth, but I went on, "Your husband could be dead in a few weeks. Caleb's got to unfurl coils of razor wire. Tomorrow! Now!"

Guiltily, Donna offered, "There is a wall along part of the property line."

"How high?" I asked. "What's on top of it? We need razor wire." I thought for a moment. "I don't think broken glass on top is legal in the Parish...bird spikes, at least. But razor wire." I heard Paul think, *I've always been a fan of broken glass.* I wouldn't be surprised if the laws were different in that yankee stronghold he comes from, West Virginia.

Cody patted his mother's hand on the table top. "She's not angry, Mother. She's just trying to help us."

"I know, dear, I know," Donna said, softly.

I rolled my eyes. "Donna. I am sorry if you took any of that personally. I guess I didn't make it clear the other day just how important it is to get these things taken care of. We have an enemy who knows where we live and already has made threats. We've—"

"I thought you were going to stop them!" She was staring at me, defiantly.

"I will. The question is, <u>where</u>. Someplace else, I hope. But it may be here. We need—"

It was Paul. Out loud, in front of Donna and Cody, he said, "Amy, take a deep breath. I'm sure Donna is hurrying as fast as she can."

Donna's jaw dropped. I was no way ready to explain to her about Paul and my dyadic life. But what he said made sense, so I didn't argue. Instead, I said, "You're right." I took a few deep breaths, and then a few more. "I apologize, Donna," I finally made myself say. "I'm sure Caleb's crew is working efficiently. I know you've been moving mountains to protect George. Razor wire would be a good idea, but I'll dial back the drama. I promise." I smiled meekly and let Paul finish the soup. I had lost my appetite, but he would still be hungry if both my legs fell off.

"I'll tell Caleb to get some razor wire," Donna said. At least I got the message across.

"Thank you for lunch, Mom," Cody said as he stood up, his plate and empty bowl in his hands. "I have to get back to work. Susan will be back in a little while."

I heard Paul think *You're supposed to chaperone*. So, I stood up; taking my cue from Cody, I picked up the debris of my lunch. "Wait, I'll come with you," I said, and I followed him into the kitchen to put plates in the sink.

As we went on to his studio, Cody said, "Your story about moving the spoon was very entertaining."

I let Paul accept the complement; he replied, "Thanks, Cody. I thought it was a fairly comprehensive explanation."

"So, why do you move your spoon from one hand to another?"

I decided on the easiest way to explain. I thought to him, *Paul.*

"Do what?"

Okay, that didn't work. *You tell him*, I thought to my dyad. Of course, I couldn't hear what he thought to Cody, since it wasn't aimed at me, but the look on Cody's face told me what I needed to know. The dropped jaw, the dazed look around the eyes, the stumble in his limping step.

When he recovered, Cody asked, "How can I tell which of you says things? Uh, out loud, I mean."

I put my arm around his waist as we walked. "If it's goofy and makes no sense, it's me," I offered. "If it's clever and amusing, it's Paul. He's quicker than I am with that sort of thing."

Thanks! I appreciate the praise. I heard Paul chuckle.

When we got to his studio, Cody checked his watch. "Susan will be back in a few minutes. Thanks for helping me with her shoot."

"I don't understand how her kids fit in with a bedroom scene," I said. Sure, bedroom scenes lead to kids, but I didn't think that was the message she wanted to get across to her soldier husband.

Cody laughed. "She's leaving the children with her in-laws. This will be negligee pictures, maybe a nude. Will you be okay with that?"

Paul and I silently laughed together. Considering his years attached to Christine, I was used to being around naked women; but I didn't see any reason to explain it to Cody. "I have a kid sister," I said. "It'll be fine."

Cody picked up his camera and began checking the data card, the shutter setting, and other things I don't know about—I still have an Instamatic that uses film. For some reason, since he was looking at his camera instead of me, it was easier for me to say, "Let's you and me go to dinner tonight."

He didn't look up when he countered, "Mother would be happy for you to eat with us. She's making lasagna that I like a lot. I'll tell her after I finish with Susan." Finally, he looked up and smiled at me.

That's not what I had in mind, but I didn't feel brave enough to protest. "No. I mean, sure, if it's a meal you like that much. Your mom has been very good to me. But sometime, I want to spend some time that's just you and me, away from your parents. Away from your house." I felt my heart going thumpity-thumpity-thump.

He placed the camera on his desk, slowly, as if he were thinking of a response. If he didn't hurry up about it I was going to have a stroke. At last he said, "I'd like that. Amy." He was smiling. "Maybe tomorrow evening?"

Paul jumped to lead, jealous of his Christine time. "Can't do tomorrow, but let's plan on Wednesday." I added, "I'm thinking Pascal's Manale. It's on your side of the park."[27]

Yes! I heard Paul shout, silently. *Me for veal!*

"I'll let mother know when we're done with Susan's pictures. She doesn't like surprises at meal time, but this should be enough notice for her. Got to keep happy family relations."

We heard Donna call from the living room, "Cody! Your client is here!"

"Shall I bring her back?" I asked. His smile broke up the sharp angles of his face, and I went to greet Susan.

She was standing in the living room, chatting with Donna. The woman had changed clothes into a pale-yellow slip dress with a dangerously low neckline and perilously high hem. The dull green backpack, however, defeated the intended impact of the dress. "Susan," I interrupted, "I'll take you back to Cody." Donna nodded approvingly.

As I walked the woman back to the studio, I asked, "Where are those darling kids of yours?" It was just to make conversation.

"Rex's folks are watching them," she answered. "It's important to have family babysitters nearby." I heard Paul think, *You stuck your nephew with a safety pin changing his diaper and Kaylee never asked you to watch her kids again.* "I can see that," I told Susan.

"Welcome back, Susan," Cody said, and he limped out from behind his desk to greet the woman. "If it's okay with you, Amy will be able to help you with your wardrobe changes, anything you need."

"Oh. Sure, that'll be great," she said as she shrugged the backpack off her shoulders. Then she seemed to continue a conversation she'd begun with Cody earlier in the day. "I'd like a few like this, and then some in my pajamas, and maybe a few more."

---

[27] *The park* is Audubon Park, a huge greenspace that separates Amy's Carrollton neighborhood from the Locaviche's Uptown section. The other comparable green space in New Orleans proper is City Park, surrounding the municipal art museum and Botanical Garden. And, as Paul notes, Pascal's Manale serves a lot of veal.

Pajamas? Paul thought to me. I thought back, *Maybe it's code for sheer naughty things.* I love it when I make him laugh.

Cody had placed a chaise in front of his blue scrim, alongside an end table that featured what I now thought of as **my** Tiffany lamp. There was a folded blanket at the foot of the divan; with my understanding of the photo shoot, I unfurled the blanket and spread it over the whole daybed. I imagined Cody's lighting would make the setting look like a bedroom.

Cody turned on two spotlights, arranging umbrellas to soften the light like a frosted bulb does. Then he turned off the overheads. "Turn away from me," he ordered Susan, "then look back over your shoulder." She obeyed, and Cody began snapping his shutter and offering ongoing encouragement and instructions. "Yes, yes...the camera likes you...turn to your right, yes, like that...okay, uh, hands in your hair—like that, yes...okay, now smolder!" She responded to his commands: frowning, smiling, looking sexy and looking innocent, all in sequence. I don't think I could have done as well, even with as good a director as Cody.

How old do you think she is? Paul thought to me.

"I don't know," I whispered. "She seems like a kid to me. Twenty-four? Twenty-five?"

Next Cody sat the woman on a bench in front of a green screen. "I'll install a nice background. The Riverwalk? Or London?" Susan seemed embarrassed as she sat, as if her husband would never believe she went to those places. I've never been to London, but I wouldn't want anyone I know to think I spent any time at the Riverwalk. Sure, New Orleans is all about tourism, but the Riverwalk is just too much for a townie like me. Maybe the Chamber of Commerce will pay me to keep my mouth shut.

I heard Paul think, *My God, her legs are five feet long!* Susan crossed them, and the yellow mini-dress left little to the imagination. But when she smiled she looked like an innocent little girl. Cody snapped a bunch of pictures as she posed. I could feel Paul's inside eyes pop when she hiked her skirt up even more.

"I think we have the ones for your family," Cody said, putting the camera on his desk. "Amy? Would you help Susan with her costume change?" I followed her to the refuge behind the Japanese screens Cody had in a corner of the studio. She was unzipping her backpack when I caught up with her.

"Do you really need help?" I asked. After all, 'helping' was a white lie to cover for my real job as chaperone.

"Tell me how I look," as she pulled the shoulder straps out and let the slip dress fall. Paul gurgled silently at the unexpected look at the naked woman. I tensed my throat to keep him from using it to answer her.

She crouched and pulled a sheer pink babydoll from her backpack. Knees still bent, she held the article over her head and slipped it on, then tugged the spaghetti straps into place. When she stood up, the effect was riveting. *I have got to get one of them for Christine*, I heard Paul think. The pink bow at her cleavage was a contrast to the see-through nylon that let her breasts show clearly despite being covered. The hem was just below her bellybutton, showing bare, shaved genitals. Paul stammered silently, then thought, *Don't let me touch her. I want to, don't let me.*

I parked my hands in my armpits and thought back, *Not a problem.*

Susan stood with her arms at her side. "So?" She didn't seem the least bit self-conscious about being virtually naked to a stranger.

"Your husband will come home the day after he sees the pictures," I said. "Any man with a pulse would. Maybe I need to get me one of those things."

"I'm ready," she called out, and I followed her as she stepped from behind the screens into the studio proper.

Cody had turned on my Tiffany lamp on the end table by the daybed. He held out one arm to herd her towards it, saying, "Make yourself comfortable. Would you like anything? Tea? Brandy?"

"Some whiskey if you've got it," she said as she dropped onto the chaise on all fours, head toward Cody and me. "That'll make this easier."

As comfortable as she is standing buck naked in front of us, Paul thought, *give her whiskey and she'll take on the whole New Orleans Saints' backfield.*

Cody responded to Susan's question, "I think so. I'll be right back." He limped out of the studio to raid George's liquor cabinet.

"It's just Cody and me," I said to Susan, trying to make her relax. "You don't have to be embarrassed."

"I'm not embarrassed," she answered. "I want to pretend Rex is about to fuck my brains out." She looked up at me. "I miss him. And I'm worried some Jap tramp is trying to replace me."

"Why? Has he, uh, said anything?"

She pulled herself to sit up on the chaise with her legs bent; her feet were next to her butt rather than under it. "He only calls, like, once a month. His parents get more news from him than I do. He never writes. We got married a few weeks before he shipped out, and I...I..." Paul thought, *I never saw a nearly naked woman about to cry. It's so sad.*

I remembered she had said her little girl was born after the husband went to Okinawa, and that the kid was maybe 18 months old. I thought to Paul, *Her son is maybe three. Do you think both kids have the same father?*

Somehow, I inadvertently let Paul get ahold of my larynx. "You are a lovely woman," he told Susan. "These pictures will remind him what he's missing."

"That's the idea."

Cody limped back into the studio with highball glasses in one hand and a bottle of Haig & Haig Pinch in the other. "Wish me luck," she finished.

Cody put two glasses on his desk, then walked to Susan and held the third glass out to her. "Here," he said, and he pulled the stopper on the scotch bottle; it made a satisfying pop. "Say when," and he poured an awful lot of the amber liquor into her glass. She finally held up her other hand to indicate she had enough, then downed the drink in two gulps. Granted, her eyes bugged out and she coughed for two minutes, but it seemed to relax her. "Okay," she said. "I'm ready."

Cody said to me, "Come get your own at the desk. So, I joined him there while he poured more modest shots for each of us. Paul said, "I was a scotch man when I had my own body." If it confused Cody, he hid it pretty well.

I let Paul lead to drink the stuff, so I didn't get any burn or buzz. My poisons are Dixie Beer and any red wine, with the very occasional Daiquiri. Hey, if you live in New Orleans, you have to drink a Daiquiri sometimes. Or a Hurricane. Since I value my liver, I choose Daiquiris.

"You've got great taste in booze," Paul told Cody. "I never could afford anything beyond Dewar's White Label, but this," he pointed at our empty glass, "this is sweet shit right there."

"Dad likes this," he replied. "It's rare that I have any liquor at all."

Oh, I thought to myself, he's not a drinker. And he's self-employed. Those outweigh the fact that he still lives with his parents. I was looking forward to being part of his family dinner, assuming we didn't pass out drunk. Who drinks whiskey at 2:30 in the afternoon?

Cody dimmed his spotlights, aiming them away from the chaise and at two umbrella diffusers. By then I was looking at the side of the chaise where Susan was fluffing a pillow and trying to use the blanket for a show of modesty. Cody called, "Okay, Susan. I'll move around to get different angles on you. We'll go over the pictures later and I'll delete anything you don't like. Ready?"

Silently the woman nodded. Mostly prone, head toward Cody, she leaned this way and that. I heard the shutter snap every four or five seconds, much slower than when she was in her yellow dress.

After a while she sat up, playing with the blanket, and then with the pillow.

I heard Paul think, *I understand, this is not pornography. This is, what, private erotica, just to get her husband to bond with her. But there isn't a man alive who hasn't fantasized about shooting porn.*

So you're going to be frisky when we get home tonight? I was unable to look away from Susan's performance.

Uh, probably.

It was gradual. First Susan put aside the pillow. A little while later she dropped the blanket to the floor. And finally the babydoll was up over her head and gone. She was touching herself in all the places Paul was hoping she would, and was exciting herself. There was a point where she stiffened and shook. A moment after that she stood up and said, "I'm done."

Cody lowered his SLR and limped back to his desk. "Amy, can you open the lights?" I heard Paul think, *Huh?* but my memaw used that expression so I knew what he meant. I flipped the wall switch and bathed the room in the fluorescent daylight glow.

Cody was reviewing the results of the shoot in the camera display. Susan was standing alongside him, still nude, watching as he scrolled through them. I heard her saying, "Yes. No, no, yes, God no, okay, yes, yes, yes..." Sometimes she reached past Cody to point at something on the display panel. It seemed surreal to me, this naked woman standing next to my fully clothed candidate for boyfriend, both behaving as if nothing about it was strange. *It seems I lead a sheltered life,* I thought to Paul. He laughed out loud.

Finally, I walked over to stand on the other side of Cody and looked at the pictures as they flashed through the display. His camera angle captured a more, uh, intimate view than I had had on the sidelines. *Later you can tell me if these are good or not,* I thought to Paul. Immediately he thought back, *I'll tell you right now: Hot as sun.*[28]

---

[28] Paul liked the expression he learned from a song on Paul McCartney's first

Susan asked, "Amy, what do you think of this one?" It was a particularly, uh, intimate picture, taken after she had removed her babydoll. *Paul?*

He answered her, "You look like a brave woman. You look comfortable and confident. And sexy as hell."

She nodded. "That's a keeper," she told Cody.

I've never seen so many dirty pictures in my life, I thought to Paul as the camera review continued with Cody and the naked Susan.

They're not dirty! he thought back. *Well, maybe that one...and that one. Nothing wrong with this kind of photography as long as everyone is a willing participant.*

I'm a lady. No nekkid Amy pictures.

I felt him shrug. *You're not a willing participant, so no, no naked Amy pictures. Nothing wrong with that. But there's nothing wrong with what Susan is doing.*

I suppose you're right, I thought back. *But I wish she'd put some clothes on now.*

I heard him laugh silently. *There's never enough naked women. Never.*

Finally, the model and the photographer finished going over one hundred and thirty-six pictures. Susan made Cody delete a bunch of them, and not just the lingerie shots. Cody put down the camera and said, "I'll have prints and the files for you next Tuesday. These will not leave my possession until I turn them over to you. Something I have to say to all my clients, Susan—if the invoice isn't paid, the pictures become my property to dispose of however I like."

It never occurred to me that a naked person could look shocked, but Susan sure did. "Of course I'll pay you. I'm no deadbeat."

---

post-Beatles album. He didn't much care for the song (or the LP), but the phrase stuck with him.

"Of course you will," Cody said, soothingly. "Like I say, I have to tell this to all my clients. See you Tuesday?" Then he turned to me and said, "Amy, can you help Susan get dressed?"

Somebody had better, I thought to Paul. *She was barely dressed in that yellow thing.*

We're all naked under our clothes, philosopher Paul replied. There are times I want to smack him but I can't figure out where.

Susan declined my aid. She wasn't behind the Japanese screen twenty-five seconds before she reappeared in that yellow dress, dragging her backpack behind her.

"Are you okay to drive?" I asked, thinking of the triple shot of scotch she gobbled down an hour earlier.

She said nothing but nodded.

"I'll walk you to the door," I offered,

We stood on the top step, looking at the semi-circular driveway where Susan's beat up Ford Ranchero was parked. I started to say, "Have a good eve—" but she interrupted to say, "You and Cody are great. You tried to make me comfortable, you didn't say anything mean or judgmental. I dance at a couple of clubs in the French Quarter and I've been called all sorts of names. Rex's parents think I'm a whore, and my landlord always has a smirk on his face when he's around me. You two—" she struggled to get the backpack over one shoulder "—you two treat me like I'm normal. Thanks."

I was too startled to say anything, but Paul picked up the slack. "You are normal. That's why we treat you that way. You're fine, Susan. I wish you luck with your husband."

For a second I thought she was going to hug me, which Paul would have loved. Instead she caught herself and just nodded. "Yeah. Thanks." I watched her slide the backpack off and toss it in the bed of the pickup part of her Ranchero. She waved, and then she was gone.

I stood there in the chilly December day for another minute or two. "This has been the strangest afternoon of my life," I whispered to Paul.

I found my way back to the studio. Cody was furling the lighting umbrellas and stowing gear. "Are you done for the day?" I asked.

He was stuffing equipment in a cabinet. "Shoots like Susan's," he offered, "you never know how long they're going to run. I didn't schedule anyone else for this afternoon."

"Oh. Makes sense. Have you cleared dinner yet?"

"I'll talk to Mom when I finish in here, let her know you'll eat with us."

"Don't forget Wednesday," I prompted.

"I'll tell Mom."

I watched him putter around the studio, tidying up. "That was the strangest session," I said. "Do you get a lot like that?"

"It never ceases to amaze me how many women want to take their clothes off for a camera." He smiled sheepishly. "I wish I'd been a photographer when I was twenty."

"It's got to be tempting," I suggested. Was Cody a secret Lothario? I needed to find out now instead of later.

"It would have been when I was twenty," he laughed. "Now it's enjoyable at a distance. But Susan, for instance—she's sad, and she's desperate. I don't find that attractive."

"When I walked her out, she thanked me because you and I treated her as if she were normal."

He shook his head. "What kind of life does she have where she thanks you for being nice to her? Like I say, that's not my idea of an appealing woman."

I couldn't resist. "What is your idea of the ideal woman?"

"Normal," the word immediately fell from his mouth. "Pretty and rich are in there somewhere, but—you know, just nice. Normal. Good to animals and old folks."

"What, no sterling sense of humor? Long walks on the beach?"

That made him laugh. "I told you how I almost got married."

"You said she was overwhelmed when you were in that car wreck."

"Oh, Rachel was fine until then. But you don't know someone until bad times hit. My idea of a good woman is one who rises to the occasion. And I hope I'm a good man if I'm ever put to the test."

I thought to Paul, *Remember when you beat up that lover boy who surprised us in my dorm hallway? I thought he acted like a boy, but you behaved like a man.*[29]

Out loud I said, "Don't we all hope that. About ourselves, I mean."

Cody nodded absently as he lined up several camera lenses for the next day's projects.

It felt like that line of conversation was over, so I changed subjects. "I need to see how Caleb and his crew are doing. I hope there's a forest of barbed wire in your back yard."

I found Donna feeding the dryer in the laundry room. I was happy to see the new back door had been installed, complete with gleaming deadbolt. "I know usually you are the chaperone for Cody's boudoir photo sessions. How do you deal with them?"

"Weird, isn't it? I find them a combination of funny and sad."

"You got that right."

"Sometimes one of the women tries to seduce Cody. Did that happen today?"

I shook my head. "No. Susan is hoping hot pictures will keep her husband from leaving her."

Donna closed the door of the dryer and twirled the control knobs. The machine began to make squeak, squeak, squeak noises. "Oh, that poor child."

"I'm guessing she's twenty-four or twenty-five."

Donna stared at me. "If that girl is more than twenty I'd be astounded." I figured her perspective on age was better than mine. *Twenty! Two kids*, I thought to Paul, *working as an exotic dancer,*

---

[29] *The Beaded Necklace* by A. Trauring. The jerk Amy had foolishly slept with wanted to 'surprise' her in a dark hallway at 2 AM. Paul beat the daylights out of him and broke his nose. The creep deserved it.

with a husband of only a few weeks before he was mobilized to Japan. Hot pictures or not, this is not going to end well.

I feel bad for her, Paul responded, *and I'm glad you've made better choices. We're okay.*

I considered that. I'm thirty-seven. I'm self-employed but at least my work doesn't depend on my looks or on taking off my clothes. No kids, no husband. And I've got my eyes on Cody as potential boyfriend material. *Yes, we are okay. Thanks.*

"Where's Caleb's gang?" I asked.

"They're out in back, putting up the barbed wire."

"Tell me they're wearing work gloves! Please!" I squeezed behind Donna to get to the window so I could see what the workmen were doing. Four men were in the back yard wrangling what looked like an enormous Slinky, like the one I used to make go down the stairs when I was a little girl. The afternoon sun was glinting off the trapezoidal pieces of metal that I knew were affixed razors. I heard Paul think, *We can hear them swearing from here. Very creative, too.*

"Razor wire is not perfect," I explained to Donna. "If you throw a couple of blankets over it you can get past it without damaging yourself too badly. But it's a big help."

"What would work better?"

Paul answered for me. "Land mines. There is no foolproof answer."

About this time we heard Cody calling, "Hello? Mom? Amy?" Donna shouted, "Back here, Dear." A few moments later he limped into the laundry room. "There you are," he said.

"Amy told me about your session," Donna said. "How did it go?"

"Susan was cooperative and did not make any fuss," he replied. "She'll be back on Tuesday to pay me and get the files and the prints." We watched his mother nod. Then he went on, "I hope it's alright, I invited Amy to stay for dinner."

"Of course!" she said enthusiastically. "Cody and George love my lasagna, and there's always plenty." She put her hand on my upper arm and rubbed it, smiling. *I think she likes me*, I thought to Paul.

I helped Donna in the kitchen until George called out, "I'm home in one piece!" from the entryway. Donna put down a wooden spoon she was using to stir some cauliflower and went to follow the voice. I kept at washing out a few bowls and pans she had used to get dinner going. I heard Paul think, *There's a dishwasher over there, why are we washing these by hand?*

"I'm so sorry if you end up with dishpan hands," I said aloud, "but some things get cleaner with the old school methods."

At least we're not taking things out to the creek and pounding on them with rocks.

"We'll do that after dinner. That lasagna pan will be a lot of work to get clean."

"What's that, dear?" Donna said. George was holding her hand as she walked back into the kitchen.

"Just entertaining myself," I answered. "George! You look like no one tried to kill you today."

"Just a client that busted my balls over a lease agreement. Donna tells me you've been a big help today."

"I try to be useful," I said as I dried my hands on a damp dish towel. "Have you looked in the back yard?"

"I tried to get in the garage from Nashville Avenue. Caleb waved me away."

Cody limped in from wherever he had been. His mother announced, "Dinner in five minutes. Everybody wash up." She was picking up trivets and potholders; she said, "Amy, dear, can you bring the cauliflower to the breakfast nook?"

"Yes'm!" But before I could turn toward the stove, Cody scooped up the pot. How chivalrous! *I think he likes you back*, Paul thought.

For no reason I walked with Cody to watch him deposit the cauliflower on one of the potholders, and then we walked back to the kitchen to wash our hands in the sink. "I'm glad you're staying," he said to me. Oh, God, that smile! It breaks up the sharp angles of his cheekbones, and seems to increase my diastolic blood pressure by twenty points. "Yes. Me too," I answered. I could feel a blush creeping up my neck and invading my face. *Crap!* I thought to Paul, *I'm so easy!* I heard him snicker silently.

When the four of us were seated in the breakfast nook, Donna pushed the lasagna pan toward me, then handed the cauliflower in the other direction, to George. The pasta smelled so good that Paul said, "Can I have a corner? I like the chewy stuff." There was laughter all around.

I passed on dessert—blackberry buckle—despite Paul's silent whining. When everyone was done, I helped Cody collect dishes and silverware and pots and pans, and ferry them into the kitchen. But as soon as I noticed George heading for his study I dried my hands and followed him.

"We need to talk," he said when I entered the room. He motioned me to one of the wing chairs while he sat in the other. "I like your attitude about safety," he began, "but I'm afraid this is too big for one person. You can't watch my family at home and me at work."

I was hoping he wouldn't notice, I thought to Paul. Aloud, I said, "You're right. I see three possibilities."

George leaned forward, elbows on his thighs, and looked at me.

"One, you involve the police. The drawback is that then the police notice you, and we're hoping the remains from your warehouse don't turn out to be human."

"Two, we bring in additional muscle. I'd recommend Duke Cranston, I worked with him at the New Orleans Police Department. He's big and he's good. We pretty much saved each other's lives."[30]

---

[30] See *The Wedding Fatality* by yours truly.

"And three?"

"I hate to say this," rolling my eyes. "Go hire Pinkerton. Security Protection. Eagle. U-S-K-9. Or At-Risk. They have resources I don't. They'd be able to give you and your family 24/7 coverage. Obviously, I can't. But with Duke I can go a long way."

He rubbed his chin, then asked, "How much do they cost?"

"U-S-K-9 charges about twelve grand a week, but that's for three or four people."

More chin rubbing. "What am I paying you?"

"$250 a day, plus expenses."

"So, if I hire this Duke, it'll be, like, $3,500 a week?"

"I don't know his prices." I reached for my wallet, saying, "I've got his business card. We can ask him."

"Okay." He stood up and went behind his desk. "I'll put him on the speaker-phone."

I stood on the other side of the desk. Looking between Duke's card and the phone, I punched in his ten digits. On the third ring we heard, "Cranston. What?"

"Hey, Duke," I said, brightly. "It's Amy Clear. I'm with a client, George Locaviche. We want to know if you're interested in some intensive personal protection work. Are you available?"

"Say what? Queenie, is that you?"

Half a smile crossed George's face when he heard that old nickname. "Yep, it's me, the one and only Queen Bitch. How's business, Duke?"

"Damn, Queenie, it's good to hear from you. Hey, I finished a job last week, so I'm open. What'choo got?"

"Some bad apples are threatening my client and his family. They've already tried some nastiness. His family needs protection at home, and he needs it at work."

"You check out the client?" I saw George's jaw drop when he heard that.

"Of course," I answered. "And his first check cleared. But the job needs more muscle."

"Ah! I've got my brother-in-law helping me on some jobs. The three of us ought to be able to cover this."

"Mister Cranston," George spoke up. "I'm George Locaviche. Give me an idea of what you charge?"

We heard Duke laugh. "I'm seventeen-fifty a week. If we include Luther, it's twenty-five hundred."

I held my breath. *Duke and me are cheaper than the big companies*, I thought to Paul. *Wish me luck.*

"What do you propose to do?" George asked me.

"One of us at home when you're gone, the other with you at work. Luther can spell us at your house."

"I'll take the house," I said, wanting to remain close to Cody. More to George than Duke I said, "He'll be a help in your business. Anyone sees Duke, they'll agree to anything you say."

"Just as long as I don't have to give him a percentage. Okay, Mister Duke, I'll try this out." Pointing at me, he added, "How long is this going to go on?"

"I got a name and address from Sergeant Francks today. Tomorrow I'll stake out his place and see where he goes."

"You got a name, Queenie? Who is it?"

I told him, but it didn't seem to register.

"When can you start?" George was drumming his fingers on his desk.

"Give me your address. I'll pick you up in the morning and drive you to work. What time do you need to go?"

A smile spread across my client's face. "Be here at 7:15," George said. "What do you drive?"

"A black Hummer with bullet-proof windows."

"Dress nice," George grinned. "See you tomorrow."

We heard Duke shout off the telephone mouthpiece, "Hey, Luther, we—" as George ended the call.

"Anything else?" he asked as he plopped himself back in his wing chair.

"This is going to sound strange," I said as I took my own seat back. "There are nights I'm going to have to sleep here." Paul added, "Luther, too. We can take turns in the same room, I suppose."

What? I am not going to sleep with Duke's brother-in-law!

"We did that in the navy," George said. "We had sleeping shifts on the submarine. The bunk was mine from two to nine AM. Somebody else had it from ten to five, and some lazy doofus from Idaho used it on the third shift." He shook his head. "I had to chase him out of the rack before I could go to sleep. What does a landlubber from Idaho know about boats?"

"Tonight I'm going home. I'll pack a case and be back in the morning before Duke picks you up. Do me a favor and keep the doors locked and the curtains drawn 'til I get back."

He saluted and said, "Aye aye, Captain." Then, puzzled, he asked, "What did—what's his name? Duke?—what was it he called you?"

Paul laughed out loud. When he was done, I explained, "When we first worked together, we had a bit of a, you'll excuse me, a pissing contest. Cops do that. Anyway, he asked me what he should call me, and I told him I was partial to Queen Bitch. I am glad he shortened it to Queenie." I heard Paul silently singing *Go, go, go, little Queenie!*[31] He is an aficionado of an obscure and ancient form of music called rocks that roll or something.

"I'm going to see if Donna can use any help in the kitchen. When she's done with me, I'm off." He nodded and grunted, and I left him in his study.

She's not in the kitchen? I heard Paul think.

"So it seems." I walked past the breakfast nook and found Donna in the living room. She was sitting in the middle of the huge sofa, with a pile of wool on her left and knitting needles in her hands.

---

[31] Paul thinks Chuck Berry was the poet laureate of America. Amy never heard of him.

Paul said, "Making a toaster cozy?" *Shush!* I thought.

Fortunately the woman took it as an innocent joke. "My niece is due in April. I'm getting a head start on a blanket."

"Is this her first?" I sat on her right, away from the skein.

"Second," she said, looking up even as her needles continued to klack, klack, klack. "We're hoping for a girl this time."

So we chatted about domestic things for maybe half an hour. I like Donna! She's been accepting of me, even though I think she's figured out I have designs on her son. She's open, she's clever, and she's interesting. Paul even got in on the conversation, asking where her niece lived and what she did. He can be open, clever, and interesting, too.

Finally, I made my excuse to go home, saying I'd be back early to talk to a colleague who was going to pick George up and keep an eye on him at work.

When I got to my car, Paul insisted on calling Christine. I didn't feel like concentrating on driving, so I sat and listened while my dyad talked to his girlfriend. "Paulette!" she cried, full of enthusiasm that had not dimmed in the, what, five years they had been a couple. "You and Amy come on over. I've got a surprise for you."

I piped up, "Okay, but I have to go home first to pack some things. I'll be bunking at my client's house for a while."

"I hope that's a good thing," the woman said. She is a considerate creature, that Christine. "Do you get a real bed? Or do you have to sleep under the sink like Harry Potter?"

"I think that was only for the first book," I laughed. "No, I get a bed. I have to share it with my old police partner's brother-in-law."

"Uh—" There was a long pause. "I thought it was the client's son you liked. I'm confused."

Paul laughed out loud and took over. "Amy's sharing a bed, all right. She gets it from ten at night to six in the morning. The other guy gets it from eight AM until whenever."

"That's a different kind of sharing," Christine admitted. For some reason it sounded as if she were trying not to laugh. "I hadn't thought of that."

I glanced at my watch: five-thirty-six. "How about we show up around seven?" I offered. "Seven-fifteen?"

"Sure, Amy. Paulette, I'll be waiting for you. Knock twice so I know it's you."

When Paul closed my phone I thought, *Would you like to drive?*

Does the Baptist church have a bus? He mashed the glow plug button. When it blinked he cranked the engine and let out the clutch. Out loud he said, "Next stop, Amyville. Please keep your hands and feet inside the vehicle at all times and do not feed the natives."

Even at rush hour, the drive between Cody's house and mine wasn't ten minutes. Freret and Cherokee were easy streets, other than the nightmare of crossing over St. Charles Avenue.

Paul parked in the gravel construction pit in front of the house. "Can I wait here while you pack?" he asked.

"Sure," I said, getting the joke. "I'll be right back."

Inside my humble abode I took my overnight case from under the bed and opened it on the bed. While I looked through my dresser drawers, tossing underwear and blouses and makeup in the general direction of the valise, Paul said, "I thought you were going to let me wait in the car."

I stopped, a tan bra in my hands. "I thought I did leave you there."

He was silent for a few seconds, long enough for me to begin to wonder if Donna had spiked the lasagna with some hallucinogen, before Paul laughed out loud. "I had you going, admit it!" he howled.

"Guilty as charged," I said. I don't know why, but I felt some relief that it was just a joke. You may think it's weird and unbearable to have someone living in your head, but after twenty-six years I've gotten so used to it, the idea of Paul being gone is unreal. Scary. Downright frightening, even. We sometimes joke about it, but at unpredictable moments like this it's something I don't think is the least bit funny.

I dropped the bra on the bed and wrapped my arms around ourself. *Don't go*, I thought. *I like you being here with me.*

It was just a gag, he thought back. *If I weren't here with you, I'd be inside that urn in the back of your closet.* I rubbed my hands up and down my arms, the way Paul and I hug each other. "I'm not going anywhere," he said; then, *You know I love you.*

"Yes," I held myself tighter, wanting Paul to feel how important this is to me. *I love you, too.*

So, I stood there for a minute, me and Paul feeling close. The fear was gone, and I was starting to relax.

"Christine's waiting on us," Paul said, so I went back to stuffing things into the suitcase. I took a quick turn around the house, turning off most lights and closing the curtains.

He didn't wait to be asked this time. Paul led to take my keys and he started up the car. It was a thirty-minute drive to go from my place near the river to Christine's double near Lake Pontchartrain.

He parked off the alleyway alongside her place, but I led to walk up the steps to her door. *Christine said to knock twice*, he thought to me. *Okay*, and so I did. Knock knock.

"Paulette?" Christine's voice came through the closed door.

"He's here," I said. I knew that she could tell I was leading.

"Let me talk to her."

Well, all right, then. I stepped back inside and let Paul say, "It's MEEEE!"

A sigh sounds odd when it comes through a door, but that's what I heard. Then Christine threw the door open.

There she was: multi-colored and multi-length hair; broad smile showing her bent front tooth that mirrored mine; and a red ribbon with a big bow around her bare waist.

"Oh, you Christine!" my dyad called as he walked through the doorway to embrace his girlfriend. Even while he was kissing her Paul lifted my right foot and slammed the door closed behind us.

They came up for air around nine-thirty.

What is it like for me when Paul and Christine get frisky and intimate? Paul leads during all the activity; Christine probably would pull her clothes back on if I were to lead for even a moment. Whichever one of us leads gets the most out of any sensation: when we eat, the leader gets full taste and satiation while whoever is in the background gets a dull version of flavor. When we drink, the leader gets tipsy or worse, while whoever is in the background barely gets a buzz (although we both can get a headache the next day). Same thing for sex. So I close my inside eyes and enjoy the filtered pleasure. And this time I was thinking about Cody. I declare, that boy will not know what hit him when I get my hands on him.

Paul and Christine cuddled for a while, until the woman said, "Amy? How are you doing?" I love how she thinks of me, even at a time like that.

"Glad to be here with you and Paul," I said. The physical activity does make me feel closer to both of them, and I like that.

Tell your lover that we have to go home soon. I need to be back at Cody's by seven in the morning.

Paul responded by going, "Ohhhhhh..."

"What?" asked Christine. "Paulette, is anything wrong?" She hoisted herself up on one elbow to look down on us.

He sighed. "Amy has to be at work at seven tomorrow." He used our right hand to rub her back and shoulder. "We'll have to leave soon."

"Not before you kiss me another twelve...no, sixteen times. And real kisses, not the kind of peck on the cheek you'd give your granny." I was relieved to see her smiling. There was a time, a few years ago, when she was still working out her medications, when what Paul said would have reduced her to tears. She's doing much, much better now.

Paul started to meet Christine's demand, so I thought more about getting that close to Cody's angular face. In fact, I just let myself pretend that's what was happening.

At half-past ten I was finally in the safety of my yellow car. Paul coaxed the glow plugs into life, and cranked the engine. One of the squirrels sounded unhappy about being awakened on a chilly December evening, but after a while it caught up with the rest of its diesel brethren.

"God, I love that woman!" Paul said as he let out the clutch. "What a welcome!"

"And she still has time to ask how I'm doing. You've got a winner, my friend."

"Mmmm."

As we headed down Wisner, along the bank of Bayou St. John, I said, "I'm getting super-emotional lately."

"How so?"

"Well, at home today. Your joke about waiting in the car, and how I needed that hug. And you and Christine tonight—all that closeness was nicer than usual."

I felt him raise my eyebrows. "And this is different?"

Yes. I pondered it. *I think, I **think** it's because I'm letting myself like Cody.*

"It's been a while since you liked a guy."

Well, there was the twin that murdered his brother and adopted his identity. And when I was still a detective on the New Orleans police department there was that partner who was estranged from his wife, but not estranged enough. "It's been a while, yes," I said. "I think it's my turn."

Paul got us through the tricky intersection where Wisner turned into Carrollton, just where City Park ended. We drove on in silence, until he asked, "So, what's the plan for tomorrow?"

"I get up at five-thirty," I said, dreading the fact that five-thirty AM was not far enough in the future to allow a decent night's sleep. "Get to Cody's by seven. Talk shop with Duke and watch him drive George off to work. Check with Donna about the security improvements—I really worry about their home alarm company. And then it's off to Chalmette to stake out he whose name must not be mentioned."

We were stuck at a red light at Tulane Avenue, with the cosmic spaghetti monster lanes that were the entrances and exits from I-10. The only saving grace was relative light traffic so late at night. I was glad Paul was driving.

"Okay. And if the creep-o gets in his car?"

I grinned. "I follow him. Three car lengths behind. Notice where he goes, and drive past it; then double back to shadow him on the ground. I've done this before. Weren't you paying attention?"

I thought I was, but I guess not. Sorry.

"Stakeout can be boring," I confessed. "Also dangerous."

Considering the hour, Paul zipped through the intersection with Claiborne. During rush hour it is the single most deadly piece of asphalt in the parish. We got through it unscathed.

"Why dangerous?"

"First, you can fall asleep. Did I say it was boring?"

I heard Paul's silent chuckle.

"Second, you're so busy looking for your quarry that a bad guy can sneak up behind you. I'm told that is the kind of nasty surprise that can ruin your day. And third, your target spots you and lures you into an ambush. Uh, also ruining your day and maybe ending your life."

Paul said, "I guess it's the 'maybe ending your life' that made me not pay attention." He ran the yellow light at St. Charles Avenue, then slowed down to avoid plowing into the drunks stumbling out of Cooter Browns. A little further and he got us to the levee, then made a left on Leake Avenue.

I've always been a fan of trains—my Pepaw had an incredible model train layout in his basement, and he'd let me and sister Kaylee run the transformer throttle for hours. But that CSX freight running between the street and the river was LOUD. So I thought to Paul, *Think about the positive: L-Y doesn't spot me, I find out where he's moved his operation, and I get away with exploring. I like that a lot better.*

"Yeah, that'll work."

What?

"I said—" *I said that will be great.*

I was glad when Paul turned onto my street, Cherokee. The sooner I got home, the less sleep-deprived I'd be tomorrow. And tomorrow will be the day I start earning George Locaviche's money by hunting L-Y.

☄ TUESDAY, DECEMBER 16, 2036 ☄

The only way to see five-thirty AM is to still be awake on a great overnight. On the other hand, an alarm clock going off at that hour is an offense against nature. Plus, I was feeling a little resentful that Paul's fun with Christine was the reason I would be drinking coffee by the urn-full all day. So, I thought to him several times before a *Hey, sunshine!* got through to him. I confess, I was disappointed that he was all chipper and happy and, and, and disturbingly perky for that hour.

"Aren't you exhausted?"

I felt him nod my head. "Yeah, I'm pretty tired. But I feel WONDERFUL." I closed my eyes and rubbed my temples. "I had such a good time with Christine. And you said you were feeling extra close to both of us. You still have that feeling?"

"A little," I said as I straightened up and opened my eyes. "It would be bigger if I had another four hours of sleep."

I started walking to the shower. He said, "A nice cold shower will wake you up. Yep, get your attention meter up to twelve-and-a-half.[32] Get you up to six thousand R-P-M." He sounded like a cross between that late night TV commercial guy selling retractable

---

[32] Spinal Tap were such amateurs. Eleven! Ha!

awnings and that priest who taught Youth Catechism my junior year at Giles Academy. Too earnest.

So, I turned on the cold water in the shower. I counted to three and stepped into the stream so I could knock Paul out of his insufferable good mood.

In my half-asleep state it had not occurred to me that, yes, Paul would get a blast of cold water, but so would I. We both lurched in the liquid ice, and started coughing because that's what happens when we try to talk at the same time.

I heard him think *Damn, that was cruel.*

Yes. I'm paying for it now. I was turning the hot water faucet. Paul used our left hand to turn off the cold water, just about the split-second when the hot got hot. There was a lot of noise, and now I've got a black-and-blue mark on my shin. I didn't get poached, but it was close.

I got a more realistic temperature shower stream and resumed a normal morning routine. Paul kept mooning over Christine, "Oh, she's great. And I'm glad the two of you are friends." I was surprised to realize I wasn't annoyed with Paul anymore; that got frozen or baked out of me in the shower.

It was five-'til-seven when Paul parked across the street from the Locaviche's semi-circular driveway. I was wearing a UNO-Lakeside sweatshirt over baggy jeans. Roskette was in a fanny pack, along with my P-I license, my old NOLA police detective ID, and a little thing of hand sanitizer.

Since George hasn't given me a key yet, I had to knock at the door. I could hear movement, but it was thirty seconds before Donna opened the door. Before she could greet me, I said, "Use the peephole. Don't let people in until you know they're okay."

Donna hung her head like a chastised puppy, and Paul thought *You have quite a talent for bringing this woman down.* Now that I was the chastised one, I added, "But you're the first person I've seen close up all day, and I have to say, I'm glad it's you." She perked up a little. "Getting George off?"

"He's finishing breakfast. Is his ride here?"

"Duke said seven-fifteen," I answered as we walked into the living room. "He's punctual."

Quietly limping into the room was Cody. His hair looked slept in, but his face had a nice smile. *That's for you, you know*, Paul thought.

And I appreciate it. "Good morning, Cody. Are you doing all right?" He stepped closer to me. "Got a lot of clients today?"

What a goofy smile, Paul thought. *No!* I thought back, *It's charming. It's adorable. It's...*

It's the same as the smile you're wearing, I bet.

I think he was right. Cody answered, "Five adults, and twin sisters for their mid-winter prom."

"I'm impressed that you are making a go of a home business. If we team up, we can probably rule the world." Suddenly I heard Paul thinking, *The same thing we do every night, Pinky—Try and take over the world.*[33]

What? A little distracted, I had to ask Cody to repeat his response, which was "Let's start small, just Orleans Parish. We can grow from there."

"Have you eaten breakfast?" Donna asked. "Cody, please set another place for Amy. I've got oatmeal on the stove."

"No, really," I said to Donna, but I was following Cody on his way to the kitchen and the breakfast nook. When we were in the next room I said, "Your mom is good to me. I'm not used to clients feeding me. Well, expenses, but I mean standing at a stove and feeding me."

"Mom likes you," he said, reaching into a cabinet for a bowl. "She's grateful that you're saving Dad from this craziness."

"I hope Duke doesn't upset her. He's black as a cave and as big as a tank."

"As long as he fits in the front door, it'll be okay."

---

[33] Another one of Paul's beloved cartoons. This was from *Pinky And The Brain*, whose every episode includes Brain declaring this to his rodent side-kick.

I followed him into the breakfast room, where George, in a blue suit, white shirt, and red striped power tie, was hunched over his bowl of oatmeal, peering at the "Greater New Orleans" section of the sloppily folded Times-Picayune. Cody put my bowl on a placemat across from his father. "Good morning, Boss," I said.

"Hmmm?" He looked up, pushing his reading glasses down the bridge of his nose. "Oh, Amy. Good morning." He started to move as if he was going to stand up and wait for me to sit. "Uh, please—"

I held my right hand out, palm forward, the universal body language known through all the explored galaxies as 'STOP'. "Don't get up on my account," I said, hurrying to sit at that funky table. "I want to let you know what I'm doing today."

He was holding the newspaper up, but his head had swiveled to look at me. "I'm going to check in with Duke Cranston. He'll drive you to work and be your shadow all day. After I see if Donna needs anything, I'm headed to St. Bernard Parish to stakeout your nemesis."

He nodded and turned back to the Times-Picayune, but said, "I hope this Duke is dressed well."

"Usually," I said. I was ready to wait in the driveway for Duke, but then Cody came back in and sat next to me. "Can I spoon some oatmeal out for you?" His eyes were bouncing between my face and the empty bowl. *I was hoping to avoid the calories*, I thought to Paul. I heard him return, *I was hoping to avoid the hunger pangs*.

So, I nodded and held out my bowl. After he poured the second serving spoonful into it, I said, "Whoa! You can stop now. I have to watch out for my figure."

His grin! It was so cute! I made Cody laugh. "Write that down, 'I made Cody laugh.'"

"Am I usually all grim or something?" He spooned so much into his own bowl that, I swear, only surface tension kept the oatmeal from making a gooey mess on the tabletop.

"I, uh, no. No, you're not grim, not at all. I'm happy that you laughed because of me."

I hate it when men squint, and tilt their heads, and give me a look like, 'I didn't know you were **this** weird.' *Uh-oh,* I thought to Paul. *Too much too soon?*

It would be nice to rewind the last twenty seconds, I heard Paul think, *but, yeah.*

I shook my head and said, "Anyway. Today I stake out the address I got for one of George's molesters. Would you like to come with me?"

"Is it dangerous?" His eyes were open wide.

I laughed. "Not particularly, unless something goes wrong." I raised my eyebrows to let him know I was waiting for a yes or no.

"I've got a bunch of shoots scheduled today. But I'd love to do it some other time."

It was Paul who spoke up, "We'll hold you to that. Sometimes one body just isn't enough."

There was a knock at the front door. Donna left the kitchen to answer it, and I heard the bullfrog voice of my old police partner, Duke Cranston. She's such an automatic hostess, she walked him back to the breakfast nook and ordered him to sit down for oatmeal. "I thank you, Miss," he said, "but my wife fed me this morning."

Then he looked up and saw me. "Well, well, little Queenie," he said with a big smile, "you are looking fine. Come here," and he opened his arms for an embrace. You have to understand, when Duke and I worked together, I saved his life, and he saved mine; that sort of thing makes you bond deep and quick. I walked into his bear hug and let him squish me good.

The man is a foot taller than me. I said to his chest, "Good to see you, Lieutenant."

He let go of me and I stepped back. Duke Cranston, in all his six-foot-six glory, wearing a dark pinstriped three-piece suit and a pair of Ray-Bans. I'd only ever seen him in police blues before.

Our face hurts, Paul thought. *Quit smiling so hard.*

He'll be gone in a few minutes. Maybe I'll frown then.

"Let me introduce you to our boss," I said. "You've met Donna—" I touched her on her arm "—this is Cody, and that's George over there." In fact, George had folded the Times-Picayune and was in the process of standing up while gulping his coffee.

"Pleased to meet you," Duke said, holding out his hand. It was three times the size of George's, eclipsing it when they shook.

"Amy told me you were big and intimidating. I didn't know she meant this big."

"I'm just a pussycat," Duke smiled, "but if needs be, I've got one hell of a bite. You ready?"

George looked at his watch. "You're on time. That's good."

"Let's roll." He turned to Donna and said, "It's nice to meet you, ma'am." He nodded at Cody, then play-punched me in the shoulder. "See you later, Queenie."

As we watched them leave the room, Cody said, "You weren't kidding about him being big."

"He makes me feel safe," I replied.

He put his arm around my shoulder and pulled me toward him. "And I guess Dad is safer now."

"All of you are." I patted his hand where it fell on my upper arm. "And you've got business to do, and so do I." I stepped away from him and said, "I hope I'm back this afternoon. Between clients I'll let you know what I find out."

Another cute smile, and he limped off to the hallway and his studio.

I found Donna in the kitchen, working a crossword puzzle. I could hear the dishwasher cleaning up all the oatmeal plates and pots. I sat in a high stool alongside her and asked, "What is Caleb doing today?"

She held up her left index finger while she penciled in an answer on the Times-Picayune grid. Then, "His crew is working on the new back fence. If Caleb can break loose, he'll start working on the, what did you call it, the safe?"

"Ah. Safe room. Good."

"And what are you up to today?"

"In a little while I'll put on a fake moustache and stake out one of the baddies that's been bothering George."

"Stake out!" she said. "Like in a spy movie? Isn't that dangerous?" Why does everyone ask that question? Especially when the evident answer is 'yes.'

"I hope not," I tried to reassure Donna. "I've done this before. And I'm armed. And that reminds me—" I leaned forward so she could hear me whisper, as dramatically as I could "—Armed. Do you or George have a firearm?"

"George does. I think he keeps it at his office. I told him I didn't want it in the house."

Even though I nodded, I said, "It's time to reconsider. George, you, and Cody need to have a gun and know how to use it. I'm afraid your husband's nemesis is ahead of y'all on that score."

Donna put a hand on mine. "Cody can't have a driver's license because of seizures. They'll let him have a gun?"

"You don't need anyone's permission to own one, only to carry it concealed. And I'm pretty sure I can get the permits for all three of you."

At this point Paul poked me inside and took the lead. "In fact, I'll take everyone to the range for some safety lessons and practice. It really is a lot of fun."

"A gun? Fun?" She looked like someone had squirted lemon juice into her mouth. I couldn't help but laugh. "I know!" I shared. "I'd never considered it before a friend—" Paul "—took me target shooting. It was so, so empowering. All at once I realized I never had to worry about getting mugged or raped or anything. I could protect myself." I lowered my voice again, "And it's almost as much fun as sex."

There was a sparkle in Donna's eyes as she said, "Well, I guess it wouldn't hurt to try." We both giggled like sorority girls comparing notes the day after the prom.

After a moment she asked, "This Duke man—he's good?"

"The best. He was a lieutenant when I did a freelance job for parish police. We saved each other's life a time or two."

"He's big."

"Yes."

Donna nodded and went back to her crossword puzzle. I heard Paul think, *It's like watching your mom. Tracey has puzzle books squirreled all over the house.*

Out loud I said, "My mom does crosswords. Whenever I did something that I knew would upset her I'd buy her a crossword magazine and a box of Mike & Ike."

"Cody used to do the same thing, only with me it's Godivas."

I like this woman. She's open and friendly. Not to mention she listens when I tell her what needs to be done for security. I think she'll have a good time at the pistol range.

Girl talk is fun and all, but I knew I had to stake out LY's property in Chalmette. I said my goodbyes, assuring her I planned to be back in the afternoon.

Let me drive, I thought as I walked out to the Benz.

Only if you promise lunch.

Promise lunch what?

Paul let out a groan that made me laugh. Usually he's the one making bad puns. Once I was in the car and belted in, he said, "How come you want to drive?" I swear, Paul lives to eat, to be with Christine, and to drive.

"I haven't been to Chalmette in a couple of years," I answered. "I want to see if I remember how to get there." I put the car in gear and headed to the next cross street. I made two lefts and was on Nashville Avenue, headed north. As I came up on the back of the Locaviche estate, I saw some of Caleb's men laying bricks to make a fence.

"Do we have a plan?" Paul asked. "I hope we have fun today."

"Fun? Not getting spotted would be fun. Finding out where LY's business lair is would be fun. Getting back to Cody's in time for dinner would be fun."

"I'm good with all that," he said, "but I wouldn't call them 'fun.'"

I came up on the back of the huge Ursuline Academy complex to the left, and the front of McMain Secondary on the right, hoping to make the green light at Claiborne. "Consider the alternatives. Hmmm?" As I entered the intersection the light turned yellow. I goosed the gas pedal.

"Let's see if the guy really lives where we're going," Paul said, being his occasional wet blanket self. "It might be a different person with the same name."

"Or he might have moved away," I conceded. I got caught at the light at Poydras, next to the hulking Superdome, in the shadow of the interstate. "But I want to find him. George is my client, so I want to keep him safe. Donna is a doll, so I want to keep her safe. And I sure want to protect Cody."

Once I was on I-10, headed north and east to the suburban peace of St. Bernard Parish, Paul thought, *We're going out with Cody tomorrow, right? Dinner?*

"Yes. Are you okay with that?"

Sure. You deserve to have a good time. And I'm working on getting used to him.

"I have a plan," I said. "I assume I'll have to shadow LY at some point. I want Cody to come with me. I'll bet he has some secret cameras he can use to, I don't know, get some evidence. Or maybe blackmail LY into leaving George alone."

I heard Paul laugh silently, but then he said out loud, "You want to blackmail the goon? That'll be interesting."

Things looked a little familiar when I got off the interstate at the North Claiborne exit. First there was the Lower Ninth Ward, then one of our hippie enclaves in Bywater. When I crossed the parish line I was in Arabi, and Claiborne suddenly was called Judge Perez Drive. Was it for Leander or Melvyn[34], who I don't think

---

[34] Leander Perez was the political boss of Plaquemines and St. Bernard Parishes from before WWII until his death in 1969. He was an outspoken (>>>)

were related—I don't know; both of them were before my time. It's just a street name to me.

As I drove over the Guerenger Canal I said, "Do you think it would be faster to get out here in a boat?" Then came the Chalmette Vista Canal, and finally the very end of the Guichard Canal. Why, you might ask, are there so many canals around New Orleans? Considering much of the metro is only about one-quarter inch above sea level, the canals hold water that otherwise would be in the roads, in the sewers, and—if your house had one—in your basement.

My visit to my old police station told me LY lived on Pakenham Drive. It was the first left after the Guichard Canal.

"Where are the trees?" Paul asked.

"There's one," I answered, tilting my head toward a short, spindly thing on the right. "And up there on the left—there's another one."

"One tree per block? Did this place get infested with super-termites?"

Actually, all of St. Bernard Parish got infested–with floods. When Katrina hit, 32 years earlier, the entire parish was under fifteen feet of water. It's said that only six houses in the parish remained habitable after that, but I think that was an exaggeration; more likely the number is no higher than two. And then Hurricane Rodrego did damage in the '20s, and Bianca did more seven or eight years later. At least Hurricane Olaf didn't get this far east. Anyway, that's why there are so few trees in Chalmette. And why there are still so many residential driveways leading to cracked concrete slabs.

(Continued) segregationist, and widely acknowledged as corrupt. Parts of state highways 39 and 47 in St Bernard Parish were named Judge Perez Drive upon his death. Melvyn Perez, who indeed was not a relative, was a state judge in St Bernard Parish. In the year Amy was born, 1999, the parish conveniently rededicated the road to Judge Melvyn without incurring the expense of buying new street signs.

The street was lined with modest private houses, brick. At this hour—8:25 in the morning—there weren't a lot of cars visible in driveways. A very few homes were two-story, one with an out-of-place Mansard roof. And there were swaths of grass and weeds where houses had been before Mother Nature wreaked her vengeance on poor Louisiana.

Next to one of those vacant fields was the address I was looking for, a simple brick structure, with a sedan and a large SUV in the driveway. "I'm going down Josephine," a convenient side street. "There's a rare tree that might hide me while I watch." I went up a ways, made a U-turn, and parked in the shade of what might be the only magnolia tree in the parish. I had a clear view of the front door and the driveway that I hoped belonged to LY.

After a few minutes Paul said, "Want to play Rock, Paper, Scissors?" It was our preferred time-waster when we were stuck somewhere.

"Nuh-uh!" I said. "I need to pay attention." An idea bloomed in my head. "How about you watch the cars, and I'll watch the front door."

Okay, boss. I kept my eyes on the main entrance to the house; I trusted Paul was using my peripheral vision to keep a lookout on the vehicles. It was a division of labor we'd discovered we could do years earlier.

Sure, stakeouts can be dangerous. But mostly they are boring. And the trouble with boring is you get careless. You might doze and miss your target's movement. Your mind might wander, and next thing you know you're looking down the business end of a double-barreled shotgun. There are two parts to Amy's foolproof stakeout method: industrial sized thermos of coffee, and, if desperate, parking my fingernails into my palms. It's a good way to ruin a manicure, but it works.

I was pouring a third cup of chicory coffee when I heard Paul think, *A woman. Heading for the sedan. Look!*

I jerked my head up to look and spilled perfectly good and not very hot coffee all over my jeans. "Crap! Double crap!" But I made myself look out at the target driveway. There was a woman about my height, maybe a little older than me, wearing a skirt that came to within an inch of her knees. She had on a grey jacket with what looked like a silver pin in the shape of a flying bird. Her hair was black, in some short, simple do. *She looks like my mother!*

Like Tracey twenty years ago, Paul corrected.

She unlocked the car door and slipped behind the wheel. Even though my hands were wet I grabbed for my binoculars. "D-R-P-zero-three-eight," I recited. hoping I'd remember the license plate number long enough to write it down. "Honda Accord. Mmm—gray? Brown? Crap, it's hard to tell." The tail lights popped on, and the woman backed the car onto Pakenham Drive, then drove north, out of sight.

"A wife?" Paul asked, surprised. "Hoodlums have wives?"

"Wives who go off to work in the morning," I added. I tossed the binocs onto the dry passenger seat, then tried to write down the tag number before I forgot it. A wet pen on wet paper did not cooperate, so I did my emergency backup and wrote it on the back of my left hand.

"May as well get the tag on the SUV," Paul said. I pulled my clipboard across my wet jeans to sop up some of the coffee off of the pad, readying it to accept my chewed-on pen. I held the binoculars with my right hand so Paul was free to use my left to write down the license plate number I dictated. In case you never have the experience, take my word for it—it is very weird to feel someone who is not yourself moving your hand from the inside.

"I'll get Walter to run a search on both of these tomorrow," I said. I folded my arms across my chest and slouched down in my seat, eyes on LY's front door.

Paul unscrewed the top of the thermos. *May I?* I heard him ask. I retreated inside to let him sip luke-warm coffee.

Excellent idea, I thought back. Except for the cold, wet spots on my pants, it was a boring morning, and caffeine might keep me upright.

It was a little before eleven when I saw the front door swing open. A short, stocky man in khakis and a pale yellow polo shirt turned to lock the door, then walked to the SUV. *What a runt!* I heard Paul think, *He's what, five foot nothing?* And he laughed inside.

He had a point. Walter's search with the police computer program said LY was five foot two, meaning I'd tower over him. On the other hand, he's a known bad guy with a reputation for slicing people who use his Christian name. *Short but dangerous*, I thought back. *We'll be cautious.*

He backed his Ford Explorer out of his driveway, then headed south, toward Judge Perez Drive. I counted to ten and started the car. Times like this I wish the diesel engine weren't so noisy.

I caught up to him at the traffic light at Judge Perez. Paul said, "Looks like he's playing drums on his steering wheel." There was no sign that he thought I was following him; I don't think he realized there was a car behind him. Good.

When the light changed LY turned right and headed upriver, toward town. Since rush hour was long past, traffic was light and it was easy to keep his SUV in sight from a few car lengths behind. "I hope he's a good little criminal and uses his turn signals," I said. "Otherwise he might shake me."

I expected him to get on the expressway, but instead he leaned to the right and went down Claiborne, the city street under and alongside the elevated I-10. He kept going past the Superdome, where the expressway veered west, but took a sudden left onto Earhardt Boulevard. He knew where he was going, so he was going faster than I was comfortable with. Still, I kept him in sight.

Paul asked, "Why does this look familiar?"

"We're near Goode At Law," I said. I ran a yellow light so I wouldn't lose my quarry. I followed LY when he made another turn, and we whipped past what everyone still called Lee Circle, even though the statue of the southern hero of the War of Northern Aggression had been pulled down twenty years earlier.

When LY turned into an alleyway off Poeyfarre, I kept going to make sure he didn't notice me. The hash of one-way streets meant I had to go around two blocks before I could return to his destination. I found a place to park about sixty feet beyond the alley. "We're here," I announced, "wherever here is." While I was feeding the parking meter, I heard Paul think, *We're at that bar.*

What bar?

That place where some geezer tried to pick you up the other day.

I could feel the mental database zipping through my half of my brain. Bar? Geezer? And then it struck me—*The 55th Fighter Group!*

Paul whispered, "I hope LY isn't tending bar. I want another one of those beers we had last time we were here."

Shush! I thought. *I'm on the job and I'm not drinking a beer now. I'm going to splurge on an overpriced oyster loaf.*

Well... I could feel the wheels turning on his side of my head. *If you let me lead for it, I'll drink the beer and you'll be fine.*

"Fine!" I hissed. *Now, be quiet so I can work.*

Someone had put a Santa hat on the mannequin soldier in the jeep, and the bar now was outlined in blinking colored Christmas lights. Even though several tables were occupied, the L-shaped bar was empty. I took the same stool I'd used last week, and waited for the bartender to notice he had a customer. *Squatters*, I heard Paul think. *That great beer was Squatters' something something.*

It was the same tattooed man behind the counter. "You're back!" he enthused. "You know, we're probably the only place in town with Squatters Outer Darkness."

"That's it!" Paul blurted out. "We want one of them."

I added, "Can a girl get a sandwich at the bar?" I batted my eyelashes, just for the practice.

"Sure enough. I'll get you—"

"A half oyster loaf," I interrupted. I watched the barkeep scramble for his order pad to write it down. "You get one side with that," he informed me.

I heard Paul think *Ooh! Fries! Or onion rings!* I imagined the calories and said, "How's your cole slaw?"

He smiled. "Barely a drop of mayo. We use vinegar."

"The magic words. Load me up."

"Let me get your Squatters—"

I interrupted again, "I'm still trying to warm up. It's chilly out there! Bring the beer with the sandwich, okay?"

He nodded as another customer sat at the other end of the bar. It was an older man, the collar on his coat turned up. He looked like a serious drinker.

I would have loved a head-start on the beer, my dyad informed me. *I'm not cold.*

I am. You'll have to wait.

From behind me I heard a man's voice say, "Paulette, is it?"

At the sound of his pseudonym Paul jumped to the lead and turned to face the man we had embarrassed last week. "Yep. That's me," he said. "Forgive me, I don't remember your name."

"Edgar," he said, as he boldly took the stool next to me. "You're the policewoman, right?"

Paul smiled and shook our head. "Private detective," he said. "I left the police force a few years ago."

There was a crash behind the bar as our tattooed publican dropped my bottle of Squatters' Outer Darkness. It was followed by a string of curses that probably made the mannequin soldier in the jeep feel as if he were back in Kuwait. Finally, he said, "Sorry. I'll get you a new one." Edgar and I watched him retreat to the corridor to the kitchen. *Hey*, I heard Paul say, *he's talking to our quarry.*

I shifted my focus. Sure enough, the bartender was huddled with the baddie I'd shadowed to this place. Paul thought, *Do you think he recognized us? Shit!*

I hope not. I'm hungry. I want that oyster loaf.

And I want that beer, he thought back. Then he turned back to Edgar and said, "I'm sorry, that distracted me. What were you saying?"

"I was saying it is a pleasure and a delight to see you again." He was fiddling with his bowtie. "I quite enjoyed our conversation last time, and I notice you do not have a file of work in front of you today."

"Yep," Paul nodded. "Finished that project. Haven't gotten paid for it yet."

Yes, we did. Melanie paid us when we turned it in. Weren't you paying attention?

Obviously not, he thought back. "What are you doing here in the middle of the day?" Paul asked Edgar.

"I told you I'm retired. The 55th Fighter Group is my Senior Center. Some of my friends—" he pointed at one of the tables in the back where three or four gentlemen were carrying on "—and I meet here most days. We're regulars."

"That's downright creative, Edgar. Beats the hell out of Bingo and origami classes."

"The food is better, too."

The barkeeper carefully placed my bottle of beer on the counter, and slid a plate with my sandwich and a ramekin of slaw next to it.

"Well, I don't want to interrupt your lunch," he said, standing up. "When you're done, you're welcome to join me and my friends. We'll take care of your drinks."

"We just might do that, Edgar," Paul replied, using that first person plural that often confuses people. It's because he thinks of him and me as being...well, I almost said 'joined at the hip,' but that barely covers it. Paul turned our attention to the meal on the bar. He lifted up the beer bottle to enjoy the color of the ceiling lights through it, then thought, *I don't remember this being cloudy.*

I paid attention. *It does look cloudy*, I thought back, *but I don't remember what it looked like last week.*

He shrugged and took a very long swallow; about one third of the Squatters' Outer Darkness now was in the inner darkness of my stomach. Paul enthused, *Every bit as good as I recalled. This—this is grade-A beer, right here.* And he took another long draught.

Easy, boy, I thought. *My sandwich is getting cold.* Born and bred as I was in New Orleans—well, Metairie, but that's quibbling—I ignored the knife and fork. I grabbed both long sides of the oyster loaf and took a big bite from one end. I could feel remoulade sauce escaping down my chin, but so what? There is nothing, absolutely nothing, as delicious as a freshly fried Louisiana oyster surrounded by lettuce, that sauce, and a crusty baguette. I don't eat an oyster loaf or a shrimp loaf often because of calories and carbs, but when I do, I absolutely savor it.

You want a bite?

Sure. You want some of this Squatters?

While Paul sampled my po-boy I thought, *No beer for me while I'm working. I need to figure out how to get inside this place.*

We are inside it. Aren't we? He drained the bottle.

I shook my head. *What's LY doing here? What does this bar have to do with a maybe white slaver making George decide to burn down his own warehouse?*

My guess iss muh-muh-money cleaning.

"What?" I was so startled I actually said it out loud.

You know, mun-mun-munnnney, uh—

I put down the sandwich. *Please tell me you're not having a stroke!*

Is it me or is the room spinnn—spinnn—spinning?

Granted, the stout was almost eleven percent alcohol, but this was unprecedented. I've endured Paul splitting a bottle of Everclear with a cajun and it took him an hour to pass out.[35] *What's wrong?* I asked.

---

[35] *The Wedding Fatality* by the one and only A. Trauring. Short spoiler: Everclear

Uh. Wow. Sleepy. Huh. Tell—tell Christine—

There was silence. I poked Paul inside, something we can do, but nothing came back. Either he was asleep or dead. I didn't like either option.

And it dawned on me. Our Squatters was spiked.

"Ready for another brew?" I wanted to reach into the bartender's smiling mouth and pull his tattooed left lung out, but I decided to pretend I was fine. After all, I was fine. And he doesn't know Paul exists.

"One's enough this early in the day," I said with a smile. "Oyster loaf is great. Can I get a doggie bag for the rest of it?"

"You're sure you're good to drive?"

"Why wouldn't I be?" I stood up and opened my wallet on the bar. "What do I owe you?"

I could imagine what he was thinking: 'That roofie was enough to knock out an elephant.' And I knew what I was thinking: If you hurt Paul I will come back and remove that death's head tattoo on your arm with a blowtorch and a pair of pliers.

The bartender took a Styrofoam clamshell from under the counter and handed it to me. "With the Squatters, that's, uh, $18.75."

Left over oyster loaf in the Styrofoam, and a twenty on the bar. "Thanks. Be seeing you."

"Are you sure you're feeling okay?"

I ignored him. I patted the manikin soldier on my way to the front door.

Crap. Double crap. I walked up Poeyfarre toward my old Benz. *How did I blow my cover? Did LY notice me tailing him?* I wished Paul were awake, I needed to talk to him.

As I drove off, I tried to rewind my time at the 55th Fighter Group. Got there. Ordered the sandwich and beer. The barkeep seemed to remember me from last week. Then Edgar came over, he remembered Paulette. And... and it came back to me. Edgar said he

---

is a cross between rat poison and napalm.

remembered I was a police detective. Granted, I'm a thin white woman, but I'm 37 years old and I doubt I'm on anyone's wish list to be sold into slavery. The bartender must have heard Edgar, he must have told LY, and spiking my drink was their response.

I was headed back to Cody's place. While I waited for the traffic light at Napoleon to change, I beat on my steering wheel. Cover blown! Suddenly it was too dangerous for me to pursue LY on my own. Crap! What was I going to do? *Paul, wake up!* I shouted silently, but there was a 'gone fishing' sign on his half of my head. Crap-and-a-half!

I parked across the street as Cody was saying goodbye to his clients, who appeared to be the two high school senior girls and somebody's mother. I stood by the Benz until the customers were safely in their car before I walked up the semi-circular driveway to meet Cody. I was in no mood to pretend to be nice to strangers.

"How did it go?" he asked, arms outstretched for a hug I needed badly. I walked into his arms and whispered, "They doped Paul."

"They what?"

I was glad he didn't release me. "I followed the man who's been deviling your dad. He's based in a bar in the CBD. I went in to reconnoiter, and the bartender put a roofie in my beer."

Cody hugged me tighter. "And you're okay?" he asked. He sounded more confused than worried.

"Paul drank the beer, I didn't have any of it. After a while he started talking funny and then he conked out." I grabbed Cody tighter. "If he leads, I don't get the impact, whether it's food or drink or—" umm, not ready to talk about sex yet "—or whatever. And I don't like it when he's out of commission like this." I shrugged one shoulder to catch a drip from my nose. So, we stood like that for maybe a minute. It helped me feel better. And Cody smelled good.

Finally, he said, "I've got one more client coming. Come help me set up." He took my hand and we walked into the house.

I babbled on, how I was angry at myself for letting my cover be blown. "Doesn't sound like it was your fault," he said while rearranging his props in front of a scrim. "And that old man, even though he said you were a police detective, he didn't know that was a secret."

"I know," I moaned, feeling a certain amount of self-loathing. "Edgar is a sweetheart. He's brave to strike up a conversation with a woman half his age. Quite the gentleman."

"See? Stop beating yourself up," he said. I looked up at Cody to see the kind smile on his angular face. "Stuff happens."

After a moment I responded, "It sure does."

We heard Donna call, "Cody! Your client is here!"

"I'll get her," I said, and went down the hall to the living room, where Donna was talking to a dark-haired woman about my age, wearing a gray wool dress with a black jacket.

"Hey, Donna," I said, "who's your friend?"

The woman turned to face me as Donna said, "Amy, this is Regan. Cody should be expecting her."

"Nice to meet you," I said, and put my hand on her arm. "Will you come this way?"

As we walked, Regan swiveled her head, taking in the dark wood paneling and framed prints in the hallway. "This is nice," she exclaimed.

"Thank you," I chirped. "We like it." I heard the words come out of my mouth and realized I was behaving as if I were a Locaviche. Down, girl; it's a little early for that.

When we got to the studio, Cody limped over to the woman and said, "Regan, is it? It's nice to meet you." They exchanged pleasantries until Cody said, "What are you looking for today?"

"My husband and I are going to Mardi Gras in Brazil next spring," she answered. "I need passport photos."

He smiled and said, "If I take the lens cap off my camera, I have to charge fifty dollars. When I applied for my passport, I paid fifteen dollars at the CVS up on Claiborne. It took ten minutes and they handed the prints to me."

The woman looked confused. "So—you don't want to do this?"

"I would have to charge you three times what CVS will." Cody held out a business card. "Save that money now, and call me when you want a portrait or a family picture or something."

Regan took the card, still holding it with her arm extended. "Wow," she said. "Since when do photographers send a customer elsewhere?"

"Since they would rather have your long-term business." He was smiling, that adorable round smile in his angular face. "I'd love to work with you when you have a need that CVS can't meet."

I realized my mouth was open. Cody must have been sincere, or why would he say no to fifty dollars? He really was looking out for his customers. Not that I had thought about it beforehand, but I guess I didn't expect this. Oh, my mom will love him when she meets him!

So, I walked Regan back to the living room and the front door. She asked, "Does he do this often?"

"He really cares about his clients," I answered. I did not add that I was as surprised and pleased as she was.

We said goodbye on the top step, then I went back to Cody's studio. He was stowing equipment and generally tidying up. "That was super considerate," I said. "Regan was impressed."

"Impressed enough to come back with a real project, I hope," he said. "Passport photos are not high art. The drugstore will do her fine."

"Now what?" I asked. He looked at me with one raised eyebrow. "I need to talk to Duke when he brings your dad back. I mean, uh—" What did I mean? "—I mean, in the meantime."

Cody laughed, then he put down the lighting umbrella to come give me a hug. "Let's go sit in the backyard. It's a decent day for December." He stopped, then said, "You can wear one of my jackets."

I nodded against him, because even though I started out early enough to be at Cody's by seven, I had neglected any outerwear. New Orleans winters have highs in the low sixties, which may sound balmy to you, but we're used to triple digits from May to September. To us, sixty degrees requires blankets, GoreTex parkas, and smudge pots.

I felt sheepish, sticking my arms in his denim jacket while he gallantly held it up for me. Considering how much taller and bigger he is, my hands disappeared in the sleeves. I wrapped it around myself and followed Cody through the kitchen, to the laundry room, and the newly installed back door.

It was sunny, but the steady breeze from the Mississippi River a mile away kept things chilly. We sat on a wrought iron bench that faced a sundial and, at the end of the yard, the barely begun new fence.

"Still no Paul?" he asked, his arm around me.

"Still no Paul," I repeated. "Thanks for keeping me company while he's unconscious. I haven't spent a lot of time alone since I was eleven years old."

I felt him nod silently. We sat, his arm around me and me snuggling against him to keep warm. Oh, who am I kidding? I was snuggling against him to snuggle against him. But the body heat was welcome, too.

Finally, I said, "Tell me about the bad girl."

"Bad girl? What bad girl?"

"That woman you almost married, but she—"

"Oh!" he interrupted. "Rachel. Not really bad. Just..." and he trailed off.

I poked him in the ribs. "Just what?"

"Just...unprepared."

I sat up, leaning away so I could look at him. "After that, you have got to tell me the whole story."

He laughed, then pulled me closer again as he told me about Rachel.

"When I was in my early 30s I worked for Stanwyck Photography. I did a lot of weddings and industrial, and a little bit of commercial. I got hired to take pictures of a new building Campus Oil had finished. Rachel was their PR person. She's the one who set up the shoot and hired me."

"Love at first sight?" I volunteered.

"Ummm—more like lust at first sight. But six months later we were living together in St. Claude. We had half a double. Funky area, but we got along with the neighborhood, and we sure got along with each other. Her family was from Venezuela, so I learned Spanish. We didn't set a date, but we knew we were going to marry each other."

Why was I feeling pins and needles? Cody was talking about ancient history. I'm not in a competition with this woman. Hey, I'm the person who accepts him, voice and all. This should be easy. Oh, I wish Paul were awake!

"Then came the accident. Three years ago. A woman T-boned my car on the way to a photo shoot. She got killed, and my left leg was crushed." He lifted his leg and slapped at it. "I was in and out of Ochner for five months. Rachel was a champ—she visited me every day, then looked after me when I got sent home."

"That sounds pretty good, under the circumstances," I said. My stomach was sinking, the way it did when I had a crush on Officer Kowalski and Paul would insist on asking after his wife's health.

I felt him nod. "Then came the voices. The voice, actually—just the one. I was sure I was going insane. It seriously scared me. I didn't handle it very well. And after a month or so of that, Rachel announced she was moving out. She just could not deal with what both of us thought was her bonkers fiancé."

"So much for sounding good."

I felt him let out a big sigh. "She moved into town, took an apartment with some of the other nursing students. I was still in physical therapy and couldn't walk much. I couldn't take care of myself, so I came back here. Mother was as worried as I was, but, you know, she was a grown woman who was better at dealing with the surprises life throws at you than Rachel or I was."

"Do you still talk to her?"

"We did for a little while, but I was a mess. She gave up. Last I heard from her was maybe two years ago. She sent me an invitation to her wedding. Some guy in Biloxi." He shook his head, then looked up at me with a grim smile. "I sent her a toaster."

I held him tighter, trying to offer some sort of comfort. I was elated that Cody had opened up to me like this, and that Rachel was safely in his past. We sat silently for a minute or two, listening to Caleb's crew laying bricks and feeling the setting December sun on our backs, while I wondered how I could return his intimacy. Before I could think of anything he said, "Is Paul back yet?"

I shook my head, then looked up at the side of his face. "This is such a relief. You know about Paul. I don't have to hide him."

"Well, you know I hear a voice."

Ahh. Intimacy equilibrium.

"Tonight Paul and I are supposed to visit his girlfriend. She won't—"

"Whoa, what? Paul has a girlfriend?" Cody pulled away to turn and look at me. I put my hand on his thigh as I started to explain. This is too early for him to ask if I'm bisexual. Crap, but I wish I could talk to Paul.

"Yes. Christine. Didn't he tell you he had a squeeze? She's my best buddy. Outside of my family, you and she are the only people I don't have to hide Paul from." I swear, I could see wheels turning behind Cody's eyes. "They've been together for years."

There was a long, ominous pause before he said, "Will I get to meet this girlfriend?"

"If you play your cards right," I answered.

Well, that was awkward. Crap, I wish I could talk to Paul! I wish Paul could talk to Cody. There was some more silence. Finally, I said, in all honesty, "I'm getting cold. Can we go inside?"

"Sure." When we stood up, Cody took my hand and led me to the back door into the laundry room. We heard Donna wrangling pots and pans in the adjoining kitchen.

"Mom, do you need any help?"

"Not unless you remember where I put the colander," she said, squinting into a cabinet next to the stove.

"Where haven't you looked yet?" I asked, and headed for the cabinet next to where she was looking. "A colander, you say?"

"Thank you, dear. Two sets of eyes work better than one. It's a red plastic thing."

Cody limped off in the direction of his studio. I ransacked three or four cupboards before Donna cried, "There it is!" She retrieved it from a drawer and held it up proudly.

"Collapsable?" I said. "You didn't tell me that. I never would have found it."

"I appreciate you looking to help," she smiled. She rinsed it in the sink as she added, "Steamed vegetables with dinner. You're staying, of course."

Oh, that made me feel good. When you like new people—and not just because they write you checks—and they like you, it's that secure feeling of acceptance, of belonging. I'm not neurotic or anything, but does anyone get enough of that emotion? Still, I had to say, "Actually, I have plans with a gal pal tonight."

"Tomorrow, then."

"Uhh—I guess Cody didn't mention it. He and I were going to get dinner tomorrow at a place I know uptown."[36] She didn't respond, so I added, "Please don't hate me. You're a great cook, and you've been treating me so well, and—"

"It's okay, Amy." I watched her shake the colander dry. "Wednesday is my night for church choir. Usually, Cody and George call for a pizza, I think."

---

[36] As already noted, the definition of "uptown" in New Orleans is upriver. Considering where the Locaviches live, uptown would be west and north. If we were in the French Quarter, it would be south. And you thought your town was strange.

I couldn't help myself: I hugged Donna. "Thank you," I managed to say.

"Off you go now," she said, shooing me out of the kitchen. "I've got to get dinner ready. George will be home soon and I know you'll want to hear if anything happened at work."

"Yes, ma'am," I said as I left the room. Why did I hug her? Why am I feeling so, so, so what? Crap, I wish Paul were awake.

I found my way back to Cody's studio, but he wasn't there. The room was tidy and dark. I sat near 'my' faux Tiffany lamp and turned it on. The multi-colored glow from the shade was peaceful. Even so, my thoughts bounced back and forth from relaxation to near panic over Paul's incapacitation.

I heard noise, loud noise, from the living room. Before I knew it, I had my pistol in my right hand and I was crouched down, carefully working my way toward the sounds while trying to present the smallest possible target. The front door opened and Duke's usually smooth voice was sharp. "...do that again and I'll leave your ass on the side of the road!"

"It was just for half an hour," George argued. "I didn't—"

"Half an hour? It would take me half a minute to shank you."

I laughed at the argument that most bodyguards have at least once with each client. I holstered Roscoe and said, "Is this a private fight or can anyone throw a punch?"

"You!" Duke shouted, pointing a huge index finger at me. "Queenie, you didn't tell me your client has the brains of a bag of hammers."

"That's not—"

"Yes it is! What kind of moron hires a bodyguard and then ditches him? I ask you, is—"

"Stop!" I shouted. Both men closed their mouths and turned to me.

"Duke. What happened?" When George started to say something, I held my palm out to him and said, "Shush. You'll get your turn. Duke?"

"Everything was going great. I checked out the other agents in his office, they're cool. I watched our client take a few phone calls and make a few hundred. Around eleven-ten I ducked out to take a leak, and when I got back to the office he was gone."

I nodded, and turned to George. "Is that what happened?"

"I think I got more calls than I made."

Frowning, I responded, "Deflection detected and rejected. Did you slip your leash?"

The man hung his head. "Well. Yeah," he mumbled. Duke, arms crossed in front of his massive chest, broke into a satisfied smile. "Damn right," he added.

"Is that a smart thing to do?" I asked, remembering how my sister Kaylee used to deal with her kids when they were little and did stupid things. "Like Duke said, to hire a bodyguard and then get away from him?"

"It was personal," George retorted.

Duke observed, "So is a knife under the fourth rib. I am not going to waste my time ruining my reputation if you won't let me guard your damn body. If you—"

I thought to Duke, *Let me go first*. He spun toward me in surprise, then remembered our case together on NOPD.[37] "Right," he muttered. "Ventriloquist."

By this time Donna was in the living room, still drying a saucepan with a dish towel. I asked, "What was so personal you had to get away from the man who is saving your life?"

There was a very long pause, while Donna tilted her head and stared at her husband. Finally, George said, "Can we discuss this outside?" Donna threw the towel to the floor, and walked the pot back to the kitchen.

A lightbulb began to glimmer over my head, and Duke looked as if he was putting two and two together. "Good idea, George," I said. "Let's."

---

[37] Surely you have read *The Wedding Fatality*. No? Do so, as soon as you finish reading this book. You know you want to...

The sun was beginning to set off towards Texas, and the breeze had gotten chilly. As we stood in the middle of the semi-circular driveway—Duke was leaning against his black Hummer—I began our come to Jesus session. "We don't care if you are having an affair," I said. "I don't pass judgement on you over the fire, although I would not lie to a judge for you. What matters is keeping you safe. That's what you pay us for."

"It's not very romantic to have a big black guy standing next to you while you're getting it on with a woman. Uh, no offense, Duke."

"None taken." My colleague was grinning. "I'm not a monster. I can wait outside your motel room while you're knocking boots, but first I want to clear the room."

"And if we can keep this among ourselves? I'd hate for Donna to know."

Duke and I exchanged looks. He was the one who said, "I think that boat has sailed."

George looked heavenward and sighed, "Oh, no." Then, "Amy, she likes you. Could you..."

I shook my head. "I'm a private investigator, not a marriage counselor. I'm afraid you're on your own for that."

The poor man stood there, dejected: tie pulled loose and to one side, sport jacket wrinkled, and eyes fixed intently on the cement of the driveway. Duke took pity on him and said, "See you at 7:15 tomorrow, right?" Without looking up, George nodded. "We good, then?" Again, our client nodded.

"I'm going inside," George said. "There's some music I have to face." We watched him walk up the seven steps to the front door, looking like a condemned man heading for the gallows.

When George was gone, Duke started laughing and hugged me. "I think we put the fear of God in him," he chuckled. "Why does every client try this shit?"

"That they do," I answered. "It must be in the contract somewhere. Thanks for calling shenanigans on him."

"I don't envy him that talk he's having with the missus."

I snorted, which surprised me—I did not know women could do that. "He brought it on himself."

Then I shifted thoughts. "Look, there's news. I'm pretty sure I found LY this morning and tailed him. He runs a bar in the CBD. The bartender heard a customer I know call me a cop, and he tried to drug my beer. I was going to describe the guy to George to confirm it, but we got sidetracked."

"A Mickey? Queenie, how'd you get past that?"

"You know me, Duke. I'm tougher than I look."

"Shee-it," he exclaimed. "I got dosed at a whorehouse in Tréme before I signed on to NOPD. Woke up with a headache from hell and a big nothing where my wallet had been."

"The headache hasn't kicked in yet," I said, "but I expect it at any minute."

He pulled his car keys out of his pocket. "I'm going to listen to music until Lester gets here."

"Great!" I said. "I need to leave, so you brief him. And tell him starting tomorrow night I'll be using the bedroom he'll be sleeping in during the day, so tell him to make the bed."

"'Night, Queenie." He hoisted himself up and into his Hummer. I heard a split second of some noise that he must think of as music before he mercifully slammed the door.

I sat on the top step and made the phone call I'd been dreading since Paul was drugged. "Good evening, Christine. Can I come over? Like, now?"

"Of course, Amy. Make sure you bring Paulette with you. Can I talk to her?"

"Actually, no, you can't. We were—"

"What do you mean, I can't? Paulette? Are you okay?"

"Paul got drugged while we were on a stakeout," I said. Lying to make myself feel better, I went on, "He'll be fine, but he isn't fine right now."

There was a whimper on the phone line.

"Getting doped isn't permanent," I went on. "He'll have a headache when he wakes up, and he probably won't remember the beer that did him in."

"You come over!" Christine exclaimed. "I want to be with her when she wakes up. Oh, Amy, are <u>you</u> okay?" Bless her heart, she cares about me, too.

"I'm fine. Maybe you can help me work up a game plan for tomorrow."

"You know I'll help if I can," she said. "But you come over right now. You hear me, right this instant."

"Yes, ma'am," I said. "I just need to find Cody to tell him I'm leaving. Leave a light on for me."

I was surprised to find Donna in the kitchen, stirring pots and finishing dinner. George was sitting on one of the stools at the island. There were no obvious signs of additional blunt trauma to his head, although his face still showed the damage LY and company inflicted. "I'm heading out," I informed them. "Duke's in the driveway, waiting on our overnight guy. Where's Cody?"

"What?" Donna asked. "Oh, he's probably meditating in his room. You can let him know it's almost dinner time."

I sidled over to George and whispered, "You all right?" He nodded with a smile that showed all his teeth were intact. Having never been married, I don't understand how couples are able to cope with things like infidelity. I hope I never have to find out.

Cody wasn't in the studio. So, I went up a flight of stairs and began to explore the mysterious second floor of Schloss Locaviche. The hall had thick, light green carpet, and a subtle flowered wallpaper. I passed the open door of what looked like the master bedroom, then went past the humongous bathroom—was that a Jacuzzi? Finally, I came to a closed door with light showing under it, and the sound of Indian raga music that Paul had introduced me to. Timidly, I knocked; then I pushed the door open, slowly.

Cody was sitting on his bed, his back to me. As best I could tell he was in that stereotypical meditation posture: cross legged, his hands on his knees, with thumbs and index fingers making circles. I hated to disturb him, but I had to leave and I needed to make sure we were okay after our little discussion about Paul's girlfriend.

I cleared my throat.

Without appearing to move, he said, "Yes, Amy?"

"Donna says it's dinner time. And I'm off for the night. See you tomorrow morning, right?"

He swung around on the bed, sitting on the edge with his bare feet touching the floor. He had changed into jeans shorts. "Sure," he said. Then he added, "Give my regards to Paul's lover. Tell her I'm looking forward to meeting her."

The eternal seventeen-year-old inside me felt a flood of relief. We were still on track to end up boyfriend and girlfriend. I ran over to him and knocked him back on his bed, planting a kiss full on his lips. "Sure will," I said. It happened too fast for him to respond; he seemed still to be a little stunned when I stood back up. "That's where I'm heading now. See you in the morning."

Cody held his arms out for me, so I walked into them while he still sat on his bed. His arms around me felt good. He nuzzled against my stomach, and I think he kissed my sweatshirt somewhere between bellybutton and boobs. "Thanks," he said.

I kissed the top of his head. "Sure. Gotta go."

One encouraging thing happened on the drive up to Christine's. I heard Paul groan a couple of times, even though he never did respond to my pokes. Christine would be glad to hear he was making progress. God knows I was.

When I parked in the alleyway alongside her double, Christine was on the porch, vibrating with anticipation. "Amy! You're finally here! Paulette! Where's Paulette?"

"In here somewhere," I answered as I got out of my car. "Help me find him."

Once inside Christine's home, I told her about Paul's groans. "He's going to be okay," I said. "Dead people don't groan. I don't remember if it's Sister Agnetha at St. Giles Academy or my dad in his emergency room taught me that."

Christine hefted a bottle of shiraz, but I shook my head. "Alcohol got Paul into this problem. I want to wait for him to wake up before I have any."

"Oh," she said, simply. She put the wine down on a counter top. While she poured water into a kettle to make tea she asked, "You say Paulette got drugged? What happened?"

I told her about shadowing LY, about following him to the 55th Fighter Group, about old sweetie Edgar, and about the spiked beer. "Paul said he thought the beer was cloudy, but he drank it anyway. Ten minutes later he was talking strange and then he passed out."

"Oh, my poor Paulette," she said. She took a chair next to mine and put her hand on my arm. "Is she waking up yet?"

I shook my head. "Not yet." Then, "So, how was your day?"

"Real estate is slow in December, but tomorrow I get to show two boys some places in town."

"I thought you stuck to the west bank."

"Yeah, usually. But they want a gay friendly area. There are some houses in Marigny and Bywater they can afford." Her smile collapsed as she added, "But in Orleans Parish I only get six percent. Still, it'll be a nice end-of-the-year bonus."

I admit I am envious of Christine's second career, as a real estate agent. When I left the New Orleans PD to hang a shingle as a private investigator, Christine was just the receptionist at her agency; I tried to bully her into working for me. But it was just as she was taking courses and working on her real estate license. Paul is proud of her success, and so am I. But I'm jealous because she is better at finding business and closing the sale and making money than I am. I don't really know how much she made this year, but I know how much I didn't. Can you be jealous and sincerely happy for someone at the same time? The answer is yes and I am exhibit A.

"Is Paulette awake yet?"

"Do you have an egg timer?" I asked.

Christine looked at me oddly. "You want eggs for dinner?"

"No, just an egg timer. And I promise I won't eat it."

She kept staring at me, even as she stood up and backed her way to that drawer every kitchen has, with all the gadgets you don't use twice in a year. Finally breaking her intense look at me, she rifled through the drawer and came up with a small hourglass. "Okay," she said as she came back to the table, "an egg timer. Now what?"

I took the little plastic tool from her, then set it down on the table with a loud bang. "When it runs out," I said, "ask me again about Paul. Believe me, I'll let you know if he wakes up before then."

"Oh," Christine said quietly. She looked smaller than usual, sitting in that chair. I had meant to make her calm down about Paul, but she seemed to take it as chastisement. "He'll be with us in no time," I said, as much to convince myself as her. "Really."

"Well, if I can't ask after her—" her eyes were on the hourglass "—can I get us dinner? I've got some sausage and potatoes and—"

I interrupted. "Paul's asleep. Can we have a salad instead?"

Christine's face lit up. She was a good sport about Paul's preference for meat with two sides of more meat, but her taste was more like mine. She opened the refrigerator door and started pulling out packages, of lettuce, arugula, tomatoes, cucumbers, chives. "I don't remember," she asked, "are you still off mushrooms?"

"Are they store-bought?"

"Well, yeah!" She turned to face me, one hand on her hip. "I'm not farming them in the crawl space by the glow of the water heater pilot light."

"Store-bought, that's good." I had quit eating any mushrooms after a client had picked some death caps to poison his nephew.[38] I will never trust another 'shroom picked by an amateur.

---

[38] See *The Strawberry Birthmark*. The author admires friend Cindy for her courage in foraging for morels, but none for me, thanks.

"I'll help," I said, standing up. "Give me a cutting board and a knife. Tomatoes?"

Christine slid them across the counter to me, and got herself fresh utensils. As she began chopping the green onions she said, "Is it time? Is Paulette okay?"

Understand, Christine is my best friend. Even so, she can be so literal that it makes me laugh. "No Paul yet," I said, and made a dramatic flourish to turn over the hourglass. "Ask me again in three minutes."

While we prepared the salad, she said, "Now the bad guys know who you are. What are you going to do next?"

"I want to draft Cody. I can wire him so I can monitor him and talk to him from my car. He's a photographer, so he can get pictures—I don't know maybe even a GoPro camera. I want to make sure the man I think is LY really is. And maybe Cody's dad can tell us who the bartender is."

Christine poured all the chopped and torn veggies into a bowl and stirred with a wooden spoon. Not the way I would toss a salad, but no one would confuse me with Paula Deen. I got plates and forks and set the table for us.

When we dug in, I was surprised by how flavorful the tomatoes were. "Are you growing your own?" I asked around my mouthful of salad.

"Not in December, no. Not even in New Orleans," Christine said. "Last week I stopped at the Crescent City Farmers' Market at Bayou St John. Heirloom tomatoes look ugly, but they sure taste good."

I dropped my fork when a headache began. Christine said, "Is everything okay, Amy?" I guess she took a second look at me, because she went on, "What's wrong? Is Paulette okay?"

I rubbed my temples, trying to massage the pain away. "I think Paul will be awake soon," I said. "He's going to have a major headache, and that's why I'm getting one."

"But—Wait. You've told me how you work. If Paulette leads, she's the one who gets drunk, or tastes the food. Why would you have her headache?"

I was still rubbing my head. "My doctor dad says dilated blood vessels cause the pain of a headache. Paul and I use the same arteries and veins."

"Your father said that? Or was it that Sister Agnes?"

Despite the pain, I laughed. "Sister Agnetha. She said she had been part of a music group in Sweden. She called herself the dancing queen."

The headache was getting worse, which was starting to frighten me. "Either Paul's about to wake up, or I'm having an aneurysm," I said. "I think—" I left the chair and lay down on the linoleum floor "—I think I'm going to retreat and let Paul take over."

"What should I do?" Christine asked, sounding scared. "Bandages? Boiling water?"

"It's a headache, not a baby. Maybe an ice pack?"

Retreating is not unconsciousness; it's just letting Paul lead. I could feel the headache, and the hard floor, and some pressure in my ears. I was thinking just how much I did not want to die on Christine's kitchen floor when I heard a wobbly *Oooh. Damn but my head...*

Paul! I shouted silently. Even though my head felt like it was breaking in half I was relieved to hear his voice. *Say something. Anything!*

What happened? Where am I? Why is there an anvil on my head?

Yes, my head hurts, too. It is wonderful to hear your voice.

Paul hadn't opened our eyes yet, but I felt him trying to lift ourself up on one elbow. "We were following that guy, and then— where are we?"

I imagine Christine was shedding tears of joy over her Paulette demonstrating the absence of death. I heard her say, "Paulette, what can I do?"

He opened one eye. "Chris—Christine! What are you doing here?"

"I live here, you big silly."

He opened the other eye, which was looking in a slightly different direction from the first one, and turned our head. Christine's Qantas poster with the kangaroo came into focus for a second. "Oh. So you do." We were sitting up on both elbows, while Christine patted our face. "Oh. Ouch! What am I doing here?"

I saw the ecstatic smile on her face before she hugged us, or her Paulette. Rocking, she whispered, "I was so worried. But you're back. You're okay. I love you."

I could feel Paul hugging her back. Christine's giggle told me he had thought something to her, which I couldn't hear. Then he said, "Honey, I need a glass of water and a couple of Advil. And why am I lying on the floor?"

I spoke up. "I put us here," I said. "I wasn't sure what was going to happen and I didn't want to fall out of the chair."

"Like The Doctor regenerating.[39] Can we get up now?"

"Sure." Christine started tugging our hands and shoulders. *Up we go, big guy*, I thought. It took a minute, but I ended up back in my old chair. The remains of my salad were in front of us.

"Do you know what happened?" he asked Christine. "Amy?"

"I missed you!" I said. "Aside from our mutual migraine, are you okay?"

"I don't know yet. Oh, thanks—" Christine had the water and pills "—I remember tailing the guy in the SUV, and then...and then nothing." I felt him shiver. "It's like when Lazlo did that hypno-thingy on me to see what I remembered from getting knocked into a coma."[40] He gulped the tablets, then drank the entire glass of water.

Inside I came forward to lead. "How's your headache?" I asked.

---

[39] The Doctor. *Doctor Who*? Precisely! As an adolescent Paul was a total geek.
[40] See *A Different Kind of Twin*. It's where the adventure began.

"Eleven or twelve on a scale of one-to-ten. Yours?" Christine was sitting next to us. When she knew Paul was leading, she rubbed our shoulder or patted our face; when I led, she just held us by the arm.

"Only an eight, but that's bad enough."

"So, what the hell happened? Oww, oww, oww."

I recapped our morning. "You said you thought that beer looked cloudy, but you drank it anyway. Next time trust your instincts."

"I don't remember any of this. So, the barkeep heard that geezer call you a cop, the barkeep dropped a perfectly good beer on the floor, then brought you one with a Mickey Finn?"

"Of some sort, yes." Even though my head hurt, I smiled as I added, "The bartender was annoyed that it didn't work on me. He kept asking, 'Are you sure you're okay to drive?'"

After a few seconds of silence, Christine said, "What an adventure, Paulette. It's things like this that make me worry for you."

"I never used to believe women who said 'Not tonight, I have a headache.' Is it too late to apologize? Please forgive me, Honey," he said. "I know I just woke up, but I feel like hammered armadillo squeezings. All I want to do is take a nap. Maybe until Friday."

"Sounds good to me," I said. "Christine, can we have an ice pack and a towel?

"Sure," and she jumped up to grab a dishtowel and to take some flexible blue artificial ice from her freezer. She followed us to the bedroom, and wrapped that stuff around our head.

You know how hard it is to fall asleep when your head hurts? But when you finally drift off, so does the pain. Besides, Paul was back. It was going to be okay.

☄ WEDNESDAY, DECEMBER 17, 2036 ☄

The next morning wasn't bad. Yes, I had a headache, but it was the kind that you forget about it as long as you're concentrating on something else. It's only when you finish a task that you remember there's a dull ache at the back of your head, just on top of your neck. Paul was not so lucky. "It's down to a six," he said on the drive to Cody's. "Improvement, but it still feels like I've been crowned with a spike right through my head."[41] Glad that's just a metaphor!

George was all contrite this morning, promising not to slip his leash again. Donna seemed her usual sunny self, so whatever George's indiscretion, it doesn't seem to have blown up their marriage. How do women deal with an unfaithful husband? I can't imagine. I don't want to imagine.

I told Cody I wanted to draft him into protecting his father. He had some sessions this morning, but said he's all mine after one o'clock. I hoped he wasn't teasing.

Paul still felt bad, and for some reason I was exhausted. I slipped into the bedroom that will be mine for a nap, but Lester got there first. So, I went into the living room and took off my shoes, then lay down on the sofa. It's big and comfortable. So much so, that I woke up hearing Cody explaining to a departing client that his

---

[41] Paul was unusual in that he liked the Rolling Stones as much as he liked the Beatles. His sister was a Beatle fan, but she hated the Stones. Too ugly.

'colleague was recuperating from a late-night assignment,' and that the staff doesn't usually sleep in the living room in the middle of the day. I pretended I was still asleep, but I have a feeling my face glowed red with embarrassment.

After he closed the door behind his client, he sat by me on the edge of the sofa and repeated, "I'm all yours."

Smiling, I opened my eyes and put my arms around his waist. "Goodie," I said.

Cody petted my hair for a few moments; it felt warm, intimate, safe. Finally, I began, "You're camera man. I've got audio gear. I want to wire you up and send you into 55th Fighter Group."

I heard Paul think, *Does he get a badge? A secret cyanide capsule?*

"You get a pretty good lunch at that place."

"Lunch is good," Cody responded. "What's the plan?"

I sat up and rubbed my face, making myself wake up completely. "We're thinking LY is probably a white slaver. We need to go to the 55th Fighter Group, and then you need to go upstairs, or wherever they keep their prostitutes, and talk to one. Get enough information to nail LY. I'll record what you see and hear."

"Okay," he said. "And then what?"

"Then you leave, safe and sound, and we go to dinner."

He frowned, creasing all the angles on his face. "Is it really that simple?"

"Sometimes." I was wearing a huge smile. "Not always. But I'm still alive and kicking, you know?"

"Olay," he said. "What do I do?"

"I've got some things in my trunk. You get your camera. I'll get the software, and I'll meet you in your studio."

That stuff's in your trunk because you didn't know where to put it at home, Paul thought.

Yes. The car is part storage-shed. That's why there's hardly room for groceries.

Paul was teasing me, but it was fair—the trunk of my Benz was a mess of overnight bags, a battery charger, two tire inflators, emergency flares, field rations, first-aid kit, fire extinguisher, a spare 9mm pistol, and clothes either for or from the dry cleaner, I couldn't remember which. Somewhere in this clutter was a thumb drive with a piece of surveillance software I'd pirated from NOPD back in the day. I stacked things on the sidewalk next to the car, with Paul's silent howls of laughter as the soundtrack. Finally, nestled in a snake's den of bungee cords, I found the yellow and white 16 gigabyte Lexar jump drive. "Come to mama," I said aloud, and put it in my left front pocket.

You go back, Paul thought. *I'll put all this crap back in the trunk*. Yes, we joke about the way we are linked together at the brain. "No, I'll stay and watch," I said.

When he was done, my trunk was just as chaotic as before— except for the surveillance software in my pocket. Before I locked the car, I retrieved my laptop from the back seat.

Cody was sitting behind his studio desk that was piled high with camera gear. "Can I push this a little," I said, shoving gently to make room for my laptop. While it booted I presented the flash drive and said, "This is what I've got for audio."

Spreading his hands wide, he said, "This is what I've got for video."

Paul said, "What, no Betamax?" I thought *Huh?* about the same time Cody made the same sound out loud. I don't know if Cody grasped that it was Paul who said, "I forget, you two are such babies."

"What?" Cody said. "I'm thirty-eight, and you're..." waiting for me to fill in the blank.

"Paul's a geezer," I offered as explanation. "He and Abe Lincoln used to argue politics. Never mind the beta-whatsits, what do you have here?"

"Go-Pro," Cody said, lifting the common movie camera.

"Hard to conceal," I said.

Next, he held up a pair of horn-rimmed eyeglasses. He stuck his fingers through the lens-less openings. "Point-of-view glasses. A camera is in the front of the right earpiece. It transmits to a computer." I heard Paul chuckle, although I had no idea why.

"That'll do," I said. "Can you make it send the images to my laptop?"

"Sure." He plugged a cable into the glasses, and the other end into my laptop's USB port. "Let me set it up."

Cody's great and all, Paul thought to me, *but you're letting him use your computer?*

In a minute I'm going to hijack his smartphone.

"There!" Cody said. "The camera transmits to a URL, and now your computer links to that." He disconnected his camera glasses. I thought he looked like a pet, waiting for its human to give over a treat for some trick. With that strong, angular face, that was fine with me.

"Excellent," I said. "I'm glad you know how to do that. Now let me have your phone for the next part of this."

He popped his iPhone out of its belt case and handed it over. I plugged the thumb drive into a cable that ended in that little nipple thing that fits into phones. "Uh, that's not how you add an app to a phone," he said.

I smiled. "Police have their own way of doing things. This is an app we use at NOPD instead of wiring an informant the old-fashioned way. We—"

I heard Paul think, *Was tin can and string the old way?*

"—Yes, Paul, we used soup cans and dental floss in the old days. Anyway, this—"

"Wait, what?" Cody looked confused. I didn't blame him; if I hadn't heard Paul's thought I'd have wondered about my response.

"Sometimes Paul thinks jokes to me," I explained. "Some of them are duds, but mostly he's quite clever. I just had to react to what he said."

Still confusion on Cody's face.

"Yes. Well, moving right along. This program is Phantom. It works like your camera, I guess, but it's just the audio. Your phone talks to the cloud, but so does your laptop. Between your glasses and my gizmo, I'll be able to see and hear you in real time. Plus, if you wear your Bluetooth I can talk to you."

"You used this when you were a cop?"

"Please," I said. "I was a detective, not a policeman. I never owned a uniform. And yes, I did. We all made use of Phantom." His phone went 'ding' a few times, and I disconnected the cable. When I handed Cody his phone I said, "Tap that new app icon and everything your phone hears is broadcast and recorded."

"Okay," he said, uncertain, as he opened the app. "How do I turn it off?"

"Take the battery out of your phone. That's the only way."

He stared at his phone. "What's next?"

"It's Paul. You two can talk to each other with that program, but what about when there are people around and Cody can't speak without blowing his cover?"

"Hmm, you're right." I mused on this. Before I came up with an answer, Paul announced, "That magic slate thing you used when you were looking after your niece. Can Cody use that when he can't speak?"

"Magic slate?" Cody responded, the look of confusion returning to his eyes.

"That's what I call thinking. It's in the back seat." I looked up at Cody. "A plastic sheet over some sticky black cardboard. You use a stylus to draw or write. Then you erase everything by lifting the plastic. Kaylee's daughter loves it."

"I had one of those when I was maybe eight years old."

"When you can't speak, you can write and aim your camera glasses at it."

Paul said, "Paul again. When you write 'Beam me up, Scotty' or 'What's that smell?' we'll call the cavalry. How's that?"

Cody stood up and began stowing the unused camera equipment. Looking over his shoulder at me he said, "How often do you need reinforcements?"

It took me a moment to decide how to respond. "Cody, I won't lie. It's dangerous. I think LY holds women in prostitution and slavery. He has a reputation for slashing people. And he's already beat up your dad." He turned to face me. "We're trying to protect your parents. Some things are worth the risk."

The man went pale, and swallowed hard. "I know you're right," he said. "I just didn't expect us to be doing something risky."

He said 'us', Paul thought.

"It's for a good cause. Let's get going before we come to our senses."

"Let me tell Mom I'm going out," he said. I followed him as he limped to the living room where Donna was curled up on the sofa with a clipboard and the *Times-Picayune* crossword puzzle.

"Mom, Amy and I are going downtown to catch Father's nemesis."

The woman looked up at us, over the tops of her reading glasses. "Is that really a good idea?"

"I think it's necessary, ma'am," I said. "I need to take the battle to the bad guy. Otherwise we give him the advantage of choosing when to surprise us here."

"You're saying I'm in danger staying here alone?" She put down the clipboard and sat up on the sofa. "I'm coming with you."

"I don't know if that's wise, Mom."

"Maybe it's not, but I'm coming with you. Amy?"

Not my favorite scenario, but maybe another human being on board will be helpful. I nodded and said, "Do you know how to drive a diesel?"

"Of course," she said, standing up. "We have one at our beach house in Pass Christian. Why do you ask?"

I edged toward the front door, trying to get Cody and Donna to move with me. "I have a diesel," I said. "It's good you can drive it, just in case."

"Just in case of what?"

I opened the door and swept my arm to urge them on. "In case I can't. Or in case I don't come back."

"What are you talking about?" The woman was not noticing my physical cues to leave the house.

"Donna, we're going to the lion's den. Cody will try to get information from inside the bar they run." Paul knocked me back, inside, and continued, "So, you can drive. Just in case everything gets...pear shaped."

"I don't know what that means," the woman said, but she resumed our convoy to the front door, "but it sounds exciting."

"Yes," I said. "Very exciting. I hope not <u>too</u> exciting."

While Cody opened the rear door of my Benz for his mother, I opened the trunk and found my spare 9mm, a Glock with a recoil like when you stumble on a dead body or a live skunk. I hated the damn thing, but the only thing worse than a gun you don't like is having no gun at all. I pulled the slide and a copper-jacketed round popped out. Okay, a round in the chamber.

Cody was next to me when I let myself in. When I got behind the wheel I asked Donna, "Do you see a magic slate back there?"

"What's a—oh, is this it?" She was holding it up—a picture of SpongeBob SquarePants and Patrick above the slate part, which still showed my darling niece's writing, 'I ♥ Aunt Amy.'

"That's it!" I said, glancing at its image in my rear-view mirror.

"That's too big!" Cody said. "Where am I going to hide that?"

He was right. But the actual magic slate part was maybe five by seven. "Do you have a pocket knife, Boy Scout?"

"Of course."

"Get to work," I said.

As Cody hacked at the cardboard, I twisted to look at Donna. "I have a present for you." I handed her the Glock, butt first.

"Oh, dear!" She looked up at me with surprise across her face. "I didn't know—I mean, you didn't say—"

"Better safe than sorry," is what I did say. Turning to face my windshield, I said, "Keep your finger OFF the trigger until you're ready to kill someone. And that includes anyone who's pointing their gun at you."

Paul cranked the engine and started the drive to the CBD. Meanwhile, I explained to Cody and Donna what we were going to do. Cody was to go in and ask the bartender if there was any action. If there wasn't, we were wasting our time; but if there was, Cody was to talk to one of the women and get her story.

Donna was puzzled when Paul said, "I'm thinking, Amy, that if Cody gets to be with one of the women, the bad guys may be listening in. That magic slate will be great."

From the back seat I heard, "That's not how I talk to myself." Meanwhile, Cody, who was beginning to understand how Paul and I work, rolled his eyes. "Mother!" he muttered.

So, I joined the party and said, "And Amy thinks they may even be watching. Cody, maybe you'd recognize a camera. Look for anything that might be a lens and keep your backs to it."

"You really have a plan!" Donna exclaimed. It made me laugh. "Protect your house? Check. Bring down the guy threatening George? Double check." And Paul added silently, *Get close to Cody? Triple check.*

It was a quick drive down and around on St Charles Avenue. We went under the imposing Pontchartrain Expressway, and a block more to Lee Circle. Paul made a couple of right turns and we were slowly going up Poeyfarre Street.

"Crap! No place to park," I said as we passed occupied parking meters and parking spaces.

Paul said, "Wait. Wasn't there an alleyway alongside the place?"

"You're right," I exclaimed. Heaven knows what Donna thinks, hearing a conversation like this, all of it in my voice.

Next to the 55th Fighter Group building were two driveways. The one nearer the bar seemed to end at a loading dock, but the other sported a beat-up sign that said "Parking," with the usual bullet holes. When Paul turned in, I tried to use our peripheral vision to examine the building.

Two stories. Brick. Lots of windows on the top floor.

Paul said, "Looks like this is public parking. I wonder how much they charge?" Good question, since the meters cost three dollars an hour. I could see another entrance, this one from the street behind that had the elaborate name of Andrew Higgins Drive.[42] *Another way out*, I thought to my dyad.

Paul parked near the 55th Fighter Group, but with a series of dumpsters screening my car. Even so, I could see my target. There were six windows across the back of the second floor.

Cody and Donna suddenly were talking at the same time, and I didn't understand a word. "One at a time," I announced. "Is someone with a weapon approaching the car?"

Donna shrugged as if it were nonsense, but Cody said, "No one. No gun."

"Okay. Now you and I need to turn on all our gear." I woke up my laptop while he fiddled with his camera glasses.

"You'll be able to watch him when he's inside?" Donna asked.

"That's the idea. Well, sort of. I won't see Cody. I'll see what Cody sees."

"Ready to go," Cody said. He was poking at the camera glasses sitting on his nose, trying to get them level.

I heard Paul think *I wish I could look at you like that.*

Huh? Like what?

Your face. Cody gets to see your face. I only get to see it in a mirror.

---

[42] Higgins was a private boat builder in NOLA who invented the Higgins boat and made a zillion PT boats during World War II. Retired President Eisenhower called Higgins "The man who won the war." Fittingly, the street passes right by the World War II Museum, not two blocks from the 55th Fighter Group. And neither Amy nor Paul had any idea who Andrew Higgins was.

Paul and I developed a fantasy when I turned into a cauldron of hormones in seventh grade. We had gotten comfortable with the impossible fact that he was a permanent tenant in *Chez Amy*. He was grateful he wasn't in his old body when it died, after he left it and came to me. And I was still excited that Paul filled what had been my childish fantasy of spending time in super adventures with super cute and super smart boys. Or at least Justin Timberlake. Anyway, about the time Sister Agnetha was telling us at St. Giles Academy that we were turning into lovely young women and that we should always wear high-collar blouses, I let myself crush on Paul. I can't imagine my life without him, since he's been with me since I was eleven. We don't much talk about it, but I love him and he loves me, and we wish we could be separate people so we could be lovers. Or hold hands. <sigh> So I understood why it was a big deal to him to see Cody look at me. He wishes he could do that.

We can sit in front of the mirror when we get home, I thought.

Let's.

"How's that working?" Cody asked.

"Peachy." I put on my headset and spoke into the microphone, "Can you hear me now?"

He nodded.

"Got the magic slate?"

He held it up; he had chopped it down to about six inches square.

"Okay, we're good. Go walk in the front door, and see if you can make contact with one of LY's prostitutes. You ready?"

"I guess. This is exciting, but it's scary."

Paul spoke up. "It's smart to be scared. It's smarter to do what needs to be done anyway. Just, you know, be careful."

"Are you sure this is a good idea?" Donna said from the back seat. "You make it sound dangerous."

"It's okay, Mom. Amy's told me what to do. Everything will be fine."

Keep telling yourself that, I thought to him. Then I twisted around in my seat to tell Donna, "It may not be the best idea, but it's the idea I'm going with. Cody's got his instructions. With luck we'll be home in an hour."

"I'm ready," Cody said, opening the passenger door. I lifted the lid of my laptop and saw his view of the parking lot, then of my car.

"Break a leg," I told him. Then I said to Donna, "Come on up front. You can help me keep an eye on Cody."

Donna slid into the front passenger seat and looked at my laptop. "Where's Cody?" she asked

"We're seeing what he's seeing. I love that soldier mannequin." We saw his right hand reach out to pull open the front door, and then GI Joe in his jeep, complete with Santa hat and a new strand of Christmas lights around his neck.

We saw the bar get closer, until Cody's hands were on it as he sat on a stool. The tattooed bartender was at the other end, putting a drink in front of another customer. "That's the man who tried to drug me," I said into my headset so Cody could hear. "I want to know who he is." The image on my computer momentarily dipped down and up; I think he nodded.

"What can I get for you?" the bartender asked as he got larger on my screen. We could see some of Cody's fingers at the bottom of the picture.

"Umm, just a, uh—what do you have on draft?"

Mister Tattoo began rattling off brands. Cody stopped him with, "An Abita will be fine."

"Cody doesn't drink!" Donna exclaimed. Her jaw was practically in her lap. "Why would he do that?"

I held a hand over the microphone boom on my headset. "Necessary to establish raport," I said.

When the beer appeared, Cody said, "Something else."

"Ah. Here's our menu," and one appeared from behind the bar.

"No, not that," Cody said. He must have leaned in, because the image of the barkeep got larger, and the angle was from Cody's seated position. Great view of the man's nostrils, perhaps the only part of his body not emblazoned with tattoo. "I'm in the market for some, uh, companionship."

The bartender's eyebrows lifted, practically meeting his hairline. "You?" he said, "You can't find your own?" I whispered to Donna, "He figures a man as good-looking as Cody doesn't need help."

"I'm looking for some strange, all right?" Cody barked back.

"Sure, sure." We saw the bartender's tattooed right hand cup his chin. "What's your preference?" I heard Paul think, *He's not even pretending his bar isn't a whorehouse.*

The image on my laptop momentarily swiveled to the top of the bar, then back up at Mister Tattoo the pimp. "Girl," Cody said. "About so high—" not that we could see where he was holding his hand "—skinny. Young. Clean."

Donna made some noise that made me look over at her. She was turning a bit green. How often does a mother hear her son order up a prostitute? Or, for that matter, does a prospective girlfriend hear her intended do the same? Paul thought, *I felt our stomach hit the floor. It's okay, Amy—he's describing you, you know.*

I'm so high? I thought back, but his observation relieved some of the anxiety I had been feeling. *Thanks.*

"I'll find out what we've got available," the bartender said. We watched him turn and lift the handpiece from an old-fashioned wall phone; he punched some numbers on the keypad, then seemed to be saying something that didn't make it to the Phantom software on Cody's iPhone. What I did hear was a splash, and then Cody's hand put his now half-filled beer glass back on the bar. "I know he's smart," I said to Donna, "but that is brilliant. He's spilling out the beer instead of drinking it. I don't know that I would have thought of that." No point in trying to explain that I let Paul do the drinking when I'm in those situations.

Tattoo Man put the phone back on the wall and turned to Cody. "It'll be a little while," he said, his face getting bigger as he stepped closer to the hidden camera.

"How much?" Cody asked.

The man leaned closer, just part of his face filling my laptop screen. "One-fifty," he said. The image jogged as Cody nodded.

"This is disturbing," Donna said quietly. "I worked for ten years before I made that much in a day."

"If it makes you feel better," Paul piped up, "the girl might see twenty-five of those dollars. The rest goes to the house."

"House?"

I replied, "The sign doesn't say it, but this is the 55th Fighter Group Bar and Whorehouse."

"But that's not—I mean, prostitution—even in New Orleans, isn't it against the law?"

Paul again: "Oh, sure. So's speeding."

The computer screen showed a panorama of the dimly lit bar. The image jogged, and a view of one side gradually got larger. While we had a closeup of what I assumed was an artificial banana tree, we heard liquid splashing. Cody must have looked down because we saw a puddle in the fake tree's pot, and an empty glass in somebody's hand. "Way to go," I said into my headset microphone. "You're smart to stay sober on a mission."

He whispered, "I don't like beer." A smile broke across Donna's face.

For a while we had a Cody-eye-view tour of the 55th Fighter Group. I particularly liked the piles of sandbags against a back wall, designed to look like an allied redoubt in a French farmhouse circa 1944. There were grainy black and white photos of men in khaki uniforms–all thumbs up in front of silver airplanes, relaying 155 millimeter mortar shells toward a howitzer, sitting in foxholes with machine guns and dangling cigarettes, passing pans of food in a group huddled under a lone tree, ripping a captured swastika flag, handing out candy bars to a crowd of ragged children, and of one man in camouflage helmet and uniform, full pack, cigarette hanging on lower lip, with a wounded comrade over his shoulder. Finally, we saw a close-up of a fireplace mantle, covered in Plexiglass, with hundreds of names. A little sign offered thanks to the veterans of all the wars who had signed the wooden mantle. I heard Paul think, *This is 2036, so World War II ended 92 years ago. Not a lot of people born then still alive; surely everyone who actually saw combat has fallen in for the final muster. I'm glad I missed World War II. My granddad refused to talk about it.*

"What kind of place is this?" Donna asked.

"It's not really a museum," I said. "Until I figured out it was a whorehouse, I used to like stopping in for a beer and letting the old men flirt with me. Really, quite pleasant." And Paul tagged, "Aside from the knock-out drops in our drink."

"You seem to live an exciting life," she said; for a second, I thought she was being sarcastic, but that's not like Donna. "Thank you," I said. "Glad to share."

The computer was showing us a framed issue of Colliers' Magazine with a cover picture of two officers in dress uniforms reading a newspaper headline, "Yanks Capture Jap Airdrome." Suddenly the image swirled around, finally settling on the bar at the front of the establishment. "That's enough to make me seasick," I muttered.

Leave it to Paul to be Mister Smartypants. "Usually your brain turns off your eyes when your eyes move. If you're drunk your brain forgets and lets your eyes stay on—that's why it seems like the room is spinning when you're drunk, your brain is letting you see while your eyes are drifting." He shivered, which means Donna saw me shiver. "I hate being hung over."

"Oh, Dear, I hope that doesn't happen often."

Paul again: "Not anymore, boy howdy." Great. Not only does my prospective boyfriend live with his parents, but now his mother thinks I'm a lush.

On the laptop screen, the bar was getting closer and bigger. The tattooed bartender was motioning and his mouth was moving. Eventually I heard, "The boss will come get you in a couple of minutes." Finally we saw Cody's hands on the top of the bar. "It's a hundred and fifty," the bartender whispered.

I winced when I saw Cody's wallet appear, and saw him retrieve his Optimo credit card. "No!" I hissed, not wanting the tattooed man to hear my voice coming out of Cody's bluetooth. "You don't use a credit card to pay for contraband!" I saw his hand suddenly cover the plastic card, and he opened the paper money part of his wallet. With my hand over my microphone I asked Donna, "How much cash does he carry?"

"I have no idea," she replied, giggling. And we both were amused when Cody took out some bills and said, "I've only got a hundred and forty. Can we work something out?"

The screen showed the bartender's face compress into a scowl. I imagined he was balancing desire for full payment against need for any payment; finally he said, "Next time you come in here, I'm charging you extra." He snatched the seven bills from Cody's hand. He turned away, but we heard him say, "Just a few minutes now."

Suddenly the laptop showed a rapid pan of the restaurant: bar; front area with jeep and Christmas lit manikin soldier; far wall with sandbags and framed pictures; dark back where I knew the old dears hung out; and then back to the bar. Again. And again. And again.

"Is your computer breaking?" Donna asked. It dawned on me that a bored Cody was making use of the swivel bar stool. "Stop that!" I hissed. "You're making me car sick."

The zipping panorama abruptly stopped, leaving a view of a middle-aged couple entering the establishment; the man saluted the uniformed manikin. "Oh."

"Sorry, Cody," Paul spoke up in my normal tone of voice. "For all the advice I've heard about seeing life through someone else's eyes, it's weird to actually do it."

"And all God's children say 'Amen,'" I added.

Cody whispered, "Okay. Now I'm just waiting."

"You're doing fine, Dear," Donna called from the seat next to mine. I heard his quiet response, "Mother...."

I let Cody eavesdrop as I told Donna, "Cody's being brave, and he's doing something he never imagined he'd get to do. Let's not distract him, okay?" Too bad he couldn't see his mother's broad grin.

"So, here's what's next," I said into the microphone. "I want you to take a good look at the guy that leads you away. Find out his name if you can. Make sure you look at every turn you take, every door you pass, every sign that might have any meaning."

I heard him whisper, "Okay."

"And when you get to the woman you're renting, remember they house may be listening to you. Maybe they're voyeurs, maybe they want to make sure the woman doesn't step out."

Paul suddenly spoke up: "And if you make use of the woman I won't reimburse you."

My jaw dropped. Donna was staring at me. Only a man would have thought to say that. Crap, only a man would have thought it. *Thanks, Paul. Let's see what he does.* When Donna started to say something, I covered my microphone with my hand. "Cody wouldn't do that," she asserted. "He's a good boy."

"Yes, ma'am, he is a good boy," I said. I heard Paul add, *Like a man is really going to fuck a woman in front of his mother.*

"Well, yes," I blurted out.

A strange man's voice came out of my laptop's speakers. "Hey, come on!" it said. Our view pivoted to the other end of the bar: a short, stocky man wearing a polo shirt with a five pointed star crest and the legend, "Republic National Distributing." The man got bigger and closer as Cody must have stepped off the stool and walked toward him. "L-Y!" Paul exclaimed.

"What's that, Dear?"

"The new person. His name is L-Y Young. He's the man who's been tormenting George." I said it into the microphone, so Cody would know this was our target. "Introduce yourself," I said, "get him to tell you his name."

Immediately I saw Cody's right hand extend into the picture. "Hey, I'm Woodrow," he said; "who are you?" Donna whispered, "That's his middle name."

Unless someone is a hard-core jerk, or hates you in particular, they reflexively smile when you do; they shake a proffered hand; and tell you their name if you've said yours. "Call me L-Y," he responded coolly. "Follow me upstairs," and he turned away to enter a wooden stairwell.

"Show me!" I barked into my microphone. The image stopped, then Cody must have stepped back. There was an ancient Jax Beer poster on the paneled wall next to the staircase. I saw the steps in front of him jog and move, jog and move; there were twelve of them. At the top I saw L-Y's back receding down the hallway to the left. The second door on the right was wide open, and when Cody turned to look, I saw three small children laughing, playing with an enormous smiling man with that distinctive face that tells you 'that boy ain't right.' I heard Cody call to L-Y, "What? You have a kindergarten here?"

L-Y replied, "Employee day-care. Come on." I watched the man go to the last door on the hall and knock. I couldn't hear a reply, but the door swung open. L-Y said, "You've got forty-five minutes" and walked out of camera range. *Where's he going, do you guess?* I thought to Paul. I heard him reply silently, *Hoodlum continuing education classes. You know, New Horizons in Kneecapping, Advanced Boot-Putting, Witness Intimidation Made Easy—that sort of thing.*

My screen showed a young woman sitting on the edge of a cot at the far end of the room. She got bigger as Cody walked toward her; she stood up and, in a decidedly un-erotic move, pulled up her skirt and sat back down. I heard him say, "No, no. It's okay. Look, my name is Woody. What's yours?"

"Que?"

"Mi nombre es Woody. Tu nombre?"

She looked down, shy. "Consuela," she said. "Mi nombre Consuela."

Donna said, "Cody's—uh, an old friend of Cody's taught him Spanish." I heard Paul comment, *Yep—the fiancé who ditched him.*

"That's a great help right now," I said, "but my linguistic ability is limited to English, a little Catholic school Latin, and Cajun."

As I saw the woman, and heard her and Cody converse, I said into my microphone, "Quiet! Remember, they're probably listening. Use your slate."

I saw the slate appear—I wondered where Cody had been keeping it—and saw him write something in Spanish. His hand swiveled the slate so Consuela could see it. She took the little wooden stylus from him and began writing a reply.

These exchanges went on for a while. I was glad the images were being recorded, so Cody could translate them for me later. This was different from something Paul showed me one day at a gym, when I was using the treadmill and he turned the TV onto a Univision soap opera. I didn't understand a word of that either, but we all know the conventions of soap opera, and the actors always overdo it, so it was obvious what was going on. Cody and the Hispanic prostitute, not so much.

Since nothing I heard made sense to me, every now and then I said into the microphone, "How's it going?" Invariably he muttered, "Going great. We'll get the guy who's been bothering Dad."

Donna and I got to look at Consuela a lot. I guessed late twenties. Dark hair swept back, dark eyes, and a broad mouth with full lips. *Is she pretty?* I asked Paul; he answered, *She's fine. Not beautiful, but not ugly. You know, normal.*

I heard noise through the speakers. Our view swiveled from Consuela to the doorway, where an angry looking L-Y was standing. "What the fuck is going on here?" he bellowed.

"My time isn't up yet!" Cody hurled back, which prompted Paul to think, *Good one. I wouldn't have thought of that.*

I tore off my headset and opened my door. Turning to Donna, I said, "Crap-and-a-half, I'm going in. Crank the engine. Lock all the doors and do not open them for anyone but me or Cody. If someone points a gun at you, run them over!" She said something back, but I was too busy running up the parking lot to Poeyfarre Street to hear. In the door, past the jeep and the soldier manikin. While I raced past the bar, the tattooed man shouted, "Hey!" I hoped he didn't recognize me from the day he spiked my drink, but if I were in charge of a place, I'd sound the alarm over any random idiot running through it. He was still yelling while I took the corner. At the Jax beer poster I ducked into the stairwell and took the stairs two at a time.

Voices thataway, Paul thought as we got to the top hallway. I heard Cody and L-Y arguing to the left. A little out of breath, I walked toward the room at the end of the hall instead of running. I passed the daycare room on the right; in person the gigantic man with the face marked by idiocy was ignoring the three children climbing all over him, perhaps trying to comprehend the raised voices from the room where Cody and L-Y were facing off. Reflexively I waved at the giant and kept going.

I stopped at the doorway of the *oda*. Consuela was standing on the bed, holding up her skirts like my mother used to do when a mouse ran through the kitchen. Cody was facing me, his camera glasses gone, and a small amount of blood under his nose. *If that monster hurt my Cody I will take him apart!* I shouted silently.

I could see L-Y's back. With Cody beyond him and Consuela standing on the bed, he looked positively diminutive. Paul thought, *I don't see his hands. Assume he's holding that razor he's famous for.*

Before I figured out how to announce my arrival Paul thought, *I got this.* He had me step back, then ran to L-Y and slid across the wood floor like the Zephyrs' player who had stolen all those bases this year. Paul stuck out our left leg and knocked L-Y down. *There!*

Cody jumped on L-Y and threw a few healthy punches at the man. "Good to see you," he said, delivering another blow. But L-Y grabbed Cody's arm and pulled him over. All three of us were lying on the floor, while Consuela shrieked and keened from her perch on the bed.

I could feel, before I could see, the giant standing in the doorway. I tilted my head back to see him, upside down, as if he were standing on his head on the ceiling. Giggling four-year-olds were wrapped around each leg, but his misshapen face didn't seem to show any notice of them. But that face gradually turned into a scowl as he heard Consuela shouting and saw L-Y trying to stand up.

Cody grabbed L-Y from behind, as the pimp obscenely threatened to send my intended to the place the nuns at St. Giles Academy used to assure me I would end up if I didn't spit out that chewing gum. Cody was lifting him a few inches and then dropping him back on the floor to bounce on his butt. Repeatedly. I want to remember that trick.

"What the hell is going on?" It was a shout from behind the behemoth, from the tattooed bartender who finally came to the party. Suddenly we were outnumbered. I thought to Cody, *Maybe it's time for us to leave.*

"I'm taking Consuela," he said, standing up and saying goodbye to LY with a kick to the side of his head. He turned to the bed where the woman was still standing, although mercifully she had stopped wailing. Cody said something to her in Spanish and held a hand out to her.

"No, no," she said, shaking her head. "¡Mi hijita!"

"She won't leave without her little girl," Cody translated for me. "And how do we get out of here?" It was an excellent question. LY was holding on to the wall, trying to stand up. The babysitter was lumbering into the room. And the bartender was smacking his fist into his open palm as he tried to get around the big man. And all of them were between us and the door.

I heard Paul think, *Window*. I grabbed Cody's hand and spun him around. "Better a broken leg than a slit throat," I hissed. I pulled him up on the bed with me, and then flung us both against the window.

Paul had taught me the formula for falling bodies, 32 feet per second per second. We were leaping from a second-floor window, so we were going to discover what was under us in less than a second. But in mid-air, with the babble of the angry bad guys fading away, it seemed like a minute or two. There was my car, my precious yellow Benz, with Donna behind the wheel; she was watching us, with her eyes open even wider than her mouth. A woman in a heavy brown coat was unlocking her car across the lot. Someone's golden retriever was retrieving God knows what from under a golden step van. The sky was surprisingly blue, punctuated with a few puffy Simpsons' clouds. And I was still holding Cody's hand.

And then we were in the dumpster, bouncing off big brown plastic bags of the morning's leavings and leftovers from the bar. I heard Paul think, *We're still alive!* I was happy about that.

"Cody!" I called. "Talk to me! Are you okay?"

"I—I think so," he wheezed.

I saw everyone leaning out the big hole in the side of the building that used to be a window—LY, the giant, the tattooed bartender, Consuela, and two giggling children who probably thought what they'd just seen was way cooler than TV. There were shouts and shaking of fists.

"Let's get out of here," I prodded. "I hope your mom is a speed demon, 'cause she's driving." It was hard to get my footing, since the many bags of garbage were uneven. On top of that, the ones that had broken open were beyond stinky. Cody managed to balance himself despite the remains of someone's Caesar Salad all over his back. He hoisted himself up on one side of the dumpster, then reached in to pull me up by my hand.

Cody got to the ground first, and let me bounce against him when I followed. "Donna!" I shouted twice, "Let us in!" She mashed the armrest button that unlocked all the doors. I scrambled into the back seat and pulled Cody in behind me. "Go!" I ordered. "Now! Fast! Faster!" Glad I told her to keep the engine running when I ran out to rescue Cody. We were just turning onto Poeyfarre when LY and the barkeep emerged from the restaurant's front door. I didn't see it, but I heard the bang! of a big caliber hollowpoint as it shattered my back window. Kernels of safety glass rained down on Cody and me. Crap-and-a-half! Will my comprehensive insurance cover that? Will the detail place I use be able to get all the glass out of the seats?

Donna's eyes were darting between the road and the rearview mirror, trying to get a glimpse of her son. "Are you two alright?"

"I'm fine, Mom," Cody said, smiling. "I haven't had this much fun in a long time."

"Fun?" I thought about it. "Well, we didn't die, that's a plus. And we have enough to put LY and his crew out of business. Don't know that I'd call it fun, though."

"I'm so glad you two are all right," Donna said as we sped down St Charles Avenue. "I saw that man coming at Cody, then the camera went flying and I couldn't see them anymore, but I heard them yelling and fighting."

"That's what happened, Mom," Cody responded. He slid his left hand along the car seat and grasped mine. "He hit me and I lost the camera glasses. After that we rolled around." He thought for a moment. "I haven't been in that kind of fight since high school."

"You seem to have done alright," Paul said. I added, "LY carries a razor."

"A razor?" Donna shouted. "You didn't say this would be dangerous!" She turned her head briefly to shoot daggers—uh, razors—at me.

"I think I said this would make them leave George alone," I said, defensively. "Cody helped me save your husband."

"Are they following us?" Donna asked, scanning the side mirrors as she ran another red light at Napoleon. Easy to miss the light when you're dodging Orleans Parish's eternal road construction that features closed lanes and open pits.

"They don't seem to be, Mom," Cody offered after looking out the December air-conditioned former back window.

Paul pulled out my cell phone, thinking *Call your old police station. They'd better work fast.*

Why hadn't that occurred to me? I was too busy feeling the exhilaration of survival and of bonding with Cody to remember I'm a trained Law Enforcement Officer. Semi-retired, it's true, but Commander Rodriguez still has me on the roster for my occasional consulting. *Thanks.* I punched the speed-dial for the inside line.

"Yeah, yeah, what you want?"

"Not the most professional greeting, Walter," I said to my old buddy Sergeant Francks.

"Sugar!" he cried. "If I'd only known it was you, I'd have gargled honey before I picked up the phone. When are you coming to visit? Are you finally ready for us to elope?"

Elope to the evidence locker, I thought to Paul. "I don't have my Daytimer out so I'm not sure when we can set a date," I teased. "Look, I've got serious business to discuss. Crime. White slavery."

"Sugar, I don't mind if you keep working after we marry. But I've got to say, white slavery? That's a strange career choice."

I love how Walter likes to play. "No, no!" I said, "it's not my business. It's some bad guy's. Do you remember talking about that man "L-Y"? The one who cuts people if they say his real first name?"

"Oh, yeah. L-Y Young. He's a mean one." There was a pause, then Walter said, "Wait–don't tell me you're eloping with him!"

I rolled my eyes. "I'm not eloping with anyone, Walter. This L-Y, he runs a brothel out of the 55th Fighter Group on Poeyfarre in the Central Business District. And I've got a recording of one of his women saying he's forced her into prostitution."

"Give me an address," he said. Suddenly play time was over, and Walter was all business.

"Poeyfarre between Magazine and Annunciation. It's just down from the World War II museum. And if you get there fast you might catch everyone."

"Who's everyone, Sugar?"

"L-Y. The bartender covered in tattoos. A huge guy who's not quite right. And the good girl is a Hispanic named Consuela, she's the one I've got recorded."

"Poeyfarre, near the war museum. Got it. Meet us there in twenty minutes? It'll be your bust."

Your bust. Such sweet words I hadn't heard in so long. "I'll be there in, oh, six minutes," I told Walter. "Save me a place."

"So, the police are taking over," Donna said. She let her foot up off the gas pedal. "Thank God. We're going home!" She turned to us in the back seat with a big smile of relief.

Paul answered before I could think of a softer way of saying, "Nope! Take us to George's place and we'll let you out. Amy and Cody and I are going back."

She pulled over to the curb and stopped. "Amy and Cody and you?" She peered into the rear-view mirror. "Who is 'you'?"

"Oh, Mother. It's like the royal we. C'mon, take us to Dad's." *Thanks for the rescue*, I thought to Cody. *You want to come back to the action with me?*

He snickered! Donna put the Benz in gear and I swear, the man snickered! And he nodded. And he put his hand on mine on the glass-littered seat. That curved smile broke up the sharp angles of his face like dawn chasing night time away.

"Well, okay," Donna said, turning north on some non-descript side street, "but Cody Woodrow Lochaviche, you are getting out with me." He replied, "Yes, Mom," but he winked at me.

"I have to get back to the bar," I said. "I'm the only one who knows what the bad guys look like." Then Paul continued, "And there might be a reward. I could use the money."

We were just coming out from crossing under the Pontchartrain Expressway, into the grim warehouse district. Poydras was only a few streets further up; Donna knew the way to her husband's office, and she stopped my car in front of the Poydras

Center building. In a flash she was standing in the street and calling "Cody! Out! Now!"

I got out to get into the driver's seat, while Cody was sneaking to the passenger side. "Donna, you were great," I said. "I'd hug you except I've got garbage and glass all over me. Stay here with George and Duke until you hear from me."

I don't think she was paying attention to me, because she kept barking Cody's name. He kept the body of my car between himself and Donna. Finally, he said, "Mom, I'm going back with Amy. I want to see this through."

She began to stamp her foot. Then Paul said, "Be careful with that pistol in your hand." I couldn't believe I hadn't noticed that she was holding my Glock by the barrel. "It's loaded."

Cody and I jumped into the car. He waved to his mother as I popped the clutch to zip up Poydras a few more blocks. Then I turned south on one-way Magazine Street, headed back to the 55th Fighter Group.

"I think Mom's mad at us," Cody offered.

"Yes, but she'll forgive you because you're her son. She's going to murder me."

The turn to Poeyfarry was blocked by an SUV cop car with cycling blue lights. I pulled over and parked with my left tires on the sidewalk. Paul hit the button for emergency blinkers while I fished out my old "NOPD" sign from under the seat and laid it on the dashboard.

"Now what?" Cody asked. He was looking at me, even with his right hand on the door latch.

"First, I talk our way past these cops." I opened my door and squeezed out between my car and the chain-link fence surrounding some parking lot. Cody had an easier time stepping into Magazine Street and then coming to the back of the car, waiting for me.

"Do you know them?" he asked me. Paul answered, much to my amusement, "There are two types of coppers—the individuals Amy knows, and all the other interchangable ones with names like 'Buddy.'" And for some reason he began to sing some strange Paleozoic era song that went, "His name was always BUDDY! And he'd shrug and ask to stay. She'd smile like Twig the Wonder Kid and turn her face away."[43]

"What?"

I shook my head. "Paul. Weird music from his youth." I showed my NOPD ID to the officer. "Did I tell you he used to talk politics with Tom Jefferson?" The policeman waved me through, but then he stopped Cody.

"Whoa!" I turned back to the cop. "He's my deputy. He's with me." I grabbed Cody by the arm and pulled him away from the officer, and we walked toward the clot of uniforms in the street in front of the 55th Fighter Group.

"You can do that?" he asked, turning his head between me and the cop we were leaving behind. "I thought you left the Police department."

"Short answer," I smiled, "is yes, I can. If you act as if you belong and the person challenging you is out of line, you can get almost anywhere. Besides, I consult for NOPD. I'm going to get paid for today."

He was shaking his head as we reached the unit outside the bar. I recognized the man in civvies with the gray ponytail, so I squeezed next to him and tugged on his hair.

"What the fuck!" he bellowed as he turned, "Who the—Oh, Sugar! It's you." Even with a cocked Beretta in his hand, Sergeant Walter Francks hugged me. "Glad you made it. This is your bust."

"Walter, this is Cody Locaviche. Cody–Sergeant Francks. He's—"

Walter interrupted to say, "She's mine, kid. Someday Sugar and me are gonna elope."

"Oh, Walter, I'll bet you say that to all the girls." He grinned and said, "I figure it'll work with one of you." Cody shook his head, but he was grinning.

A uniformed lieutenant turned to face the bulk of the dozen officers and bellowed, "Listen up! We talked about this on the way here. Second group?" Quiet. "Second group? Hands!" Four men and one woman raised a powder-blue-sleeved arm.[44] "You all, up the

---

[43] "Drive In Saturday" by ~~Ziggy Stardust~~ David Bowie, with a tip of the recording console to one-time modelling superstar Twiggy. Amy was not alone in the year 2036 having never heard or heard of the man—or the model.

[44] God bless the New Orleans police, the only cops in America whose uniform is powder blue. I don't know who came up with that idea – maybe the same person who renamed the baseball Zephyrs the Baby Cakes.

alley and around the back. Be ready for the perps coming out."
There were nods, and those officers trotted away.

I poked Cody and thought, *We're in the main group. Stick with me.* He had an amused look on his face when he turned to me. I heard Paul observe, *He's getting used to us. Good.*

"Hey! Hey hey hey!" the lieutenant barked. "Detective Clear, get your ass up here." There were murmurs, as some of the rookies didn't know me or my history with Commander Ramirez and NOPD. "And the rest of me," I said as I went to the front, dragging Cody with me. "Uh, who are you?" The officer said, "Lieutenant Rockforte. Good to meet you, Detective. Now tell everyone what's going on."

"This bar is a front for prostitution and white slavery. The brain is a short, wiry guy called LY, and he's quick with a straight razor. There's a taller guy with tattoos up to his neck, Ricky Young, he's second-in-command. And there's a giant of a guy who's some kind of developmentally challenged—" *He's a retard*, Paul thought; I responded silently, *Yes, Paul, he's a retard*, and we can do that so fast that I didn't stumble or slow down my presentation—"he's always smiling, and once he gets going he can do you some damage. There's at least one girl in there, Consuela, speaks Spanish. And there are three little kids. We—"

"Protect the girl and the kids," Rockforte interrupted, "and let's get the scumbags. Osborne and, and Wilkins, stay out here to clean up anything that tries to get away. Clear, you lead. Let's go!" With that he pushed me toward the front door. The lieutenant was right behind me, and Cody was next. I think there were another eight uniformed officers behind us, as well as Walter, who I have never seen in powder blues.

I pushed the door open and walked past the manikin soldier in the jeep, now wearing a Santa hat and Santa beard. There was a half-glass of maybe an Abita, light yellow, and a few bites left to a loaf, but no one was behind the bar. About then I heard a pistol fire behind me, and the soldier manikin now had a bullet hole in its left shoulder; since the manikin was hollow thin plastic, the bullet kept going until it snuffed the life out of a bottle of Monkey 47 gin. Paul thought, *This place, they probably filled the bottle with New Amsterdam.* I heard Walter bark at the trigger-happy officer, but I didn't look.

"Is that you, Paulette?" I heard from the far reaches of the bar. Paul jumped to the lead and said, "Edgar, good to see you. I'm working right now, we'll talk later. Uh, you and your friends might want to wait outside for a while." Rockforte was pushing me forward—no time for social chit-chat.

Around the corner, and the familiar Jax Beer poster. I stood aside to let Rockforte charge ahead of me up the stairs, and for Cody to catch up with me. "Just like old times," he grinned as we went up. The farther up we got, the louder I heard some argument coming from the top floor. Lieutenant Rockforte waited in the hall, unsure which way to go, so I pointed and whispered, "This way." At the first doorway the big idiot was playing with the children who seemed to love him. I told the lieutenant, "He's like a tank. Get the kids away from him and it'll take three guys to take him down." Paul added, "At least three." Quietly, Rockforte sent four officers in the room. Then we went to what had been the *oda*, with the unseen argument as loud as an overhead airplane. I felt the cold wind that I knew was coming in through the big hole in the wall that used to be a window.

LY and Ricky were calling each other delightfully obscene names. The bigger man, the tattooed wonder, was sitting against a wall. He was holding his right hand over his left bicep, with lots of blood coming through his fingers. *Looks like LY used that razor*, Paul thought. The wiry runt was standing over him, hurling insults; the straight razor in his left hand was adding drop-by-drop to the little puddle of red under it.

"I want to pay back a debt," Cody said. Before Rockforte or Walter or I could do anything, Cody went up behind LY and grabbed him from under the armpits, lifting him into the air. Ricky's face went from surprise to fear to a smile. I thought maybe he was seeing us as the cavalry, saving him from LY.

Rockforte and Walter ran up to relieve Cody of his burden. The lieutenant squeezed the hand holding the razor until it fell to the floor, while my friend Walter took one of LY's arms and did something to it that I'm sure my arm wouldn't do without unpleasant noise and worse pain. Cody stepped back, then turned toward me with an enormous smile.

About then LY kicked back, hitting Cody in a leg, and somehow shaking Walter off. The last remaining officer, who was behind me, started yelling that "Down! Now!" that some cops love to shout. LY turned his head to the sound. "You!" he spit at me. And 'And you!" to Cody. Rockforte grabbed for him, but LY jumped up on the bed and used it like a trampoline; he was out the hole in the wall.

Of course, we all rushed to the opening to watch, just like LY and Ricky and the big baby and Consuela and the kids did when Cody and I jumped an hour earlier.

We heard a quick *fwapp* as LY landed on the same trash bags full of lunch leftovers that Cody and I bounced off. I started to say to Cody, "When we did that it seemed—" when we heard a gunshot. A very loud gunshot. A gunshot from just behind us, where the same rookie who fired at the soldier manikin downstairs was already lining up a second shot. Walter, who is the armorer at the Rampart Street station house, grabbed the man's gun hand while he said, "Wait a sec, Murphy. That gun looks like it's missing its frammits. That's bad. Let me look." The officer handed the cocked pistol to Walter. My sergeant buddy decocked it, quickly pretended to examine it, and said, "Yeah, the frammits is completely wacko." He shook his head while he stuffed the gun in his waistband. "The barrel could have blown if you'd fired again."

Paul was in silent hysterics, but I was impressed at how smoothly Walter had prevented Murphy from letting off another shot, and without escalating a potential fight with a fellow officer, let alone a hearing with the citizens' committee. Still, I didn't want Murphy to realize he'd been played, so I thought to Paul, *I'll complement Walter later. That was just ace work.*

Out the window, most of the second group had scattered, trying to round up giggling little children. I saw LY, with Cesar salad dressing in his hair, jump out of the dumpster and head for Andrew Higgins Drive, out the back of the parking lot. No one on the ground noticed.

"Crap!" I yelled. Rockforte and Walter and even Murphy were running back down the hall, down the stairs, and out to start hunting for our bad-guy pimp. Cody asked, "What just happened?"

"It's Paul. You were great, that was crazy brave, what you did. But it looks like the guy who beat up your dad is still on the loose."

I took a last look out the hole Cody and I had created where a perfectly good window had existed just a few hours earlier. Down in the parking lot Rockforte and Walter, pistols in hand, were shouting back and forth and running around. Even Murphy, now disarmed, was partaking in the running and shouting. Paul said, "I don't think the powder blue boys are gonna find LY." He went, "Huh! More like the Keystone Kops."

"The who?" asked Cody. I thought the same thing to Paul.

"Before your time," he said. "Hell, they were before <u>my</u> time." I added, for Cody's benefit, "Paul was born sometime in the 1950s, if you can believe it. If the Keyhole Crops were from before that, it's no wonder I never heard of them." I took Cody's hand and started for the door. "Let's go home, Cody. I need to face the music with your mom."

"Was every day like this when you were a detective?" he asked as we went down the stairs.

I shook my head. "Like firemen say, it's a job of boredom punctuated by blasts of sheer terror."

"It's Paul," he interrupted. "Amy exaggerates. There were some scary times, but mostly—really, it was just a job."

I snickered. "Please, please, please, I beg of you: don't ask me if I ever killed anyone."

"But you'll tell me some time, right?"

Sigh. "Probably."

Outside the front door of the 55th Fighter Group was the Black Mariah, and it was bouncing like the cars Paul had told me about from his prime, vans or SUVs with stickers that said 'If this van's a-rockin', don't come a-knockin'.' I recognized the Yeoman who was guarding the vehicle. "Flambeau," I called, "what's going on in there?"

"Benji. The big retard?" A look of amusement crossed his face but did not linger. "It took three of us with an animal tranquilizer gun to bring him down. I tell you, make copies of him and put them in the army. We'll beat the Chinese in a week." He looked up Poeyfarre Street as if he were hoping a commanding officer was about to relieve him. "Sounds like he's waking up. I hope this paddy wagon can hold him."

"Well, good luck with that, Yeoman."

"Oh, I got promoted. I'm an Officer II now."

"Well done, my friend, well done. I only ever got to Detective Officer III."

Holding hands, Cody and I walked towards Magazine Street where I'd left my poor Benz with its absent back window. It had gotten dark, and the chill of December was upon me.

"You were great," I told Cody. "The way you grabbed LY, it was like what I did to my kid sister a few times when we were small." I watched a rose tint start up his neck and get to his cheeks. "Really. It was brave, and it was useful, it let Walter and Rockforte get the razor away from him."

We were close to the intersection where I'd parked when I felt Cody pulling at my hand. He had stopped walking. "Everything okay?" I asked.

He took one step toward me and enveloped me in his arms. I felt him breathing deep, and his heart could have been the drums for a Second Line parade.

"How...how do you do this?" he asked.

"Do what?"

"You know all this stuff, house security for Mom, and you talk your way past cops to be part of a confrontation, and it's like you never miss anything."

I heard Paul think, *You seem to have overwhelmed him.*

"Oh, Cody." I returned the hug the best I could, considering he's so much bigger than me that I couldn't get my arms all the way around him. "I'm glad you came with me today." He was rubbing his hands up and down my back, and it didn't feel the least bit erotic. *Not ready to say the L word*, I thought to Paul. Instead, I said, "I'm proud of you."

My hunky about-to-be boyfriend...was he crying?

Abruptly he let go of me, and turned away. He leaned his face against his hands holding the chain link fence along the street.

"Cody?"

I heard him breathing hard. It's not like he was sobbing or acting like a little girl, but I guessed he was trying to hide some tears. I thought to him, *It's okay, Cody. I'm not scared of what you're doing. You do what you have to, I'm right here and I'm not going away.*

He let out one weird snort and stood away from the fence. I saw him run his shirt sleeve across his face. Then he turned to face me with a shy, little boy smile. He picked up my hand and started us walking the rest of the way to my four-wheeled home-away-from-home. "Thanks."

"Time to face the music," I said as I pulled the parking brake across the street from Shloss Locaviche.

"My mother is going to hate me," Cody said as he got out of the car. "You know the worst thing? It's when she says, 'I'm so disappointed in you.'"

"Yes," I nodded, "my mom pulled the same thing with me."

Holding hands, we walked across the street in the dark, then across the semi-circular driveway and up the seven marble steps to the double-door entrance. Paul said, "At least Donna and George are locking the door."

Cody banged his fist on the door. A moment later it opened, and we were looking at the business end of a 9mm Glock. From this perspective, the hole in the barrel looks as wide as a dinner plate. "Friend! Friend!" Paul shouted, our voice breaking.

"Mr. Cody? Amy?" Standing behind the weapon was Duke's brother-in-law Luther. The man lowered the pistol and waved us in. "Your folks was worried about you, come in." He turned his head and shouted into the rest of the house, "It's Mr. Cody and that detective lady!"

"In here," I heard from somewhere in back. Cody said, "That's Mom's 'you're grounded!' voice."

"Let's get it over with. I'm desperate for a shower after our dumpster dive, let alone all the excitement since then."

We found Donna in the breakfast nook. There were three mugs on the table, and a percolator on a trivet. On Donna's face were a bunch of creases above and between her eyes, like she was trying very, very hard not to explode. I heard Paul think, *Shit. We're boned.*

"Hey Mom, I'm home." I was glad to see Cody doesn't shrink from the obvious. Crap. Maybe we should have stopped to get some Dove bars as a peace offering.

Donna looked up at her son. She made a sliding down motion with her right index finger and said one word that was colder than a SnoBliz[45] in August: "Sit." He dropped onto the bench.

Then the woman looked at me. "You! You are impossible." I could feel the inner Amy quaking and whispering, 'Yes, ma'am,' but I was too busy gulping to say anything. After what seemed like two days in Slidell she made the same hand motion and spit out "Sit" like another ice cube. I fell on my butt next to Cody like I'd been pole-axed.

Donna began with her son. "You're a grown man, I know that. But that doesn't mean you can lie to me. You said you would stay with me at your father's office, but you left." She stared at him for a good ten seconds before she added the magic words, "I am so disappointed in you." I could see Cody hang his head, his face turning red. I thought I saw steam coming out of his ears.

"And you!" she turned to me, eyes blazing. "How could you expose Cody to such danger? He doesn't have training like you do. Why would you drag him into a police action? He could have been hurt." She let out a loud "Tch!" and turned her head to stare out the nook window into the Louisiana night.

Paul thought, *Can we go home now? Shush,* I replied silently.

"Donna. I was protecting George. You should be proud of Cody, that he wanted to be part of helping his dad." The woman shook her head silently, eyes still averted. "And he was a huge help. You remember the computer stream when we all were in the car at the bar? The man who started to fight Cody? That man had just slashed a partner with a straight razor, and Cody grabbed him so the uniformed officers could disarm him. He's very brave, ma'am. I'm proud of Cody."

She turned to look at me, still not a happy camper, but not looking quite so furious.

"You should be proud of him, too."

"I am," she whispered. "I always am proud of my son. But I worry for him." Her face softened a little more, and she asked, "Do you have children?"

"No, Ma'am." No need to explain that I hate children, that if I had any I'd sell them to Tulane for medical experiments.

"So you don't know that a mother's job is to worry about her children."

---

[45] Hansen's SnoBliz is a local brand of snoball confection. It is cooling on a summer day. From Donna right now, though, it's like swimming in liquid nitrogen in the midst of an arctic winter.

I couldn't help but smile. "I have a mother," I said. "I know she still worries about me and my sister."

Now what? Paul thought.

Donna picked up her mug. And looking and sounding as if it was a normal day in this, the best of all worlds, she said, "Your coffee must be getting cold."

What a relief! The tension was gone. Cody began to tell Donna about our experience at the bar, about watching LY finally escape the same way she watched him and me go through the window. But she sniffed the air a few times and interrupted, "What's that smell?"

"That would be us," I said. "We're still wearing what we jumped into in that dumpster."

"Please do something about it," she said, smiling as she stood up. "You can tell me the rest of what happened in the morning."

"We need a burn bag for our clothes," I said as Cody and I unpeeled clothing impregnated with the restaurant debris from our dumpster dive. The smell was rancid: sharp, unpleasant, insistent. When we got down to our underclothes we both paused. Now what?

Cody said, "We can save water if we shower together." I liked the shy smile he was wearing.

"I'm not usually a recycling kind of girl," I replied as I unclasped my bra, "but that's a good idea." I heard Paul think *Go Amy! Good for you!* He used to go apoplectic when I slept with a man, but since his time with Christine he's a lot more supportive. *Thanks,* I thought back.

So, we stood in the middle of Cody's bedroom, stark naked and stinky, with goofy smiles on our faces and hormones raging. "Where's your shower, Big Guy?" I asked. I reached out to hold his hand.

"This way, my lady," and he led me into the tiled emporium of ablutions.

An hour later we were clean again, happy, and exhausted, without a drop of hot water left in the Locaviche household. We dried off and fell onto his bed.

I need to call Christine.

Not now, Paul. Whenever I wake up will be plenty of time.

Oh. He paused, then thought, *Happy?*

I only got the first half of '*happy*' out before I was asleep.

I woke when the December daylight was high outside Cody's window. I turned my head and found him, wide awake, smile on his angular face, staring at me.

"Welcome back to the land of the living," he said. He poked his head toward me and kissed me.

Nice to see you again, I thought to him, as I returned the kiss and embraced him. Then I snuggled, head against his chest, listening to his heart beat and to all those internal white noises that came from three years of police firing line practice. Out loud, "We're alive!"

"And well," he responded, kissing the top of my head.

I heard Paul think, *Hate to interrupt, but I need to call Christine.* He is inflexible about his Christine dosage.

Before I could disengage from Cody's welcome encirclement, my phone went off. The sound was faint because of all the dirty, foul, and stinky clothes piled on top of it. But Cody leapt over me, out of bed, and found that electronic ball-and-chain. For some reason he looked at the display, then handed the phone to me.

"Christine!" Paul crooned.

"Sugar?"

Oh. It's for you.

I was well aware that Cody was sitting on the edge of the bed right by me, stark naked, while I was laying under the covers, equally bare; I was thinking about—oh, who am I kidding, you know what I was thinking about. Still, I talked into my phone. "Walter?"

"Honey, there are times I worry something fierce about you. Everything okay there?"

"Uh, yes. Peachy. What's up?"

"Okay, you were gone by the time we finished up last night. We picked up the guy with tattoos everywhere, he won't say anything but 'I want my lawyer.' And we got that big retard you mentioned? You know, three officers tried Tasers on him and the guy dragged them all halfway down the street. Our weapons man opened the squad car trunk and nailed him with an elephant tranquilizer dart."

"Yes, Officer Flambeau told me about the big baby. I guess the paddy wagon held him when he woke up. What about Consuela?" It was hard to concentrate while Cody rubbed me through the blanket.

"Oh, we got that woman, and four others. All of 'em, Hispanics smuggled in to be sex slaves. We got seven little kids, too."

I grabbed Cody's active hand to make him stop, uh, arousing me, so I could pay attention to Walter. "I watched you and Rockforte and Murphy run around the parking lot. Did you find L-Y?"

"That's what I wanted to warn you about, Sugar. He got away."

"His house in Chalmette?"

"Way ahead of you. His sister lives there. She says she has no idea where Elias is."

I was startled by that last bit. "She called him by name? I thought—"

"If anyone can get away with that, it's a big sister."

"Well, crap. Crap-and-a-half." I sat up, bare arms resting on the blanket over my bent knees. "He's got to have figured out George's people are behind this."

"George who, Honey?"

"George my client, George Locaviche. Remember, I told you about L-Y throwing an empty gasoline bomb through the window?" Cody was leaning away from me, a creased look of worry on his angular, geometric face. His chin was bouncing off the bed; that's how slack-jawed he was. "Something tells me he's going to pay us a visit soon."

There were some 'tch-tch-tch' sounds over the phone. "You know we can't set up a police perimeter or anything. Damn, Sugar, you better be careful."

Paul piped up, "Well, I guess. Any advice?"

"Nothing below 9 millimeter."

The call over, Cody seemed to forget no one was wearing clothes. "The guy we were fighting with? They didn't get him?"

"No, siree." I was out from under the covers, reaching for my bugout bag with the clean clothes. "And I'm guessing he's going to drop by any minute."

Dammit, I need to call Christine! She's going to be worried about us.

"Oh, all right. Call her." I put the phone in my left hand, 'Paul's' hand. While he placed his call to his girlfriend, I struggled to put on clothes with one hand.

"Paulette! Where are you?" I heard worry in the woman's voice, not annoyance.

"I am so glad to hear you," he answered. "You won't believe what the last two days have been."

"Are you okay, Sweetie? Amy, are you okay?"

"We're fine," he said; I added, "We're peachy."

"Then where are you? You're supposed to be here, at my place. You didn't call. I'm so worried—" Her voice was rising in pitch, and the words were coming faster and faster. *She's upset*, Paul thought to me. *In spades*, I thought back.

"Christine, Honey," Paul said, "it's okay. Here I am. I love you. I haven't forgotten you—" that was a ticklish issue for Christine, dating from the days before medication had tamed the poor woman's schizophrenia "—I want to be with you. And so does Amy, you're her very best friend." Through the phone I could hear Christine's breathing slowing, calming, listening to her Paulette and—for very good reason—trusting him. He really is crazy about her.

"Well, can, uh, can I, uh, uh, let me come to your place! I can be there in twenty minutes! If something's going on and you can't get away, let me go to you!" Again, her speech was rising in speed and pitch.

And Paul said, "Let's find out. Amy, can Christine come here? That way we're still protecting George and the family. What do you say?"

Cody was standing not five feet away from me, mouth hanging open at what he was hearing. Since Paul was leading, I couldn't smile or wave to acknowledge my beau. So, I thought to him, *Looks like you're going to meet Paul's girlfriend sooner that we thought.*

"Christine, it's Amy. I love how you worry about me and Paul, so I have to tell you it's going to be dangerous at the client's place. The main bad guy got away, and I'm expecting him to pay a visit any minute. Are you—"

"Yes!" she yelled into the phone. "Tell me the address. I'll be right there! I'd rather be dangerous with Paulette than safe without her."

I heard Paul think, *Please?*

I let out a big sigh. "Okay. I mean, Cody and his mom already have volunteered, so you can join the Amy Posse." I dictated the address to her twice, and waited while she configured the GPS in her phone.

And the proof that Christine is a darling, and an ongoing surprise, she said, calmly, "What can I bring? If that boy and his family are having me over..." Her voice got faint as she must have turned her head to look around her double, then came back to normal volume. "...I've got a bottle of Shiraz I was saving for Christmas with Paulette. Will that be okay?"

Paul answered, "That would be excellent. That's so thoughtful of you, Honey. Yeah, come on over. You can meet the client and Amy's b—I mean, that man's she's mentioned to you."

Paul ended the call and said out loud, "It's Paul. Our arrangement is I get alternate days with Christine. Thanks for honoring the deal."

Cody had not moved. He was still naked, still open-mouthed in amazement or horror, I couldn't tell which. I had managed to get one sock on and one foot through a leg hole in a pair of clean underpants; when's the last time you tried to get dressed with only one hand? Oh, sure. And how did that work for you? I went to Cody for a hug and a quick kiss. Wow, did he feel good! "Christine will be here soon, so we'd better put some clothes on. Uh, she will not be joining us for a threesome, so don't even think about it."

"I never considered it," Cody said. Then he grinned, a happy semi-circle in the middle of all those sharp angles of his face. "And now I don't know how to stop thinking it."

I play slapped at his bare arm. "Put some clothes on, Lothario. Christine matters to Paul and to me, so be on your best behavior."

Once we were presentable, or at least street legal, we went looking for Donna to tell her the bad news about L-Y's getaway.

I found her in the kitchen, pouring batter from a Cuisinart mixer bowl into a cake pan. "There you are," she said, smiling like she'd won the lottery, as if her son and I hadn't disobeyed her orders about yesterday's police escapade, and like she couldn't guess the two of us had been exploring physical intimacy under her very roof.

Cody showed his relief by hugging his mother from behind and kissing her cheek. Paul spoke up, asking for the obvious to make sure he understood: "So, we're forgiven?"

"This time, Dear," she said with a wink. I guess I still have my job as bodyguard. And I seem to have gotten a boyfriend out of the adventure. Thanks, A Trauring.

"I'm making a cake to celebrate you saving us, Amy."

"Crap-and-a-half. Donna, I talked to one of my colleagues with parish police. The ringleader is still at large."

She stopped pouring batter, even as some dripped off her wooden spoon onto the island countertop. "Which one is he?"

"The short guy who got into it with Cody. I expect we'll get a visit from him soon."

She put down the half-full bowl and sat in one of the high chairs. As bright as her face had been at first, now she looked as if someone had just run over her dog. "You did a great job getting us out of trouble, Donna. And like I told you last night, Cody was a big help when we nabbed the second-in-command and freed a bunch of women who were in slavery. You've got a future as a stock car racer."

"Listen to her, Mom," Cody chimed in. "They shot at us. You saved us."

"Thank you, Dear," she replied weakly. I don't think she believed us, but what we said was true. If she hadn't wheeled us out of that parking lot and run some red lights, the day's entertainment might have turned out very different.

Cody put his hand on Donna's shoulder, and kissed her cheek again. "Really," he said.

"I've got to deliver the news to George," I announced. "Is he in his office?" She nodded, weakly, as she reached up to put both her hands over Cody's, still on her shoulder. I left them and considered how I was going to explain developments to my client.

When I knocked at George's office the door swung open. He seemed to be restoring the paper files that a day ago he was preparing for the shredder. "George!" I called, and he swung to look at me. "How'd things go with Duke?"

"Better," he said. "We didn't get into another pissing contest, and I believe him being with me made a difficult client much more agreeable. He's huge!" I walked in and sat myself down in one of the wing chairs, while he went on, "I was going to tell you when I got home, but I couldn't find you—my pal Lucky—"

"Ah, Lieutenant Lucky," I interrupted. "He's your inside connection with the Jefferson Parish Sheriff?"

"—Yep, that's him. He called to say the remains weren't human."

Paul said, "Tell me it wasn't E.T.!"

"Who? No, no. He said it was two of the biggest damn nutria[46] he'd ever seen."

This was so unexpected that it was taking time to sink in. *Nutria?* Paul thought. *The state owes George five dollars a tail, right?*

"So... so no fatalities. No people hurt. No—"

"No charges," George smiled. "Lucky said I'm off the hook."

What a pleasant turn of events! You better believe my next resume will give me all the credit for it. "Great!" I exclaimed. "You won't get in trouble for chasing LY away." I held my hand up for a high-five, but George was too involved with his file folders to notice or respond. "Uh, you did cancel the insurance claim, right?"

The man ignored my comment to go on, "Last night Donna told me you and Cody were going after the people who beat me. So, you've wrapped everything up? How much do I owe you?" Even though he was still standing, with a bunch of manila folders in one hand, he groped at his desk drawer where I knew he kept his checkbook.

"As much as it goes against my religion to say 'no' to money," I began, "things are not wrapped up. Last night we got the junior partner and the big idiot, but L-Y got away. A short, runty looking guy? Is that him?"

"Uh-oh." The files fell out of his hand, back onto the floor from whence they came. "Yeah, about five-foot-nothing, kind of wiry man." He sat at his desk, but wasn't reaching for his checkbook any

---

[46] Known in their native South America as coypu, nutria are an invasive species with destructive habits in wetlands and riverfront areas like Louisiana. Although the Zephyrs minor league baseball team has adopted Boudreaux D. Nutria as a mascot, most locals think of them as overgrown water rats. Rarely they get up to about 35 pounds of hungry rodent. The occasional human, like the Zephyrs' marketing team, thinks they are cute. They are wrong. The state of Louisiana offers a bounty on the animals as part of an eradication project.

more. "You finally convinced me my family was in danger. Then my wife says she and Cody were part of your great escape. And now you say the danger isn't over?"

I nodded with a sigh. "Yes sir. That's what I'm saying. I expect LY is going to make a courtesy call any minute now."

George stared at me, with the remains of the bruises all over his face. "Well, fuck a God-damned duck."

"Donna told me you have a gun. Do you know how to use it?"

"I was stationed on a submarine, so it's not like I ever had a chance to kill some Islamocrazy. But landside, yeah, I did training. Last time I went to the range—" right hand rubbing his chin "—ooh, maybe this time last year?"

"That'll have to do," I said. "Get it out, load it, and keep it with you all the time." Paul piped up, "Uh, please tell me it's not a .22 or a .25. Please?" Silently I laughed at Paul.

"No! It's a real gun. It's a .45. Ten round magazine and one in the chamber. Why?"

Smiling, I said, "I am relieved that you know what you're talking about. Go get it."

"Uh, it's at work. Donna doesn't want a gun in the house."

"Well, that's too bad for Donna, now, isn't it? Bring it home tomorrow and glue it to your hand. Until L-Y is caught or worse, you must be armed. Duke is armed. I just found out his brother-in-law is armed. I know I'm armed. And I can arrange for permits for Donna and Cody. Do you know L-Y has a reputation for taking a straight razor to people who call him by his real name?"

A blink. No, two. "How bad is his real name? Donna's is Eustacia, and she hates it, but she's never threatened mayhem over it."

"Donna is not a white slaver. That's the difference." Paul stood up, thinking *Christine should be here any minute.*

Hang on a sec, I thought back. I reminded George "Luther will be here again tonight, to cover—" There was a vacant look in his eyes, a total absence of recognition "—Luther, that's Duke's brother-in-law? Part of the holy bodyguard trinity of Amy, Duke, and Luther? Didn't you meet him last night when he was here?" There was a flicker of either recognition or of the desire not to hear any more about it, it could have been either. "He'll be here again, maybe around ten o'clock. He'll keep us alive overnight."

"Right," a memory kicking in behind the man's multi-colored and bruised face. "Part of the package deal. I remember now."

"Good. Anyway," flapping my arms against my sides and legs, "Hodges is dropping in, too."

There was a frown. "I thought he didn't do, what did you call it, field work anymore."

"That's mostly right. SHE doesn't do field work anymore. We have a little company business to discuss and I can't get away to the office, so she's coming here."

Christine would be mad if she heard that, Paul thought. *She's barely forgiven you for trying to dragoon her into being part of your P-I business.*

We'll just have to make sure she doesn't hear it, then. Or should I tell George that the lady lover of the invisible man who lives inside me is coming over for a social visit?

Truce. We lead a complicated life, Paul and me. And Christine. And maybe now, Cody.

I left George to decide for himself if he should put his files back in their drawers and cabinets, or if he should go back to shredding and burning them. I'm glad I don't know what evidence might be at issue—not my problem. Keeping him alive, and Donna and Cody—that is my problem.

I left George's office and softly closed the door behind me. I turned and caught a glimpse of Cody limping toward the kitchen to help Donna with dinner, so I sat in the living room, on the sofa where the freshly beaten George had recuperated just a few days ago. It was the first time I really looked around the room. Granted, I had noticed the fireplace, which was getting some use in mid-

December; and the big, colorful Christmas tree, and the dark wood paneling that extended into the hallway.

"This is a pretty room," I offered. "I never really looked at it before."

"Did you say something, Dear?" Donna was standing in the hall doorway, holding a Pyrex baking dish in a folded dish towel. "It's almost dinner time. You wash your hands, now."

"Did Cody tell you? I asked, hoisting myself up from the comfortable couch. "A business associate is coming over to discuss a few things with me. Nothing to do with George and you, it's some other case."

"That's nice," said the ever-gracious Donna. "He can join us for dinner. I'll just throw some more rice in the cooker." What a sweetheart!

"Can I help?" I asked as I walked toward her.

"Cody did all the work. Will your colleague be here soon?

Paul perked up at the reference to Christine. "She'll be here any minute. I was just waiting here—" And right on cue, there was a timid knock at the door. Donna nodded at me, so Paul opened the door to find Christine, hugging herself against the December chill, and with a bottle of something red and vinous dangling from one hand. "There you are!" he said, and stepped back to let her enter the house.

"Paulette!" She embraced me—well, Paul, since she always could tell which of us was leading—and planted a deep kiss on our mouth. Not the kind of kiss you want to get while your prospective boyfriend's mom is watching. Paul must have thought something to her, something I couldn't hear, because Christine let go and stepped back, eyes cast down, and said, "Oh. Sorry. Sure. Uh, Amy." Despite my curiosity, I was glad I could not see Donna.

"And it's good to see you, Christine." I put a hand on her shoulder to lead her into the living room. "Let me introduce you to these nice people. This is Donna—" the woman nodded, her hands busy with the casserole dish.

"Hello," Christine said. "Thank you for letting me come over." She held out the bottle of Shiraz.

"Of course, Dear!" Donna was grinning. I think she really likes to entertain people, or at least, to feed them. "My hands are full, so you just bring that into the dining room with you." She turned to go back to the kitchen, then stopped; Christine walked into her, and I walked into Christine. "Go wash your hands first," she ordered. In a ragged unison Christine and I both said, "Yes, ma'am."

"What am I supposed to do, Paulette?" she said as we stood before the guest bathroom sink, obeying Donna's orders. "That woman seems nice, but—but am I not allowed to be me?"

I couldn't hear Paul's thoughts to Christine, but I saw the woman smile, then frown, then look up at me—well, at her Paulette. "If they don't know you exist," she said, "why am I here?"

With my voice Paul answered, "Because **you** know I exist. I need you, Honey."

She looked at her hands as she scrubbed them. "I can't hug you?"

I sighed. "Not a good idea while they're watching. Christine, George and his wife are paying me almost $2,000 a week to protect them. I don't want to get fired."

"If they don't like two girls being together, maybe you shouldn't be working for them."

"I doubt they care about the lesbian thing," I smiled. "It's the crazy thing that'll lose me the job. They don't know Paul exists, and I think they've figured out I'm sinking my claws into their son." I shook my head as I grabbed a hand towel. "Don't want to confuse them."

I passed the towel to Christine. She made some noises I took to mean she was hearing Paul—God! but I wish I could hear him when he thought to other people (A Trauring, can you fix this in the next story?[47]). Finally Christine said, "As long as I get to be with you tonight. After all this, I need a hug. A lot of hugs."

---

[47] We'll see, Amy. At least you have a boyfriend now!

"Here you go," Paul said, and he embraced her. It was a tight, long hug. I think it calmed Christine a bit; it sure calmed me. She's not my lover, but she is my best, dearest friend.

We joined the Locaviches in the dining room, which I hadn't explored before. It was twice the size of the breakfast nook, with a shiny wooden table that easily could hold eight people. The walls had the same dark wooden paneling as the rest of the house; there were some family photos on the walls, and a huge print of a Van Gogh still-life of apples and pears in a bowl.

I sat between Cody and Christine; she was alongside Donna, and George was across from me. "This is my colleague, Christine Hodges," I announced. Then I pointed and said names, and Christine responded: "George." "Hello, young lady." "Nice to meet you." "You've met Donna." "Thank you for feeding me." "And this is Cody." I added silently, *This is the man I like.*

"Amy has talked about you a lot," he smiled at her as he hefted a bowl of black beans and rice.

"Yeah. She's talked a lot about you, too." When he motioned with a serving spoon, she nodded and let him dish out some. It smelled good. I heard Christine laugh, and Paul thought to me *I told her about the threesome conversation.*

As everyone passed the serving dishes around—rolls, asparagus in cheese sauce, and is that lamb? Lamb? Yes! It's been forever since I've had lamb—George volunteered that it was a good day at work. "That Duke," he said. "With him standing there, no one disagrees with any prices or codicils. I may hire him after all this drama is over."

"I told you about this last night," Donna said to her husband as she cut the asparagus on her plate, "but Cody and Amy weren't here. I had a new and different day yesterday. Somebody pointed a gun at me."

"And you wonder why I love you?" George responded. "You have a fascinating life, just fascinating."

"Oh no!" Christine whispered, leaning toward me. I assume Paul thought something to her, just as Cody said, "He did more than point, Dad. He shot out Amy's back window."

"What?" George swiveled toward his wife. He was holding a roll in one hand and a knife loaded with butter in the other, but suddenly they weren't moving. "You didn't tell me that. Donna, are you all right?"

"Nobody hurt," I said; Paul added, "It's all good." Have I said how much I hate that expression? On the other hand, this lamb is incredible. Have I said how much I love lamb?

And have I said how much I enjoy Cody's family? They all like each other. Maybe that's not rare; my mom and dad and my sister Kaylee and even her husband Eddie like each other and me, and I return the sentiment. But considering how much doom and gloom and anomie is talked about—did all journalists and pointy-headed intellectuals grow up in miserable family situations? —it's a pleasant surprise to participate in a Locaviche love-in, or, at least, dinner. And Donna went out of her way to include Christine, asking about her life and expressing admiration with her bootstrapping from receptionist to agent at the real estate brokerage. *Christine is having a good time!* Paul silently enthused to me. My fantasy about being open about Paul with his lover and mine seemed to be approaching reality.

At ten o'clock the doorbell rang. George went to answer the door. "Make sure you know who it is!" I cautioned, and he actually looked through the peephole.

"Why is a black man at our door at this hour?" he asked.

"Oh! That should be Luther," I said, reminding him of the protection trinity we'd set up with me, Duke, and Duke's brother-in-law.

"Who's there?" George called.

"Luther," we heard in a soft voice. "I'm here for the night shift."

Satisfied, George opened the door and we all saw Duke's kin by marriage.

Considering Duke's appearance—tall, wide, well-muscled—Luther was a surprise. He was a hair over five foot two, and looked as if he weighed a hundred and thirty pounds. He was wearing a dark grey polo shirt, chinos, and leather loafers, and was holding an overnight case in his left hand. Yes, he was a good-looking man, with clear brown eyes, a thin nose, and a wide mouth; it just seemed like his head was on the wrong body. *He's a bodyguard?* I heard Paul think. *He's going to protect us overnight?*

"Luther!" I called. "I'm Amy Clear. I'm the P-I who got Duke involved in this. We sort-of met last night when Cody and I showed up so late."

The man smiled and held out a small hand with unusually long fingers. I shook it. *Whoa*, Paul thought. *I did not expect such a strong grip on such a wimpy looking guy.*

"I appreciate the work," he said, then turned to George. "You're still okay. Good."

"We all are," George replied. "It seems my son and my wife and Amy had a, uh, an interaction yesterday with the guy who's after me."

"Young man," called Donna, "would you like to join us for dinner?"

"Thank you, ma'am, but no," he said. "My sister—Duke's wife—made pork chops tonight. I'm good."

"I took the bottom drawer in the chest," I said, "You can use the rest of them."

"You know, my girlfriend had a fit this morning," he smiled, showing off a gold tooth. "I told her, this new job, I'm sharing a bedroom with this cute white chick." Then his smile collapsed. "Maybe tomorrow she'll let me explain it to her."

As Luther excused himself to stock more clothes in the chest of drawers, I thought to Paul, *I'm a cute white chick?*

Damn right you are!

After dinner Cody washed dishes and I dried them, and Christine sat at the kitchen island to be part of the conversation. She and I—and Paul—did our best to make sure the Shiraz she brought was put to good use. As he had told me the day I chaperoned the young woman trying to patch up her marriage with erotic pictures, Cody was not much of a drinker.

What's our sleeping arrangement? Paul thought to me, interrupting my train of thought while regaling Cody with the tale of one of the cases I worked when I was a New Orleans police detective. *It's my turn for Christine.*

"Oh, crap!" I blurted out.

Christine narrowed her eyes and tilted her head to stare at me, while Cody exclaimed, "What's wrong?"

"You got any graph paper?" Paul asked. Christine smiled because she knew it was her Paulette who said that, but Cody assumed it was me.

"Graph paper? What ever for?"

"Quarter-inch," Paul said. "No, maybe eight to the inch."

Cody turned off the water in the sink and wiped his hands on the bottom of the towel I was holding. "I don't remember what size it is, but I have some in my studio."

"Nah, never mind," Paul said, holding up my free left hand to stop the man from going to fetch what he thought I'd asked for. "It's Paul. I just mean, we have to do some thinking."

"Think about what, Paulette?"

"Who sleeps where."

Suddenly the kitchen was silent.

I said, "Any suggestions, Paul?"

"We're all friends, right?" He made my head turn to look back and forth between Cody and Christine. "Right?" Christine face broke into a smile, while Cody, tentatively, replied, "Riiii-ght. Uh, right." I was curious what derailment this train of thought was headed for.

"Okay. Cody, Amy, you two have already, uh, knocked—no, uh, umm—"

It's not like you to be so tongue-tied, I thought to him since he was the one using my mouth.

I don't want to say you two have already made the beast with two backs today, but I don't know a better way to say it.

I fell back onto a stool, laughing. Paul must have thought something to Christine because she joined in. Cody, meanwhile, was standing at the sink with his hands on his hips. "What is so funny?" he asked, his words uncharacteristically clipped.

"Paul has a way with words," I finally was able to say. "But not always polite." Sitting up, I stuck my index finger in Cody's belly and said, "We've already slept today. Together. It's Paul and Christine's turn."

"You wanted graph paper to figure that out?" Christine asked. She always knew which one of us was leading, but not necessarily that we were kidding.

"Yeah," Paul answered. "It was too abstract, I needed to make it visual."

Cody cleared his throat. "Is this going to happen a lot?"

"Every other day, Kiddo," my dyad said. "It's the deal Amy and I made years ago. We have to take turns."

At that Christine stood up and hugged me. Uh, hugged Paul. "I love you bestest," she said.

Cody rolled his eyes while she went back to her chair. "This—this is going to take some getting used to." He was not smiling. I reached a hand out to grab his. "For me, too. And for Paul. And for Christine. Please, let's all get used to it. I like you, Cody. I like you a lot. But Paul is actually a part of me. He and I must take care of each other before either of us is worth a crap to anyone else."

"What do I tell mom and dad?" he asked. He pulled out another stool and joined Christine and me at the kitchen island. "Yesterday mom said she was happy for me that you and I seemed to be getting close. This is going to be very strange to them."

Christine spoke up. "You know about Paulette. She's my girlfriend. Even though I know she's really a boy, but I met her as Paulette and that's who she is to me. I like Amy—she's the sister I never had; she really is my best friend. But it's Paulette I'm in love with, not her. I'm not a threat to your time with Amy," she went on. "Please, Cody, don't you be a threat to me and Paulette." She turned toward me and smiled. "My Paulette."

Paul jumped to the lead to squeeze her hand.

"Yeah, but what do I tell my parents?"

I shrugged. "Tell them I'm bisexual. I promise, George will love that. I'm not bi, but that seems like the easiest answer." I shook my head and added, "God, I did not anticipate having this conversation with you quite this early."

"It's a good thing I like you," Cody said, finally smiling again. "You are the strangest person I've ever known."

"Yes, I probably am. You know, I hear that a lot."

So, Cody trundled upstairs to his bedroom, where earlier today he and I had enjoyed one another. Christine and I went to the spare bedroom on the main floor, the room I'd explained to her (badly) that I'd be sharing with Luther. Paul told his lover, "You were amazing. You were firm with Cody, but considerate. I'm proud of you."

"I was afraid he wouldn't like Amy anymore. I need Amy to be happy."

"You're a dear," I said, channeling Donna for a moment. "We'll see what happens."

After a while Paul and Christine started talking about their things that didn't have much to do with me, so I zoned out. *I'm thinking of you*, I tried to think to Cody upstairs. I don't know if this ability Paul and I have to think into people's heads goes that far. The best I've tried before was when I was on the force, with Kowalski. Like with Duke, I'd convinced him I was a really, really good ventriloquist. One time I thought to him when he was in the men's room to hurry up because our quarry was making a move, and he was still zipping up as he ran out to return to the stakeout. But upstairs? Tomorrow I'll ask Cody if he heard me. Like Paul says, we didn't come with an instruction manual.

℅ THURSDAY, DECEMBER 18, 2036 ℞

"...to work. We'll talk tonight, okay?" I woke up to the sound of Christine talking to my dyad.

"It was great, you coming over last night," Paul replied. "Cody likes you. I think Donna is crazy about you."

"Good morning, lovebirds," I butted in. "What time is it?"

Christine was kneeling by the bed. "Oh, hi Amy," she said, and hugged me.

"Did you have a good time at dinner?" I asked. I was rubbing my face to wake up, while I heard Paul silently mutter, *What? Why are you—hey! Stop that!*

Ooops. Sorry. What did I miss?

"It turned out great, Amy," and she rocked back on her feet to a crouch. "I was worried at first when you said I shouldn't have kissed Paulette, but nobody cared about that and everyone was nice. The lady was 'specially nice to me." She was smiling.

Paul elbowed to the lead, uh, internally. "I'm sure your client will sign the contract today," he said. "What a Christmas present to themselves."

"I hope so. If they do, I'll take you and Amy to dinner tomorrow. How about Dockside?[48] They have a nice oyster loaf."

---

[48] Dockside was a glorified meat-and-two-veg place in Harahan that specialized in shrimp, oysters, crawfish, and crab. Decent po-boys at moderate prices, but with all the ambiance

"Go get 'em, Tiger," Paul said. Then I tagged on, "Your office must be happy over all the houses you sell. Good for you."

"Thanks, Amy," and—my God, who blushes at 7:45 in the morning? If you look up the word 'humble' in the dictionary, there's a picture of Christine Hodges. She's a lot more confident than when we first met her, but she still has no idea how smart she is, how cute she is, and how exceptional she is for going from the receptionist to a Lincoln Properties gold jacket production winner. Sure, the jacket is atrocious, but what it means is that Christine is good at what she does.

She left to close a contract with two young men who fell in love with a double they could afford in a less-than-genteel part of the lower 9th Ward. Afterwards Paul asked, "What's on the docket for today?"

"Laundry," I answered

"I'm torn," I said. "Part of me thinks I need to be wherever Donna and Cody are, you know, as protection."

"Only part of you? Which part?"

I laughed. "The part of me that likes to yank your chain. No, the rest of me thinks I need to be here, to protect the house. LY won't know if Donna is at Rouses or if Cody's buying camera stuff somewhere, but he knows where the house is." I sat up in the bed and looked around for my clothes. I was going to have to clear out so Luther could sleep here.

Paul said, "Caleb and his crew will be here most of the day. They can protect the house."

"Nuh-uh," I said as I pulled a sweatshirt over my head. "Caleb being here should make LY think twice about an attack, but Caleb's not a soldier. That's not his job."

I shuffled into the hallway and followed the smell of coffee and bacon to the breakfast nook. George was asking Luther if he had

---

of the laundromat that used to be in that location. Alas, the Covid plague killed Dockside before Amy and Paul could eat there in 2036. This anachronism brought to you by Unforeseen Events.

seen anything overnight. Meanwhile I sat on the bench next to Cody and put my left hand on his forearm. "Good morning," I whispered; when he glanced at me, I smiled.

"Not a damn thing," Luther was saying. "I kept seein' lights out the back windows, but I figured out they were cars on the street back there. Y'know, you really oughta seal off the back of your property. I'm just sayin'."

"Where's your colleague?" Donna asked, hefting a bowl of scrambled eggs and passing it around the table for me. "She was quite the delight."

"Yes, Ma'am," I said, and let Paul scoop the equivalent of an ostrich egg onto our plate. "She's got a contract closing early this morning, so she left a while ago." I handed the bowl to Cody so it would continue its around-the-table journey, to Luther and George, and back to Donna. "She told me she was knocked out how nice everyone was to her."

George laughed. "Anyone bringing wine is welcome in my house."

A knock at the door announced Duke's arrival. Cody limped into the living room to let the man in. "Good morning, Mister Cranston," he said.

"Shit, man," holding out his enormous right hand, "I'm Duke. You're...you're Coyote, right?"

"Cody," he corrected, shaking the hand. "Come on in, Mom will want to feed you."

As they entered the breakfast nook, George looked up and said, "Ah! My silent partner!" Donna offered food, and Duke again declined, praising his wife's cooking. Around a mouthful of eggs Luther offered, "You're missing some good chow, my man."

I stood up and went to Duke to check in. As I walked us into the living room, I told him about my, uh, meeting with L-Y and my dumpster dive. "Anything happen on your end yesterday?"

"Probably not, Queenie. But there were three or four phone calls with no one on the line. George there says that happens sometimes, but four? In one day? I don't know."

My hand was on his shoulder and my head was somewhere near his armpit. Crap-and-a-half, he's a big one. "Our target may be testing the waters," I nodded. "I figure he has two options: leave, or attack quickly. Do you think he's a runner?"

Duke smiled. "If he's smart, he is. But how many sleazeballs like that are smart?"

Paul spoke up, although Duke assumed it was me. "I'm thinking...if he approaches George at work and sees you, he'll be smart enough to run. To run here."

"That sounds right, Queenie. You stay on your toes."

"Let's get going, Duke!" called George as he came into the room. "That Desrosiers client is bringing a check at nine."

"Break a leg," I said to my client.

With those men gone, I went back to the breakfast nook. *Let's see if there's any bacon left,* my dyad thought to me. Donna was back in her kitchen, and Luther had retreated to our time-share bedroom, but Cody was sitting quietly in front of his empty plate. He was just sitting. *Uh-oh,* I thought to Paul. I sat next to him and put my hand out next to his on the tabletop. *Is he upset because of Christine?*

Threatened, more like. Insecure, Paul thought back. *Ask him.*

"Cody?" I was feeling mighty insecure myself.

"I don't understand." He continued to stare at the plate on the table.

I leaned my head against his shoulder.

"I—I really thought you liked me."

"Cody!" I exclaimed. "I do!"

He pushed his fork through some remaining yellow liquid on his plate. "I guess. I imagined you thought something to me after I went to my room."

"I did! I wasn't sure I could cover so much distance, but you heard me!" I hugged his arm. "Paul was busy with Christine and I was thinking about you."

"But you wouldn't be with me last night. I don't understand."

I think he needs to hear from me, Paul thought.

I sat up, next to but not leaning on Cody, so Paul could have his full attention. Much of the next few minutes was a mixture of anxiety and bordom. Anxiety because I didn't know what was happening. And boredom because A Trauring, in all her compositional authority, doesn't let me hear when Paul thinks to another person. That's got to change in the next book. Please.

Mostly I heard Cody say disjointed things, like "Oh. Yeah" and "not really" and "uh-huh" and "I don't know." But then Cody said, "I was engaged before the accident, and Rachel broke it off. You— uh, Amy—Amy is the first woman I've been with since then. Three years!" He finally turned his head away from that soiled breakfast plate and looked at me. "And now I feel like a yo-yo. I feel like a stupid schoolboy for feeling jealous and abandoned and needy. I hate being like this." He paused—maybe Paul was thinking something to him. Then, "Yeah, that's it. I'm scared."

All yours, Paul thought to me.

Silently, I replied, *I want a transcript.*

"It's okay to be scared," I said to Cody. "You know, I'm scared, too. I'm just getting to know you. I like you, and I can't help imagining the two of us being together. And I'm scared that I'll say something stupid that makes you realize what a loser I am and that..." And what? "And that'll be the end of it."

"Yeah, right"

"Cody. Really. That's what scares me."

A smile broke out on his angular face. "Does everyone think if someone knew the real them, they would run for safety?"

"Pretty much."

What a relief! So, I threw my arm around him and hugged him from the side. "I don't know what Paul said to you, I can't hear him when he thinks to people. Are we okay?"

"I guess. I'm going to try for us to be okay." He snaked his arm behind me and returned the sideways hug. "He explained about the woman. That it's him, not you." I nodded against his arm. "It's just so weird!"

I couldn't help but snicker. "You think it's weird! Imagine what it's like for me and Paul on the inside." I pointed my index finger at my temple. "It's taken us a long time to, uh, come to grips with the weirdness."

"So, I can see you every other day?"

"Not Sunday. I don't see anybody on Sunday. On Sunday I do laundry."

"Amy?" Donna called from the kitchen. "Caleb's here and is ready to start on that, what, security room?"

"Safe room. Yes, Ma'am," and I stood up to get to work, trailing my fingers across Cody's back. "I'm on the time clock," I said to him. "I'm glad we talked." I stood still for a moment, looking down at that sharp, geometric face full of anxiety and relief, all at the same time. "The more I know you, the better I like you. Thanks." I patted his face, careful not to cut myself on that sharp cheekbone, and went into the kitchen to work with Donna and her maintenance man.

You know what's uncomfortable? Being in someone else's house, and the phone rings, and nobody answers it. It just keeps ringing and ringing. It's all you can do not to answer it yourself except, well, like I said, it's not your house. Donna and I were upstairs, showing Caleb how we wanted him to install a metal door with a three-inch deadbolt. So Donna didn't answer because she was busy with Caleb. I didn't answer it because I was the one explaining. And I knew Cody was with a client in his studio, so I guessed he was busy with them and didn't want to interrupt his photographic magic.

Mercifully, it quit ringing. For twenty seconds. Then it started again.

This time Cody got it, because we heard him shout, "Amy! It's Duke! He wants to talk to you."

I ran downstairs to the only phone location I knew, in the kitchen. For a second I was sixteen years old, back home in Metairie, with nosy parents and an annoyingly extra-nosy kid sister. The old words came so easy as I picked up the handset: "Got it! You can hang up now!"

"Queenie!" Duke's voice leapt five feet beyond the phone earpiece. "I just chased that son-of-a-bitch off. He's probably headed your way."

"Everyone okay? You? George?"

"Shit, yeah. He never got close. Found him trying to jack my Humvee. If he hadn't run so fast, I swear I'd have killed him. Don't fuck with the Duke's wheels!"

"I'll keep that in mind, I promise. Does George know?"

"I'm gonna tell him in a minute. Thought it was more urgent to warn you."

"Thanks. I'm going to fetch the shotgun out of my trunk. You be careful, my friend."

As I hung up I heard Paul think, *When did we get a shotgun?*

Tomorrow, honest. No, just an extra 9mm, and a couple hundred rounds of hollow-points.

He said, "Okay, what's plan B?"

One hand on Roscoe's butt, I opened the front door. Crap, it was cold for a New Orleans December. "The other pistol. Load it and put it in Cody's hand. Give him the fifteen second safety lecture and then...then we wait."

It wasn't even noon yet, and the residential Richmond Street in front of the Locaviche home was deserted. I crossed the asphalt to where my wounded Benzmobile was resting, shards of safety glass at the edges of the opening that used to be the back window. With no one around, Paul spoke. "Cody proved himself yesterday, dealing with L-Y. But so did Donna. Another gun for her?"

I opened the trunk and felt around under the crap that mysteriously accumulates back there. "I only have one extra gun. I'm going with Cody." I found the black plastic case with my spare Taurus and put it on my back bumper. Then I climbed in the trunk to rat around for boxes of ammo.

"What about that revolver in your purse?" he asked.

That brought me up straight—whacking my head against the underside of the trunk lid. "I forgot about that," I said, surprised. See—Paul and I really are two different people.

I went back into the house, rubbing the back of my head, with the pistol case under my arm and two boxes of hollow-points in my free hand. Then to Cody's studio, where his client was behind the Japanese screen, changing clothes.

"Got something for you," I announced, and sat the pistol case on his work table.

When I popped the case open wide, Cody's eyes popped even wider. "I don't want that in here," he said.

"Too bad," I answered, picking the Taurus up and racking the slide to make sure it was not loaded. "Duke says L-Y is probably on his way here. I've got a revolver for your mom, too. It's all hands on deck, Cody."

His frown actually fit the geometric patterns of his angular face—that set, square jaw, and that solid line of his disapproving lips.

I opened a box of ammunition and began loading the fifteen-round magazine. "Keep your finger off the trigger until you're ready to fire," I began, reciting Colonel Cooper's[49] basic safety rules,

---

[49] Jeff Cooper rose to Lt. Colonel in the US Marines during the Korean War. He is considered the father of the modern technique of handgun shooting. His innovations include the Weaver stance and color-code preparedness for self-defense, as well as the four golden rules of firearms safety that Amy abbreviates for Cody.

"don't aim at anyone unless you're willing to shoot them, and make sure what's behind your target is expendable. Oh—and every gun is loaded until you demonstrate to yourself that it's not." I handed the pistol to him and smiled. "Yesterday you enlisted in Amy's army. Today you get a promotion."

A young woman emerged from the screen, leading her seven- or eight-year-old son for the next set of pictures. She froze when she saw what Cody was holding, and shoved the boy behind her.

"Hi," Paul called in my voice, "I'm Detective Clear. Cody here is in training. Didn't mean to alarm you." Cody, meanwhile, placed the loaded pistol back in its case and closed the lid. "Sorry, Miriam," he said to his client. "Is Donnie ready for the next shoot— uh, the next round of pictures?" He slid the box across his desk, towards me.

"We'll continue later, Cody," I said as I picked up the gun case and carried it out of the room. I hoped I hadn't ruined the session, or, worse yet, chased off the client.

I tip-toed into the dormitory bedroom, trying not to disturb Luther while I fetched my revolver from my purse. *No extra ammo?* Paul thought to me.

It's just a backup gun, I thought back. *I can't fit the entire Louisiana Armory in my purse.*

I closed the bedroom door quietly, then headed upstairs. Donna and Caleb still were in the bedroom, discussing her proposed color scheme for the door. They both looked up as I approached, holding the revolver with the muzzle pointed down.

Donna rolled her eyes and sighed. "Amy, now what? Put that thing away." But before I could say anything, Caleb held out his hand and said, "Is that a .38 or a .44? Can I see?"

"Give me a sec," Paul said aloud. I swung the cylinder open and let the half-dozen shells fall to the floor. "Here you go," I added, letting Caleb take the empty revolver. Then, to Donna, I said, "Duke called to say he scared off the bad guy from George's parking garage, and he's likely headed this way. You were a great

getaway driver yesterday, so you're in the Amy Army now."
Abruptly Paul added, "You're not behind a plow." *What?*

"Getaway driver?" Caleb asked. He was hefting the unloaded
gun, trying the sights.

"I don't know," Donna said, stepping back and shaking her
head. "I told you, I don't let George keep his gun here."

"Getaway driver?"

"The man who beat the stuffing out of your husband is
probably on his way here. My job is to stop him. I need your help."

"Mrs. Locaviche," Caleb interrupted. "Getaway driver?" His
fists were on his hips, the open revolver still in his right hand.

"Yes, Caleb. Amy and I had an adventure yesterday. Really,
it's quite all right."

Paul spoke up, "It's not like we knocked over a liquor store or
jacked the Qwik-E-Mart. Honest."

He didn't look convinced. Still, I held out my hand and said, "I
need to give that to Donna."

"I've got a .45 in my truck," he said as he handed over my puny
snub-nose .38. Then he turned to the door frame and went back to
measuring the opening for the replacement metal door.

"You take that thing down to the kitchen," Donna said sharply.
"When Caleb and I are done up here I'll come down and we can
talk." Despite her tone of voice, though, I am sure I saw her wink.

Did you see that? I thought to Paul.

I sure did, he responded. *Considering the conversation y'all
had a few days ago, I think she'll be fine with this.*

I put the revolver on the island countertop, cylinder open. Then
I found a ramekin in one of the cabinets and dropped the half-dozen
.38 cartridges into it.

My phone ringing startled me, but instead of barking 'What?' I
remembered to say "Clear, Hodges & Owens. How can I help you?"

"Amy!" I heard Christine shout, "They signed the contract! I
sold the house!"

Paul jumped to lead and answered his lover, "That's great! You really are doing a great job selling houses. And this one is in the city, good for you!"

"Let me take you and Amy to dinner," she said. "This check is starting to burn a hole in my purse."

"Sounds great," Paul said. "Uh—Amy?"

"I'm proud of you," I made myself say to her. It was true, but also true was my own envy or resentment over her success. I mean, I was still struggling to get enough work to pay the mortgage and buy the wine, and she was going to take us out. "We should be able to go to dinner soon," I added. "This case is coming to a head. We're waiting for the bad guy to come here for a showdown."

"But—"

I waited, but she didn't go on. "But what?"

"I'm not a brave girl like you, so I'm probably full of baloney, but why are you just waiting? Shouldn't you be hiding outside to see him when he's getting close?"

Her common sense left me speechless; even Paul could only manage a belated, "Wow." Finally I was able to say, "Brilliant. Absolutely brilliant." To Paul I thought, *your woman is a genius*.

"Christine, we were looking at all the trees. You just reminded us of the forest," Paul said. "I think Amy is revising her strategy. Wow!"

"Just be safe, Paulette. You too, Amy. I need to be able to take you to dinner."

"If it's alright with Paul, I think we're going to cut this call short. I've got to give new orders to the Amy Army here, before Voldemort shows up."

"Patronus," Christine intoned. "I think that's the spell that got him."

I was on my way to Cody's studio when the lights went out. The sound of the central heat blowers ceased. And I barked my shin on some invisible table in the darkened hallway. I could hear cries of surprise from Cody ahead of me and from Donna and Caleb above.

"...to check the breaker box in the kitchen," I heard Cody telling his client as I got closer to his studio. *Convenient,* Paul thought to me. *Or has LY made his long-awaited appearance?*

"Crap!" I shouted. "Double crap! Cody?"

I could make out his silhouette as he neared me in the hall. "I'm going to reset the breaker," he said as he limped along.

"Don't bother," I said, grabbing his upper arms to make him stop walking. "I'm sure LY cut the wires. Hide your client somewhere safe, then you and me and Donna have to do battle." I wished I was able to see the expression on his geometric face. "Are you ready for that pistol yet?"

"I'll meet you in the kitchen," he said, then retreated to look after the woman whose little boy he had been photographing.

While Paul used our left hand to grope for his little LED flashlight in my pocket, I shouted upstairs: "Donna! Come on down! We got trouble! Meet me in the kitchen!"

What if it's not LY? Paul thought. *What if it's just a power failure?*

Then I turn in my PI license, refund George's money, and go back to running Z-Scores for market research. You know I don't believe in coincidence.

Paul flicked on the flashlight and lit our way to the kitchen. The gun case that held the semi-auto that Cody had declined was where I had left it, on the island counter; I unsnapped the latch and opened it to make the man's reconsideration go a little faster. While I was at it, I reloaded the spare revolver I had offered to Donna, but left it on the counter top with the cylinder open.

"Let me get the hurricane lamp," Donna said when she and Caleb joined me in the kitchen. As she took it from its perch over the refrigerator—where I had never noticed it—she said, "I see the Delacroixs next door still have power." She removed the glass chimney that was the inspiration for New Orleans' most famous potable, the Hurricane, to hold a match to the mantle; when it caught, she trimmed the wick and restored the chimney.

By then Cody had limped in, with his client and her obviously frightened little boy. Donna said, "Dear, will you check the fuse box?"

"I hope it's tripped," I said, "but I doubt it. I think LY has announced his visit."

As Cody removed a red-and-white sampler that said "As for me and my house, we will serve the Lord" to access the electrics, I looked at his client. "You're Miriam, right?" She nodded. Her son was clutching her around the hips, clearly alarmed. I let Paul reach out to touch the boy's cheek and say, "You're a brave little thing. You protect your mama."

"Breakers all look normal," Cody reported as he came back to the group.

"I'm afraid the man that's been terrorizing George has arrived," I said. "If we're lucky he electrocuted himself when he cut the wires, but I've never won anything on a lottery ticket, so he's probably just peachy."

"I want to go home, mommy," the little boy whispered as he buried his face in his mother's hip.

"Yes. Miriam, we need to get you and sonny boy out of here. This conflict has nothing to do with you."

"I'll walk her out," Caleb volunteered. "I want to get my gun out of the truck anyway."

Nice of him, Paul thought to me.

No cigar, I thought back. "I'll do it," I made myself say. "I'm the paid bodyguard, it's my job to take the risks." I went on, "This LY is a razor man. I doubt he's got a gun, but that's no reason for us to be stupid. Caleb, you can try the back if you want to fetch your weapon. Cody, take the damn semi-auto. And Donna, are you finally ready for the revolver?"

"I—I guess."

Paul spoke up. "Okay, these are the rules. Don't shoot me. Don't shoot each other. We all clear about that?" There were nods all around, although Caleb was on his way to the laundry room and the brand-new back door.

I turned to Cody's customer. "Do you have all your gear?" Her boy was silent, but tears were pouring down his face.

"Yes. Please, get us out of here."

Paul aimed the flashlight ahead to the living room. I pulled on my denim jacket, and let him unzip our holster and heft my 9mm carry gun. "Stay behind me," I ordered Miriam. "If the bad guy comes at me, you run for your car and skedaddle."

I took a deep breath and unlocked the front door. Motioning the woman behind me, I stood behind the big wooden door as I opened it slowly. The distant sound of cars from St. Charles Avenue to the south filtered in, or maybe from Jefferson Avenue to the east. I didn't hear anything nearby, so I crouched down to look around the door and out to the driveway and the street.

It was around four o'clock on one of the shortest days of the year. Compared to the Locaviche's now non-electric house it was bright outdoors, but it really was a dim, dreary, nearly-winter day. *You see anything?* I thought to Paul.

Nothing useful. Nothing scary. No.

"Come on," I whispered to the woman. I stood up and slowly went down the seven marble steps to the half circle driveway. "Is that your car?" I asked, stupidly motioning with my gun hand toward a late model Lexus; it was about thirty feet away.

Her "Yes" barely reached my ears, it was so soft. "Come on," I repeated, and grasped her wrist to make her stay close to me. By years of practice, I kept my eyes straight ahead and let Paul monitor our peripheral vision. *Anything?* I asked him silently. *Nope. Nada. Nein. Zilch. Uh—nope.*

Miriam clicked her key fob and the lights on her Lexus blinked twice. The little boy ran to the back door and dove across the seat, then reached back to close the door behind him. As his mother got behind the wheel, Paul said "Call Cody in a couple of days. If we're still alive he'll be glad to make up for today." Her driver's side door wasn't closed yet when her tires squealed and she headed out into and down Richmond Place toward her idea of safety: some place where the lights were on, where seemingly nice people didn't wave guns around, and where adults knew better than to worry about a boogieman. Out loud Paul said, "I'm afraid Cody's lost a customer."

He holstered my Ruger and zipped it closed. We stood in the dim, chilly December afternoon, looking at the place where Miriam's car had been. "It's nice to relax," I said to the world.

Suddenly my back and butt felt warm. Before I could comprehend that unexpected change, and just about the time Paul was thinking *Uh-oh spaghetti-o*, I felt hot and cold—hot breath on the side of my neck, and cold steel at my neck.

"Don't move, sweetheart."

I recognized the voice. It was LY.

"You and me, we're going to wait for George. I've got a little something for him."

Shoot him! I heard Paul shout silently. *We can end this!*

As much as I love Paul, and even though he's the one who taught me to shoot and handle guns safely, he was never in law enforcement; in fact, although he's never explained the details to me, it seems he spent some time in his youth evading the law. People who don't get immersed in firearms skills mistakenly think a gun is an all-purpose tool, like an umpteen blade Swiss army knife. No. A chainsaw is a wonderful tool, but not when you're climbing a ladder. A hammer is great, but not when you're dealing with screws. And a gun is no help when a bad guy with a straight razor has the drop on you. *I could shoot him,* I thought to Paul, *and his dying reflex would slit my throat and I'd die on top of him. We wait for a better moment.*

Oh. I'm glad he takes me seriously. He listens. Have I mentioned how I love—

"Introduce me to your friends," LY said, as he began pushing me toward those marble steps and the front door that I foolishly had left standing open. "I've got a score to settle with you and that limping guy."

I hoped I wasn't too far away from that limping guy when I thought *Cody! LY has me. Hide so he doesn't find you. Later you can surprise him and take him down.* After all, he heard me last night when I thought to him up in his bedroom.

"So, how's the bar business these days?" Paul said. I'd never have tried to provoke the man holding a razor to my throat. He has different ideas of negotiating tactics.

"Shut up, bitch!" LY growled as he pushed me up the stairs. "You and that friend of yours are the reason I'm broke and on the run. I could kill you for it." He pushed some more. "I can kill you for it."

Paul thought, *He's in for a shock when George and Duke get here.* I answered, *I hope I'm still alive to see it.*

I thought of something else Cody could do while he was hiding, assuming he heard me think to him from outside the house. *Call George. Have him tell Duke LY's holding me hostage with a razor and is waiting on your dad.* Duke and I had worked some nasty cases together and we saved each other's lives—a common enough story for working cops or detectives. I trust him. If anyone can get me out of this in one piece, it's Duke Cranston.

LY pushed me up the steps. Paul thought, *He's shorter than we are. He's having trouble keeping his razor in the danger zone while we're going up stairs.*

Maybe he'll make me climb a ladder inside. Then I can take him.

Sure! Paul enthused. *If a ceiling light blows, you can climb the—oh, right, he cut the power. Never mind.* I swear, if I were being marched to a hangman's noose, Paul could make me laugh over the trapdoor. It takes a morbid sense of humor to get through things like this. Well, it's our way of doing it.

Once we were inside, LY kept shoving and marching me toward the light of the hurricane lantern in the kitchen. Donna was alone, but she was holding a regular drinking glass that seemed to be half-full. On the island counter-top was an open bottle of Chateau Bayou Rouge. Paul said out loud, "Wine? We've got company. Get some more glasses."

"Shut up!" LY barked, and pushed me down onto one of the chairs. The razor stung at my neck, and I felt a drop of blood bead up.

"Who are you?" he said to Donna, in a remarkably calm and social tone.

She drained the glass and put it back on the counter top. "I'm Eustacia," she said. "Who are you?"

"Oh, call me LY. Do you have another glass? May I have some of your wine?"

Amazing, Paul thought. *He sounds like this is a Rotary Club social.*

Without speaking, Donna retrieved a wine glass from one of the cabinets and brought it to the island.

"Could I trouble you to pour me some?" He chuckled. "My hands are busy."

Can we think to Donna? I mean, without freaking her out?

I thought about that. When I worked with Duke on a few cases I convinced him I was the best ventriloquist in the world. Did that with Lieutenant Kowalski, too. But at the start they always were startled and confused.

Then I had an idea.

Since LY was standing behind me, he couldn't see my face. So I mouthed the words I thought to Donna, hoping she'd think I was whispering. *Donna, he can't hear me like this. Did Cody hide?— show me your palm if it's yes. Back of your hand for 'no.'*

A small smile flew across her face while she poured wine for my captor. As she put the bottle back on the counter top she held her right hand up, palm out.

Caleb too?

She rubbed her cheek with the back of her hand, showing me her palm.

What's going on? Paul thought to me. I explained my little ruse, to which he silently expressed obscene approval.

"Excellent wine," LY said pleasantly, "thank you. I appreciate it. Now, tell me, do you have some clothesline I can use? Rope? I'd hate to have to rip up your towels."

"Rip up...what on earth are you talking about?" Donna asked. I think there was as much curiosity as anger in her voice.

"Why, I have to tie you up. And this lady here," tapping me lightly on the top of my head.

I was surprised to hear Paul say, "No."

"What?" LY moved his razor and I felt another drop of blood bead up. Oh, crap, he was going to get blood on my UNO sweatshirt. That's a tough stain to remove. Of course, if he went much deeper with that razor, my mom and dad could just bury me in it.

Paul! I shouted silently. *This man wants to kill us! Don't provoke him!*

I've died once, he replied.[50] *Next time I die I'll be on my feet, not on my knees.*

"I don't remember asking for your opinion," LY said, and his pleasant social voice was replaced by a raspy snarl. He took the razor away, then clamped his other arm around my neck. He looked up at Donna and said, "Rope. Now."

"No!" Paul said again. LY tightened his grip on my throat.

"You know I can kill you right here," he hissed in my ear.

"Then what?" Paul croaked.

I saw Donna's face go pale. I knew she didn't want to see a bloody mess all over her kitchen, but there was something else in her expression. I started to think to Paul, *What is she—*

---

[50] Invisible man ~~speaks~~ thinks with straight, uh, neuron. Read *A Different Kind of Twin* by A Trauring and it all will make sense.

"Stop." It was Cody's voice!

I could feel LY turn, probably to look at the source of the voice. His grip on me loosened just a little, so I was able to turn, too. Cody was no more than six feet away, holding my revolver with both hands, but shaking uncontrollably, like a can of cranberry sauce that's just been emptied onto a Thanksgiving platter. I heard Paul think, *Oh no! He looks like the kid at the beginning of* Pulp Fiction*. We're all gonna die.*

"Well, what have we here?" LY drawled. He extended his free hand, razor outstretched, toward Cody.

Cody's eyes were darting everywhere: LY, me, his mother, me, the clock. *This is not going to work*, I thought to Paul.

At which point Donna landed a rolling pin on the side of LY's head. It made a satisfying *thunk!* and some blood spurted, and LY dropped to the floor like, well, like he'd just been pole-axed. Paul said to Donna, "Williams Sonoma needs a customer testimonial from you."

Cody fell into a chair, letting my revolver fall to the floor; I was guessing his adrenalin was spent.

Freed from LY's sharpened steel, I knelt by the chair where Cody sat. "You are one brave man," I said, putting my hands around his available arm. "You saved me."

Very softly he said, "I have never been so scared in my life." Paul thought, *It showed.*

"Courage isn't the absence of fear," I counseled. "It's doing what needs to be done even when you're terrified. You are my hero," and I hugged his arm.

Donna was on the wall phone. From her end of the conversation I was glad to hear she was talking to Orleans Parish police. Good. The sooner they got LY out of here, the sooner we could call an electrician to fix what the son-of-a-bitch broke.

"Hey," I asked, "Where's Caleb?"

Donna chuckled, "He went out the back door. He may be in Arkansas by now." Then she turned to her gas range. "I'll make some coffee while we're waiting." She moved the hurricane lamp to have a better view of the jars in her cabinet.

"It's over, Cody," I said. "You were brave to distract LY. And your mom was brave to whack him. Thanks."

He finally opened his eyes, looking down to where I sat next to his chair. "I need to know—is every day with you like this?"

Paul laughed and said, "More than I like, but no, not very often at all."

"It's Amy. And with this job done, now I'm out of work."

He leaned over and planted a warm, wet, wonderful kiss on my lips. *Yes,* I thought to him. *Yes yes yes.*

Balanced against that physical warmth was a cold spot on the nape of my neck. As I heard LY growl something unpleasant, Paul said, "Oh, great. Our spare revolver. The one Cody dropped." Cody's head jerked up, and he kicked his chair away from me.

Slowly I turned to face LY. He kept the gun barrel pressed against my head the entire time, until it was fixed to my forehead while I looked at him. His eyes were all pupils, all black. Just like his heart.

"Now what?" Paul asked.

"Now we wait for George to come home. Then I kill you all."

"Now, young man!" Donna blurted.

When he swiveled to point the weapon at her, I threw my right arm up against his gun hand. By reflex he pulled the trigger, putting a .38 caliber hole in the kitchen ceiling. You always forget how LOUD it is when a gun goes off indoors, how it makes your ears tighten up and interferes with your hearing for a while. Sometimes it even hurts. Like now.

At that point it turned into a wrestling match between LY and me. I'm taller than him, but he's probably got sixty pounds on me. And he still had my revolver. So I did what any well-mannered retired little-lady police detective would do: I bit his gun hand. I mean, bit it hard enough to taste blood. He shouted, although it sounded like a muffled cough, and the gun fell to the hardwood floor. Cody kicked it away and then piled on me and LY. There was a vague buzz in the background that I took to be Donna screaming and wailing. I hoped she still had a good grip on that rolling pin.

Shoot him! Paul screamed silently. Ah, another thing people without law enforcement or combat training don't realize is that at close quarters, there is no such thing as *your* gun. In a hand-to-hand melee like I was in, it's *all y'all's* gun; it's impossible to be sure of your control of a weapon when your opponent isn't even six inches away from you. *Don't draw,* I shouted back at Paul.

Do men understand how much it hurts to get punched in a boob? Ouch! I mean, OUUUUCHH!

LY twisted to face Cody, who was a bigger physical threat to him. I threaded my right arm in front of him, and managed to raise it up to his neck. Then I had my right hand grab my left shoulder for leverage, and began squeezing the man's throat. *That serial killer at UNO Lakeside,* I thought to Paul, *the detective said just five pounds of pressure in the right place could kill someone.*[51]

Yeah. This would qualify as self-defense, he thought back. *But I still want to shoot the fucker.*

Apparently my pressure was not it the right place, because LY wasn't dying. He squirmed, he kicked, he parried the punches Cody was throwing at him, he was gurgling, but he was definitely conscious and alive.

I squeezed harder.

More gurgling. Cody continued to pound him.

I squeezed as hard as I could; I thought my left shoulder was going to fall off.

Even more weird sounds from him. And then Cody planted a roundhouse against his jaw.

At that LY stopped struggling.

---

[51] Paul's West Virginia Boy Scout troop may have taught him about quarterstaff (see *The Strawberry Birthmark*), but not judo. Amy didn't know the detective had talked about 'blood choke,' and she really didn't know how to apply it. No wonder it didn't work.

Out of breath, I managed to wheeze, "Donna." Pant. "That rope." Pant.

Cody hoisted himself up to his knees, and lifted the limp LY off me. He threw the man down on the floor beside me and landed a gratuitous punch on his nose. LY didn't respond, unless you consider starting to bleed a response.

With LY's weight off me, I caught my breath. "Cody. Great. But stop hitting him, he's down." Even if you're into punishing an opponent, what's the punishment if they are unconscious and can't feel the pain you're inflicting?

Cody let himself fall onto the floor on the other side of me, facing up and breathing heavily. "I can't believe it. I can't believe what I just did." He turned his head to look at me, our noses only inches apart. "I can't believe what you've done."

"Yes," I said. "You were great. I'm—I'm proud of you, Cody. Thank you." I pushed my face forward and kissed him.

Donna cleared her throat. "The police should be here any minute. I want to clean up this mess before they get here."

Sheepish, I looked around. Chairs were on their backs and sides, and there were blood spatters over LY, and the floor, and Cody, and my precious UNO Lakeside sweatshirt. At least it wasn't our blood. "Okay, Donna," I said, standing up. My left boob still hurt, and for some reason, so did my left knee.

"Yes, Mom," her son said. He was up and straightening furniture. Donna smiled and said, "The coffee's ready. Do you take sugar and cream, Dear?"

I hugged the woman. "Thank you, Donna. You helped save us. Thank you thank you thankyou." I felt her patting my back. "Of course, Amy. You're important to Cody, and that makes you important to me. Now drink up your coffee before it gets cold."

I didn't know any of the four New Orleans police officers who showed up halfway through the cup of Cafe du Monde's finest. They seemed startled to see the three of us at the kitchen island, drinking coffee by the light of a hurricane lamp, while LY was stretched out on the floor with clothesline binding his hand and feet. My revolver was sitting on the countertop with the cylinder open.

The officers were taking basic statements from Donna when there was noise from the living room. Duke burst in, his hand inside his jacket where I knew his shoulder harness held his .45 pistol. "Damn, Johnson," he said, "what are you doing here?" Scurrying behind him was our client, George Locaviche.

One of the policemen, a light skinned black man who looked to be in his 30s, said, "I could ask you the same thing, Cranston. How the hell are you, anyway?" The other officers turned to greet their one-time compadre. Many police fantasize about going independent as security agents or private detectives, but Duke Cranston had the courage to make the change. So did I, but these cops didn't know me.

George embraced Donna. The two of them hugged, and I could imagine expressions of concern, and gratitude that the ordeal was over. I heard Paul think, *Sweet, isn't it?*

Yes.

Officer Johnson and his crew eventually turned back to work. Two of the men handcuffed the prone LY, then splashed water on his face to revive him. His face was swelling from the pounding Cody gave him, and he wasn't resisting the police.

I raised my hand like I was back in Sister Caligula's Social Studies classroom at St. Giles Academy. "My name is Amy Clear. I'm a former NOPD detective, and I was hired to protect this family from that creep—" pointing where the other officers were hoisting LY up "—Elias Young."

"Queenie, what happened?"

"He cut the power lines somehow," I answered Duke. "Then he got the drop on me when I was outside, escorting Cody's photography client to safety. He pushed me back in here and we had a struggle."

Paul added, "Actually, a couple of struggles."

"A couple?" Johnson was writing in his notepad.

"Yes. First he held a razor to my neck and demanded rope so he could tie us all up. Cody distracted him with my revolver, and Donna KO'd him with a rolling pin. But then he came to and got my gun off the floor. He said he was going to wait for George to come home and then kill us all. I managed to disarm him, and we had a wrestling match. Cody did him in." I snorted. "That time we tied up the creep and waited for you."

Donna nodded, even while she was still embraced by her husband. "I called 911. Would you men like some coffee? It'll only take a few minutes to get some more going."

The dazed and handcuffed LY came alive when he noticed George. "You!" he bellowed, trying to twist away from the two officers holding him upright. "This is all your fault! You ruined my business and you ruined my life! I swear—"

Duke pushed himself in front of LY, arms folded across his chest. The six-foot-four private detective looked down on the five-foot-two captive. "What's that?" he challenged. "You swear what?"

"Not you," peeking around Duke to where George was standing with his wife, "him. That son-of-a-bitch. I had a great base of operations and he burned it down."

Duke cocked his bratwurst-sized index finger against his thumb and let it go with a *thump!* against LY's forehead. "You want him? You have to come through me. You ready for that? You want those cops to let go of you so you can take me on?" Duke nodded at the two officers holding the man, and they let go of LY's arms. Of course, the handcuffs were still in place.

There was no answer. "Right."

"Cranston," one of the officers said softly as they resumed their grips on LY. "I can't let you mess with him while he's in custody."

"He ain't worth my time." Duke turned away and walked to George. "Yo, client," he called. "About my invoice..."

George let go a laugh of relief. Donna and Cody were safe. He wasn't going to get beaten up again. True, he was out a warehouse, but the man who had been hounding him was in handcuffs, disappearing into the living room and out the front door in the company of two uniformed policemen. I was relieved my client finally was safe.

Lieutenant Johnson spent a few minutes questioning each of us, then shook Duke's hand and showed himself out.

Donna took to the wall phone and pushed buttons. When her call went through she said, "Caleb, it's all clear. You can come back now. We need you to fix the lights."

Cody was sitting next to me at the island while Donna and George still stood, holding hands. Come to think of it, that's what Cody and I were doing, too.

George said, "Too much excitement. Let's go out for dinner. I think we can get in at Upperline. Their rack of lamb is good eating.[52] Cody? And you come with us, Amy. And Duke, please let us take you, too."

"Y'all have treated me great," the big PI said. "But I've got a wife who would like to know I ain't dead yet. Uh—I'll mail my invoice, it's payable on receipt. We good?"

George smiled. "We good," he said, and held out a fist to bump Duke's. They both laughed.

Cody can't think into my head like I can do to people, but he sure read my mind. "I have to pass on dinner, Dad," he said, tightening his grip on my hand. "Amy and I are kind of bushed after all this."

I thought to him, *Thanks! We can do better than dinner.* He shook his head in puzzlement and said, "What?" Then I heard Paul think, *I just told him he's the smartest man you've ever dated.*

To Cody: *Paul may be right.*

"Well, you kids take care," Donna offered. "We'll bring you back a doggie bag." Paul thought, *Look at that smile! I think she's glad Cody's interested in a woman again.*

---

[52] Don't know if the restaurant or the street it's on was named Upperline first. They specialize in *prix fixe* dinner, and the rack of lamb lives up to George's description.

As George and Donna left, Paul said, "I need to call Christine. She's bound to be worried about us."

"Can't it wait?" Cody said; he was nuzzling my ear and whispering some delightfully naughty things.

I kissed Cody and put my hand against his chest to hold him off a little. "No, it can't. And tomorrow Christine is taking us out to celebrate selling another house." I smiled weakly at the man. "Give me a minute. I'll meet you upstairs, okay?" I may not be the smoothest femme fatale, but I know that telling a man you'll be in his bedroom shortly makes him forget any anxiety, frustration, or disagreement. He mussed my hair as he stood up and went into the hall towards our trysting place.

Paul dug out my phone and pushed the speed dial for his lover. I didn't hear even one ring when Christine's voice came over the line, rapid and high-pitched. "Paulette are you okay is Amy all right tell me you're okay and, and, and—"

"I'm fine, Honey," he interrupted. "You had a great idea for Amy, but we got started too late. The bad guy ambushed us and—"

"Oh, no! Paulette, no!"

"We're okay, Christine, honest. There was a fight, and there were some scary moments, but we won. The cops have been here and taken LY away."

"So—so, so, what does that mean?" I could hear her panting with worry.

"It means I'm safe. Amy, too. We're not hurt. And Amy's boyfriend and his mother were big helps, too."

"Whew!" Christine exhaled for what seemed like two minutes. "So, I can relax now?"

"Sure thing, Sweetie. Hey, how did your day go?"

"I got to the bank before they closed so I deposited my commission check. You and Amy are coming to dinner with me tomorrow, right?"

"Absolutely."

And I chimed in, "It's Amy. You bet, Christine. You earned a celebration and I'm going to be there with you and Paul."

I let the lovebirds coo for a minute or two, then broke in. "Christine, Cody's waiting for me upstairs and—"

"I know!" she chirped. "Tomorrow it's Paulette and me, but tonight it's you and your boy. I love you, Amy, you have fun. And I love you, Paulette!"

When the call was over, Paul mused aloud, "She still gets scared if she doesn't hear from me on 'our' days. But for the other days, absolutely no jealousy." He shook our head. "I am the luckiest man in the world."

Consider that. Paul Owens was mugged on the Decatur Street levee and kicked into a coma by a pair of New Orleans thugs. And a few years later, as his comatose body was finally shutting down, his mind was miraculously transferred to my then-eleven-year-old self by a splash of body fluid when the intern taking him to the Emergency Room bumped me with the gurney. And he calls himself the luckiest man on earth.

"I hope things go that well with Cody," I responded as I went towards the stairs. "Now I want to think about what to get him for Christmas."

How about a little revolver and some lessons?

I giggled. But then I had a serious thought: "Crap. I need to get something for Donna and George, too. Double crap!"

When I was halfway up the stairs, excited about heading for Cody and his bedroom, I heard Paul think *Are you in love?*

I remember your advice, I thought back. *I hope we end up in love, but for now I'm hugely, enormously, outrageously infatuated. Not to mention in lust.*

Aloud, he said, "Ah, not to mention it."